Praise for the no
New York Times bestselling author Beth Kery,
recipient of the *All About Romance*
Reader Poll for Best Erotica

"An intensely sexual love story."   —*Kirkus Reviews*

"Addictive, delectable reading."   —*USA Today*

"Wicked good storytelling."
          —Jaci Burton, *New York Times* bestselling author

"Holy hell HAWT."   —Under the Covers Book Blog

"One of the sexiest, most erotic love stories that I have read in a
long time."   —Affaire de Coeur

"A sleek, sexy thrill ride."   —Jo Davis

"One of the best erotic romances I've ever read."
          —All About Romance

"Nearly singed my eyebrows."   —Dear Author

"Fabulous, sizzling hot."
          —Julie James, *New York Times* bestselling author

"Action and sex and plenty of spins and twists."
          —Genre Go Round Reviews

"Intoxicating and exhilarating."   —Fresh Fiction

continued . . .

GLOW

BETH KERY

BERKLEY BOOKS, NEW YORK

BERKLEY

An imprint of Penguin Random House LLC
375 Hudson Street, New York, New York 10014

This book is an original publication of Penguin Random House LLC.

Copyright © 2015 by Beth Kery.
Penguin supports copyright. Copyright fuels creativity, encourages diverse voices, promotes free speech, and creates a vibrant culture. Thank you for buying an authorized edition of this book and for complying with copyright laws by not reproducing, scanning, or distributing any part of it in any form without permission. You are supporting writers and allowing Penguin to continue to publish books for every reader.

BERKLEY® and the "B" design are registered trademarks of Penguin Random House LLC.
For more information, visit penguin.com.

Library of Congress Cataloging-in-Publication Data

Kery, Beth.
Glow / Beth Kery.—Berkley trade paperback edition.
p. cm.
ISBN 978-0-425-27966-3 (paperback)
1. Romantic suspense fiction. 2. Erotic fiction. I. Title.
PS3611.E79G65 2015
813'.6—dc23
2015017874

PUBLISHING HISTORY
Berkley trade paperback edition / December 2015

PRINTED IN THE UNITED STATES OF AMERICA

10 9 8 7 6 5 4 3 2 1

Cover images: woman by Maksim Toome / Shutterstock;
glow/flare by Godruma / Shutterstock; background by Igor Zh. / Shutterstock;
pattern by siam sompunya / Shutterstock.
Cover design by George Long.
Text design by Kristin del Rosario.

This is a work of fiction. Names, characters, places, and incidents either are the product of the author's imagination or are used fictitiously, and any resemblance to actual persons, living or dead, business establishments, events, or locales is entirely coincidental.

Penguin
Random
House

ACKNOWLEDGMENTS

As always, I'd like to give thanks and love to my husband, who gives me everything from rich factual information to much-needed support while I'm writing a book. My thanks also go out to my wonderful readers, whose encouragement, feedback, and good wishes offer much-needed daily fuel for a career that is mostly carried out in solitude.

Dear Reader,

I'm so excited that the sequel to *Glimmer* is finally making its way to your bookstores and e-readers! This marked the first time in my writing history that I had a story arc that I felt was just too big to squeeze into one book. After writing *Glimmer*, I knew there was much, much more to tell about Alice and Dylan. In *Glow*, I wanted to give Alice the opportunity to surmount the incredible challenges associated with her past and grow to a self-confident woman who is learning how to trust . . . and love. I hope you are as thrilled with the conclusion of Dylan and Alice's intensely passionate and emotional romance as I am.

Thank you for reading!
Beth

ONE

The night after the fierce storm, Alice dreamed while she lay in the circle of Dylan Fall's arms.

She was again sitting in front of the vanity mirror at the Twelve Oaks Inn—that lovely home overlooking the lake where Dylan had first told her she was special to him, where she'd first realized she was more than passingly pretty in an edgy, "I don't take any shit" kind of way. She was beautiful. Desirable. That was a truth she'd read in Dylan's eyes that night.

In the dream, Deanna Shrevecraft, the sophisticated, kind owner of the Twelve Oaks Inn who had been so knowing and compassionate of Alice's awkwardness during the romantic getaway, was once again applying her makeup.

"Your eyes are so pretty," Deanna murmured as she gently stroked on eye shadow.

"Dylan doesn't like the way I wear my makeup," Alice confessed impulsively, once again experiencing a sharp pain of embarrassment at the memory of Dylan's words. *I hate that you darken your eyebrows. And you shouldn't put so much liner and mascara on your eyes.*

"He doesn't like to see you hiding yourself. He knows there's something special underneath," Deanna said matter-of-factly.

"If you think basket-case geeks are special," Alice mumbled.

"Some are," Deanna assured with a glance of amusement. She

reached for a tray of eye pencils. Something glittered on her wrist, capturing Alice's attention. An uneasy feeling coursed through her.

"How did you get that bracelet?" Alice demanded. She noticed Deanna's startled expression. "I mean . . ." What *did* Alice mean, snapping at Deanna that way? "It's so pretty," she faltered awkwardly. The vision of the unique bracelet on Deanna's wrist felt wrong somehow. Out of place. But Alice's dreaming brain struggled to recall *why* exactly.

"My husband gave it to me," Deanna said, stepping toward her with an eye pencil in her hand. Alice lunged back when she saw the stains and burns on her gripping fingers, the dirty fingernails. A familiar chemical odor entered her nose, toxic and foul. She looked up, startled, and saw the gray pallor of a ravaged face. Deanna had disappeared. In the magical way of dreams, Sissy had taken her place.

Alice's mother, Sissy Reed, was forty-five years old. She could easily pass for seventy. It was one of the many hazards of being a methamphetamine cook and abuser.

Anger flooded Alice, not because of the vision of her mother, but because Sissy dared to wear the exquisite rare bracelet. She grabbed at her mother's bony wrist, lifting the bracelet with the ridge of her finger.

"This isn't yours. You stole it. Your husband didn't give it to you! You don't even have a husband, Sissy." She pushed at the other woman's arm disdainfully, guilt mixing with disgust when she realized how hollow and insubstantial Sissy felt . . . when she saw how she stumbled back at her shove.

"You never would call me Mom," Sissy accused, her passive-aggressive whine an all too familiar splinter under Alice's skin.

"You never did earn the title."

Her disgust and guilt stung like acid at the back of her throat. So did her longing for something different. Something *more*.

Before her eyes, Sissy altered, transforming into a beautiful pale-faced woman with large blue eyes—eyes that looked very much like Alice's, except they were wide with terror. Alice realized with her own sense of dawning horror that there was bright crimson liquid wetting the side of the woman's cheek and neck. She reached out to Alice, desperate in her intent, and Alice again saw the delicate gold bracelet on her wrist.

"*Run*, Addie. Hide!"

Alice awoke, gagging in fear.

She looked wildly around the shadow-draped bedroom, searching for a threat. Her heart was beating like it might explode any second now.

Within seconds, Dylan's embrace penetrated her anxiety. Eased it. She was in Dylan's suite at Castle Durand. She was in his arms.

Safe.

She exhaled shakily, willing her racing heart to slow.

With waking rationality and returning memory, Alice recognized that the unique gold bracelet belonged to neither Deanna Shrevecraft nor Sissy Reed. The last woman in the dream, Lynn Durand, had been the true owner of it.

She'd seen that bracelet and the wearer in dreams before tonight. In fact, she'd *thought* she'd seen the woman walking right in front of her while she was wide awake. At the time, she'd wondered if it was a ghost. Later, she'd realized it was her own long-forgotten memory resurfacing within the familiar setting of the Durand mansion.

Lynn was the wife of Alan Durand, the maverick brilliant businessman who had founded Durand Enterprises, the multibillion-dollar international company that manufactured everything from candy to yogurt to sports drinks. Durand chocolates and confections were a mainstay across every candy counter in the world. Just through the surrounding woods was another Durand legacy: Camp Durand, an acclaimed summer camp that served at-risk children from Chicago and Detroit. Camp Durand was Alan and

Lynn's favorite charitable endeavor. Alice was a Camp Durand counselor, one of fifteen MBA graduates who had been hand-picked by Durand executive officers to compete for nine highly coveted Durand junior management positions.

Was she really just going on her third week at Camp Durand? Time had become so difficult to gauge. Especially since a few days ago, when Alice's life had been heaved completely upside-down.

Really, the first shaking of Alice's known world came the moment she'd walked into the business department's dean's office months ago for an interview with the impossibly gorgeous, light-years-out-of-her-league CEO of Durand Enterprises, Dylan Fall: the man who currently held her naked body against his own.

The man who currently held her naked heart in his hand.

"I knew I would care about you. I had no idea I'd fall in love with you."

She pressed her fingers against her breastbone. Her heart squeezed with anguished wonder at the memory of Dylan saying those words just hours ago, following their stormy lovemaking. The memory felt very beautiful to her: fragile and tender, new and raw, the weight of the reality of his words seemingly too big to hold inside her. She was desperate to believe him, but she wasn't sure she *could*.

Especially given the magnitude of all the other information she'd been told in the last few days. The nightmare from which she'd awakened brought it home to her. She was very confused.

Very afraid?

In his sleep, Dylan shifted slightly and pulled her tighter against him. Unnamed emotion swelled in her chest, feeling like an expanding balloon. For a few panicked seconds, she couldn't breathe from the pressure of it. *Jesus.* How was it possible for her to have acquired this level of feeling for him when she'd barely known he existed these last few months, and only been intimate with him for an even shorter period of time?

You've known him longer than a few months, that's why. You've known him for most of your life, a firm, authoritative voice in her head said. She flinched instinctively at the harsh reminder, air popping out of her lungs. Alice could only withstand the truth in small, rapid doses. It was like her body and her brain weren't entirely her own. Her weakness mortified her. She needed to do better. She needed to be stronger.

Alice Reed didn't run from the truth.

The comforter and sheet had slipped beneath her breasts. The air conditioner felt chilly against her bare skin, but Dylan warmed her backside. Alice craved the sensation of sinking deeper into his embrace, of melting into him. He made her forget everything. His heat and touch were the sweetest addiction.

But just like the first time she'd awakened in his arms, she furtively eased out of his embrace.

Abandoning her defenses and submitting to comfort was something Alice had been nearly hardwired to resist. As a child, she'd forced herself to sleep with the windows open, even in the most frigid nights of a Chicago winter, warding herself against the toxic fumes inherent to Sissy's "business." Although the trailer resounded with the abrasive, harsh voices of her uncles and Sissy's customers, Alice never used a fan, radio, or television to trick her brain into the safety of solid sleep. She needed to hear a threat coming to her locked bedroom, to prepare herself for a fight or an escape. A potential fire from Sissy's meth lab was yet another nightly reality for which she had to prepare herself. Escaping her history was proving to be a challenge.

She shivered as she stood next to the bed, and then cautiously moved through the dark room. Earlier, she'd seen Dylan hang her clothing in the bathroom. The thunderstorm had caught them in its first furious lash. They'd only arrived at the rear entrance of Castle Durand several seconds after the rain began to pour down in torrents.

Her T-shirt was still a little damp. She hauled it on nevertheless, willfully ignoring the fluffy, cozy, dry robe Dylan had bought
her. Her shivers amplified as she unrolled the damp fabric over her
breasts and belly. She ignored her jean shorts and sufficed with her
mostly dry underwear.

When she silently exited the bathroom, she paused for a
moment in the still room, listening. Everything was silent. Dylan
slept on. It was for the best. He wouldn't approve of her mission.
Or at the very least, he'd insist on being there by her side while she
undertook it. She vividly recalled his words during their heated
lovemaking last night as the storm raged around them.

*"I don't like you being down at that camp, Alice. I can't con-
trol what happens to you."*

*"You can't control what happens every second of my day,"
she whimpered, because he'd pressed her to him, her back to his
front, and was reassuring himself of her existence and safety in
the most elemental way.*

*"Maybe not," he rasped, running his teeth over the skin of her
neck and molding her breast to his hand. "But right now I can."*

Mixed feelings of renewed arousal, irritation, and stark compassion at his concern swept through Alice at the volatile memory.
She'd struggled to be independent and self-determined for her
entire life. Dylan's proprietary attitude over her nettled a little. His
possessiveness also thrilled her a lot, a fact that often had warning
sirens going off in her head.

But Dylan had a *right* to his worry, didn't he? He'd earned it.
He'd been consumed for more than half his life at the idea of finding Alan Durand's kidnapped and assumed-dead daughter, Adelaide "Addie" Durand. Everyone else had long ago accepted that
Addie had been murdered and lay in some long-forgotten makeshift grave. It was Dylan's unwavering conviction—a stubborn
refusal to concede defeat, a bullheaded determination even against
horrible odds that had been born and bred in his youth in the

rough, unforgiving streets of Chicago's West Side—that had eventually led Dylan to Addie.

But Alice had no such personal ties or strong feelings toward Adelaide Durand. To her, that privileged, adorable little girl was a distant tragedy. If anything, that child was relevant primarily because of the singular effect Addie had on Dylan's life.

That's what Alice told herself, anyway, as she stood in that cool dark room, chilled to the bone.

She wavered on her feet, suppressing a powerful longing to get back into bed and cuddle against Dylan's solid length. The vision of Lynn Durand's exquisite bracelet flashed into her mind's eye again.

Bizarre as it seemed, that bracelet was not just a random dream created by Alice's unconscious mind. Her recollection of that bracelet was a genuine memory. Because as much as she was struggling to believe it, Dylan swore it was the absolute truth.

According to Dylan, Alice Reed and Adelaide Durand were one and the same person.

IT was the second time in a week that Dylan awoke in the dark room to find his arms empty. Instinct told him that it was still too early for him to escort Alice to the camp, a clandestine ritual they went through every morning before dawn. Neither of them wanted the Durand managers or the VP of human resources, Sebastian Kehoe, to know that Alice had taken up with the CEO of the company. What was between Alice and him was complicated and powerful.

And it was their business alone.

At least for now it was.

Dylan wasn't sure how long he could keep Alice and Durand Enterprises in separate spheres. For all intents and purposes, Alice *was* Durand Enterprises. She just didn't want to—or couldn't—accept that reality as of yet.

"She'll let you know when she's ready to hear certain things, Dylan. She won't ask what she doesn't want to know. That's nature's way; the unconscious mind's attempt at shielding her from the truth until she's ready to handle it."

It was his friend Sidney Gates's voice that he heard in his head. Sidney was a psychiatrist, and an old friend of Alan Durand's. He was very familiar with Addie's—and Alice's—history. Dylan trusted his opinion more than anyone else's when it came to Alice's state of mind at that point.

The problem is, Sidney had also compared Alice to an undetonated cache of explosives. No one knew for sure what would set her off at this point.

Alarmed by the thought, he reached blindly, finding his cell phone on the bedside table. He squinted at the time. No, he'd been right. It was only a few minutes past two in the morning, way too early for Alice to be up and preparing to return to the camp.

He rose from the bed with just as much haste and alarm as that first time, but on this occasion with more certainty that he knew where to find her. The knowledge didn't quiet his worry any. He switched on a bedside lamp and hauled on some jeans.

He found Alice standing square in the middle of the empty large bedroom suite in the west hall, her fists clamped tight at her sides. Her long toned legs were naked. They looked strangely vulnerable in the bright glow of the overhead chandelier.

Tension coiled tight in his muscles. On that other night when he'd found a disoriented Alice standing in the hallway, she'd claimed to have seen a woman; a woman Dylan knew to have been dead for nearly twenty years. It was as if her long-buried, resurging memories were too foreign for her to process, so they'd leapt into the solid surroundings of her waking world, like a weird unconscious hologram effect. Or at least that's how Sidney Gates had tried to explain it to Dylan.

It was so hard, not knowing what to expect from her from one moment to the next. He felt like he could only be certain of her when he was making love to her, when she was entirely present in the moment with him, abandoning herself to pleasure.

To him.

"Do you remember who this room belonged to now?" he asked from behind her, his voice echoing off the bare walls of the large, mostly empty suite. She'd accused him of manipulation and lying when she'd realized he'd purposefully kept her from entering this room. That was before he'd told her the truth about her identity.

He was glad when she started slightly and turned her head, meeting his stare. She looked fully alert. Since Alice had come to Castle Durand, there were a few times when she'd go still in his presence, and it'd been like the ghosts of her past flickered in her eyes.

Is that what *he* was to her? A ghost?

"Was it Addie Durand's room?" she asked slowly, her low hoarse voice causing his skin to roughen.

His heart knocked against his sternum, even though he knew his appearance remained calm. No matter how hard he was trying—no matter how much he understood—he couldn't entirely adjust to Alice's distant, disconnected attitude about Adelaide Durand. It was . . .

Eerie.

He nodded and stepped toward her. "It was originally the nursery, and it had just been remodeled as a bedroom before Addie was taken. Addie's 'big girl' bedroom," he added with a small smile. "Are you remembering?" he asked her again cautiously.

She shook her head adamantly. Her short dark hair was growing. Her spiky bangs fell into her eyes. She stuck out her bottom lip and blew up on her bangs to clear her vision. The uncontrived, sexy gesture distracted him.

Just like most things about Alice did.

"I don't remember."

Despite her quick, firm denial, he wasn't entirely sure he believed her. "Then why did you come here?"

"I was curious," she replied, eyebrows arching in response to his quiet challenge.

"And how did you guess this was Addie's room?"

She shrugged. "You tried to keep me from it. And it's the best situated in the house, so large and airy . . ." She faded off, glancing around at the ornate crown molding, the bluish-silver-colored silk wallpaper, and the enormous bay window with a built-in curving cushioned bench that looked down on the gardens and the sharp drop-off of the craggy limestone bluff to Lake Michigan. Because it was night, their reflections glowed brightly in the opaque black glass. The room was nearly empty, only a few of his personal items remained from his recent occupancy. "You and Sidney had suggested how the Durands prized Addie so much, always giving her the best," she continued. "So I guessed the best bedroom suite had belonged to her. And it belonged to you. Alan Durand prized you, as well," she added, once again meeting his stare squarely.

Slowly, she spun to face him. She wore only the fitted T-shirt she'd worn at the bonfire and a semitransparent pair of white cotton panties. Instinctively, his gaze dropped over her, trailing over her elegantly sloping shoulders, the full thrusting breasts that stood in such erotic contrast to her slender limbs, narrow waist and hips. His gaze lingered between her thighs. Alice dyed the hair on her head to an obscuring near-black color, but her true shade was a dark red-gold, a combination of her father's blond and her mother's rich auburn. Despite the tension of the moment, he felt his body flicker with arousal at the vision of the auburn triangle of hair beneath the see-through fabric. There was something about the contrast of Alice's tough-girl strength and her potent vulnerability that lit a fire in him, something elemental and strong.

He dragged his gaze to her face.

"It must be strange for you, thinking of me living in Addie's room. Here. In the Durand's house," he added, taking another step toward her. He was often approaching Alice like he might a half-wild animal, highly aware that she might bolt at any moment.

He was determined to catch her, no matter what move she made.

She shook her head. She wore not a trace of makeup. Without the heavy eyeliner and mascara she often wore to hide herself or intimidate—or both—her dark blue eyes looked enormous in her delicate face. God, what he'd experienced when she'd walked into that office last May, so awkward and yet so defiant in her inexpensive new interview suit. The truth had slammed home, jarring him, rattling him to the center of his bones, even though he'd taken great pains to hide his shock. He had seen those sapphire-blue eyes before. But even if it *had* been the first time Dylan had ever seen her, he suspected he might have been nearly as shaken. No wonder she'd been drawn to the eye goop. Her eyes would draw men with the noblest intentions.

And the foulest.

"No, it doesn't seem strange to me at all. I can see you in this room. Did Alan suggest you take it?"

"He did, yes. Just before he died."

"You moved out of it"—her chin tilted and her eyes sparked in that familiar defiant gesture—"because of me, didn't you?"

"I didn't know what to expect. Sidney thought we should cautiously expose you to the surroundings," he admitted. Sidney had suggested bringing her to the estate under the pretense of hiring her as a Camp Durand counselor when they discovered that—miraculously—she was a business major. In those circumstances, Dylan could determine what she recalled about living there—if anything—and see how she reacted to the environment. If not Dylan personally, then the two Durand security employees he'd ordered to covertly watch her while at the camp could give him insights as to her state of mind.

"I was familiar with Addie Durand's habits," he said slowly.

"There are a few places that I worried might be more likely to trigger memories too quickly. This one, even though it's been redecorated. Alan and Lynn's suite. The den, the stables, the library . . . and the dining room. The entry hall, the kitchen, the living room, the terrace gardens, and the media room have been extensively renovated, so I didn't worry as much about that. Most of the other bedrooms here weren't used much—either by the Durands or me, so they weren't of any concern."

He hesitated. "I never imagined you'd inadvertently find your way into the dining room that first night at the castle. Or the stables the next day," Dylan told her, choosing his words carefully. Alice had made it very clear to him that while she would discuss the details of Addie Durand, Addie's kidnapping, and Dylan's part in the tragedy, she wouldn't talk about Addie and herself as if they were the same person. Currently, they were treading on volatile ground.

Her eyelids narrowed slightly, and he knew he'd made some kind of misstep, despite his caution. "You suspected I was going to be in your bedroom, even before I came here? And so you moved suites, in order not to trigger any . . ." She faded off uncertainly, aware she was skimming close to the fire. Her defiant expression made a quick resurgence. "I thought you said that you hadn't planned for anything sexual between us . . . that it just *happened* that morning in the stables?"

"That's true. And since you seem to need a reminder, *you're* the one who seduced *me*, Alice," he said with a stern, pointed glance meant to quash her suspicion immediately. It didn't work. He damned her defensive posture and closed the space between them. Satisfaction went through him when he took her into his arms, and the tension melted from her muscles. She pressed against him.

"If that's what you want to call the first three seconds of what happened in those stables. It was all you after that, baby," she grumbled under her breath.

"I didn't hear you complaining."

Her eyes flashed up at him.

"I'm telling you the *truth*," Dylan said succinctly. "I didn't plan for us to be together in the stables that morning. How could I have? I didn't know you'd show up there. I *didn't* plan for us to get involved in that way when you came to the Durand Estate."

"Then why would you worry about me being here . . . in this room? Why did you pack up most of your things and decorate a whole new suite, if you didn't *plan* on us sleeping together from the first? Why else would I be in the CEO of Durand Enterprises' *bedroom* if you didn't expect us to become lovers?" she demanded.

Dylan suppressed a sigh. Despite the fact that she grasped his waist and lightly pressed her breasts and belly against him in a tempting gesture, her trademark wary expression remained as she stared up at him.

"I didn't do it because I had plans to seduce you," he told her with an air of finality, mapping her elegant, supple spine and the tight curve of her hip with his hands. He felt his need for her mount. How would all of this have played out, if this powerful attraction hadn't been there? It was so hard to say, but he would have contrived something to bring her closer to him.

"*Why*, then?" she insisted, undaunted by a tone that Dylan used regularly to cow some of the most tried and hard-boiled executives in the world. Of course it didn't faze Alice. He closed his eyes briefly. Damn it, she could be impossible.

"Dylan?"

"I felt like an interloper, being in here . . . knowing you were about to come to the Durand Estate."

"You felt like an *interloper*?" she asked slowly, looking dazed. "Because this was Alan Durand's house? Because of your history with him?"

He held her stare. "Because it was no longer my room, Alice. No longer my home, really. Not since you came. Period."

Regret sliced through him at his harsh tone when he saw her lush lower lip quiver.

"I'm sorry," he said, frustrated. "It's just that sometimes, you keep pressing. And it's hard to know when you want the truth and when you don't."

"I know," she said quickly. She, too, looked regretful. "And it's not true, what you said. Of course Castle Durand is your home. You own it, don't you? You bought it?"

"Yes, but only because Alan Durand offered the house to me as part of the special contract he created to make it possible for me to purchase Durand shares when he made me the CEO. I wouldn't have been able to afford it at that time in my life if he didn't offer me certain concessions." He exhaled at the memory of their negotiations for his taking over Durand Enterprises. Alan had been so stubborn. So insistent. So *generous* in contriving a way to set terms that would allow Dylan to smoothly and completely take over the helm of the company. He missed Alan Durand, more than he liked to admit.

"Once, a lord's title was tied to the land. That's what Alan explained to me. Alan loved his European history and traveling," he recalled with fond, wry amusement. "He insisted that I'd be taken more seriously as the head of Durand Enterprises if I was master of the company's symbolic domain."

"The castle and the estate," Alice said, a small smile flickering across her lips. She sobered. "I don't think I've ever heard what he died of. Alan Durand."

"Testicular cancer."

He saw a shadow cross her face. He tensed. But she'd asked, hadn't she? She'd been prepared for that truth? He was wary of her asking more questions. Instead, she inhaled and looked away.

She's not ready to discuss their deaths any further yet. He didn't know if he should be worried or relieved about that. He did know one thing. If *he* ever made the bizarre discovery that he'd once had a loving mother and father, he wouldn't be too eager to plunge into the topic of losing them before he'd ever even known them. Her denial was the only way she was coping right now, and he had to try to respect that while she slowly assimilated to a new reality. It'd only been a few days since he'd told her about Addie Durand, after all.

He felt as if he navigated a minefield with no map.

"You *are* the master of this house, Dylan," she said, sounding subdued.

"No. Not entirely."

He cupped her jaw, trying to ease her sudden troubled expression . . . her abrupt fragility. She looked up at him through her spiky bangs, her glance reminding him again of a cautious, wild thing.

"It's just so impossible to believe," she said in a rush. "I mean, it's not that I think you're lying. Why *would* you? It's just . . ." Her expression grew a little desperate as she seemingly searched for words to explain. "You can't just start thinking of the world as round in a second when you've thought it was flat for your whole life." She gave a sharp bark of laughter, as if she'd just absorbed the meaning of her words only upon hearing them. "It's not a bad analogy, really," she mumbled to herself. "I sort of feel like I might fall straight off the earth into nothingness every time I think about what you told me. Please understand."

"I *do*," he assured quietly, his fingers delving into her silky short hair. He cupped her skull. It was hard to be the rational executive when it came to Alice. It was hard to be clearheaded in this situation period. But he had to try. So much was at stake.

"What do you think would help you to make it real?"

She shook her head. "I don't know for sure. Just time, I guess."

He nodded, lowering his head until her upturned face was just inches from him. "Do you think it might help to see tangible proof?"

She blinked. "Like what? More photos?"

He pulled her tighter against him. Her T-shirt felt cool and slightly damp against the naked skin of his torso. Despite the chill of the fabric, it was the sensation of her full breasts pressing against his ribs that made his skin roughen. Her erect nipples were a distraction. He forced himself to focus.

"Not just photos. You've said yourself you don't experience any connection to photos of Adelaide Durand."

"What, then?" she asked in a hushed tone.

"Alan and Lynn Durand's physician still practices at Morgantown Memorial. He's in possession of some of their genetic material. Alan arranged it that way before he passed, because he wanted to make sure there was a potential means of identifying Addie. You could find out without a doubt if the Durands were your parents."

She stared up at him blankly. "You want me to go for genetic testing?"

"Only if you're up for it. It doesn't have to be now," he said, caressing her neck. He'd learned from experience in the past week that his touch helped to ground her. Soothe her. Distract her from her phantoms. It was selfish, too, but he wasn't above using that fact proactively to help her through this process.

He wasn't above using *anything*, in that cause.

"You mean . . . it doesn't have to be *now*, but it does have to be *sometime*."

He strained to keep his expression impassive, very much aware that he was once again walking through a minefield.

"I knew the truth almost the first second I saw you. I don't need any proof that what I told you is one hundred percent true," he said, holding her stare.

"But there *will* be those that demand the solid proof."

An imagined vision of a roomful of somber Durand executives and attorneys—all the potential doubters and naysayers, people who were panicked at the idea of possible upheaval at Durand Enterprises—flew into his mind's eye. "There will be plenty who eventually want to see those test results," he repeated as calmly as possible.

She bit her lip and glanced aside. Aside from all these bizarre circumstances she found herself in, Dylan knew Alice Reed was typically a practical, down-to-earth young woman with a brilliant brain for mathematics and business. Never let it be said that genes weren't telling. Alan Durand had possessed one of the finest business minds he'd ever known, and Lynn had been an outstanding scholar. She'd been an assistant professor of mathematics at the University of Michigan when Alan had first met her. He was glad to see Alice focus so rationally on the difficult topic.

"I don't want anything of Addie Durand's, so why should it matter?" she asked.

"You don't know that yet."

"I know what I want and don't want, Dylan."

"Then do it for yourself," he suggested without pause. He'd been prepared for her response. He'd been prepared for her stubbornness.

"Myself?"

He nodded. "That's what I meant before. *You* need tangible proof. Not just my word. You need firsthand evidence. It'll be something firm to grasp onto."

"A solid start," she whispered.

"A solid start," Dylan agreed, relief sweeping through him because he'd seen something click in her gaze, and knew she'd go for the genetic testing. He needed that tangible proof as a shield against potential challenges.

He leaned down and brushed his mouth against hers. His kiss was meant to be gentle and reassuring, but Alice was having none of it. She put her hand on the back of his head, pulling him farther down to her and going up on her tiptoes. He responded to her invitation as always.

Wholesale.

Their kiss deepened. His lust flared high on the fuel of her reciprocated need. So sweet. So Alice-like, to be wary and doubting one moment, and then taking him to the center of the flames within two seconds flat.

He would have to have her again tonight, experience her melting beneath his touch, laid bare and submitting to the bond between them. He needed it for Alice's sake.

He required it for his own.

TWO

Dylan leaned down over her, their mouths melding, their tongues tangling. His hands were greedy and sure as they molded her back muscles and hips, and then slid beneath her underwear to cup her buttocks. Alice pressed closer to him, becoming desperate at the evidence of his growing erection just behind the fly of his jeans. Her hands mimicked his, sliding beneath the low waistband of his jeans and caressing the round hard globes of his ass. Arousal spiked through her, demanding and sharp. She thought it must have been the same for Dylan, because he groaned roughly into her mouth and shifted his hands as if to lift her.

She knew him well enough to guess he was about to carry her to bed and consume her utterly. One thing about Dylan: He never did anything halfway.

"No," she whispered hoarsely against his lips when she abruptly broke their kiss.

"No *what*?" he muttered, his dark brows slanting dangerously as he looked down at her, his mouth set in a grim line. She also knew Dylan well enough to know he didn't like being denied what he wanted, *when* he wanted it.

How he wanted it.

"In here," Alice coaxed, cupping his whiskered jaw and urging him back down to her mouth. She didn't know why she'd said it, precisely. There wasn't a single piece of furniture in the room.

Or maybe she *did* know. She hadn't liked what he'd said about this house and this room not being his. She wanted him to claim this space in the most elemental way.

Maybe she wanted to stake her claim, too. This room, this house, this world . . . none of it belonged to her. The only way she seemed capable of navigating this alien new territory was with Dylan as her guide. Her link. Sometimes, their passion, their intense hunger for one another, was the only thing that seemed real to her.

For a few seconds, he resisted her urging, his expression going hard and unreadable as he looked down at her. She rubbed her breasts seductively against his lower chest and ribs, circling her pelvis against his cock. Something sparked in his lustrous dark eyes. *Gypsy eyes*—that's how she thought of them. She gyrated her hips more firmly. Triumph surged through her when she saw the telltale snarl shape his mouth. She slid her fingers into the cleft in his chin and then over his firm lips, tempting him.

Still, he didn't move.

She slid one hand down the smooth skin of his torso, relishing the way he roughened beneath her touch. She looked down to where her fingers touched him, watching herself caress the two scars just below his ribs. Powerful emotion surged through her. Dylan had been stabbed there by Addie Durand's kidnappers. He'd almost died as a boy of fourteen, trying to save that little girl. She clenched her eyelids shut, but almost immediately opened them, aware of Dylan's hawk-like stare and not wanting to betray her vulnerability.

Her fingers lowered, looking for a distraction to lighten her emotional weight. She immediately found it.

He was the most beautiful man she'd ever seen, let alone touched. She loved to taunt him, but that didn't mean she still didn't fear the result a little. She knew more intimately than most that Dylan's polished business exterior shielded a fierce, sometimes savage, always magnificent spirit. Her knowledge of that sharp edge of his personality added a dash of the forbidden to her arousal.

She ran a fingernail over a rib, taking note of his slight flinch. Her fingertips skimmed his taut abdomen, trailing down the silky, thin strip of dark hair beneath his belly button. She pushed her forefinger beneath the waistband of his jeans and stroked his skin in that vulnerable sweet spot: up and down, up and down. His expression grew hard as stone, his stare on her narrowing. She grasped the top button of his jeans, feeling his tension and her own anticipation mounting. Very deliberately, she slipped the button free of the hole while holding his stare.

Leaving most of his button fly fastened, she reached beneath his jeans, finding his velvety-smooth cockhead where it pressed below his hip bone. She slid her fingers over the well-defined, succulent crown and gave a firm, abrupt upward tug beneath the rim.

He jerked and hissed. The next thing she knew, he'd pinned her hands at the small of her back. She gasped and then laughed shakily when he roughly turned her in his arms.

"You get your way far too easily, do you know that?" he told her, his low, silky voice and warm, firm lips on her ear and throat sending a potent thrill through her. He pressed against her backside and transferred her captured wrists to the front of her. He flexed his hips, pushing his cock against her ass, a steel-hard demand. She moaned. His teeth rasped gently against the pebbled skin of her neck, and her moan turned shaky. "But sometimes, you're bound to get more than you bargained for, Alice," he hissed near her ear before his mouth closed on the opening, and pleasure rippled through her.

He pushed her from behind, urging her to move toward the bay window. Alice caught a glimpse of her face in the dark mirror of the shining glass. Her eyes looked enormous, her expression a strange mixture of anxiety and arousal. She'd recognized that warning in his voice just now. She *did* love to tease him, and there was always a price to pay for taunting a tiger. But it was what she needed at that moment, the forgetfulness of his demanding passion.

"Bend over and put your hands on the seat," he growled softly. Her heartbeat leapt into double time.

Yes. This is *precisely* what she wanted.

She bent at the waist, placing her palms down on the cushioned seat. The action sent her ass even tighter against his crotch. She bit off a moan and pressed closer. She could feel the outline of his erection and the subtle throb of his arousal. A cry leaked past her lips when he placed his hands on her ass in a possessive gesture. He stepped back, sliding his palms against her skin, lowering her cotton underwear to her thighs in the process.

"Spread your legs," he instructed shortly. Alice opened her thighs several inches. The action stretched her panties tight just above her knees. She knew she'd taken the position he desired when she heard his rough groan. He opened one hand on her right buttock and caressed her.

"Something tells me you need a good spanking," he told her. "Am I right?"

"I don't deserve it," she said with shaky defiance. His touch on her bottom was highly distracting, but she wanted to make sure she didn't sound like too much of a pushover.

"But you need it," he corrected, his blunt fingertips lightly feathering down the crack of her ass. She gasped, her pelvic and thigh muscles tightening around the sharp twang of arousal she experienced at his touch. "Don't you?" Dylan demanded gently from behind her.

"Yes."

"And you know I'm here to give you what you need."

She glanced up into the black window before her, hearing the small smile in his voice. If he wasn't humorous at times during his dominance, she didn't think she could take it, no matter how much it turned her on. Dylan always did things just right.

He'd already been watching her reflection. His mouth twitched even wider when he saw her gaze on him.

"How fortunate for me," she murmured with wary amusement. He reached with his other hand, cupping her from below. He molded both cheeks to his palms in a taut, greedy gesture.

"How fortunate for both of us," he added thickly, massaging her lewdly—knowingly—for a moment before he dropped his hands. His smile vanished.

"Spread your thighs again, and keep them that way this time," he said, tapping her inner thigh gently. She made a miffed sound at his brisk correction—she'd only closed her legs some because arousal had stabbed through her at his touch, after all. He placed one hand on her left buttock, holding it possessively, and swatted the cheek with his other palm. Alice jumped slightly. "Hold still, Alice," he warned softly. Her breath sticking in her lungs, she met his glittering stare in the dark glass. Slowly, he moved his hand back, his muscles flexing.

He popped her bottom.

"Ow," jumped out of her throat at the brisk sting of skin against skin. He never spanked her hard enough to cause any lasting pain. The experience was still new to her, however. It surprised her every time, how exciting it was.

"No more grumbling." In the reflection, she saw his brows slant in dark amusement at her frown. He rubbed her flushed ass cheek with his spanking hand. "You agreed that you wanted this, didn't you?"

She swallowed thickly, because he'd begun to massage her bottom with his other hand, as well. Her pussy was growing very wet. Her clit ached. She longed to clamp her thighs together, but knew she had to hold position for the spanking.

"Alice?"

"Yes," she snapped. She saw his expression go hard at her tone. He lifted his hand and spanked her right buttock once, then twice. Alice moaned and shifted her hips instinctively when he raised his hand again. He captured her squirming ass by looping one arm beneath her belly and bracketing her far hip. He pressed her other hip firmly against his crotch, holding her in place. In that position, he spanked her several more times. The nerves in her ass began to burn and tingle, the sensation transferring down her perineum to her sex and simmering clit.

He paused and rubbed his hand over her ass, soothing the firing nerves.

"Yes *what*, Alice? What is it you want?" he growled softly from behind her.

She gasped shakily because his long fingers were stroking near the crack of her ass between her thighs. Her clit gave a twinge of arousal.

"I want more," she grated out.

He cupped a buttock from below, squeezing it. The action pulled slightly on her sex—on nerves that needed stimulation *so* badly. She clenched her teeth together.

"And?"

"Fuck me," she whispered hoarsely. "Make me forget everything but this. Make me forget everything but you."

In the dark window, she saw him transfer his gaze from her bare ass to her face.

"I can do that."

"I *know* you can."

HE turned her bottom a vibrant pink, relishing her increasingly desperate moans as he swatted and caressed her, intoxicated by the heat emanating from her smooth, taut skin and firm cheeks.

He loved both her slight defiance at being spanked combined with her complete immersion and submission to the experience. He walked a tight wire. At any moment, he might cross the line and infuriate her. Pricking her defiance sexually was a risk, but the challenge goaded him. It intoxicated.

Alice did.

And every time she submitted to the bond between them, he drew her closer to him.

He placed both of his hands on her hot buttocks and lifted slightly, revealing her pink, glistening sex. Arousal tore through him. His cock twitched uncomfortably. He dropped one hand, still leaving her partially parted for his gaze. He rubbed his raging erection through his jeans, trying to alleviate that sharp ache. Her harsh moan made him look up. Her eyes looked enormous in the reflection on the window.

He handled his cock more slowly, highly aware of her stare on him in the shiny glass.

"Is *this* what you want to see when you walk in this room? Is this the memory you want?"

"Yes. God, yes."

"You're never going to forget me again, Alice."

He slid his hand off her buttock. She lowered her head and gasped loudly when he thrust a finger into her pussy. So warm. He saw the slight sheen at her nape and experienced an urge to slick his tongue through her sweat. His greediness for her was epic; his hunger for her complete submission unparalleled.

"I'm not going to forget you. I never did," she added desperately.

He pushed higher, cupping her tender, wet outer sex with his hand, his finger still penetrating her. He circled his hand, stimulating her clit. She made a choking sound.

"Are you remembering more than you're admitting?" he demanded grimly after a moment.

"No," she cried out. "I meant that of all things, you're the most familiar to me. You . . . you bring me the closest," she finished raggedly, panting. He felt a ripple go through her flesh, and knew she was very close to climax.

He froze, still applying a firm pressure to her sex, absorbing her admission. He understood instinctively what she'd meant. It was his presence that brought her closest to the threshold of memory, to the deep, perhaps unbreachable split between her present and her past.

He bent and lowered her panties to her feet.

"Step out of them and get up there on your knees," he prompted. He lowered his hand and grasped her naked hips, guiding her onto the curving bench built beneath the triple bay window. It was a narrow cushioned seat, meant for gazing out to the Great Lake and the magnificent gardens below. "Scoot right up next to the windows."

"But what . . ."

"Just do what I say," he said quietly, urging her toward the wooden frame between the two on the far right and the center window. "Now bend forward and put your hands over your head. Brace them on the wood frame. Don't worry. It's solid. I saw how this window was manufactured during the remodeling of the room before I moved in."

A measure of satisfaction and amplified arousal went through her when she followed his instructions without further hesitation, bending at the waist while she was on her knees, exposing her pink round bottom. Unable to resist the temptation, he spanked her briskly but softly on one buttock, letting his other hand roam up her belly beneath her snug T-shirt. She moaned his name shakily when he cupped a full breast and smacked her bottom again. She turned her face so that it rested on her upper arm and he could see her profile. Her cheeks were as flushed as her ass; her eyelids heavy. She was exquisite. Slowly, erotically, she circled her hips, waving her ass in an eye-crossing temptation.

Beckoning him.

He swatted her firmly, squeezing taut, hot flesh, punishing her for trying to set the pace yet again . . . rewarding her for her singular beauty.

"Alice," he hissed, tested by the vision of her arousal. Her abandon. "Open your eyes."

He saw her eyelids flicker.

"Look at yourself in the window," he commanded. Deliberately, he peeled her T-shirt over the globes of her breast and her head, exposing the beautiful stretch of her naked back. He tossed aside the shirt, his gaze trained on her. Her skin was such a lovely color—peaches and cream where she didn't tan, a coppery apricot where she did. The vision of her pale suspended breasts in the window made him clamp his teeth hard. He'd never known another woman to compare to her. He watched himself in the glass as he stroked her taut belly and suspended breasts for a moment. His cock raged for her.

"You're going to watch me fuck you. You're not going to forget that, are you?" he asked, ripping at his button fly and jerking down his jeans. Despite his hasty actions, he kept his eyes pinned to her luminous face in the black pane.

Her lips framed an emphatic *no.*

He kicked aside his jeans and moved behind her, his cock a heavy ache. She instinctively bent several inches when he held her hips, positioning herself. He grasped his cock and pulled back a hot ass cheek, feral arousal shooting through him at the vision of unspanked white skin in the crack of her ass and her glossy pink sex.

He moved his cock toward her slit. The angle wasn't ideal, but he was determined to make it work. He'd understood Alice's unspoken desire somehow. She wanted to be branded here. She wanted to make this space her own. Theirs.

He was more than happy to give her what she wanted. They'd create more memories, but this was a damn good start.

He lifted his foot, placing it on the cushion next to her knees. He lodged his cockhead at her damp, clamping channel. The angle was much more hospitable now.

"Say it out loud, Alice," he ordered tensely, holding her hips firmly.

"I'll *never* forget."

He plunged his cock into the heaven of her. Her whimper segued to a loud wail.

"Oh God. I'll never forget this. You. Never. Never," she chanted as he began to drive in and out of her sleek body, and their mutual, volatile passion was broadcast like a blazing beacon onto the dark window.

HE saw the light and the figures and immediately plunged into the hedge to hide himself, alarmed he'd be seen. Cautiously, he looked again. A sweat broke out on his brow and neck. He couldn't believe what he was seeing.

Thad Schaefer didn't *want* to believe it, but he couldn't look away nonetheless. It was something no man should ever be forced to witness: the woman of his dreams being utterly sexually consumed by another man.

Damn Fall.

He'd been ordered here for a specific purpose. It'd never been *his* mission, but hadn't life proved to Thad so far that he'd always be at the mercy and bidding of someone else? Although he'd been labeled a natural born leader on many occasions, the truth was he'd been bred into the role of follower. Not the follower of just *anyone*. He performed optimally when the disapproval or approval of a single alpha male was at stake, all thanks to his damn father—the original alpha.

Thad couldn't complete his assigned task if he left, no matter how much part of him longed to run until he collapsed from exhaustion. Another part of him couldn't have walked away even if he'd used every ounce of his will.

He'd known what Alice was doing at the castle night after night with Dylan Fall. But he hadn't guessed *this*. It was one thing to experience the simmer of jealousy at the thought of Alice in another man's bed. But what he was watching at the present moment flayed him down to the bone.

Her naked body rocked and shuddered as Fall took her from behind, her breasts bouncing at the crash of flesh against flesh. Fall's possession wasn't violent, but it *was* forceful. Precise. Total.

To think you ever thought you had a fucking chance.

Her arms were suspended above her head on the frame between the two windows, but he could see the majority of her naked body through the glass. The skin over her ribs was stretched tight, her breasts a full, succulent contrast to her slender carriage. She was amazing; beyond even what he'd fantasized. But it wasn't just her exposed body that held him spellbound. It was what he could see displayed on Alice's face: the pure unadulterated lust and abandonment to the eroticism of the moment.

He thought he saw her wince as Fall became even more demanding. Thad started impulsively, nearly spilling forward onto the stone path and breaking his cover. Was Fall *hurting* her? He stilled, holding his breath, a snarl shaping his mouth.

No. His worries were for nothing. Alice reached between her thighs, still bracing herself with one hand, seeking the relief of release from intense pleasure, not pain.

No sooner had she buried her fingers between her thighs than Fall was grabbing her wrist and putting her hand back on the frame. *Bastard,* Thad thought, although his scorn didn't begin to fracture his focus on the unfolding scene.

Then Fall's hand was between her thighs, and he was thrusting powerfully again. A strange combination of respect and flaming jealousy tore through Thad. *Fall* had wanted to be the one to make her climax. Or he'd been worried about her getting hurt if she didn't support her body adequately, as hard as he was taking her.

Or both, Thad acknowledged with a sinking feeling. It was bizarre and unprecedented for him to feel both sick and sharply aroused at once. Leave it to Alice.

Leave it to Fall, he thought bitterly. Why couldn't Alice see how he was controlling her with his allure of power, money, and sex? He'd been learning a lot about Fall's ruthlessness. His skill at manipulation. Everyone in the business community knew he was used to getting precisely what he wanted. Previously, Thad had respected that characteristic . . . until he'd understood Fall had set his sights on Alice Reed.

Fall's hand moved faster between her thighs, and Alice tilted her head to the side. Thad could almost feel her peaking arousal. The night was pitch dark. Deep cloud cover remained after the storm, obliterating starlight. He could see the erotic tableau with surprising clarity in the lit large bay window. Alice's eyes were shut, as if her entire consciousness had narrowed down to the sensation of Fall taking her by storm. Even at this distance, Thad sensed her focus was absolute. In mixed dread and fascination, he watched as her lush lips parted and her face went tight.

Distantly, he heard her high keen of pleasure.

The sound was like a sharp screw twisting straight through flesh and bone to his very core. Thad wasn't sure how he survived that novel, distilled form of torture. But he stayed.

Until the bitter end.

HE was rocking her so hard, slaking his lust on her, pounding his essence into her deep. Alice wanted it. She *loved* it. At the same time, it was almost too much pleasure and emotion for her to withstand. It hurt in a way that was beyond pain, such a sweet, unbearable agony. She reached with one hand between her thighs, desperate to end it.

"Your job is to keep yourself steady," she heard him rasp. Her eyelids sprung open. Both her palms pressed against the solid frame again. He removed his hand from her wrist and slid it down her belly between her thighs. His cock jumped inside her. She whimpered, arousal cutting at her, as he rubbed her lubricated clit.

"It's mine to give you pleasure," he added hotly near her ear as she crested.

"Oh God," she moaned.

He thrust again. She turned her head to the side, the tense friction mounting with his hand and his pounding cock forcing a high cry from her throat. She climaxed, her raw emotional state and Dylan's effect on her too powerful to suppress. She quaked as he continued to take her hard, hearing his tense erotic praise as if from a distance.

As she quieted, he slid his hands over her belly and ribs, firmly grasping her breasts in his hands. He slowed some in his possession of her. He molded her flesh to his palms. She sagged slightly against the wood frame, panting.

"I told you to watch in the window, Alice," he said, his voice low, a rough threat that both aroused and soothed somehow. "I told you I wanted you to remember."

She opened her eyes sluggishly, turning her head, seeking his image in the glass. His eyes were as black as the night outside the window. Still . . . she made out the glitter of lust in them, the spark of feral possession. His stance—one long leg planted on the floor, the other one bent, his foot on the bench next to her knees, only added to his aura of stark dominance.

"Tense your arms. Hold steady," he said quietly, molding her breasts to his palms, his fingertips gliding over her rigid nipples, pinching them lightly, before he slid his hands to her hips. He waited until she'd firmed her sagging muscles, bracing herself for him. She couldn't take her eyes off him as he began to fuck her again. He owned her in those moments, perhaps more than her past did. Her present.

Maybe even her future.

ALICE felt wrung out by the time Dylan turned out the chandelier in the room and closed the door behind them. His luxurious, mussed bed was a familiar delight, his weight next to her sublime. Sex with Dylan had that effect on her. Afterward, she was usually too sated and exhausted to think.

Or so she'd thought. The past few days had changed her expectations about herself, even about the most basic workings of her mind and body.

A thought kept squirming around in her brain, preventing her from succumbing to sleep.

"Dylan?" she mumbled, her lips brushing against his hard chest.

"Yeah, baby," he replied drowsily, his fingers moving against her scalp. She loved the sound of his deep rough voice in the darkness.

"What about the gong?"

His fingers stilled. When he didn't reply immediately, she elaborated. "There really was a gong, wasn't there? Once? I've been meaning to ask you. Did Addie Durand play with it or something? You know . . . when she lived here?"

She referred to an incident that had occurred when she'd first come to Castle Durand with the rest of the Durand managers and counselors for a dinner party. Alice had left the rest of the group upon hearing a gong struck, walking alone through the large ornate home. The sweet, mysterious note had drawn her unerringly. Dylan had found her in the dining room. At first, Dylan had insisted she couldn't have heard a gong sounding, furthering Alice's humiliation at being caught wandering around his house alone. Later he'd made up a story about his cook, Marie, being responsible for the mysterious sound. A few days ago Alice had discovered his lie about the gong and confronted him with it, which had eventually led to Dylan telling her the truth about Addie Durand.

"Yes. There really is a gong, but no one has struck it in a very long time," he said quietly after a pause. "Alan found it at an antique store once while he was on business in China and gave it to Lynn as a gift. Addie liked some of the unusual items he'd bring home from his trips—"

"Like the knight knocker," Alice said, her voice just above a whisper.

Dylan lifted his hand and then plunged it back into her hair, rubbing her scalp. "Like the knight knocker," he agreed, both of them referring to the unique brass doorknocker on the entryway door to Castle Durand. "He brought the knocker from a trip to Scotland, when Addie was three years old. Addie took a liking to it because of some of the fairy tales about knights Lynn and Alan read her. But the gong?" he asked quietly, his fingers against her scalp creating a drugging effect. "You can't guess what it meant to Addie?"

"I have no idea," she insisted. She fastened on another topic that had been bothering her. "Dylan . . . are you sure that there wasn't any truth to Matt's ghost story at the campfire tonight? Are you *sure* Lynn Durand wasn't there when Addie was taken?"

She tensed when she felt him sit up slightly in bed. "I've told you what happened that day. I was the only one with Addie when she was taken in those woods. *Why?*"

She hesitated. She shouldn't have brought it up, but her curiosity had gotten the best of her. "It's nothing. I just . . . I had a bad dream tonight. It was different than ones I've had before, though. Maybe it was just a nightmare."

He waited intently. She sighed, knowing he expected to hear the details.

"In it, a woman who looked like Lynn Durand was telling Addie to run and hide. She looked kind of banged up, and there was . . . blood on her." She twisted her chin over her shoulder when Dylan didn't immediately respond. He cupped her hip.

"It was just a dream," he said quietly. "That story by the bonfire got to you tonight. Given everything you're going through, that's not too shocking. But I assure you, the story that kid was telling is an urban legend, a ghost story that's been built up and embroidered until only the tiniest part of reality remains. I've asked Kehoe to try to quash the telling of that story, but it always seems to resurface, usually with some sensationalized new twist to it. But what I told you is what actually happened," he said steadfastly. "What you had was definitely just a nightmare. Addie never saw Lynn like that. Never. Okay?"

"Okay. Night," she said softly after a pause. His mouth covered hers in a brief, hot kiss. She twisted back around and held her breath. Thankfully Dylan remained silent. Still, she sensed his sharp attention on her. He didn't entirely believe that she wasn't remembering other things.

Or that she was "fine."

He *should* believe her. Alice only had a few ephemeral snatches of memory that seemed to relate to Dylan's story about Addie Durand. Those snippets didn't really feel like personal memories at all. It was more like she'd undergone some science-fiction surgical technique for having another person's memories stitched into her brain. That handful of tiny, jagged bits of memory created a jarring contrast to the billions of other Alice recollections she'd accumulated through the past two decades of her life.

Sometimes, she felt like a computer that had downloaded a virus. What would happen if those fragments of another's person's

mind—of another person's world—began multiplying and expanding inside her?

Would Alice Reed disappear altogether?

The thought terrified her in the most primitive way, a way she
couldn't convey to Dylan. It was hard to put it into words.

And there was an elusive *feeling* that kept mounting in her. A
suspicion rose in her that if she tried to communicate to Dylan
what that amorphous feeling was, it might take shape and solidify
even further.

Maybe the feeling would become tangible memory?

Leave it in the dark.

Addie Durand and Alice may have been joined once, but the
rift was complete. They were two separate people now. Alice was
a mathematician, after all. Numbers cleaved, they carved out
clear-cut, rational, predictable realities. *That* was how Alice Reed
saw the world. She was overreacting in regard to her fear.

*Of course you can discover a few interesting facts about Addie
Durand without losing Alice. Don't be so nutballs about this.*

Feeling relieved by her self-scolding, she allowed her heavy
eyelids to drop. She sent up a silent prayer for dreamless sleep.

UNFORTUNATELY, a sound night's sleep was just not in the cards
for Alice or Dylan that night.

She startled awake at the jarring sound of a loud, high-pitched
alarm. Before she could utter a single stunned syllable, she felt
Dylan leap out of bed.

"Dylan, what the hell—"

"Stay right there. I *mean* it, Alice, do as I say for once," he
growled tensely. She gasped in disbelief. Did the man have night
vision? How else had he known that she was untangling her legs
from the sheet in order to jump up and follow him? She thought

she heard him moving in the room in the fractions of the seconds between the swelling shrieks of the alarm.

She blinked when the bedside light switched on. She squinted at the vision of Dylan standing next to the bed. He'd pulled on a pair of dark gray pajama bottoms with stunning speed. His face and torso looked tense and hard as he handed her the phone.

"I want you to get up and lock the door after I leave."

"But—"

"There's someone in the house, Alice. If you don't do exactly what I say, I swear I'll—"

"All right, all right," she said in a beleaguered fashion, convinced by his snarling intensity. She threw back the sheet.

He started toward the wood-paneled door. "Call nine-one-one as soon as you lock the door after me," he said over his shoulder. "The police should be on their way since the alarm was triggered, but see if you can have them inform the officers that I'm downstairs in the house. I don't want to be accidentally mistaken for the intruder by the police."

The reality behind his words penetrated. What if the police shot Dylan? What if the burglar did?

"Dylan, wait, *no*—"

"I can take care of myself," he said, pausing briefly with his hand on the doorknob. "Now *lock* this door and stay in this room *until I come to get you*. I'll be distracted if you don't do exactly what I asked you to do. *Alice*." He said her name like an ominous warning. She realized he saw her defiance stamped on her face. The heavy crease of worry on his brow and his fierce glare nudged at her.

She nodded in agreement. He disappeared.

She knew what he said was true, even if it didn't calm her any. Dylan had grown up on the streets. He was no stranger to confrontation or violence. He was no fool. She didn't want to be responsible for him worrying about her safety, distracting him, while he investigated the potential break-in.

She hurried to the heavy carved door and locked it. A few minutes after she'd called nine-one-one and yanked on her robe, she heard approaching sirens mixing with the screeching alarm. She jogged to the window and pulled back the curtains, her nerves crackling in anxiety. Over the top of the long, steep road leading to the castle, she saw the pulsing reflection of red lights against the opaque night sky. Not three seconds later, two police cars topped the rise and zoomed onto the circular turnabout in front of the entrance, their sirens wailing. Alice saw one cop get out and run around the house while the other—a big man—approached the front door. Straining her ears, she thought she heard the sound of banging, and then distant male voices.

The teeth-grinding wail of the security alarm abruptly ceased. A heavy, suffocating silence followed. Remembering her promise to Dylan and feeling like a trapped animal, Alice hurried to the locked door, pressing her ear to the wood, desperate for signs of what was happening below.

After a tense minute of hearing only her own pounding heartbeat, her few remaining threads of control snapped. She jogged to Dylan's walk-in closet. Flinging open the door, she found the light. The room was illuminated fully to her eyes for the first time—and it was a room *not* a closet, at least in Alice's limited experience with luxury. She sought among immaculately organized cedar shelves and what seemed like hundreds of hung suits and tuxedos. Her gaze latched on a potential target.

Several seconds later, she padded silently on bare feet down the enormous, curving grand staircase, a golf club gripped in both hands.

THREE

Dylan conferred quietly with Jim Sheridan, the sheriff of Morgantown, in his den. Alex Peterson, one of Jim's deputies, was still doing a cursory check of the house and grounds. Jim was convinced it'd been a false alarm, however. Every point of entry was intact, and everything appeared to be in order.

Jim was an old friend, despite the disparity of their ages. He was in his late fifties while Dylan was thirty-four. Jim had been the sheriff back when Addie Durand had been taken. Under those stressful and nightmarish weeks and months that followed, Dylan had gotten to know Jim quicker and more completely than most people become familiar in years.

Jim Sheridan had been an all-state linebacker back in his high school days and still had the heft of one—more so, now that the years and his love of the food at the local diner had put sixty pounds on a once lean frame. Jim wore both the experience and the extra weight well. He possessed a friendly, craggy face and a down-to-earth warmth that might initially fool some into thinking he was just a good-old-boy small-town pushover with a badge. Others might be tricked into thinking it was his physical stature that earned Jim so much respect around Morgantown, but Dylan and those closest to the sheriff knew differently. The fact of the matter was, hidden beneath that amiable quick grin and the fading glory of a high school football star, Jim Sheridan was a shrewd observer and a damn good cop.

To this day, Dylan thought Jim had a better understanding and more keen insights into the details and nuances of the Adelaide Durand kidnapping case than any of the FBI agents sent to investigate the crime. Those FBI agents had failed completely, while Jim had been the one to encourage Dylan to never give up. He'd supported Dylan's trips to regularly visit Avery Cunningham, one of Adelaide's kidnappers, every year in prison until Cunningham had finally confessed to the crime just before his death. That refusal to give up had been what eventually gave Dylan clues to Addie's whereabouts twenty long years after she'd first been taken from the Durand Estate.

Of course, Jim didn't know about Cunningham's confession yet, and Dylan wanted to keep it that way for a while.

"Odd that the alarm would malfunction tonight. It's never gone off once—with or without cause—since I moved in here six years ago. I have it regularly serviced," Dylan was saying to Jim.

"The storm caused some power outages down south," Jim said from where he leaned against the edge of Dylan's desk, arms crossed over his broad chest. "Maybe it was some kind of electrical anomaly." He noticed Dylan's skeptical look and shrugged. "Stranger things have happened. Trust me. After thirty-seven years on the force, I can't tell you the number of false alarms I've raced to in the middle of the night caused by faulty security systems. You know better than anyone how many Durand execs live in Morgantown. Lots of big houses. Lots of fancy security systems. Lots of malfunctions," Jim said with a small smile.

"I still don't like it."

"Have someone come and take a look at the system—"

Jim paused and blinked. His stare at the door widened. Dylan spun around. Had Jim been mistaken in thinking it was a false alarm?

Alice stood warily several feet back from the open door, her short hair wild and mussed, her robe tied haphazardly and bunching awkwardly around her slender frame. Her face was set and pale, like she was ready for battle. She had a death grip on his five iron.

"*Alice.* Damn it," he mumbled under his breath. He crossed the distance to the door rapidly. "I thought I asked you to stay put until I came back." He grasped her forearm and pulled her into the den after him.

"You might have come up and told me what was happening sooner, instead of leaving me up there to worry all alone while you sit down here having a friendly chat," she hissed under her breath. She jerked her arm out of his hold and cast a half-apologetic, half-resentful glance at Jim before returning her burning stare to Dylan.

"We *just* determined there wasn't an actual break-in a few seconds ago." He resisted a strong urge to lift her over his shoulder and lock her behind a closed door somewhere. Jim was studying her with avid interest, only adding to Dylan's sense of growing unease.

Damn Alice for her impulsivity. He didn't want Jim to suspect the truth. He wasn't dead set against Jim knowing about his finding Addie in general—the sheriff had been one of the few who had known about Dylan's continued search all these years, after all. Jim deserved to celebrate the amazing truth with him at some future date. It was just that as soon as Jim knew about Addie, the sheriff would be obligated to inform the FBI. The kidnapping wasn't Jim's case. It was a federal one.

Alice wasn't ready yet to have police and agents swarming around her and asking her a slew of questions. She claimed that she was fine, but Dylan was much less confident about her emotional and mental well-being. It was only two days ago that she'd been told she'd been born a completely different person than the one she'd believed herself to be.

She certainly wouldn't be prepared if her "mother," Sissy Reed, and some or all of her many uncles were implicated in colluding with Avery Cunningham, one of Addie Durand's kidnappers. She hadn't asked him about the Reeds' involvement in the past few days and Dylan hoped to spare Alice that reality until some future date. In Sidney Gates's professional opinion, Alice suspected the Reeds' collusion and was repressing it. Her silence on the matter was an indication to him that she wasn't ready to tackle that painful territory yet.

Don't ask. Don't tell. That was the course of action Sidney was recommending for now.

To have the Reed clan thrown into prison right this second might give Dylan a rush of sweet vengeance, but it would only leave Alice feeling more torn, confused, and alone. She despised the Reeds, but they were family, too. Dylan knew better than most that feelings toward family members could be a tangled, confusing mess.

He unclenched his jaw and exhaled his frustration. "Jim Sheridan, I'd like you to meet Alice Reed."

"Do you have a license to carry that five iron, ma'am?" Jim asked, stepping forward with his hand extended in greeting. Alice glanced dazedly at the golf club she gripped like she'd forgotten it was there. She grimaced and unpried her hand, shaking with Jim.

"It was the first likely candidate I saw in Dylan's closet."

"I've always preferred a seven iron for a fight myself, but I can see how the five might give you a little more maneuverability in a pinch," Jim joked.

"You wouldn't have needed either if you'd done what I'd asked you to do and stayed put," Dylan reminded quietly, leaning against his desk with forced casualness.

That wild, cornered-animal look leapt back into her eyes. "What if you needed help? I couldn't just wait up there without knowing what was going on!"

"I told you I could handle it myself, Alice," he said, his pointed stare meant to remind her of what else he'd asked her to do. She looked a little abashed, but clearly was not subdued.

"So what *is* going on?" she asked, shifting on her bare feet and glancing at Jim.

"Nothing much. And unless you can fight the aftereffects of an electrical storm with that golf club, there's nothing here to do," Jim said.

"The storm set off the alarm?" Alice asked, lowering Dylan's club slowly. "But the storm has been over for hours."

"Maybe it was some kind of residual electrical burst," said Jim. "Hard to tell."

"The point is, everything is fine," Dylan said. She pulled her bathrobe tighter around her, as if she had just become aware of her disheveled appearance. Dylan didn't care for the way Jim stared at her face fixedly, a slightly bemused expression on his face. Again, Dylan experienced that sharp urge to hide her. "The house was never breached. Why don't you go back upstairs? I'll be up in a minute," he added when she furtively met his stare from behind the partial shield of her spiky bangs.

"Yeah, okay," she agreed huskily after a moment. "I guess that alarm clock is going to go off soon."

"Have to work early in the morning?" Jim asked.

"Yeah," Alice replied.

"There was some pretty serious flooding a few miles south of town in the vicinity of Chandler Creek. I hope you don't have to drive far to work," Jim said concernedly.

"Oh no. I'm just down at the camp."

Dylan resisted an urge to roll his eyes at her giving Jim exactly what he'd angled for with his fishing. She gave Dylan one last fleeting glance and walked out of the room.

THE next morning her kids were still riding high from being the top team in accumulated points after the first week at Camp Durand. It was a good time to have everybody so cheerful, because the morning mandatory activity was the zip line challenge—the activity Alice had struggled with most during her training. Alice was terrified of heights. Worse yet, she'd been paired up for the zip line during training with Brooke Seifert, who had been Alice's nemesis since the first day she'd arrived at camp.

Today Alice was more fortunate.

"At least I don't have to do the zip line myself this time around. *And*, I'm with you instead of Brooke," Alice said quietly to Kuvi Sarin as they walked side by side through a meadow toward the woods, the twenty kids from both of their teams spread out around them. Kuvi was her cabin mate and friend. She was warm, genuine, funny, and smart. Except for the smart part, she was pretty much the exact opposite of Brooke Seifert.

"Brooke's team got paired up with Thad's for this challenge," Kuvi said wryly. "She'll be in heaven."

"From what I saw yesterday, so will Thad," Alice replied under her breath. Kuvi gave her a sharp, knowing glance. Yesterday, Alice had spied Thad and Brooke kissing in the woods. She'd immediately told Kuvi what she'd seen. The accidental sighting had shocked her, because in the past Thad had only publically demonstrated a platonic interest in Brooke. In fact, Thad had previously not even attempted to hide that he was very interested romantically in her—*Alice*. She considered Thad a great guy and a friend, so what she'd seen between him and Brooke had left her feeling confused and disturbed. She'd been subtly avoiding Thad all day. Why was he purposefully misleading his friends when it came to Brooke? Was it because he knew how much Alice disliked her?

"Hey," Kuvi whispered. "You promised yesterday that you were going to tell me where *you* have been disappearing to at night."

Alice glanced around warily, assuring herself that their conversation wasn't being overheard. Until yesterday, Kuvi had assumed she was sneaking away from their cabin at night for trysts with Thad. Alice had never admitted to that, but Kuvi and Dave Epstein—their other friend—had just assumed a relationship between them, given Thad's obvious attraction to Alice.

"I'll tell you tonight, after the night supervisors take over," Alice said quietly. "I promise," she added when she saw the question and concern in Kuvi's eyes. Kuvi nodded.

Alice wasn't exactly looking forward to confessing for the first time that she was having an affair with Durand Enterprises' CEO. Kuvi was sure to tell her that she was out of her mind. If they were discovered, the ramifications for both Alice and Dylan could be serious. But part of her was relieved at the prospect of telling the truth as well. She respected and liked Kuvi too much to keep lying to her.

Alice spotted Sebastian Kehoe, the Durand vice president of human resources, a minute after they entered the woods. Kehoe stood at the bottom of a wooden flight of stairs that led to a forty-five-foot-tall zip line platform. He looked at them, pointedly checked his watch, and continued to write on a clipboard that Alice suspected was surgically attached to his hand.

Uh-oh. Were they late? Alice couldn't really afford to get on Kehoe's bad side, although she constantly felt like she was scrambling not to land there with a resounding thud. Kehoe was a longtime Durand executive. He was the top boss here—at least he was when Dylan wasn't around. It was generally acknowledged, even grudgingly by Dylan himself, that Camp Durand was Kehoe's baby and had been for as long as most people's memories went. Camp Durand was held up as a model example of Durand Enterprises' strong community and philanthropic ideals as well as being an innovative, fresh practice for finding the best of the best young executives in the world. Kehoe certainly held court at Camp Durand like some kind of village potentate. Which was unfortunate, because Alice couldn't rid herself of the uneasy feeling that

Kehoe didn't like her at all. She thought it might have something to do with the fact that Dylan hired her, when Kehoe usually did all the hiring for the elite group of counselors and future Durand executives. On a more worrisome note, she dreaded that Kehoe suspected something was going on between Dylan and her, and didn't like that fact at all.

She and Kuvi approached Kehoe while the other kids spread out in the clearing, talking among themselves.

"Hello, ladies. May I have your assignments for your zip line pair-ups?" Kehoe asked Alice and Kuvi briskly. Alice's stomach dropped. Kuvi reached into her backpack and retrieved several pieces of paper. She handed them to Kehoe.

"Alice?" Kehoe asked unsmilingly, glancing up and peering at her through a pair of preppy black-rimmed glasses. Everything about Kehoe was neat, his appearance as exacting as his manner. Even in his camp sportswear, Kehoe was meticulously groomed. He was trim and sinewy, his athletic build making him look much younger than a man in his fifties. "Your assignments, please?"

"I, uh . . . I forgot to type them out," she said in a rush. "But I know all of my pair-ups by heart. I put a lot of effort into it."

"But not enough thought to give me the paperwork I asked for. I wasn't just asking for the names and teams, Alice. I wanted your rational for how you paired up the kids. The zip line is a significant challenge for a lot of our new campers, and a few of the older ones as well. It's important that we put some planning into how we're going to comfort and empower them for what could potentially be an anxiety-provoking activity," he said quietly.

"I'm sorry. I can type up my list this evening," Alice said, humiliated. How could she have forgotten? It wasn't like her. It'd been a crazy past few days. Was she a lot more preoccupied and distracted by the news about Addie Durand than she realized or cared to admit? Maybe Dylan was right to be so concerned about her mental state.

"We don't approach a potentially dangerous challenge like this in a careless or thoughtless fashion," Kehoe said.

Rebellious anger spiked through her embarrassment and irritation at herself. True, she'd screwed up, but it wasn't because she was thoughtless. Having been terrified at the mere idea of zooming across the top of the forest while suspended from a skinny little wire, Alice had put significant planning into how she'd match up her kids to empower them for the challenge. During her own training, all Kehoe had done to alleviate her blind panic over completing the activity was match her up with a useless Brooke Seifert. All Brooke had done was simper saccharine platitudes for her safety, and even escalated Alice's anxiety by tricking her to look down at the forest floor, mounting her vertigo until she'd been mindless with fear by the time she flew off the platform.

Some help Kehoe had been.

Although the truth was, Alice had never *confessed* to the fact that she was scared shitless of heights to Kehoe, allowing him or anyone else the opportunity to comfort her during the experience. Alice didn't speak of her weaknesses easily, let alone babble on about them to a man like Kehoe.

"I know it's important. I messed up," Alice admitted stoically, looking Kehoe square in the eye. "I'm really sorry. Like I said, I have put a lot of thought into my team's pair-ups. I can name them easily. I can give you the rationale for my pair-ups right now—"

"I don't have the time to listen to an oral report. I want the typed list and your rationale *first* thing after dinner tonight," Kehoe interrupted sharply. He made a rapid note, his writing so pressured it looked like his ballpoint might drill all the way through the multiple sheets of paper to the clipboard itself. He turned and stalked a short distance away, calling out to gather the scattered, chatting teenagers. Alice glanced at Kuvi abashedly.

"It's okay," Kuvi whispered hearteningly. "It was a little thing, comparatively. Gina Sayre forgot that anti-bullying workshop agenda we had to do, plus lost track of Mark Drayner and Shayna Crawniac during the kayaking activity she led. Kehoe was furious when he found the pair of them tied up to shore and going at it in Martyr's Cove, both of them half-naked."

Alice smirked. "We should rename it Sinner's Cove."

"I should have reminded you. I know how distracted you've seemed lately."

"It's not your responsibility," Alice muttered, frowning.

She really needed to pull it together. It sucked, having Kehoe lecture her like that. Until now, his disapproval of her had remained vague and difficult to pin down. Alice's team was top in points, and she'd avoided making a major mistake so far, despite the fact that either Kehoe or one of his manager minions was watching them like hawks. She'd clearly just received her first black mark in Kehoe's meticulous notes, however.

Thankfully, Kehoe only stayed with their group long enough to assign them a Durand manager before he walked off rapidly through the forest in the direction of the next zip line platform. He was obviously intent on gathering more documentation of counselor screwups, Alice thought darkly. Only nine of the fifteen counselors would be selected to become a Durand executive, after all. Kehoe had to find rationale for making cuts somewhere. Alice feared she'd just conveniently gifted him with a nice sharp knife.

THE challenge itself went as smoothly as could be expected. There was only one rough patch—when Judith Arnold, a pretty, stubborn, talented seventeen-year-old whom Alice had just recently made the student team leader, called Alice out in front of all of the Red Team.

"What do you mean I'm paired up with *Noble D?*" Judith demanded when Alice called out the pair assignments. "I should be with Jill!"

Here we go, Alice thought.

She'd wondered how long her and Judith's relative peace would last. Despite the fact that Judith had been rude and insolent toward Alice since the moment she'd arrived at camp, she had also demonstrated true strength and compassion at times with the other campers. Alice had made the decision just days ago to challenge the girl with the team leader position. Judith was smart and strong. Alice's instincts told her that Judith could lead her peers effectively. She'd been feeling cautiously optimistic about her risky Judith selection. The first days of Judith's reign had been relatively conflict free. Alice had even shared a couple nice moments with the girl at the bonfire last night when the Red Team had been declared top in points. Things had been looking up.

Until now, *anyway.*

"Jill is with Terrance," Alice said, picking up her backpack and flinging it over her shoulder. "Terrance is an expert. He did the zip line at a church retreat," she said, referring to the custom by which Camp Durand tried to match up campers with experience at a task—"experts"—with the uninitiated "novices."

"When he was twelve years old and nearly two hundred pounds lighter," Judith snapped.

Alice noticed Terrance's head jerk around at Judith's scornful exclamation.

"Shut it, Judith," Alice ground out furiously under her breath.

Judith's eyes flashed in mixed anger and regret. Her chin went up defiantly. "Jill will be scared shitless without me being there with her. You know that," she hissed tensely. Judith had taken on the role of protector and defender of the vulnerable girl since the first day of camp. Alice was thankful for it. But she thought maybe it was time for Jill to move out of Judith's tall shadow and begin to experience her own strength.

"Jill and Terrance, you're up first," Alice called out loudly, ignoring Judith's glare.

"Come on, midget," Terrance said resignedly to Jill, nudging the girl on the shoulder. "You're the size of a gnat. *You'll* fly over those trees even without a wire."

Terrance and Jill walked toward the staircase, a Durand manager leading them. A more oddly matched pair Alice couldn't imagine. Terrance Brown was six foot several inches tall and weighed in at around three hundred pounds. He was diabetic. With little to no parental supervision, he regularly gorged on sugary snacks and fast food. Alice was trying desperately to show him the benefits of exercise and a balanced diet in order to set him on a healthier path post-camp. He was a smart, ebullient teenager, a jokester who was always the life of the party. And if he continued as he had before, Terrance was at risk of becoming mortally ill. Alice hoped she could get Terrance hooked into an activity that helped improve his health, and had talked him into jogging with her while at Camp Durand.

Jill Sanchez, on the other hand, was a slight, waifish thirteen-year-old who had become withdrawn to the point of almost muteness after witnessing the shooting death of her mother last year.

"Alice said the anchors and the equipment are state of the art here, and will hold more than five hundred pounds. You'll be fine. At least you've done this before," Alice heard Jill murmur shyly to Terrance as they started up the steps. Alice experienced a surge of warmth and gratitude toward the girl. She noticed Terrance's slightly bemused, anxious glance down at Jill. Despite his joking bravado, Jill had sensed his worry. As Alice had suspected, beneath his nonchalant kidding, Terrance was worried and self-conscious about doing the zip line, given his weight. Jill had come out of her shell in order to reassure him.

Suddenly, Terrance bent and swooped Jill into the air, plopping her down on the landing of the stairs in front of him.

"Yep. Light as a flea. You're gonna fly all the way to Detroit on that thing," he declared, releasing a startled looking Jill. Jill laughed. Alice gawked. It was the first time she'd ever seen the girl smile, let alone laugh. Jill jogged slightly to keep up with Terrance's lumbering gait as they rose up the rest of the stairs, asking the boy an enthusiastic question that faded off into the forest.

Alice glanced sideways at Judith, who had been watching the pair as well. When Judith met her stare, Alice saw her bewilderment.

"The right choice isn't always the obvious one," Alice said very quietly, echoing what she'd told Judith when she'd selected her as team leader. "Besides, you've forgotten you're as much of a novice as Jill when it comes to the zip line. I paired you up with Noble D for a reason. He'll have quite a few things to teach you." She nodded subtly. Judith glanced over her shoulder, her gaze landing on the handsome, tall, and somber teenager who stood several feet away, waiting for his partner. Mutiny had returned to Judith's eyes by the time she met Alice's stare again, along with a hint of something else.

Panic.

Alice knew that Judith was very much aware Noble D was attracted to her. She'd been avoiding him vigilantly, but Alice didn't think it was because she found D unattractive. Just the opposite, in fact.

Judith protested a bit too loudly and too often about Noble D's supposed faults. She had a feeling Judith found the idea of attraction and dating nearly as intimidating as Alice had at her age.

"Good luck," Alice said sincerely to Judith before she followed Terrance and Jill up the steps.

FOUR

Soothing her campers' jitters helped to distract Alice from her own fear up on top of the tall platform. It was hard to be too anxious about her own well-being when she was so concerned for her kids.

Justin Arun and Rochelle Phelps were the last pair to successfully fly across the treetops. Just as she lost sight of Justin, she heard a quick step on the stairs.

"Alice."

"Yeah?" Alice asked Kuvi, her brow wrinkled. Kuvi sounded tense.

"You'd better come down. There's someone here to see you."

"Who?" Alice wondered, walking toward Kuvi.

"The sheriff of Morgantown," Kuvi whispered, her tone hushed to prevent Aidan Salinger, their supervising Durand manager, from hearing.

Alice blinked in surprise. She saw the question in Kuvi's hazel eyes, but had no answers for her friend. What was the man she'd met last night in Dylan's den—Jim Sheridan—doing *here*? She and Dylan were keeping their relationship private. No one at the camp was supposed to know they were engaged in an affair. Hadn't Dylan warned Jim of that fact after Alice had left? Dylan had mentioned once that the sheriff of Morgantown and he were old friends. Surely he'd asked Jim to be discreet.

So what was Sheridan doing here in the woods asking to see Alice while camp was in session?

Jim looked just as relaxed and amiable standing in the midst of the forest as he had last night in the den. He was chatting with two of Kuvi's Diamond Team campers.

"Keep in mind, I can't guarantee what mood Camp Wildwood might be in from year to year. If I were you, I'd give some serious consideration to whether or not the goat is worth the glory," Jim drawled with a wink. The boys laughed.

"Mr. Sheridan?" Alice asked warily.

"Call me Jim," he said, turning at the sound of her voice. He stuck out his hand in greeting. "Good to see you, Alice. Sorry to bother you like this, if I could just have a moment or two of your time? Excuse us, won't you?" Jim said cordially to the two kids. He tilted his head toward the left, and Alice followed him several yards down a path to a solitary clearing.

"Your kids all off successfully on the zip line?" Jim asked, turning to face her.

"Yeah. Mission accomplished," she replied tensely, not trying to hide the question in her eyes.

"I can see you're not going to be satisfied until I explain why I'm here. No idle chitchat for Alice Reed, am I right?" he asked, his pale blue eyes sparkling with amusement.

"I'm just a little confused. Does this have to do with the alarm going off last night?" she asked quietly. "I thought you said it was just an electrical malfunction."

Jim nodded, suddenly more serious. "It was. I think."

"You *think*," Alice emphasized slowly. "But you're not *sure* like you were last night?"

He shrugged broad shoulders. Alice had the fleeting thought that he must have to have his sheriff's uniforms special-made for his big body. "Let's just say that Dylan's concern about the whole thing ramped up my worry a little. I haven't seen Dylan that tense in a long, long time. It got me wondering—what's got the iceman so ruffled?"

"He didn't seem ruffled to me," Alice said dismissively. She felt uneasy, though. What Jim was suggesting was true. To most observers, Dylan would have appeared the picture of control last night. But he *had* been worried about that alarm going off, tense at the idea of a threat. He'd made no effort to disguise that very thing after they'd both returned to the bedroom suite last night. He'd *definitely* not appreciated her venturing out of the locked bedroom on her own. She'd thought his worry and tension were out of proportion to the circumstances, and obviously, so had Jim Sheridan. The only difference was Alice knew *why* Dylan was so vigilantly protective of her.

Jim Sheridan didn't know, though. But from the looks of things, he was bound and determined to find out.

"It seemed to me he was worried about *you*," Jim said, glancing casually around the wooded clearing as though sincerely interested in the foliage. "Very worried."

"He wasn't worried about *me* specifically," Alice insisted. "He was worried because he thought his house had been broken into. Wouldn't you be concerned about that?"

"Sure," Jim agreed, nodding thoughtfully. "But why's it a bad thing for Dylan to worry about your safety, too?"

Alice blinked, taken off guard by his question. "It's not a *bad* thing—"

"It's pretty clear he thinks you're special. Most young women would be flattered to see Dylan so anxious for their safety. Most every young single woman I know in Morgantown and a good portion of the older married ones, as a matter of fact," Jim said with a disarming smile.

"I . . . I don't think—"

"You two are an item, right?"

Alice exhaled, exasperated. "Is that what you came for? To find out if Dylan Fall and I are an *item*? What, did you run out of good gossip to barter with at the local donut shop and thought you'd dig up some here? I've got more important things to do than feed your salacious curiosity."

She spun to go, but paused mid-turn at the sound of Jim's low chuckle. She glanced back. His pleased expression made Alice's frown deepen.

"*Salacious?* I guess Dylan has his hands full with you."

Alice gave a disbelieving bark of laughter, a comeback forming on her tongue.

"You aren't helping matters much, Jim," a man said. Alice started, her retort forgotten. Dylan strode into the clearing, Sal Rigo trailing behind him.

For a stunned second, she just stared in shock, sure she was hallucinating Dylan's tall, impressive form. He wore an impeccable dark blue suit, a pristine white shirt, silver cuff links, and a silver and navy striped tie. Even through her amazement at his presence, Alice distantly acknowledged he looked downright amazing. His bold masculine features seemed tense and determined. His near-black eyes flickered over her quickly. She was so keyed in to him she knew instinctively he was making a quick thorough assessment of her well-being. He seemed both bizarrely out of place in the midst of the sylvan setting, and yet completely at home at once, like he utterly owned these woods.

Which he did, of course.

"*Dylan,*" both she and Jim muttered at once. Jim sounded just as surprised as Alice. Seemingly having decided all Alice's limbs were where they should be, Dylan locked his attention on Jim. Sheridan had labeled Dylan the iceman earlier, and Alice had often had reason to suspect he would be intimidating when pressed. Seeing him at the moment, Alice knew she'd been a hundred percent correct in her assumption.

"Why are you questioning Alice out here in the woods?" Dylan demanded quietly.

"You make it sound so unusual. I just had a few questions about last night, that's all. It hardly warrants an emergency trip from the office on your part," Jim said incredulously. The sheriff's gaze ran over Dylan and then Rigo, lingering on Rigo. Rigo was nearly as tall as Dylan's six-foot-three-inches, but bulkier. He reminded Alice of a rock. Alice now knew that Dylan had personally commissioned Sal Rigo and another man from Durand's security division with the task of watching over Alice at the camp. Dylan had originally done it without her knowledge. Alice was being followed— spied on, in truth. To see the evidence of her surveillance so blatantly paraded in front of her raised her hackles.

"What's all this about?" Alice hissed, her question for Dylan.

"That's what I'm trying to find out," Dylan replied with seeming calmness, still pinning Jim with his stare. "What is it that you feel is so crucial to question Alice about while she's working?"

Jim sighed and took a step back. "The truth? I guess I came to ask her what's got you like this," the sheriff said, waving at Dylan.

"Got me like *what*, exactly?"

"What's got you rushing out of your office and traipsing through the woods the second Mr. Security Guard here says the word," Jim said mildly, nodding at Rigo. Alice saw Jim's glance slide over to her, his eyebrows arched expectantly. Dylan's gaze followed the sheriff's lead, flickering over her. For a split second, his gaze locked with hers.

Stop this, Dylan. Stop making more of this than there is! If you insist on highlighting the Addie Durand situation, how can I keep up this constant effort to minimize it and deal with the everyday details of my life?

Dylan's features stiffened as if he'd heard her panicked thoughts. He turned his shoulder to Alice and faced Jim. Feeling utterly dismissed by him, Alice's anger and helplessness swelled.

"I see you *think* you already know the answer," Dylan said to Jim.

"I wouldn't say that. If it's anything close to what I'm thinking in my wildest imaginings, though, I can't quite make out why I've been left in the dark."

"You haven't been left anywhere. But if you *had*, surely there would be good reason for it," Dylan replied. "Whatever you're thinking, coming out here to the woods and badgering Alice isn't warranted."

"Stop talking like I'm not even here!" Alice blurted out, their private little conversation infuriating her.

All three men gave her startled glances. She met Sal Rigo's gaze straight on, zeroing in on the most comfortable target. The man had been her watchdog for the past several weeks, slinking around, following her every move on Dylan's request. The reality of her invaded privacy suddenly seemed all too real. After she and Dylan had made love in Addie Durand's old room last night, she'd suddenly had an unpleasant thought and asked Dylan about Rigo's and Peterson's nighttime duties. He assured her that her "bodyguards" were finished for the day once she was with Dylan, a fact that had relieved her greatly.

Certainly, she wouldn't have made love later on that night in that window if she'd thought otherwise.

But had Rigo or that other Durand security manager—Josh Peterson—been skulking in the trees every time she met up with Dylan in the woods at night? Did they exchange information about it and smirk knowingly to each other? Had one of them been secretly watching on that day when she threw up after completing the zip line when Thad had comforted her, holding her against him while they talked?

Had Rigo run and told Dylan about her seemingly private interlude with Thad? Is that why Dylan had been so prickly that night when he'd found her on the beach with Thad? Nothing major had happened between Thad and her, but just the idea of her privacy being breached at such a vulnerable moment suddenly felt like a hand tightening on her throat.

"Look, I don't know what you hoped to gain by coming here today," she told Jim in a pressured, quiet tone, "and I don't know why *you*," she glared at Rigo, "felt it was important to run and tell Dylan about it, or why *you*," she glanced at Dylan, "thought it was necessary to come here to the woods, but I do know one thing: I'm *working*. I don't have time for whatever game you three are playing." She started to walk off, then paused, frowning at Rigo. "And don't follow me right now. *Got* it?"

"Alice, wait," Dylan called tensely. He clearly wasn't faking his concern, but she was too angry at that moment to feel any compassion for him. For the first time since she'd known him—for the first time since she'd begun to fall hard for him—she ignored his request to stop. If Dylan had his way, he'd keep her under wraps for an eternity, treating her like a fragile piece of glass that would shatter with the smallest pressure.

He still had a lot to learn about Alice.

She hauled up short with a gasp, stopping just shy of the wooded path back to the zip line platform. Sebastian Kehoe stepped into the clearing, his curious gaze running over her face. She held her breath when she saw his eyes move rapidly over the other three men.

"Dylan. This is a surprise," Kehoe said after he'd gathered himself. "And Jim. It's good to see you," Kehoe said, stepping past Alice's frozen form, hand outstretched. He shook hands with Jim. "To what do we owe this honor? I hope nothing is wrong at the camp?"

"No, everything is fine from what I've seen so far," Jim said, returning Kehoe's handshake. "As usual, you have Camp Durand running like a well-oiled machine."

Kehoe looked bemused. An awkward silence fell in the clearing.

"Then what, may I ask, are the sheriff of Morgantown, the CEO of Durand, and one of my managers doing standing in the woods with one of my counselors? It must be something important. I hope Alice isn't in any kind of trouble."

"No, of course not. It's nothing to worry about," Dylan said evenly. "Jim came to see me at the office. He said he'd heard reports of extensive storm damage in the woods nearby."

"A couple trees fell onto electrical wires, causing some outages," Jim added, playing along with Dylan's slight of hand admirably. "Thought we'd better come out and have a look."

"So . . . *you* came out to the camp woods to check?" Kehoe asked Dylan incredulously, his tone making it clear he found the idea of the CEO of Durand Enterprises checking on possible downed trees in the woods ridiculous.

"Do you have a problem with that?"

A shiver rippled beneath Alice's skin. Dylan's tone was quiet, but chilling. In combination with the palpable ice in his stare, she was surprised Kehoe wasn't frozen to the spot.

"Of course not," Kehoe assured quickly.

After a pointed pause, Dylan spoke. "I checked the camp schedule and knew the kids were in the woods today, so I wanted to be sure everything was safe. We saw Sal up at the lodge and he said he'd show us the way to where all the activity was."

"Thank you for the concern," Kehoe backpedaled. "I've been in the woods all morning, and I haven't seen any storm damage. Have you, Alice?"

"No, I'd already told them," Alice said. She swallowed thickly when the four men's attention transferred to her. She shifted on her feet awkwardly, wishing that the forest floor would swallow her whole. "I better get going to meet up with my kids for lunch," she said, pointing in a vague direction in the forest.

Her gaze landed on Dylan before she turned. His handsome

face was frozen into a steely mask, but his eyes shouted all sorts of messages at her.

Just as she entered the woods, she heard Sebastian Kehoe speak in an annoyed tone to Rigo: "I'd like a word before you go, Sal."

ALICE arrived at the distant platform only to discover the Gold Team counselor and some managers had taken her hungry kids to lunch along with a bunch of others. After another five minutes of walking quickly but aimlessly in the woods, she still hadn't blown off enough steam to calm down very much.

"Alice, wait up!"

The call tore through her chaotic thoughts, bringing her to a halt on the forest path. She spun. Despite her frayed emotional state, she gave a small smile when she saw the man jogging up to her. Thad wore a pair of long khaki cargo shorts and a gray T-shirt that showed off his athletic build and toned body. Just beneath the short sleeve she saw a portion of his tattoo on a bulging bicep: a shark slicing through blue water. Thad loved anything associated with the water: boating, diving, swimming.

Over the past two weeks at camp, his skin color had deepened to a golden bronze. His dark blond hair was attractively mussed and there was a burnished scruff on his jaw. He looked good to Alice, and not just because Thad was good-looking. There was something normal and reassuring about his appearance at that moment.

He came to a halt on the path just feet away from her.

"You okay?" he asked, eyeing her with a bemused smile.

"Fine."

"You're sure beating the path to get somewhere in a hurry. I called out to you a half-dozen times before you stopped."

"Oh . . . sorry," Alice mumbled, thinking about how she'd been stomping through the woods. "I was just thinking about things."

Thad's eyebrows rose expectantly. He exhaled when she didn't elaborate, but didn't seem surprised by her refusal to do so. He really was getting to know her well.

"Your kids already off to lunch?" he asked.

"Yeah, Dave took them with his team," she said, referring to Dave Epstein, their friend and Thad's roommate.

"He took mine, too." After a tense pause when his green-eyed gaze roamed over her face, he waved his hand toward the woods. "This must be our spot."

"Huh?" She glanced around, only then recognizing their location. Just to the left of them was the hidden, sun-dappled glade where Thad had comforted her just over a week ago.

"Oh yeah," she mumbled. "I hadn't really noticed where I was."

Thad eyed her suspiciously. "You look a little pale. You're not going to"—he waved in the vicinity of his taut abdomen—"be sick again, are you?"

Her cheeks burned at the memory of him watching her vomit. "Do you think I'm going to hurl every time I walk by this place in the woods?" she asked with amused exasperation.

He shrugged dubiously. "Just checking."

Alice shook her head and laughed. Her mirth faded when she noticed the somber way Thad was watching her. He gestured toward the glade where he'd held her. "Do you mind? If we go back? Just for a minute," he added, probably noticing her trepidation. "There's something I want to talk about with you. It's important."

It all came back to her in a flash of memory why she'd been avoiding Thad: Thad and Brooke's secretive meeting in the forest. Thad's softly uttered question to Brooke, *Then why are you here with me?* Thad leaning down to cover Brooke's mouth with his in a kiss that looked very much to Alice like one between familiar lovers.

"Oh, I guess maybe . . ." She trailed off uncomfortably,

glancing around the woods. She stood very still for a moment, holding her breath. The woods were quiet. Had Sal Rigo listened to her demand in that clearing and not followed her, for once? Not likely, with Dylan there. It'd been Sebastian Kehoe who had unintentionally assisted her cause when he insisted Rigo stay put for a dressing down while Alice made her escape. It wasn't the first time Kehoe had grown impatient with Rigo for abandoning his assigned post. Rigo took orders from another man besides Kehoe, though.

Dylan.

It annoyed her that she even had to consider her God-given right to privacy at that moment.

Screw Rigo, and Dylan, too.

Alice straightened at the volatile thought. "Yeah. There's something I want to talk to you about, too."

She noticed his green eyes narrow, and realized she'd unintentionally sounded a little condemning. She put out her hand in a "lead the way" gesture, a wry apology in her glance. What right did she have to judge Thad, when she herself was involved in a secret affair with Dylan? True, Brooke was one of her least favorite people, but maybe Thad saw something in her Alice didn't.

Despite all her rationalizations, Alice admitted the truth to herself as she followed Thad on the almost invisible, weed-choked path that led to the glade. She was disappointed in Thad because he'd been lying to her. She'd made it clear she wasn't interested in a relationship with him, but maybe her pride had been pricked by the fact that he'd publicly demonstrated a preference for her—Alice—while he'd secretly been fooling around with Brooke.

Alice had held Thad up in her mind as an example of a sincere, normal friendship. Ever since coming to Camp Durand, she'd been swimming in a choppy sea of confused emotion. She was the outsider in a group of born insiders, a girl who had grown up in a shabby trailer park, the daughter of a sick, trembling drug addict who was the object of pity, fear, and disgust to many.

But of course, there had been more to her disorientation at Camp Durand. Much more. Now she was starting to get a glimmer as to just *why* the Durand Estate was so unsettling to her. Ever since she'd arrived in this overwhelming setting, however, Thad had been a sure, reliable thing.

She was mad at him for not being what she needed him to be. *And that's just plain not fair to him, is it?*

She came to a halt several feet away from him when he stopped and turned toward her in the center of the glade. For a few seconds, they just looked at each other.

"Your hair—it's getting longer."

She raked her bangs out of her eyes self-consciously. "Yeah. It's a wreck."

"It looks good. It's getting lighter in the sun, too. I like it."

Alice shrugged uneasily, studying the long grass swaying around their feet. She needed to color her hair again, but hadn't had the opportunity here at camp. Not only were the telltale red-gold roots starting to show, the sun was bringing out highlights even through the dark brown color she usually used. It made her feel naked somehow—vulnerable—knowing Thad noticed her emerging true color.

"There's something I need to talk to you about. Something important."

She glanced up, snagged by Thad's somber tone. His gaze was so warm on her. So caring.

Why can't things be simple? Why can't things be what they appear to be? God, her life was a seriously fucked-up mess.

"It's okay," she said huskily. "I know about you and Brooke."

"*What?*"

"I saw you two together in the woods yesterday."

He appeared dumbstruck.

"It's all right, Thad," she assured, inhaling for strength. "You probably didn't want to tell me because . . . well, because it's pretty obvious Brooke and I aren't the best of friends. What's between Brooke and me shouldn't matter to *our* friendship, though," she reasoned, gesturing between them. She hesitated when he just stared at her. "At least I hope it won't," she added doubtfully.

"God, no. Of course not," he said, reaching out and gripping her upper arm. "I'm sorry. I just wasn't expecting—"

"Me to know already about you and Brooke?" she laughed mirthlessly. "Yeah, I figured."

His hand tightened on her arm. "I want you to know that if things had been different between us . . . if you had shown any interest in me . . . I mean, I've known Brooke since we were four years old. We've hooked up once in a while for nearly ten years now, but it's not like she's the *one* or something—"

"You don't have to explain, Thad. I understand. Really, I do," she assured, his obvious discomfort paining her.

"No, Alice, listen," he insisted, stepping closer to her. Alice stared straight ahead at his chest when he moved his hand on her arm, stroking her. Her heartbeat started to thump loudly in her ears.

"I *do* have to explain," he said hoarsely. "Because the thing is, I think *you* might be the one."

Her chin went up sharply. Her eyes widened when she realized how close his face was to hers. A robin keened loudly in a nearby tree and went abruptly silent.

"I know," he said dryly, obviously seeing the shock on her face. "Pretty lame on my part, to say that when I've been sleeping with Brooke. I'm weak. What can I say? I've always been weak. Spoiled rich kid. That's what most people would say, right? It's certainly what my father says," he added bitterly. He shook his head in obvious frustration at himself. "And I deserve it. Every word. I was feeling lonely. Rejected, because I knew you didn't feel the same way about me as I do you. And Brooke was there. She's pretty. Attractive. *Familiar.* My parents love her. And she has some good points, believe it or not. I know she's never bothered to show them to you, but—"

"I'm sure she does," Alice said bracingly. She gave him a determined smile. "And you know what? I'm going to try harder to get to know her. You're right. If you like her, she's got to have some good— *What?*" she interrupted herself when Thad's expression turned hard and he grasped her other arm.

"You don't get what I'm saying," he bit out, leaning down toward her so that his breath struck her lips. "I don't care that much about Brooke. I'm an ass. I just started up with her when I realized you were involved with Dylan Fall."

The name seemed to echo and vibrate in Alice's ears in the silence that followed.

"How . . . how did you know . . ."

"Do you think a guy doesn't notice when the girl he's fallen for is completely in love with someone else?"

"I'm not in love with Dylan," she denied automatically. Inside her head, an alarm started to blare. A flash of heat went through her, a prelude to panic, because it wasn't like a lie she'd ever told before. This lie *mattered*. It felt utterly wrong, like a breach of nature, saying what she'd just said.

"You're *crazy* about him," Thad stated, his mouth twisting in bitter anger. He stepped closer. "And that's what I wanted to talk to you about. You need to be careful of Fall. He's manipulating you. He's hiding things from you, Alice."

"No he's not," she defended Dylan automatically, her voice going high. The front of Thad's body was brushing against her now, and she was so confused. "Not *anymore*, he's not!"

"Don't trust him, Alice."

And then his mouth was on hers, at first hard and angry . . . then warm and coaxing. In her worked-up state, Alice lost herself for a moment. It was a good kiss.

It wasn't Dylan's kiss.

She *hated* that Thad had voiced her deepest fear. She didn't know if she could trust Dylan or not, but she *was* hopelessly in love with him. It was a horrible, awesome realization.

She staggered back, gasping. Staring at Thad, she touched her mouth dazedly. Regret flickered across Thad's face.

"Alice—"

She shook her head adamantly, cutting him off. She spun and hurried out of the clearing.

"Alice, you've got to listen to me about Fall. He's not being honest with you!"

"Who *is*?" she muttered bitterly under her breath, never breaking stride.

She would've thought the day Dylan told her about Addie Durand would have been the most disturbing day she'd known in her life, but it wasn't.

That morning in the woods took the grand prize.

FIVE

Kuvi stared at her, her hazel eyes wide with blank shock. Night had fallen. Alice had left her kids safely in the night supervisor's charge. She and Kuvi sat in their luxurious cabin's small living room area, still wearing their day's camp attire. Her roommate was flabbergasted because Alice had just told her with whom she'd been spending her nights.

"Dylan Fall," Kuvi repeated with blank incredulity.

Alice laughed.

"*What?*" Kuvi asked, no doubt surprised by Alice's burst of amusement after such a tense proclamation.

"Nothing," Alice said between jags of laughter. "You just sounded exactly like I did when Maggie, my advisor at grad school, dropped the bomb last May that I'd be interviewing with the CEO of Durand Enterprises instead of the vice president of human resources. I was floored, too."

"But this is different. It's *bigger*," Kuvi defended, glancing around their cabin like she'd never seen it before. She met Alice's gaze. "You've been sleeping with *Dylan Fall*?"

Alice wiped a tear off her cheek from her short jag of laughter. She was bordering on hysteria, no doubt.

"I know. I couldn't believe Dylan was interested in me, either," Alice replied.

"It's not that," Kuvi insisted. "Why wouldn't he be interested in you? You're brilliant and naturally beautiful and you've got all that going on," Kuvi said, waving vaguely in the vicinity of Alice's breasts. "I'm not saying that's what Fall is after, although I'm sure it doesn't hurt matters any," she added when she saw Alice roll her eyes. "I just mean—*you're sleeping with that bloody gorgeous man*?" She picked up a pillow and threw it at Alice, a grin breaking through her disquietude. "I *knew* there was something between you two that night at the castle. What's the sex like?"

"Kuvi," Alice muttered repressively.

"Never mind. It's fantastic, isn't it? You only have to look once at Fall to know it'd be smoking and a little dangerous, too. How did you get so *lucky*?"

"Shhh, keep it down," Alice said, glancing around nervously to the front door. The door was closed, thank goodness. Alice squeezed the caught pillow next to her belly in an anxious gesture. "I told you, no one else can know about this, Kuvi. Can you imagine what would happen if Kehoe found out?"

Kuvi sniffed. "He'd have a cow, the bloody tyrant. But what could he do, really? He can't fire Fall. If he fired you, he'd have to face Fall's wrath. Am I right?"

"Kehoe could potentially tell other members of the board. Dylan is the main shareholder. They couldn't fire him, necessarily, but they could censor him somehow . . . smear him in the business community, if they chose to . . . possibly make things so unpleasant for him, he'd retire? And who is going to take *me* seriously, even if Kehoe doesn't fire me? Let's say that for whatever reason, he even hired me as a Durand exec after camp. If word got out I was involved with the CEO of the company, I'd be considered a joke, wouldn't I? I'd be thought of as the company whore or something," Alice said miserably, leaning back into the corner of the couch and still clutching the pillow.

"No one who gets to know you for more than two minutes is ever going to consider you a joke."

Alice grimaced. "Thanks. To be honest, though, we don't

know what would happen if Kehoe or anyone on the board found out. Dylan told me he's never done anything like this before."

"Do you believe him?" Kuvi asked intently.

Alice met her friend's stare. "Yes."

She exhaled in relief. Despite all the doubts she'd been having about Dylan today, she honestly believed him when he'd said he'd never slept with a Durand employee before. Alice was the exception to the rule. The *reason* for his making her the exception was what created this feeling of rising panic in her stomach. Unfortunately, there was no way she could bear her soul to Kuvi about Addie Durand.

"This thing between you two must be really unique, then. It *is*, isn't it?" Kuvi asked, still studying Alice's face. Despite her teasing, Kuvi was brilliant and a shrewd observer of character.

If only you knew how unique Dylan's and my connection really is.

Alice nodded. "I tried to keep away from him. I just . . . couldn't," she said, throwing up her hands, disgusted by her failure. "I'm crazy, aren't I? For going to him every night?"

"No," Kuvi said with a sense of having just made a final judgment after deliberations. "It may not be wise. But I have a feeling this is a rare type of attraction . . . something too powerful to deny. I caught just a whiff of it that night at the castle, and even that was pretty convincing." She picked up another throw pillow from the couch and began to turn in it in her hands distractedly. "Some things are bigger than logic, and karma is one of them."

"I don't believe in karma or fate."

Kuvi shrugged. "What *do* you believe in, then?"

"Myself." She sighed heavily, feeling like a bundle of stretched threads that were about to break. "Or at least I used to."

"Anything that makes you second-guess yourself deserves some serious examination. So . . . are you going? Tonight?" Kuvi asked cautiously.

Alice studied her friend's face. Kuvi had a point.

"No," she said suddenly with more confidence than she felt. "You're right."

Kuvi blinked. "I wasn't trying to make a point. I was just asking a simple question!"

"But you're right about giving some serious consideration to anything that's making me second-guess myself," Alice said determinedly, grasping onto Kuvi's vague insinuation that she should be cautious about her relationship with Dylan. She stood and tossed the pillow she'd been clutching onto the couch.

"I'm going to take a shower and go to bed. It's been an exhausting day," she said, heading toward the bathroom.

"You're really just going to leave Dylan Fall standing there in the woods, waiting for you?" Kuvi demanded, sounding amazed.

"You said I needed space to examine this thing with him," Alice said over her shoulder.

"*I* never said that. But if you aren't going to meet up with Fall tonight, maybe that's what you needed to hear."

Alice plunged into the bathroom, too overwhelmed to say exactly what she needed at that moment.

Too overwhelmed to *know*.

SHE checked the bedside clock as the illuminated dial changed from 12:02 to 12:03. She'd only slept in the counselors' cabin that first week during her training, before she'd taken up with Dylan. Kuvi was silent in sleep. The complete quiet unnerved her, for some reason. It seemed to increase the volume level of the thoughts in her head to shouts. She'd lain in bed for the past two hours, the room draped in darkness, wakeful and alert.

Miserable.

What was Dylan thinking about her refusal to meet him at their assigned spot in the woods? Every minute of the past two and a half hours had been spent asking herself that question, over and over. The fact that she couldn't fasten on any sure answer only added to her insomnia.

She flipped over to her other side, leaning up on her elbow to restlessly punch at a flattened pillow. She paused at a squeaking noise, going on high alert with her fist planted deep in the feathers.

The outer screen door gave another screech. Her heart jumped into her throat at the sound of the lock sliding back. She heard the soft sigh of the front door opening and then the quiet thud as it shut again. Alice sat up in bed, her back ramrod straight, prepared to fly off the far side of the bed.

The overhead light came on.

Dylan stood just inside the room, his hand still on the light switch. In his other hand she noticed he held a ring of keys. *Of course* he had a key to this cabin. He owned this property, didn't he?

They'd been having a cool spell. He wore a pair of jeans and a soft-looking denim shirt that stood in marked contrast to his long hard body. His jaw was shadowed with whiskers, giving him that dark piratical look she loved, but which also intimidated her. His mouth was pressed into a grim line.

Her stunned brain left her temporarily mute.

"Let's go," he said simply.

"*What?*" she squeaked, her voice just above a whisper. Both she and Dylan glanced over at Kuvi's bed. *Shit.* Kuvi was sitting up partially, rubbing her eyes and staring incredulously at the vision of Dylan Fall standing in their cabin.

"Sorry to wake you," Dylan apologized. "This will just take a moment. Alice?" he addressed Alice levelly. "I waited until the camp was quiet, but I'm not going to wait anymore."

"You can't just break in here and expect me to get up and go with you!" Alice exclaimed, barely managing to keep her voice at a low volume.

"I do expect it. Because that's what we agreed to, wasn't it?" he asked quietly, taking a step toward her, the glint of anger in his shining dark eyes making her skin roughen in trepidation and mounting excitement. *Yes*. Excitement. The sight of him in her cabin, so solid and beautiful and demanding thrilled her, despite it all. "I agreed to let you go on as if everything was normal, as long as you agreed you'd spend the nights and weekends with me up at the castle. You've broken your promise tonight."

She glanced anxiously at Kuvi, who was now watching their tense exchange with wide hazel eyes.

"You don't have to worry about Alice," Dylan said to Kuvi, a small smile curling his mouth. "She made an agreement with me."

Alice gritted her teeth in the silence that followed as both of them looked at her expectantly. "I'm not going with you," she insisted.

"Would you like me to carry you?" Her anxiety ramped up when she couldn't gauge if he was joking or not.

"Just *try* it," she hissed.

"Maybe you'd prefer I spent the night here then?" Dylan asked, taking another step toward her bed.

She cursed under her breath and threw off the covers.

"Convenient of you to go to bed dressed," Dylan said when she stood jerkily, his gaze running over the length of her in what struck Alice as an insolent manner. He was insinuating she'd known he was going to come and claim her like some kind of caveman. She was wearing a pair of soft running shorts and a T-shirt.

"It's what I wear to bed."

His slight shrug seemed to say it all. *Not anymore, you don't.* He knew perfectly well she didn't wear a thing to bed when she was with him.

"Alice?" Kuvi asked uncertainly.

"It's okay," Alice assured, glaring at Dylan all the while. Kuvi couldn't know that she and Dylan verbally sparred like this at times, and that it was harmless.

Well. Relatively speaking, anyway.

She stalked over to the bathroom and shut the door behind her with a muted bang. She'd left her tennis shoes in there earlier. Let Dylan stew in uncertainty about what she was doing. He was far too smug in his confidence that she'd go with him.

He was far too right.

After she'd washed her hands and face unnecessarily, she swung open the bathroom door now wearing socks and shoes. Dylan glanced over her, pausing in whatever he'd just been saying to Kuvi. Her roommate sat up in bed, her sheet fastened beneath her armpits. She looked much more calm and was even smiling. Whatever Dylan had been saying had reassured her.

Dylan's gaze dipped to her tennis shoes.

"Kuvi said you'd told her about us. If you trust her, I do. She told me where your keys were," Dylan said, holding up Alice's key ring. "We'll lock up behind us."

Alice gave Kuvi a "thanks a lot, traitor" glance. Kuvi made a helpless face and shrugged. Alice rolled her eyes. She couldn't really blame her roommate. Not many could resist Dylan's charm and smoldering good looks when put to the test.

She certainly couldn't, she acknowledged to herself bitterly as her hand slid into his and Dylan shut out the light. No matter how high the stakes, she couldn't say no to him for long.

She followed him out of the cabin, their hushed, furtive movements once again joining them somehow. The power of their shared bond seemed to vibrate in the still air as they moved stealthily down the path to the coverage of the woods. Or maybe it was the knowledge of Dylan's anger and concern in regard to her edgy behavior today and her own highly volatile state that added to the sense of electricity crackling between them. Her anxiety boiled up in her until she couldn't suppress it anymore. She halted, pulling on Dylan's hand once they reached the unlit trail leading toward the stables.

"Don't ever do that again," she challenged quietly.

"Don't *you* ever do that again. Defy me if it makes you feel more in control, Alice, but don't think I'm going to roll over if you deny me *this*."

She swallowed thickly at his quick, succinct reply. It'd obviously been right on the tip of his tongue. He'd made it clear he would only agree to her resuming her life as a counselor at Camp Durand if she spent her nights with him at Castle Durand. She was reminded yet again of how anxious he'd been for her safety. Not just tonight.

For twenty years of his life.

Dylan seemed bizarrely convinced that a threat to her safety still remained. It was like after all those years of worrying, he couldn't stop the habit now.

When she didn't reply, he resumed their hasty, silent journey through the dark night. Their terse exchange had only amplified the tension between them. Alice's heart began an erratic race. When they reached Dylan's bedroom, she knew what was going to happen. Their frothing emotions would find an outlet in volatile lovemaking. She dreaded it.

She wanted it so badly, it felt like she'd shatter from the force of her need.

SIX

She and Dylan didn't speak during the increasingly familiar, dark, furtive trek through the woods, up the slope of the hill and through the terrace doors of Castle Durand. He didn't even utter a word once he'd closed his bedroom door, locked it, led her to the side of his bed and switched on a lamp to a dim setting.

Nor when he silently began to undress her.

By that time, Alice trembled from the force of anxious desire.

She reached to help him unfasten her bra, but he merely grasped her wrists and placed her arms back at her sides. She looked up at his face, seeing his fixed expression as he watched himself undress her. He was still angry with her. She could see it etched on his bold rugged features. She was still angry with him.

But as always, this electrical need, this inexplicable pull they experienced for one another, trumped everything else.

Despite his obvious irritation at her, his touch was gentle as he unfastened her bra. His fingertips lightly skimmed the side of her breasts as he removed the cups. She winced reflexively, her nipples pulling painfully tight, even at that subtle caress of skin against skin. She noticed his gaze on her bared breasts and shut her eyes, embarrassed and aroused by the exposure, knowing he witnessed the sharpness of her need.

By the time he'd fully undressed her and she stood before him naked, her trembling had amplified.

"Lie down on the bed," he said.

Relief swept through her at his demand. Lying down, perhaps he wouldn't notice her shaking. The sense of relief intensified when she reclined against the pillows, and he reached into a bedside table drawer, lifting out two black cuffs with attached straps.

It both soothed and aroused her, to feel the soft leather against her wrists . . . to feel their strength and solidity. She'd resigned herself to the fact that surrender was her only option when it came to Dylan. It helped, though, knowing that with the restraints, she had no choice but to submit.

He restrained her wrists to the bed. When he was done, she lay naked with her arms above her head, her elbows bent slightly and resting comfortably on the pillows. He straightened upon finishing his task and paused next to the bed, looking down at her bound body . . . taking his time.

Something in his gaze made her eyes clamp tight again.

So hot. So possessive.

He came down over her, still fully dressed, and straddled her hips on all fours. She made a muffled sound of arousal when she felt him plant his hands on the mattress above her shoulders, and knew he towered above her.

"Look at me."

He said it bluntly, a hint of impatience in his tone.

She stared up at him, trying desperately to even her choppy breathing. He held her gaze as he bent his arms. His dark head lowered. She cried out in helpless, cutting arousal when he sucked an erect nipple into his mouth and laved it briskly with his tongue. He lifted one hand and molded the breast on which he sucked, his actions focused and greedy. Her hips shifted restlessly on the bed as arousal swelled between her thighs.

"Dylan," she called desperately after a moment, but he was lost in his task of consuming her. He squeezed her breast lasciviously while he tortured her nipple with his tongue. He kissed her flushed skin with gentle, worshipful lips, then sucked on her again hungrily. Alice writhed beneath him, moaning his name until her cries grew desperate.

"*What?*" he asked abruptly, and she realized her chanting of his name had finally breached his single-minded lust.

She unclenched her eyelids, her breath catching at the vision of him. He held both of her breasts in his large hands possessively. His mouth was twisted slightly in a snarl—not one of anger, Alice recognized, but one of interrupted appetite. The globes of her breasts looked pale next to his hands, the nipples reddened and damp. She nearly shut her eyes again at the potency of the vision.

"What is it?" he repeated, his thumbs sliding slowly over her nipples.

She struggled to capture the ends of her fraying purpose.

"I'm not sure I trust you," she accused in a tight whisper.

She almost bit her lip to still her anguish when his stroking thumbs stilled on her damp nipples.

"What do you mean?" She experienced a blast of the cold sharp anger Sebastian Kehoe must have felt this morning coming face-to-face with Dylan's wrath.

Why had she felt the need to tell him now, in this intimate moment? She was so raw. So vulnerable to him.

That's why you did it.

"Alice?"

She shook her head on the pillow. "I realized it today. That's why I didn't meet you tonight."

His expression darkened. "What happened? Did someone say something to you? Jim Sheridan? Kehoe?"

"No. It's nothing like that. No one said anything to me. Why did you have to act like a paranoid Neanderthal today in the woods? Don't you trust Jim Sheridan? I thought you were friends."

"We are friends. And I do trust him. I had my reasons, Alice."

She waited for the rest, her brow cocked. She sighed in frustration when he remained silent and implacable.

"There. *That's* why I don't trust you. You keep things from me. *Still*. Besides . . . I'm not sure I trust anyone. Not completely."

Her defiant words sounded feeble to her own ears. They seemed to hang in the air between them, inadequate and limp.

"Do you want to be here? With me?" he asked.

"You know I do. I'm just so confused."

"Do you think I don't know what it's like? To be told to trust, just because an authority figure tells you to?" He shook his head. "I'm even more accomplished at doubting than you, Alice."

His gaze lowered over her throat and chest, to where he held her breasts in his hands. Her nipples prickled at the weight of his gaze.

"Your body trusts me. Even if your mind doesn't," he said grimly after a moment. "For someone like you—for someone like *us*—trust doesn't come wholesale. It comes in stages. And this"— he nodded at her flushed, naked body—"is a start."

She knew what he meant. He'd had it every bit as rough as Alice growing up. Both of them had learned the hard way that to trust was to eventually hurt.

To *not* trust hurt, too, though. Dylan was teaching Alice that lesson for the first time in her life.

"I'm sorry," she said miserably, because she'd seen the flicker of pain on his face when she'd said she didn't trust him, despite his tough response. She'd caused him pain, and that knowledge hurt her, in turn. "I just thought I should tell you. It only seemed fair."

"But you came tonight. For this?" he asked, and his hands on her breasts tightened slightly.

"Yes." She bit her lower lip when he resumed massaging her breasts and stroking her nipples with his thumbs. He was crouched over her, his strong thighs spread, his crotch suspended less than an inch above her lower belly and sex. As he resumed caressing her breasts, she felt his cock come into contact with her skin as the weight of his erection mounted. She moaned, the elusive touch of his desire tormenting her. "I came for you," she confirmed in a heated rush. "I came because I need you."

"Even if you don't trust me?" he asked in a hard, dry tone, still molding her breasts to his hands and teasing her nipples with his fingertips.

Heat swept through her chest and face. "Isn't it enough? That I'm here? That I let you tie me to this bed. That I'd let you do anything to me here?" she asked desperately.

His magical hands slowed. Holding her stare, he lifted his hand and pushed his blunt fingertips against her flushed lips.

"Anything?"

"Anything," she whispered, arousal swelling in her.

"And you say you don't trust," he said so quietly, for a moment Alice thought she hadn't heard him correctly.

His head lowered again, and her thoughts splintered as he kissed her breasts and ribs and heaving belly, pausing to taste her with the tip of his tongue or bite gently at the curve of her hip. Her skin roughened. She pulled on her restraints, squirming on the bed, but the straps remained secure—holding her in place for pleasure.

Making it impossible to run. She loved him for knowing she required that. Especially tonight.

There was no teasing or build-up to ecstasy—or at least very little of it, anyway. One second, Dylan was feathering his tongue across her hipbone, and the next, he was dipping it between her labia and laving her clit hard. Alice's body tightened and jerked. Her shout of surprise segued to a moan. The pleasure was hot, flooding, and intense. She twisted her hips, not wanting to escape necessarily, but instinctively flinching from such an onrush of sensation.

Dylan captured her hips and held her down on the bed, demanding a steady target. He turned his head to find a new angle with which to torture her with the firm mastery of his tongue. She lifted her head from the pillows, watching him. He lashed and agitated her clit, his actions bold and lewd one moment, gentle and soothing the next. His mouth applied the most concise, yet subtle suction. Her entire body seized in pleasure. It felt like he filled her with it, every movement, every second that passed, mounting the unbearable friction

Finally, she broke and shuddered in his hold.

Even as she struggled to recover from her orgasm, she felt him slide a finger into her slit. She clamped him without thought, still in the clutches of her climax.

"That's right. I can feel you coming for me."

Alice opened her eyes to find him staring at her face. His eyes shone with lust. His sensual, firm lips, chin, and nose glistened from her juices. She whimpered at the sight of him, another shudder of pleasure rippling through her. He stroked her higher with his finger, his mouth slanting with arousal. He had lowered over her, and now knelt between her spread thighs. She suddenly felt a pressure behind her knee. He rolled her hips back, urging her to bend her knees, her feet hanging in the air. At the new angle, he plunged his finger into her more firmly. She whimpered at the sound of him moving in her aroused sex. He growled roughly.

"You hear that, don't you? You're soaking wet." He leaned down again between her spread thighs and kissed the damp hair above her clit, the slight pressure and the promise of more flooding pleasure making her moan and pull on her restraints. He continued to stroke her deep with his finger.

She became so lost when she was with him. Alice had fought against the feeling of helplessness her whole life. She couldn't imagine why she craved abandonment so single-mindedly when it came to Dylan.

He withdrew his finger and rose onto his knees, still positioned between her thighs. She watched him closely, holding her breath, anxious for his next move. Craving it. He slid his forearm between her calves and thighs to the back of her knees and pushed back slightly, exposing the backs of her legs and buttocks. He lowered his other hand and again slid a finger into her sex, his actions deliberate and firm. As he finger-fucked her, he used his thumb to press little circles on her slippery clit.

"Oh," she groaned, because her clit began to burn again beneath his sure touch.

"Feel good?" he muttered.

She pressed her hips rhythmically against his stroking thumb and plunging finger. "Better than good. Fucking fantastic." His small smile was sex distilled.

"Do you want to come again?"

"Are you kidding? *Yes.*" She circled her partially suspended hips more strenuously against the divine pressure of his fingers.

"In a minute, then. First, I want you to do something for me," he murmured.

Her gaze flickered to his face when he slid his finger out of her and stopped the delicious circling on her clit.

"What?" she demanded, a little sharp at being deprived of such sweet, building pressure. He moved his lubricated finger to her ass.

"Trust me in this," he said quietly.

Alice went entirely still, her focus narrowing to the sensation of his fingertip pressed against her ass and his four words. A moan escaped her throat. Had he just applied a firmer pressure? The stimulation felt good to her aroused body, a different, forbidden kind of friction. Her cheeks flooded with fresh heat and the burn in her clit became a sizzle.

Little slut, said an amused voice in her head. *You're hungry for even this with him.*

"Alice?"

She blinked at the edge in his tone. It struck her that he was as tense and anticipatory as she was at that moment—maybe more so. She met his stare.

"I told you I'd trust you to do anything in this bed," she whispered.

Without altering his expression in the slightest, he pushed his fingertip into her ass. She gasped.

"It's more than a majority of women would trust, even after spending years with their husbands," he said, watching her face closely. "You realize that, don't you?"

"What can I say?" she asked shakily, because he'd just pushed his finger into her to the first joint. It felt strange, having him touch her there. Having him penetrate her ass at the same time that he pinned her with his stare was almost overwhelmingly intimate . . . although she'd never tell him that. "I'm not most women."

"You're not as tough as you act sometimes."

"Neither are you," Alice defended.

He pushed his finger farther into her. Alice suppressed a whimper. A muscle leapt in his cheek.

"You're hot and tight."

"Are you going to fuck me there?"

His mouth slanted at her attempt at bold flippancy. "So determined to prove your point, aren't you? So determined to be fearless."

"Are you saying I should fear you?"

"No. I'm saying you should trust me. It's *you* who finds that prospect frightening."

He withdrew his finger and came down partially over her, reaching and opening the top drawer on the bedside table. Alice just laid there, his reply silencing her soundly. He straightened and opened the cap on what she recognized as a bottle of lubricant. His expression appeared hard and focused as he liberally lubricated two fingers. Alice found the vision of his long thick fingers shining from the fluid both intensely erotic and intimidating at once.

He fastened the cap and moved it aside on the mattress. He

placed one hand on her shin and gently rolled back her hips several inches.

"Try to relax," he said.

She started to say something sarcastic, but the sensation of him pushing his forefinger into her ass silenced her. At first, it felt a little uncomfortable. Her gaze locked onto his like she thought it would save her. His eyes were so deep and enigmatic. So compelling. He slid his finger in her to the knuckle and then slowly began to fuck her with it.

Her lips parted in aroused wonder, and a moan slipped between them.

"That's right, just give in to it," he said, watching her expression like a hawk. "Keep your hips rolled back," he demanded, letting go of her knee.

She moaned loudly. He'd started to rub her clit with the thumb of his left hand. She was very slippery. Hot. It felt delicious. He penetrated her ass more firmly. Faster.

She looked up at him incredulously. He looked pleased.

"I know you're a virgin in this way," he said after a minute of stimulating her.

"How do you know that?" she squeaked.

"Your reaction. The first time I touched you there."

She recalled the incident of which he spoke. It'd been the first night she'd come here to Castle Durand. Dylan had touched her ass during a particularly intense moment of lovemaking. Alice had started at the unfamiliar sensation, betrayed her naïveté.

"I was just surprised," she said through a soughing breath. Something about the anal stimulation in combination with the clitoral was making her *hot*. Her cheeks and the bottom of her suspended feet began to burn. Her nipples were hard and achy. Her clit positively sizzled.

"You aren't surprised now," he said, and she noticed his gaze fixed on her breasts and erect nipples. "Take another finger."

Her eyes sprang wide as he inserted his second lubricated finger into her along with the first. She gave a shaky cry.

"Push against me, baby. Don't resist. It'll make it easier on you," he instructed. Alice struggled to comply. His thumb pressed harder on her clit. Faster. As if he pushed a magic button, both of his fingers slid fully into her ass.

"Oh," she exclaimed softly at the sensation of fullness and pressure. He immediately began to fuck her with his fingers.

"Nice tight little ass," he said thickly. He watched himself penetrate her. Alice's excitement pitched higher.

"Fuck me there. I'm ready."

"You're horny. That's not the same thing as ready," he shot back, still watching his fingers slide in and out of her ass with a narrowed gaze.

"No, no . . . I'm ready," she gasped. She bobbed her hips, getting more friction on her ass and clit. She shut her eyes, reveling in the pleasure, reaching for release. "It feels so good. I'm going to come. Fuck me with your big cock. *Please.*"

Crack.

Her eyes sprang open at the stinging slap on her buttock. Dylan stared down at her, his eyes stormy, his nostrils slightly flared, his mouth clamped tight.

"You fucking little hedonist."

Her mouth fell open in surprise at his words. She couldn't decide if he was angry at her or praising her. Knowing Dylan as she did, she'd guess both. There was a savage edge to his tone. He reached between his thighs and rubbed the considerable bulge there.

"It might hurt," he said, holding her stare as he massaged his erection through his jeans.

"A lot?" she asked, uncertainty trickling in to her thick arousal.

"Not a lot. I'll be as careful as I can this first time. But now isn't the time to test me. Do you understand, Alice?" he asked through a clamped jaw.

"Yes," she said, a little cowed by his intensity.

"Don't sabotage this. Don't try to prove to yourself that you shouldn't trust me."

"What? I wouldn't!" she denied hotly. It took a moment for his meaning to settle in. He was worried she'd goad him until he took her forcefully, and then use it as another reason for distrusting him.

"No," she said, somber now. "I won't. I promise."

He removed his fingers from her ass and peeled back his button fly. Alice froze at the vision of his erect cock straining against white boxer briefs. He looked enormous. *God, what have you gotten yourself into now?*

Her anxiety mounted as she watched him extricate his cock from his underwear. His cock was stiff and flushed, the head smooth, fat, and delineated from the staff. She hungered for it, even as she feared it. He grasped the bottom of his rigid erection and stroked the length of it. He glanced up, cock in hand, and noticed her expression.

"I'll be as gentle as I can be. This time."

Those last two words sounded a little ominous, but also exciting. Her sex clinched tight. He glanced down, as if noticing her tension. His face looked grim as he unfastened his shirt and whipped it off him with a flex of ridged hard muscle. He didn't remove his jeans and underwear. They remained bunched beneath his round shaved balls, making his jutting cock look all that much more intimidating.

Watching him lubricate his erection, knowing what he was about to do with it, had Alice skating on a ledge between boiling need and frothing anxiety.

His body looked as tensed as a coiled spring as he edged up between her thighs. Again, he used his left forearm to push her knees further into her chest and roll back her hips. She gave a little cry when he plunged his fingers into her ass again. His gaze fastened on her face as he finger-fucked her firmly.

"I'm not going to take you deep or hard. But I *am* going to fuck your ass, and it's going to feel so damn good, Alice."

"Okay," she managed, a bit awed by the power she sensed in him at that moment, the incipient restrained energy. Was she crazy for wanting to see it break free?

He paused and leaned over her. A moment later, the tension in her right hand lessened. He'd released the leather wristlet she wore from the restraining strap.

"Touch yourself," he said, straightening again between her thighs. "My hands are going to be full."

She gladly did what he asked, her fingers taking up his former task. Things felt very slippery and warm between her thighs. He watched her with a tight focus for a moment as she rubbed her clit, his lustrous eyes glittering. He used his left hand to roll her hips back farther. Her knees were now less than an inch from her nipples, her feet suspended in the air. He moved closer between her thighs.

"Don't stop," he said succinctly when she paused in stimulating her clit because he'd just slipped his fingers from her ass and pressed the tip of his cock against her. His gaze leapt to her face.

"It's not going to work," burst out of Alice's throat. Surely Dylan realized that. Her ass was a lot more sensitive than she'd ever before realized. She could perfectly feel the outline of his cock against her opening. "It'll never—"

"It will," he bit out. "With a little time and some patience. Trust me."

"But—"

He merely shook his head once and she went silent.

"Touch yourself. Please. You'll need it," he said.

Slowly, she began to move her fingers. It felt good, no matter how precarious her situation. Or maybe she was excited *because* of the risk. Alice had never considered herself a daredevil, but since sleeping with Dylan, she'd come to realize she enjoyed the spice of a sexual challenge.

He firmed his hold on her right shin, keeping her body still. "Push against me," he said. She did. He flexed his hips.

"Ouch," Alice muttered. A flash of intense pain shot through her.

"I'm sorry. It's done."

"Are you in?"

She blinked when he made a snorting sound. She stared up at him, intoxicated by the vision of his grin. He looked so beautiful to her in that moment: his muscular body drawn as tight as a wire; a glistening sheen of perspiration on his rigid torso telling her not only how aroused he was, but how much he held that arousal in check. His flashing smile was such a striking contrast to his former grim expression.

You are so far gone.

"Affirmative. Phase one mission accomplished," he said, teasing her for her practical question about the mechanics of what they were doing.

By that time, Alice already knew the answer, though. She could feel the head of his cock in her—full and throbbing. Her hand moved faster between her thighs. It was indescribably exciting, feeling Dylan inside such a private place.

"Are you okay?" she asked him, because she thought his face was drawn in pain.

He turned his chin, wiping some gathered sweat from his upper lip on his shoulder. "You feel extremely good," he said, and she realized his expression came from the pain of restraint. "More importantly, are you okay?"

"It doesn't hurt anymore."

He nodded once and used his free hand to grasp the back of her thigh. Holding her securely with both hands, he flexed deeper. Alice groaned as he filled her more.

"Okay?" he asked, pausing.

"Yes," she assured quickly, afraid he'd stop. Her clit sizzled beneath her rubbing fingers. Her suspended feet twitched in the air. The soles were hot. She moaned deeper as her arousal peaked. "More, Dylan. More."

He pushed his cock into her mid-staff. Oh God, she felt so full of him. So damn horny. She flexed her hips, pressing against him, wanting more—

His hand slid from her thigh to her lower buttock. He spanked her. Twice.

"Hold still," he ground out from between clenched teeth. She stilled in pumping her ass against his cock, but her hand moved faster between her thighs. Dylan noticed.

"Put your hand on the mattress. Now, Alice," he said harshly. She ground her teeth together. It took a monumental effort to do what he asked, akin to willing herself to jump in an ice-cold lake. He must have noticed her rebellious expression when the back of her hand thumped against the comforter. "I'll tell you when you can put it back."

Then he started to flex his hips, pumping her ass gently. Alice's mouth fell open in incredulous arousal. It felt so good; yet the intimacy was so intense, it was almost unbearable. Overwhelmed, she turned her face, pressing her cheek against the pillow. She thought he'd demand she look at him, like he often did when they were in the thick of lovemaking, but he didn't. Instead, he just kept fucking her with short fluid strokes in the ass. Maybe he knew precisely what he was doing, because Alice found that turning away didn't lessen the profound carnality of the experience in the slightest.

She became vaguely aware that she couldn't stop moaning. She was so filled with him. He pumped and pressed himself into every cell of her being in those moments.

It thrilled her that she could accommodate him in this. Even though she felt so full of him, she was aware that he held back. With each thrust into her, he went slightly deeper, but he still didn't fully penetrate her. Even though he held her firmly at thigh and shin, she began to bob her hips subtly. He felt huge inside her. Huge, and exciting, like he'd burst at any moment from the volatility of the moment.

"More," she moaned. "More, Dylan."

"You'll have what I give you."

She turned her head on the pillow to see him, compelled by the tension in his deep voice. For a moment, she just stared at him, panting, trapped by his glistening eyes as he fucked her.

"Your cheeks and lips are so pink. You like it, don't you?"

"Yes," she hissed. He smacked her buttock with his palm, and then massaged it, using his hold to firm his thrusts.

"Yeah, that's so fucking good," he muttered thickly, watching himself penetrate her. Then he looked at her face. It struck her full force, the monumental effort it took him not to slake his obvious lust like the savage she knew he could be. "Tonight, I'm going easy on you," he rasped. "Another night, I might take you harder. But you'll take it, either way. Do you understand? Because you'll trust me."

She just nodded, too overwhelmed to argue or question him. She wanted to beg him to take her harder now, to give him free rein. But she knew he wouldn't. It was *he* who held the reins, not she. He was proving a point. He was teaching her a lesson, and she had no choice but to lie there and take it.

She experienced no more pain, but the pressure was intense. It made her grit her teeth. Her moans vibrated her throat as he continued to thrust firmly, but shallowly, not allowing her to move a fraction of an inch as he plunged in and out of her.

"Do you want to touch yourself now?" he asked thickly after a moment, his thrusts inside her growing a bit faster, betraying mounting excitement.

"*Yes.*"

She opened her lips and exhaled in shaky ecstasy when she rubbed herself. She trembled. Her cream gathered around her fingers.

He looked so awesome to her in those tense moments, his

muscles bulging and defined, strained to the breaking point on the edge of raw lust and restraint. He thrust faster with a tad more force. Alice moaned in satisfaction.

She was so hot, so ready to combust. Her body tensed.

"Oh God. It feels *so*—"

She began to shudder in orgasm, her feet flexing in the air.

"*Good*," Dylan growled, finishing her sentence through gnashed teeth. He thrust more forcefully, making Alice whimper. His hands tightened on her shin and thigh. "If you had any idea what I wanted to do to you right now, Alice."

Another wave of pleasure tore through her. In the midst of her climax, she was still aware that he held back. She hated it. "*Do it*," she moaned, shaking. "Fuck me hard."

"*Quiet*," he demanded, still pumping her ass with firm, but measured strokes. She shuddered again, her head coming off the pillow, pulling hard on her single restraint. His hold on her tightened.

"Oh Jesus, it feels so *good*," he grated out.

Alice sagged back on the pillows, panting, shivers of residual pleasure still running through her. She drew a soughing breath. The hand she'd been using to rub herself slid limply to the mattress. She stared up at him, entranced by the chained savagery evident on his handsome face as he continued to fuck her. A longing welled up in her, a powerful emotion difficult to name.

A ripple of tension coursed up his left jaw and cheek.

"Come," she demanded. She *begged*.

A guttural moan tore out of his throat. Despite her satiated state, her perspiration-damp skin roughened with excitement.

She could feel him so perfectly inside her, even more acutely than she could in her pussy. Her excitement ratcheted up to a thrill of anxious anticipation when he gripped her tighter and his cock swelled huge.

He held her stare as he came. He kept his mouth clamped tight, but she saw the jerk of his muscles as he climaxed. She loved that he kept almost entirely still as he ejaculated, pumping only minimally through his pleasure, exhibiting awesome amounts of control.

She hated it.

The savage in her, that secret wildness that she and Dylan shared, longed for him to take her hard and ruthless.

Although he'd certainly taken her thoroughly, Alice acknowledged a moment later. She'd lost herself to pounding lust, while Dylan had remained in control at the helm.

He lowered his chin to his chest, trying to catch his breath. She lay still, watching in fascination as his rigid, heaving abdomen muscles slowed and his bunched sinews loosened. Again, she was reminded of how much energy he'd expended, not just from the exercise of making love; but from spending so much effort in restraint.

After a moment, he looked up and withdrew.

Alice whimpered in slight discomfort once he was gone. She'd only been excited when he was joined to her, but now . . .

Perhaps he'd been right to go easy on her.

"You didn't have to spare me," she said, her voice thick and hoarse from satiation. "But thank you, anyway."

He ran his gaze over her face slowly. What was he thinking? Sometimes she felt like she could read him like large print. Other times—like now—he was a closed book.

He eased his grip on her legs, letting her feet lower.

"Come on," he said gruffly, bending over her to release her single remaining restraint. He hovered over her and lowered, his mouth brushing against hers. Alice responded instinctively to the delicious kiss, sliding her lips against his. "Let's get in the shower," he rumbled.

Despite his words, he paused to gently bite at her lower lip and linger. His scent and taste filled her, making that inexplicable feeling of desperation and longing swell.

SEVEN

After a shared, languorous hot shower, Alice felt like her muscles were melting. As usual, Dylan had effectively worked all of her unrest, doubt, and uncertainty right out of her.

When he came down in bed next to her and shut out the light, she curled into the arc of his naked body like a warmth-seeking kitten.

"Alice?"

"Yeah?"

"Are you concerned at all about the Alumni Dinner being held for the counselors here at the house tomorrow night?"

Her heavy eyelids sprung open.

Shit. The Alumni Dinner: a semiformal affair held at Dylan's home. Several prior Camp Durand counselors and present-day successful Durand executives were invited in order to meet the current counselor class. Word had it, a few key words from an influential alumni could make or break a counselor's career at Durand. Alice had known about the event—in theory, anyway— since she'd first received her Camp Durand informational packet upon being hired as a counselor. But with everything going on, her second official visit to Castle Durand had always seemed far off in the future.

"Did you forget about it?" Dylan asked her when she didn't immediately respond, because her brain had started spinning in that increasingly familiar vortex. It would be so strange, to walk in the

halls of Castle Durand as though she were only vaguely familiar
with them . . . to treat Dylan like the distant top boss who was too
far out of her sphere to be considered even an acquaintance.

"No," she lied. "Are *you* concerned about it?"

"Not it. You," he said with his typical succinctness. "Did
everything go all right today?"

She frowned upon hearing the cautious tone in his voice.

"It was a perfectly normal day—all except for that whole incident in the woods," she added darkly under her breath.

"Insert my apology here? Is that what you're waiting for?" he
asked, humor tingeing his tone. She just scowled into the darkness.

"Okay, I guess neither of us is going to fall over apologizing at
the moment. I don't expect you to apologize to me for running off
into the woods alone today." Alice rolled her eyes and made a
disgusted sound, which Dylan ignored. "On another note, I've
made an appointment for you at Morgantown Memorial for a
blood test. It's for four o'clock on Saturday afternoon. I'll take you
over to the hospital. Dr. Shineburg will transfer all the samples to
a specialist clinic in Chicago for the actual genetic testing. It takes
four to six weeks to get the results, so we might as well get things
started."

She remained silent, but perhaps he noticed her tension because
he began stroking her upper arm and shoulder.

"Have you changed your mind about the testing?"

"No. I want to do it. I want to know for certain."

"Then what are you thinking about?"

"Dylan, why are you so worried about me? I can understand
why you have been in the past, but why *now*?"

"Do you mean why did I come to the woods today, when Rigo
told me Jim Sheridan was there? You're still waiting for me to
defend myself?"

"I think I deserve an explanation, yes."

Again, he didn't speak.

"Dylan?"

"Jim was the sheriff of Morgantown when Addie Durand was kidnapped," he began slowly. "He's supported me over the years . . . encouraged me not to give up in looking for Addie."

She lay still, absorbing not only his words, but trying to decode what he wasn't saying.

"That's a good thing, isn't it?" she asked.

"Of course it is. I don't know what I would have done without him."

"So why did you come out to the woods and jump all over him? I thought you were friends."

"Jim is a good cop. Excellent, in fact. Last night, he noticed how tense I was. Around you," he added after a pause. "He went out to see you today, because he sensed something was going on with me. He was digging for answers."

"You *were* surly last night when that alarm went off," Alice mumbled, uncomfortably aware she was skirting the relevant topic. She frowned into the darkness, attempting to firm her resolve. "You *can't* be thinking that Jim Sheridan actually was connecting last night to Addie Durand. Connecting *me* to Addie Durand," she added reluctantly.

"What if he did? I told you, he's an excellent cop. He likely noticed the similarity between you and Lynn."

She started. "I look like Lynn Durand?" That seemingly casual statement felt like a little bomb had gone off in her.

"Yes. It seems like you do a little more every day."

"What do you mean?"

"As your hair grows and lightens and you give up on some of the heavy eye makeup," he replied gruffly, and she sensed his distraction. "My point is, are you ready to answer Jim Sheridan's questions? Are you ready to have the FBI notified, and deal with the ramifications of them coming here to finally close a twenty-year-old investigation?"

"No," she exclaimed, alarm making her jerk up and turn partially toward Dylan.

"There you have it. *That's* why I didn't want Jim to find out the truth. Yet."

For several seconds, she remained in the tensed position, her mind working over what he'd told her. No. Alice definitely was *not* ready to have various law enforcement officials interrupt her life with questions she wasn't ready to answer.

That she *couldn't* answer, because she hadn't fully faced the reality of those questions herself.

Dylan had stormed into those woods with a purpose. He'd been trying to shield her.

She eased back onto the pillow.

"I think you might have made things worse with Jim by acting that way. He seemed even more suspicious by your heavy-handedness."

She heard his soft grunt of irritated agreement. "I realize that. Maybe I have mixed feelings about telling Jim. He deserves to know the truth, but I knew you wouldn't be ready to face the consequences of him knowing it yet. When it came down to it, no one else could have stopped him from interrogating you except for me. I was worried."

"I'm fine," Alice said in a pressured whisper. His hand flexed on her arm, and he drew her closer to his body. She clamped her eyes shut as emotion expanded in her chest. It seemed to rise to her brain until it throbbed in her ears.

I'm fine. Her voice replayed in her head, making her cringe. She'd sounded like she was trying to convince herself as much as she was Dylan.

ALICE was dead on her feet when Dylan awoke her in the predawn darkness. She dressed in a half-conscious daze. When she walked

out of the bathroom, she saw Dylan waiting for her by his bedroom door. When she neared him, he handed her a bag without a
word.

"What's this?"

"It's for tonight. The Alumni Dinner."

She opened the bag and peered inside. She saw a black gar-
ment. When she drew it out, she saw it was a lovely sophisticated
cocktail dress, an elegant item that she'd never have the taste to
choose, let alone the money to buy. It was one of several dresses
he'd bought for her last week.

Crap. He'd noticed how awkward she'd felt in her sundress at
the last semiformal event held at Castle Durand. The thought
mortified her.

"There's more," he said, his low rumble emanating above and
just to the right of her making the skin of her ear prickle.

Unable to look at him because she was afraid he'd see her
mixed shame and excitement, she reached into the bag and pulled
out a rectangular black velvet box. Inside nestled a beautiful rope
of pearls. She just stared at the necklace for a moment before she
swallowed thickly and met his stare.

"Yes. You *can.* They're yours," he said succinctly, preempting
her response. He'd known she was about to tell him she couldn't
take the items.

Several days ago, Dylan had surprised her with a small yet
stunning new wardrobe. That was before he'd told her about
Addie Durand. It made her uncomfortable now, to consider his
gifts, in retrospect.

Maybe Dylan expected her to look and dress the part of an
heiress.

She wavered about whether or not to refuse the items. In the
end, she accepted the dress: frowning, exhausted, and highly
uncertain. The simple fact of the matter was she didn't have anything else to wear. She'd been so distracted, she'd forgotten the

Alumni Dinner, and both of her sundresses were in the dirty-clothes hamper.

"One more thing," Dylan said before they headed out the door. "Give me your keys."

She gave him a dubious look, but handed him her key ring. He took a key from his jeans' pocket and worked it onto the metal ring. He lifted her right hand in both of his, pressing the keys gently to her palm.

"You know the security code. Now you have the key to get into the castle. If it feels strange to you tonight, being here as a guest, this is just a reminder that you're anything *but*."

A few hours of sleep were definitely not sufficient. She remained zombie-like for the entire walk through the grounds with Dylan and as she furtively entered her cabin, washed, and pulled on new clothes. She was still out of it by the time she met up with Terrance Brown for their early morning jog. The rising sun was making the eastern woods look like they were catching fire. Terrance immediately took note of her pale face and blurry eyes.

"Come on, Alice. You're supposed to be the healthy one here. Are you hungover or something? You out partying last night?" Terrance teased her, dimpling up with a wide grin.

"*Partying*," Alice mumbled with dark sarcasm. "Who's got time for *partying*?"

She perked up a moment later as she joined Terrance in stretching on the white side beach. Terrance didn't appear to be phoning it in, but genuinely trying to warm up his muscles for their run. Maybe her attempts at hooking Terrance into the benefits of exercise were paying off. At least he'd shown up independently for their early morning jogs, which was something. It wasn't easy getting a fifteen-year-old boy up at dawn.

After they'd returned from their morning run, Alice walked

into the Red Team's cabin with Terrance, wanting a word with the night supervisor before she left. After she'd met up with Crystal, she opened the door to the nearly empty common room. Immediately, she overheard Terrance, Matt Dinorio, and Justin Arun muttering conspiratorially together where they sat at a corner table.

"They say they've set up some kind of secret alarm system this year to stop people from stealing it," she heard Matt hiss. "It's not as easy as it was for Ormitz and McCaron and those guys from the Gold Team in the past. I don't think we can do it."

"You're full of it. No one would waste so much money and effort on a damn goat. You two said the Red Team has never got it! We've got to try," Terrance insisted.

"I'm *serious*. If you get anywhere near it . . . *Boom*. Alarms start blaring, and the next thing you know, you're behind bars at the Morgantown jail."

Alice stilled, both concerned and mystified by the boys' conversation. Justin and Matt were both "expert" Durand campers. They were bright, energetic, and often mischievous, but not any more so than most teenage boys. She considered Terrance in the same light. Alice didn't think any of them were capable of serious law breaking. True, Matt had been involved in several petty crimes years ago. He came from a pretty rough neighborhood and had fallen in with a bad crowd. But since first attending Camp Durand, Matt had been clean as a whistle and his grades had significantly improved.

"What are you guys talking about?" Alice demanded loudly, fully entering the room.

The boys started like they'd been goosed.

Of course she got nothing from them after that but uncomfortable laughter and some unintelligible mumbling. Alice was considering separating them for a more thorough interrogation, but stopped herself at the last minute. Something told her it would be wiser to go about this in a different way.

I mean . . . a goat? *Seriously?*

And hadn't she heard someone say something about a goat recently? It came to her when: Jim Sheridan in the woods yesterday, sporting with the two kids from Kuvi's team about a goat.

Sure, it was alarming to hear her kids talking about a theft, but there had to be something more to the story, something Alice wasn't getting. She was mystified, more than anything.

She brought up the incident at lunch later that day while she was sitting at a table with Kuvi, Thad, and Dave Epstein. Dave grinned.

"I know what they're talking about. Salinger told me after I heard some of my kids making some sly references to it and acting like I was too stupid to notice," Dave said, referring to Aidan Salinger, a Durand manager. "There's another camp down the shore called Camp Wildwood, and their mascot is a goat. They call it Bang."

"Bang?" Alice asked blankly, pausing with her chicken sandwich a few inches from her mouth.

"The whole thing is based on an old story. Camp Wildwood puts on a firework display on the last night of camp. One summer decades ago, a wild goat broke into the shed where the fireworks were being stored and ate some of the fireworks." Dave shrugged. "You can imagine the rest. Bang went *bang*." He made an exploding sound and motioned with his hands to imply fragments shooting in all directions.

"Disgusting. You Yanks have the most warped sense of humors," Kuvi declared when Thad and Alice snorted with laughter.

"Seriously? A wild *goat*? Around here? Where do they find those, right alongside the wild cows and sheep?" Thad asked, glancing from Kuvi to Alice incredulously. Alice choked on her laughter and set down her sandwich.

"Yeah, I know," Dave assured, hushing his voice to mute the spectacle of them in the crowded dining hall. "Whether it really happened or not isn't the point. Bang is a big deal around here. It's become a tradition for a couple Durand kids to sneak over and steal Bang one night while both camps are in progress. They return him the next day in a canoe, so no real harm is done."

"They got *another* goat after they blew the first one to smithereens?" Kuvi asked, looking scandalized.

"No," Dave managed between jags of laughter. Thad, Dave, and Alice had busted up again at Kuvi's wide-eyed question. Sometimes, Kuvi's Britishness made her seem more sophisticated than any of the other counselors, but occasionally, she was adorably naïve when it came to their American idiosyncrasies. "They have a little statue of Bang," Dave continued. "It sits in the middle of their common, right in the center of all the cabins. Because the Camp Wildwood kids and staff know the Camp Duranders will try to steal Bang one night, it's gotten harder and harder to do it. The Wildwood kids have made an art of defending their mascot. Last year's attempt failed, and resulted in two Gold Team experts being taken to Morgantown jail. It was the Durand kids' fault. They got mouthy and rude when they were caught. A fight almost broke out. They got out of jail quick enough with a slap on the hand. Camp Wildwood didn't press charges and everything was okay. Before that happened, the Durand managers and Kehoe sort of smirked and turned a blind eye to the Bang phenomenon, considering it a Camp Durand tradition, kids will be kids, yada yada. They've been doing it for years now. Rumor is, secret points were even allotted to the team who successfully stole and then returned Bang. Lots of Durand alumni are pretty nostalgic about Bang."

"Glorifying the tradition of thievery as long as no one gets caught at the scene of the crime," Kuvi said. "Lovely."

"Oh come on," Alice disagreed. "They're fifteen- and sixteen-year-old kids having some fun at summer camp. I can think of a kid on my team who could benefit from a little teenage rule-breaking for once. We're not talking about jumping someone in the hood here." She was thinking of Noble D. He was way too serious. His teen years were going to vanish very soon. Since he was ten, D had assumed the male leadership role in his family after his older brother had been shot and killed. D planned to become a minister following his four years at a Baptist college. Before he knew it, D would find himself a pious reverend, his chance to be a goofy carefree kid gone forever.

"I agree," Dave said. "But after the two guys got caught last year and started mouthing off, things have changed. This year, they're discouraging any Camp Wildwood forays. I think Kehoe started that rumor about Bang being booby-trapped with an alarm, just to deter Camp Duranders from getting into any more trouble. I'm going to be having a talk with my kids about it this afternoon, but I'm not sure it'll make much difference. Apparently, the Gold Team is known for being the most strategic *and* success-ful at Bang acquisitions."

"You must be so proud," Thad said drolly.

"His kids must think so," Alice defended Dave, who *did* look a little proud talking about his team. "Matt, Terrance, and Justin sounded completely envious, and were *not* happy the Red Team had never won the honor."

"If you want to call going to jail an honor," Kuvi said, popping a fry in her mouth.

"Since no charges were ever brought, I think that's exactly what my kids think. It takes some balls to do it. I just need to convince them there's no honor in being a rude jerk. So what do you guys think about the Alumni Dinner tonight?" Dave asked quietly, glanc-ing casually from side to side to assure himself no Durand managers were hovering nearby. "Think we should be nervous about being put under the microscope by the Old-Boy Network?"

"As long as we're using oxymorons, there'll be some Old Girls there as well. And some that aren't so old," Kuvi said, giving Dave a pointed glance. He shrugged a concession. Kuvi grinned at him. "I don't think it'll be so bad," Kuvi continued. "I'm getting the impression Durand executives who were counselors here have a serious nostalgia factor going on about Camp Durand. Look at this Bang example. They'll probably be more interested in telling us stories of the good ol' days than anything else. I'm not too worried about it."

"What about you, Alice? Up for another shindig at the big house?" Dave asked, using his fork to shovel up the last of his salad. Since he was otherwise occupied, he didn't notice both Kuvi and Thad cast anxious glances at her. Why did everyone think she was such a basket case?

Because you've kind of been acting like one lately.

"I'd rather go to the dentist. It's just something I have to do. What are you wearing tonight, Kuvi?" Alice asked, her offhand, casual manner discouraging further unsolicited concern on either Thad or Kuvi's part. Alice was worried enough on her own about playing the stranger in Dylan's home tonight . . .

. . . About playing the stranger in a house where supposedly she'd once lived and been loved.

EIGHT

You look beautiful tonight, Alice."

Alice blinked in surprise and turned.

"Sidney. I hadn't realized you'd be here tonight," she said, sounding both flustered and pleased when the psychiatrist leaned down to kiss her briefly on the cheek.

"I'm way too old to be a Camp Durand alumnus myself, but I've been advising alumni for years, given my place on the board."

Alice smiled. "Well the man who advises the top men and women definitely deserves a place of honor."

She hadn't seen Sidney since the day Dylan had broken the news to her about Addie Durand. It seemed a little surreal—and embarrassing—staring into Sidney's handsome lined face and kind gray eyes now. She'd fainted in front of him. Plus, seeing Sidney standing there in the glamorous setting of the Durand grand dining room emphasized the reality of the day Dylan had broken the news to her about Addie's kidnapping. The vision of the psychiatrist seemed to collapse her two separate worlds, creating an internal jarring sensation for Alice.

Sidney smiled at her and nodded cordially to another gray-haired man who was passing with a bejeweled woman on his arm. He put his hand on her elbow and smoothly maneuvered her to an unoccupied part of the room.

"I've told a few people in passing that I knew your father from my Navy days in order to explain my familiarity with you," Sidney said very quietly, the volume of his voice kept lower than the general buzz of the chat of the cocktail party. "It was Dylan's idea. I hope you don't mind. It's not a lie, after all."

Again, that strange crashing sensation in her spirit. Alice cleared her throat and fingered the rope of pearls Dylan had given her. She found the sensation of the smooth cool globes running across her skin reassuring somehow.

"I'm sorry. Perhaps I shouldn't have said that," Sidney said, his gaze sharp on her face.

"No, of course not," she assured. "So . . . you really served in the military with Alan Durand?"

"Yes. We met while we were both stationed at a naval base in Guam. I was his commanding officer there for a year and a half. Such a good man. Full of energy and purpose. Incredibly innovative, a born risk taker. You would have liked him."

"I understand he liked to travel quite a bit."

"Alan was a gypsy at heart," Sidney said with a fond smile. "Only Lynn could have ever hoped to settle him down."

"And Addie," Alice said very quietly.

Sidney nodded. His stare on her was intent, but not cautious like Dylan's often was. It was a little comforting, to know that the psychiatrist didn't believe she was going to go over the edge at any moment.

"Although, Addie only came to Alan and Lynn thirteen years after they found each other. They wanted to start a family right away, but they couldn't conceive. All the years of trying with no result nearly crushed Lynn . . . and Alan, in turn. He felt so helpless watching her suffer. She longed to be a mother. For a period of time, she became a shadow of herself. I worried their mutual grief would pry them apart."

"Oh. That's terrible."

"It all came out all right, in the end," Sidney assured with a smile. "After years of being undecided, they eventually resolved to adopt. They'd begun the process when Lynn discovered she was pregnant. That's the way of these things sometimes. Once an alternative decision is made, some of the stress goes, and *voilà*. The couple finds themselves pregnant."

"They must have been so happy," she said numbly. She was determinedly trying to ignore a rising rush of air in her ears. But she was curious, too—

"They were ecstatic. I've never seen two people so transported. They *truly* believed they'd been granted a miracle. That sense of being blessed never lessened. It only grew, every day Addie was with them."

And then it all came crashing down on them one horrible day.

A tremor of emotion went through her. What those poor people must have experienced on the day their daughter was kidnapped. How their panic and fear must have mounted in the ensuing days and weeks. Years. The grief must have been crushing.

"Excuse me," she said to a passing waiter, who paused. She placed the half-full wineglass she'd been clutching on his tray. "Thank you," she murmured before he continued on his way.

Her gaze strayed past Sidney's shoulder, her eyes unerringly finding the tall formidable figure in a black suit across the room holding court among a small circle of three women and two men. She hadn't spoken to Dylan all evening, and wasn't sure she wanted to even attempt it with so many curious people at the dinner. Alice swore eyes had been tracking her movements all night. In the next second, she'd accuse herself of being paranoid. She wasn't being observed, at least not any more so than any of the other counselors who were vying for permanent positions at Durand Enterprises.

Even though Alice knew she shouldn't be obvious in her glances at Dylan, her eyes just seemed to move in his direction of their own accord. He pulled at her attention like a magnet.

Maybe it was unfair to say that he was holding court at that moment, because that would have implied an attempt or eagerness on his part to be the center of attention to a circle of avid listeners. Alice couldn't hear what he said, but she recognized his manner; that absolute yet muted sense of confidence. Dylan's power was such that he never needed to bluster or grandstand.

Even given his focus on his listeners, his gaze suddenly fixed unerringly on her from across the room. Was it her imagination, or did she see something flicker into his eyes? A question? A concern?

"I hope I haven't upset you with talk about Alan and Lynn," Sidney said, interrupting her thoughts and nodding in the direction of the departing waiter and her wineglass.

"No, of course not. I'm a little hungry, that's all. The wine was getting to me on an empty stomach."

"Yes, I can imagine the physical exercise you get every day at camp would lead to a healthy appetite," Sidney said, smiling.

"Nothing like chasing after teenagers to increase your metabolism."

Sidney chuckled. "You know, it would be understandable if the topic of the Durands *did* leave you unsettled. But I'm not sure it's advisable to avoid it entirely forever."

Alice was a little startled that he'd returned to the topic of the Durands. "Yes, I think you're right. But just because I agree with you doesn't change the way I feel when I hear about the Durands," Alice said pointedly. Sidney nodded, and she thought he'd understood her. She was telling him she still felt no personal connection to the child Sidney and Dylan claimed she—Alice—once was. It struck her with a sagging feeling that she was trying awfully hard to convince other people of that fact lately.

"It's sometimes hard to speak of these matters in the mundane world, where there are so many things to distract us. I'd like to extend an invitation to you to come and see me at my office in Morgantown, anytime you like. I'll find a slot for you, even if I'm booked. It might be nice for you to have a little distraction-free space to explore things. Or I could refer you to a good local therapist."

Alice blinked. "Oh . . . I don't think that'll be necessary, but thanks for offering it."

"Think about it," Sidney said, his gray eyes soft, but compelling. "You have a lot of things to come to terms with in your life, and twice as many things that might get in the way of your focus."

He glanced around the large dining room. Did his gaze land on Dylan?

Alice didn't respond, because she wasn't sure how to. The spell of Sidney's somberness broke when he glanced around. "Ah, good. They're calling for us to be seated."

He placed his hand gently on her back and urged her to the candlelit tables.

THE dining room Alice had wandered into on her first visit to the house had undergone a transformation. The entire wood-paneled far wall had been moved back to expose an additional area, doubling the square feet and expanding the already spacious dining room into a ballroom of sorts. The long formal dining table had been removed. A dozen or more large circular tables dressed with white cloths and silver candelabra had been put in its place.

There were name cards at the place settings. She was less than thrilled about being seated next to a venerable-looking Durand Alumni named Jason Stalwalter, but glad to see Thad appear on the other side of her. Sort of glad, anyway. Yes, what happened in the woods yesterday was still leaving her prickly. But Thad was a friend, after all, despite all of the other . . . *stuff.* She couldn't help but feeling comforted by his familiar face.

"I bribed Dave to switch seats with me," Thad leaned over and whispered directly next to her ear after introductions were made and there was a rustle as they all settled in their assigned seats.

"Stalwalter is the northeastern region's vice president of marketing and sales. I've been trying to meet him all night."

Alice wilted a little at this. She hadn't been very proactive about networking and putting herself forward tonight. Alice despised the idea of promoting herself. If only she possessed Thad's, Kuvi's, or Brooke's breeding and polish, that social ease that came from interacting with movers and shakers since first crawling out of the cradle. That was a large part of what the Durand Alumni Dinner was about: getting your face and qualifications in front of some of the most influential Durand managers and supervisors in the world.

"Oh, we should have switched places," Alice whispered to Thad. As she spoke, the image of Brooke Seifert's anxious face suddenly came into focus in the crowd. Brooke sat two tables away. It bizarrely struck Alice that they were dressed alike; Brooke also wore black with pearls tonight. Alice wasn't sure how she felt about the fact that she could pass as one of Brooke's peers.

Her gaze flickered and stuck on Sebastian Kehoe's face. He sat at the same table as Brooke, and he, too, was staring at Alice. She blinked in momentary indignation. Was he staring at her *breasts*? No . . . Kehoe frowned as he looked at the pearls she wore.

Unsettled by the brief observation, she forced herself to focus again on Thad. "Maybe it's not too late for us to switch places—"

"Alice."

She started in surprise at the sound of the brisk, booming voice and turned in her seat. Jason Stalwalter was regarding her with benevolent warmth as a waiter set a highball glass on the table in front of him.

"I've heard rave reviews about you from our CEO. We've completely revamped our VitaThirst campaign on a nationwide basis, thanks to you. I think Mr. Fall would patent that brain of yours if he had a chance."

"What?" Alice asked stupidly. For a few seconds, she couldn't draw breath. Was Dylan *crazy*, talking Alice up in front of other

Durand executives? Her gaze shot to the head table, where Dylan sat. She wasn't surprised to see his dark eyes pinning her, but then his gaze flickered to the man on the right of him and they began talking. Alice was left hanging in confusion.

"I . . . uh, I'm not sure what you mean," she said awkwardly, uncomfortably aware of Thad leaning forward and listening to the exchange.

Upon her arrival at Castle Durand, Dylan had requested that she have a look at some Durand annual and quarterly reports. He was aware that Alice was a trendspotter, that she possessed an ability to absorb large amounts of data and statistics and quickly break them down into meaningful trends, spot anomalies, and even predict outcomes. Alice had gladly jumped at the chance to lose herself once again in the comfortable world of numbers.

Was that why Dylan asked me to look at the reports? Because he realized it would calm any disorientation I might be having, coming to the castle?

The thought only increased her unease.

Stalwalter smiled knowingly at her fumbling. "Modest in addition to being brilliant, I see. Don't tell me that Mr. Fall didn't tell you how much he appreciated the analysis you did on the VitaThirst campaign," he said, grinning and taking a swig of his drink. "I have my eye on you, Alice Reed. I expect very good things."

Alice glanced aside and noticed Thad's stunned expression as he stared at her.

"They weren't *recommendations*, really. I just looked at the reports and mentioned my thoughts on them," Alice assured. Her head was swimming. Why hadn't Dylan told her he'd made such sweeping decisions based on ideas she'd murmured to him in bed one night after making love?

"I didn't mean to embarrass you," Stalwalter said, leaning toward her and speaking more kindly. "Just know that Dylan Fall is quite taken with your unique skills, and it's not easy to impress him. *That's* nothing to be embarrassed about. You should be proud."

Alice took a nervous sip of her ice water, willing her scalding cheeks to cool. Stalwalter's words had mortified her. Was he insinuating he knew Dylan and her were lovers? Are *those* the skills to which he referred?

No, surely not, the voice of rationality said, dimming her panic. Dylan would never expose her in such a way.

She glanced at Thad, who wore a part-puzzled, part-concerned expression. *Stalwalter* might not have drawn the conclusion that Dylan was insinuating she was his personal plaything.

But she had a sinking sensation that *Thad* had.

"ALICE, can I talk to you? Privately?" Thad added pointedly in a tense whisper.

The dinner was over. Dessert and coffee were being cleared following a short speech by Mary Spear, the Durand vice president of international operations. Alice nodded reluctantly. Even though she was dreading what Thad was going to say, it was best just to get it over with. She needed to assure Thad that whatever he was suspecting about Dylan being untrustworthy wasn't true.

Sure . . . Alice had been having her doubts about their relationship, but that was about *her* issues with intimacy, wasn't it? *Other* people shouldn't mistrust Dylan.

Thad sprung up and immediately pulled her chair back when she started to stand. He took her hand and swept her in front of him. Against Alice's intentions, their shared actions appeared graceful, a natural action between a familiar couple. She glanced furtively at the head table. Dylan was listening to the man on the left of him, but his gazed tracked her.

Great.

She sighed in mounting frustration and led Thad out of the dining room. Lots of people had gotten up at this point. They were stretching their legs with a stroll on the terrace or in the gardens, milling around in groups talking, and using the restrooms. Not wanting to be overheard, Alice led Thad to the hushed, empty grand foyer. Alice caught a brief glimpse of herself in a gilt mirror as she turned to face Thad. The magnificent crystal chandelier blazed with light tonight, revealing some of the emerging red highlights in her hair.

"What is it?" she asked him, unable to stop herself from sounding short. Her arms folded above her waist in a defensive gesture.

"We never got to finish our conversation yesterday in the woods."

"I think we did. I heard you saying that you don't think Dylan is trustworthy. That's your opinion."

"Don't you want to know why I think that?"

"You misunderstood about Stalwalter in there, Thad," she said, pointing to the dining room.

"You looked as surprised as I did when Stalwalter started going on about stuff Fall had told him about you!"

"I was surprised, but how does Fall using my input for the VitaThirst campaign make him untrustworthy? He obviously gave me credit for it." *Although it might have been nice if he'd told me he was bragging about me to Durand bigwigs.*

"There's more about Fall, Alice. My father is a lot more familiar with the workings of Durand Enterprises than he'd let on before I came here," Thad began, glancing around the large open entryway, his manner edgy. He referred to Judge Schaefer. From what Alice had gathered so far, Thad's dad was a very influential and well-connected man. According to Thad, it was Judge Schaefer who had determined Thad would be a high-powered businessman, and not the teacher and coach that Thad himself aspired to be. In Alice's opinion, Judge Schaefer sounded like an uptight tool.

"There's more to Fall's assuming leadership of Durand and the surrounding consequences than I realized when we talked before," Thad said in a muted tone. "Sebastian Kehoe had a *right* to be sharp with us for assuming that Fall was made the head of Durand Enterprises because he was related to Alan or Lynn Durand. There were those on the Durand board at the time that felt that Fall had undue influence on Alan Durand, especially at the end of Durand's life when he was so sick."

"*Who* thought that? Kehoe, no doubt," Alice said, rolling her eyes. "It's pretty clear Kehoe is jealous of Dylan."

"Not just Kehoe," Thad whispered heatedly. "I saw you talking to Dr. Gates before dinner. Sidney Gates, the psychiatrist?"

"Yeah," Alice said, shifting uneasily in her heels.

"Sidney Gates voiced his doubts about Fall's fitness as CEO at the time, as well."

Alice's folded arms collapsed, falling at her sides. She couldn't believe that. Weren't Sidney and Dylan close? She shook her head.

"No. That can't be right. Besides, even if Kehoe or Gates had doubts about Dylan's worthiness to be the CEO after Alan Durand died, they've been proven wrong. In spades. You know as well as I do that Durand Enterprises is more diverse and financially robust under Dylan's regime than it was under Durand's management, which was brilliant in and of itself."

"Maybe so, but there's more, Alice," Thad said, holding her stare. "There are those at Durand who feel that Dylan's interest in you isn't . . ."

Alice waited tensely, holding her breath when Thad trailed off. Her heart had sunk to the vicinity of her navel at the words *those at Durand*. Had Dylan's and her secret been discovered and was now generally known? Or did Thad just mean that Dylan's exclusive hiring of her, his high praise of her to people like Stalwalter, and his brief but notable attention toward her at the previous house party at Castle Durand had set some Durand higher-ups on edge? It was obvious Thad was struggling to be tactful, but Alice wasn't all that sympathetic.

"Spit it out, Thad."

"They feel his interest in you isn't entirely honest. There's something behind it," he finished, his gaze running over her face.

"*Who* thinks that?" Alice demanded, her voice trembling with emotion. She took an aggressive step toward him. "Who is thinking about Dylan and me at all? You never did tell me how *you* even found out we were involved. No one is supposed to know about us!"

Thad grimaced. "It's a reliable source, Alice. This person is concerned about Fall taking advantage of you."

"Because I'm so far out of his league?" she asked, her voice shaking uncontrollably.

She was on high boil all of a sudden, and she hadn't even realized she was growing hot. Everything in front of her eyes seemed to be cast in a red haze. "Because no one can figure out why he'd be interested in a girl from the wrong side of the tracks, a girl who comes from the wrong family, and the wrong school. The wrong fucking *life*," she grated out between bared teeth. "Well, maybe Dylan knows more about my life than you think, Thad."

He looked shocked by her sudden flare of temper. She wasn't surprised. Alice herself was a little shocked.

"Jesus, Alice, I'm sorry. I wasn't trying to imply that you aren't in Fall's league. You know how I feel about you. If anything, I think the opposite." He reached out and grasped her elbow, his expression fierce. "Fall doesn't deserve you."

She whipped her arm out, throwing Thad's hold off her. "I don't deserve *this*," she hissed, only vaguely aware of what she meant. "I never thought I'd say this in a million years, but sometimes I wish my life could just go back to what it was before I ever set foot in this damn place."

"Alice, what the hell—"

"Just leave me alone, Thad."

She turned and made a beeline for the grand staircase.

WHEN Dylan stepped into the entry hall, the only person he saw standing there was Thad Schaefer, his back turned to him.

"Where's Alice?"

Schaefer spun at his sharp question. The hair on the back of Dylan's neck stood on end when he took in Schaefer's stunned expression.

"What did you say to her?" he ground out, stepping toward him rapidly. Schaefer blanched beneath his tan.

"Nothing! I mean . . . I don't know *what* I said," Schaefer said, clearly at a loss. "She just got upset all of a sudden and told me off."

"All of a sudden?" He suppressed a nearly overwhelming urge to wring the kid's neck until his pretty-boy face turned beet red. "Where'd she go?" he demanded instead.

Thad pointed at the grand staircase. "She looked desperate. Like she was—"

"What?"

"Running from me, or from *something*. I don't know what I said that upset her so much."

"You made this mess, you can help clean it up. This is a big house. Come on," Dylan ordered, his rapid stride fueled by rising alarm. Distantly, Dylan realized he'd been waiting for some kind of explosion on Alice's part. He was afraid it had just occurred outside of his watch. From the edge of his attention, he noticed that Thad Schaefer was even further surprised by Dylan's terse command to join him. But he came after a pause, jogging up the steps behind him.

"You continue up to the third floor and look for her," Dylan said when they reached the second level. He started to stride down the hallway but paused. "Check every room. Come and find me the second—and I mean the *second*—you locate her. If you finish looking before I do and come up short, then go up to the fourth floor and start searching for her there. And keep your voice *down*," he bit out quietly over his shoulder. Surely the kid wasn't so insensitive or stupid that he'd send up an alarm with all these people in the house. "Let's keep this simple, don't talk *at all* unless you've found Alice and are calling out to me. Got it?"

Schaefer's mouth slanted irritably, but he nodded.

Dylan's own bedroom suite was empty. Skipping all the bedrooms in between, Dylan headed straight for the suite where he'd found Alice the other night: Addie Durand's former one.

It, too, stood hushed and devoid of life.

"Alice," he called out when he was in the hallway again, torn between wanting to bellow her name so that he could be heard in every corner of the mansion and muting his shout to prevent being overheard by someone at the cocktail party downstairs.

"Alice?" he called out a moment later, switching on a light. He stood at the entrance of Alan Durand's suite. It had once been Alan and Lynn's, before Lynn had passed. Dylan hadn't been in the room since Alan had finally succumbed to cancer seven years ago. Most of the furniture was covered in dustcloths. It struck Dylan as empty as a tomb, and yet filled with memories: dead and alive at once.

He entered the room farther and stood stock still in the middle of it, listening. After a moment, he turned and shut off the light, closing the door behind him.

Part of Dylan still existed in that room, the memories of Alan Durand kept alive forever inside of him. Alice, however, wasn't there. He'd bet his life on it. But being in that room reminded him of something Alan had told him in passing a few times.

He approached the back staircase, suddenly highly aware of

the sound of his hard leather soles on the wood floor of the hall. He came to a halt at the side of the stair rising up to the third floor. He held his breath, listening. Unlike in Alan's room, he experienced a full, hushed sense of anxious anticipation.

He knelt by the wooden paneling beneath the stair. Recalling both Alan Durand's references and something Deanna Shrevecraft had once shown him when she'd visited Castle Durand, he used his hands to pry back a portion of the wood paneling. The three-by-two-foot panel slid aside.

Peering into the black void, he heard slight rustling and then a barely audible sound like a gasp or a whimper.

"Alice?"

Silence.

He awkwardly tried to maneuver his large body partially into the opening, squinting his eyes. A whisper came from the darkness.

"Dylan."

A shiver snaked under his skin. She'd sounded odd. Distant. Spooked.

"I'm right here, baby," he said evenly, even though alarm had started to bubble in his veins. He backed out of the cramped opening in order to go back in a more navigable angle. "I'm coming in, Alice. Everything's okay."

"I know."

He blinked.

"I remember Addie."

His skin pulled tight at her whispering voice, the hairs on his arm and nape springing to attention.

"I mean . . . not everything," she continued breathlessly.

Dylan barely contained a blistering curse because he couldn't see even her shadow. She was a disembodied whisper in the darkness.

"I ran up here, and I wasn't really thinking . . . just feeling cornered by everything, you know?" She continued in a tiny, shaking voice. "And I had this thought that I wished I could hide and stay there forever, but I needed a good spot. Then it just came to me in a rush, how she and I would play hide-and-seek. She knew all my spots, because she was the one who had shown me the good ones . . . all the secret, hidden places like this one. They were *her* hiding places, too. I'd hide and she'd look for me like she didn't know where I was, but I knew she did. She'd call out to let me know where she was as she looked around in the area, to let me know when she was getting close. *Aadddie, where are you?*"

She made a sound like a choked laugh or a sob.

Dylan jerked at the eerie sound, banging the back of his head on the paneling.

"Dylan? Are you okay?"

He pried his eyes open from a wince of pain, because her voice sounded closer. Suddenly, her pale face emerged from the shadows. She was crawling toward him on her hands and knees. He reached for her single-mindedly and propelled himself back, as if he thought he could manually pull her out of her disturbing memory like he could haul her out of that secret compartment. They landed with a thud just outside of the opening, his body taking the impact of their fall.

"Dylan?"

He was on his ass, and she was sprawled on top of him. He was tensed somewhere between lying down on the floor and sitting up.

"Yeah," he muttered, pulling her tighter against him. She put her hands on his shoulders. He rose to a sitting position. Alice was in his lap, her legs bent and sprawled on either side of his hips, her black cocktail dress ruched up to her thighs, her pearls flung behind her shoulder. Her fingertips touched his jaw.

"It *wasn't* that bad. You don't have to look like that," she said feelingly, and he realized belatedly she'd witnessed his naked alarm.

"I mean . . . I thought it was going to be bad, too, to remember something about Addie, and to *know* I was remembering while I did it. Addie Durand is a completely different person. I thought it'd be like being possessed by someone else or something. But it wasn't. It was—"

"*Stop*, Alice."

"What?" she asked, appearing incredulous and hurt by his abrupt interruption of something that was obviously new and amazing to her.

"If you so much as mention a word of this to your pillow, let alone another human being, I'll make you pay," Dylan promised.

Alice turned, her mouth hanging open in shock. She'd realized he wasn't addressing her.

"Thad," she gasped. She tugged on her hemline, trying to cover her exposed legs.

Schaefer stood there at the end of the hallway, looking bewildered. Who knew how long he'd been there, listening to them? *Shit.*

"Alice, are you okay?" Schaefer asked.

"I'm fine."

"What did you hear?" Dylan demanded.

"Nothing."

"*What* did you hear?"

"I told you. Nothing! I just walked up."

"You've given me no other choice. If you speak of anything you've seen here tonight or reveal to anyone what you know about Alice and me, I'll be forced to send you home immediately from Camp Durand. Your father wouldn't like that much, would he?"

"*Dylan*," Alice gasped, staring at him like she'd never seen him before, her eyes enormous. "What—"

"Do you understand me, Schaefer?"

"I understand *perfectly*." He took several steps back, his gaze darting to Alice's face and then back to Dylan's. "And my father might not like it if you sent me home, but he wouldn't be surprised that you acted like a ruthless son of a bitch. I know *I* wouldn't be."

"I'm glad to hear you're not entirely an idiot."

Dylan willed him with his stare to turn and walk away. Schaefer complied, if reluctantly. Dylan watched him as he grew smaller down the hallway, turned, and disappeared.

He became uncomfortably aware of Alice's disbelieving gaze on his face.

ONCE she'd scooted off him, Dylan sprung up from the floor. She refused to take his hand when he offered it. Instead, she pushed herself onto her hands and knees and stood gracelessly. Once she'd gained her balance in her pumps, she stepped into him aggressively.

"Are you out of your mind?"

"No. And I'm not going to apologize, either," he said in a clipped tone, and she sensed the residue of his cold, furious blast of anger at Thad. He smoothed his hand over his silk tie, straightening it, and then he hitched his jaw slightly, like someone readjusting his face after a fight. Despite her stunned anger, she recognized his edge—the thrilling paradox of the sophisticated executive and the street tough she'd been undeniably attracted to from the very beginning. A thrill went through her, amplifying her confusion and anger.

"You shouldn't have threatened him like that."

"He could very well have overheard what we were talking about. Would you *like* him shooting his mouth off to the others?"

"He wouldn't have said a word if I asked him not to! Besides, he probably didn't hear, and certainly couldn't have understood if he did. How could *he* understand it, when *I'm* so confused?"

He shook his head once, his thoughts clearly elsewhere. "That kid is trouble."

"Thad is one of the best counselors at Camp Durand! He's smart and funny and a natural leader," she spat. "Everyone loves him."

He stilled and met her stare slowly. A shiver rippled through her. "Everyone?"

Despite the sudden glacial quality of his dark eyes, she couldn't look away. She grasped wildly for her resolve.

"Everyone," she managed in a choked voice before she broke his hold and followed Thad down the hallway.

NINE

Dylan stood at the opened French doors in his den looking out onto the gardens and yard. The unseasonably cool weather continued. A fog had begun to rise over the distant limestone bluff. It was just past midnight. All was hushed and quiet on the Durand Estate. He could just make out the muted sound of waves hitting the rocky beach below the drop-off at the end of his yard.

"I'll have to bring in a couple other men from the security division, if you want Ms. Reed watched at night."

"Only one for now," Dylan replied. He turned and faced Sal Rigo, who stood in front of his desk. Like Dylan, he still wore his suit from the Alumni Dinner. "Bring in Janocek. I've already reviewed his file and he was on my original list before I narrowed it down to you and Peterson. I know I don't need to emphasize again the importance of absolute discretion in regard to this."

"Of course. I'll see to it myself when I brief Janocek that he's completely on board. No one will lay an eye on him."

"Make sure of it," Dylan said, giving the other man a pointed glance. Rigo looked a little abashed. Dylan hadn't disguised his annoyance with Rigo and Peterson recently because they'd allowed Alice to see them during their surveillance of her. On one occasion in the woods, Peterson's ineptitude had caused Alice considerable distress when she'd thought someone was following her with malicious intent.

"I will, sir. I know we disappointed before, but it's fairly tight quarters there at the camp. Plus, as you know, watching over Ms. Reed isn't our only responsibility. Kehoe keeps us pretty busy."

"I realize that," Dylan acknowledged. He'd originally directed Rigo and Peterson to observe Alice more than anything, not *guard* her. He needed to know if she was having any unusual or adverse reactions to the Durand Estate, any memories from her childhood. But he'd also wanted to be assured of her general safety. The problem was, despite his doubts about the direction of a threat, Dylan increasingly wanted Alice not just watched, but protected.

"Plus, Ms. Reed is very observant and . . . mobile," Rigo added with a small smile.

"Are you calling her fast?" Dylan asked dryly.

Rigo shrugged. "She's a good athlete. And she notices things. She's more aware of her surroundings than most."

"She had to be, where she grew up," Dylan muttered. "I assume you and Peterson can trade off tonight until you bring Janocek in?"

"Yes, sir. I'll take over for Peterson in a few hours, so he can get some rest."

"And you? When will you get your rest?"

"After tomorrow is over. There were plenty of times in the Army I went two nights without sleep."

Dylan nodded slowly, well aware of Rigo's stellar Army special operations record before being hired in Durand's security division. "Anything else significant happening at the camp?"

"Thad Schaefer is still meeting up with the Seifert girl at night, but he's all eyes for Ms. Reed every day at the camp."

"And Ms. Seifert doesn't appreciate that much, does she?"

"No, sir."

"Is she a threat to Alice?" Dylan asked bluntly.

"I don't believe so, but I learned early on in my training that one of the most unpredictable things in nature is a jealous woman. Schaefer is more of an issue. He's following Alice at times."

"With what intent?"

"The obvious one, I think," Rigo said with a bland glance. "I've never seen him behave in any aggressive manner toward her."

"He's a problem. More so because Alice refuses to see it," Dylan mused. "She leaves herself wide open to him, and that kid is being poisoned by someone."

"Yes, sir."

Dylan scowled. They both knew to whom he referred. He hadn't briefed Rigo or Peterson on the Alice Reed–Addie Durand connection. He'd only emphasized that Alice was important. Rigo and Peterson were also aware that Kehoe and his interactions with Alice were a prime object of interest for Dylan. He knew that the two men were probably frustrated by a lack of more solid information for their mission. The fact of the matter was, however, Dylan didn't have a specific reason for suspicion when it came to Kehoe. True, Kehoe was generally known to be bitter and disapproving of Dylan's position as CEO. But he wasn't the only one who was a Fall dissenter at Durand. Universal popularity was rare for a person in a position like his. But Kehoe was also a top-level performer and leader for Durand Enterprises. Just because Kehoe wasn't a cheerleader for Dylan was hardly damning evidence against him.

He hesitated to tell Rigo or Peterson that he'd given the two security operatives a mission mostly based on intuition and a hazy but powerful feeling of unease.

"Have you seen Schaefer with Kehoe much?" Dylan asked.

"I see him talking to Schaefer at times, but maybe only a little bit more than the other counselors."

"Is Kehoe still giving Alice a hard time?"

"It's more of a silent disapproval than anything too overt. He's not as open and friendly with her as he is with the other counselors. He knows you've taken an interest in her."

"Nobody ever accused Kehoe of not being intelligent. And after yesterday in the woods, he *definitely* suspects that you've been given the job of keeping an eye on Alice."

"Yes."

"It was inevitable. If he gives you a hard time again, please let me know.

"I can manage Kehoe."

"Good. I realize it's not an easy position I've put you and Josh in, having to report both to Kehoe and myself. Anything else about Kehoe?"

Rigo hesitated. "I catch him looking at Ms. Reed at times."

Dylan narrowed his gaze. "Like Schaefer *looks* at her?"

"No. More like . . . he's trying to figure something out about her or see some characteristic that's invisible. He *studies* her."

Dylan nodded slowly. "Yeah. I think I've caught him at it a time or two."

"Sir, I'd like to suggest again that we consider phone surveillance."

Dylan closed his eyes briefly at Rigo's familiar urging. "I'm the CEO of Durand Enterprises, not the head of the FBI, Sal."

"You're the CEO of an extensive, privately held company. You have a right to know what's happening in your domain."

"You call it 'right to know,' but *I* call what you're talking about corporate espionage. I have no grounds for ordering something like that at this point. The other problem with your argument is that I'm not worried about Durand Enterprises. I'm worried about Alice. And unfortunately, no one, including the sheriff of Morgantown, believes I have any solid grounds for being concerned about Sebastian Kehoe at this point. By all accounts, he's an upstanding, respected citizen." He noticed Sal's upraised brows. "We'll proceed with my plans for the present," he said levelly. "Did you have any other observations?"

"Just one other thing. I noticed Sidney Gates talking very intently to her tonight at the cocktail party, but I couldn't get close enough to hear what they were saying. I do think Ms. Reed became . . . *upset* in a subdued kind of way at one point."

"I noticed that, too," Dylan said thoughtfully. He'd also wondered what his good friend had been saying to Alice when he noticed her stiff expression and tense posture. He exhaled. "Well, I think that's it for now. Thank you for the briefing. I'll see you out," he said, starting to walk around his desk. He noticed Rigo's hesitation and paused. Is there something else?" Dylan asked.

"I was just thinking it might be best to bring in *two* other people from Durand security for Ms. Reed's night watch so they could have days off. I could recommend another good man."

"That won't be necessary. The fewer people involved in this the better. I don't expect this situation of Alice sleeping beyond the security of Castle Durand to last for long," Dylan said grimly.

"Of course, sir. And I can see myself out. Good night."

"Good night."

Dylan doubted very seriously it would be a *good* night. Certainly it'd be a sleepless one.

Several images flashed into his mind's eye like a video clip: Alice's pale, shocked face when he'd threatened to send Schaefer home, her determined refusal to meet his eyes as she left the house tonight. As she'd walked out, she'd been surrounded by Schaefer and her friends in what irritably struck Dylan as a protective cadre.

He recalled her disembodied whisper emanating from the darkness.

I remember Addie.

He was desperate to know what she'd experienced, but she'd denied him. One look at the stubborn tilt of her chin and the suppressed fury on her face had said it all. Alice wouldn't be returning to the castle for any clandestine meetings with him for the time being. She was angry, yes, but he knew her well enough to recognize her confusion, as well. She was having trouble telling up from down in this new world in which she found herself.

For now, he had no choice but to accept defeat. But it would definitely be a temporary one.

* * *

THE night after the Alumni Dinner, Kuvi walked out of the bath-room and caught Alice peering between two closed blinds.

"Do you think he's out there?" Kuvi asked in a conspiratorial whisper.

Alice started and the blinds snapped shut. "Jesus, you scared me."

"You've been awfully jumpy. You didn't sleep last night, did you?" Kuvi asked as she crossed over to her dresser.

"I don't know how you can possibly know that since you were sleeping like a baby," Alice said, rolling her eyes.

"This morning, your bed looked like you'd been holding a wrestling match in it," Kuvi said loftily, shutting a drawer with a snap. "As if your grouchy mood today wasn't enough to tell me that I wasn't the one you wanted to be spending the night with. And you never answered my question. Do you think Dylan is out there in the woods?"

"No," Alice replied quietly. "Not Dylan."

Kuvi did a double take at her solemn answer. Somehow, Alice would know if Dylan was nearby. Maybe she knew that because part of her wished like hell Dylan *was* nearby. She hated to admit it, but she was disappointed that he hadn't come to claim her last night in the cabin like he had several nights ago, when he'd made her face up to her promise.

She missed him. Bad. And Alice knew what that made her. A spineless hypocrite. She was still confused and angry about what he'd said to Thad. She wanted to apologize to Thad for her flash of temper at him, as well as console him about Dylan's threat. Thad wasn't giving her much of an opportunity, however. Since this morning, he'd been avoiding Alice. Thanks to Dylan, he'd probably decided his friendship with her was a black mark on his record.

There was something else bothering her. She longed to return to the castle for another reason. She kept reliving the memory of playing hide-and-seek with Lynn Durand. That memory continued to amaze her. Nourish her.

As she stood there in her cabin with Kuvi, she thought of the woman in the memory as Lynn Durand. But when she'd been experiencing it, Alice thought of her as *mommy*. The warm, sweet sense of absolute security that unfurled inside her at that memory continued to be a source of wonder. Alice had never known she'd been capable of such a feeling.

The fact of the matter was, she craved more of it. Another part of her dreaded recalling, though, fearful of *needing* those memories, afraid of the moment they evaporated like mist and she realized she was alone.

"Do you think it could be Sal Rigo out there?" Kuvi asked presently, walking toward Alice. Kuvi had been with her the time Alice caught Rigo secretly observing a group of them while they were at the Lakeside Tavern. Later, Alice had learned that Dylan had sent Rigo to watch over her—Alice—not the whole group of counselors. But if she explained that to Kuvi, she had to elaborate on a lot of other things, like why Dylan was so paranoid about her safety.

"It might be," Alice said, flipping back her covers. "There's someone out there, though. I can feel it."

"Maybe it's just your nerves," Kuvi consoled, getting into her own bed. "Like I said, you've been crazy jumpy since last night."

Alice heard the unasked question in her friend's tone. She knew Kuvi was curious about what had happened after the Alumni Dinner. It was clear to both Kuvi and Dave that something had gone wrong last night. Alice and Thad had been unusually tense and uncommunicative as all of them walked back to camp. If Kuvi couldn't guess from that, Alice's presence in their cabin last night told her loud and clear that *something* was wrong between Alice and Dylan.

"It's not just my nerves," Alice said shortly, reaching for her bedside lamp switch. "And it's not just a feeling. I saw a shadow out there last night and the glow of a cigarette. Whoever it is sits out there just past the tree line, smoking and watching. He's out there again tonight. I saw his cigarette. I'm going to figure out who it is in the morning."

Kuvi shut out her bedside light. *"How?"*

"I'll find a way," Alice replied doggedly.

"Let's suppose what you say is true, wouldn't confronting the person be dangerous?"

"They're not dangerous," Alice said scornfully under her breath. *They're just following orders.*

"Alice, do you think Dylan Fall sent someone to spy on you?" Kuvi asked, as though she'd read Alice's mind.

Alice hesitated. "Yes. Probably," she finally replied.

Kuvi was silent for a moment. Alice sensed her puzzlement and amazement. *"Why* in the world would he do that? Is he some kind of stalker?"

"He's not a stalker," she defended bluntly. "It's a long story."

"I figured. I have a long attention span, you know."

Alice held her breath. When it became clear that Alice wasn't going to reveal anything else, Kuvi sighed resignedly. Guilt swept through Alice. She really had been grumpy with Kuvi lately, and Kuvi didn't deserve it. Not by a long shot. Alice heard her turn over in bed.

"Night."

"Night," Alice mumbled. "Kuvi?"

"Yeah?"

"I'm sorry I've been such a bitch lately."

"I can take your moodiness. I just wish I knew what was really bothering you."

"Yeah," Alice whispered.

Kuvi sighed again. Alice listened as her friend's breathing grew regular and soft. She lay there, wide awake, envying Kuvi's peaceful sleep.

The next morning wasn't a day that she'd scheduled to run with Terrance, but she got up anyway and put on a jogging bra, socks, and shoes. She quietly exited the cabin and locked the door behind her. A minute later, she was jogging along the white sand beach. The sun was rising, but the woods to the left of her were still blocking much of its light. The beach was still draped in a murky gloom. She looked around, but saw no one on the beach behind her. Determined, she ran full out, racing toward the entrance to the woods that led to the stables.

Her breath was coming fast and ragged by the time she reached the path. She wasn't crazy about the idea of taking the dim trail. She'd been trying to avoid the path as much as she could, highly aware of its significance.

Dylan had informed her that it was on that very trail that Addie Durand had been kidnapped and Dylan himself had been stabbed as he tried to defend her. At the time, he'd been a fourteen-year-old boy, and Addie a child of four. When she'd first arrived at the camp, Alice had thought she'd been chased by a ghost on that trail. The ghost had turned out to be a man Dylan had hired to follow her. The flesh-and-blood, secretive man and Alice's unconscious, hazy, yet atavistic fear of what had happened in those woods twenty years ago had blended to create Alice's phantom.

She didn't feel afraid today. She was too out of breath and focused on tricking her prey.

Several hundred feet down the trail, she decided it was time to make things a little difficult for Mr. Cigarette Man. Spotting a particularly thick growth of underbrush and trees, she ducked off the path, careful to mute her footsteps. Once she was sixty or so feet off the trail, she used a thick oak for cover, pressing her back to it and willing her escalated breathing to slow. She listened for a tread on the path.

Any second now . . .

Was that a rapid footfall in the distance? She twisted her neck, craning her head around the tree to capture the elusive sound. Yes. Her follower was coming. Alice tensed in preparation to follow him and then confront him. She had a few choice words in mind. She hoped like hell Mr. Cigarette Man conveyed them verbatim to his boss.

Suddenly a glove-covered hand was covering her smirk. She spun around, her eyes springing wide.

Dylan eclipsed her vision. He pressed his big body tighter against her, pinning her between him and the tree. Alice realized she'd been struggling in panic and went still.

"Shhh," he hissed.

They both listened as the footsteps grew louder on the path in the distance. Alice stared up at Dylan's tense face. He hadn't shaved yet. His thick hair was mussed. It had fallen forward, parenthesizing his dark, narrowed eyes. He looked scruffy and rugged and delicious.

Shit.

He looked like he did every morning when he left his bed and escorted her safely to her cabin. She'd forgotten that he went horseback riding every morning after that. The gloves pressed against her lips were his riding gloves. But she hadn't heard a horse. How did he know to find her here?

He wasn't watching her, but instead staring into the distance. She knew he was tracking the approaching footsteps. It was hard to focus on the man on the path, however, with Dylan's long hard body pressed against hers. He wasn't allowing her to move or look down, but she could tell he was wearing jeans, like he did most mornings. The fly of them was pressing against her lower abdomen.

His body felt dense and unforgiving against her flesh. His masculinity was flagrant . . . pervasive; about as impossible to ignore as a blow to the head. She caught his scent.

Against her will, arousal blazed in her body. Two nights away from him. Too long.

His stare suddenly zipped to her face, as if he'd sensed the flash fire inside her, like the spark of lust had jumped into him. He pressed his crotch closer. She felt his cock harden against her. The man was on the path directly in front of them now. Alice hardly cared. She twisted her head angrily. Dylan lowered his head until his face hovered an inch over hers, and removed his hand from her mouth.

Instead, he used his mouth to silence her. It was a good thing, too, because Alice whimpered in stark longing at the hard pressure of his kiss. He grabbed her shoulders and bunched her to him, his actions a little angry and a lot possessive. He plunged his tongue between her lips, a thirsty man slaking himself. In that moment, Alice knew for certain that he was every bit as desperate as her.

She tried to pull her hands up so that she could touch him, but he pressed even closer, preventing it. Her hands remained pinned against the tree. His cock felt fuller now, the sensation of it commanding every fiber of her attention that wasn't already ruled by his demanding kiss. Time passed. The man on the path was forgotten. She drowned in his taste. Her head swam. *God*, she needed air.

She needed him more.

She twisted her head, moaning softly. He moved his hands to her jaw and kept her face steady while he fucked her mouth with his tongue. He plucked at her lips forcefully with his own and bit the lower one, scraping the sensitive skin between his teeth. Alice quaked against him.

"Always rebelling, even when you don't know what against. I ought to spank your ass red, do you know that?" he breathed out in a husky whisper next to her parted lips. Arousal shot through her at his dark threat. His eyes glittered with angry lust between narrowed eyelids. She squirmed against him and tried to break her chin free of his hold on her face. He grasped her more firmly, the feeling of the soft, well-worn leather against her skin only amplifying her excitement. "I *ought* to spank you good and hard and then fuck you even harder." He plucked at her mouth hungrily and she felt his cock swell against her belly. "I ought to fuck you so deep and come so hard, you feel me inside you as a constant reminder as you go about your day of rebelling. Would you like that, Alice?"

"No."

"Yes, you would," he growled, recognizing her lie instantly. Holding her stare, he reached between them and began to jerk down her running shorts. Her heart leapt.

"If you spank me, whoever you had follow me will hear it," she said in a panicked, choked whisper.

"Then I'll have to save the spanking for later. The other part isn't going to wait, though. If that incompetent jerk is stupid enough to come back here while I'm having you, he can just be fired sooner versus later."

"But—"

He shoved unceremoniously at her clothing and she felt her shorts and panties fall against her shins to her ankles. He grabbed her hand and pressed it against his erection. She bit her lower lip, air hissing between her teeth. Her hand moved of its own accord, cupping and massaging large, round testicles, and then the heavy, protruding staff of his cock. He snarled at her touch. "You've asked for it before against a tree in the woods. Ask for it now, little girl," he taunted. "Ask for the nice hard fuck you deserve."

His crudity was arousing her. He knew it had on other occasions in the past. Her cheeks burned and her breathing was coming fast and erratic. The ability to think rationally was fogged by lust.

"Say it," he bit out softly, nuzzling her lips with his nose and then his mouth.

"I deserve a nice. Hard. Fuck."

If there was such a thing as defiant begging, Alice had just done it.

He grunted softly, his mouth slanting into a hard line. He turned her in front of him forcefully. When she staggered because her clothing had gotten twisted on her ankles, he steadied her, his hands cupping her shoulders. He pressed his face to her neck, his hot, openmouthed kiss making her gasp and put her hands on the tree trunk to steady her swaying world. She sensed him working to unfasten his fly.

A moment later, his naked cock slid between her thighs, the top of the rigid shaft rubbing against her sensitive, damp outer sex. He gave a restrained, rough groan that vibrated in his throat. Biting her lower lip to suppress her own arousal, she leaned into the tree, bending at the waist. The feeling of the bulbous head of his cock pushing into her channel felt exciting and forbidden.

So damn good.

He held her hips steady with his hands and firmly pumped his cock into her. The fact that she couldn't scream her pleasure made her want to yowl like a cat in heat. Her choked wail burned her throat. His cock felt huge and heavy inside her. When he finally pressed his full testicles to her outer sex and paused, squeezing her to him, she opened her mouth in a silent scream.

"Quiet," he muttered tensely behind her, and Alice wondered confusedly if she'd whimpered aloud after all. In the distance, she heard the footsteps on the path. Her follower had realized he'd lost her and was retracing his steps, his pace faster than it had been previously.

They went still in a tableau of frozen, incendiary pleasure. It was unbearable. Dylan throbbed inside her, his cock steaming into her flesh. God, she needed to *move*. She couldn't stop her muscles from convulsing around him, from squeezing his rigid length.

Behind her, she heard him make a small, choked sound. Somehow it helped, knowing she didn't suffer alone.

But not much.

Her follower's footsteps faded while they mutually sweated. Just when she thought she couldn't take it anymore, he began to thrust in and out of her, his strokes deep and even a little harsh. Alice loved it. Her body jolted at the impact of him against her. His unrelenting cock plunging into her and the sharp friction he created became her sole focus. *Dylan. Dylan. Dylan.* She chanted his name in her head like a mantra every time his pelvis thumped against her. She closed her eyes, bit her lip, and counterstroked with a firm, fluid pump of her hips. It felt hot and forbidden. So *right*.

She was so deep in the zone, it jarred her to the core when Dylan suddenly stilled her bobbing hips, his thumbs digging into her buttocks. She heard distant footsteps approaching. The man was back, retracing his trail.

"Damn," she heard Dylan say behind her, the single muted word practically bursting with sharp frustration.

"You put him up to it," she hissed over her shoulder, her whisper barely audible.

He squeezed both her buttocks in a taut reprimand. Alice tried to get air, but it was like her body had grown confused under the influence of rampant, stifled arousal. Her lungs didn't seem to want to expand, even though she needed oxygen desperately. Dylan's hands moved slightly on her ass, peeling back her ass cheeks, making some kind of lascivious display of her. There was nothing she could do about it, either.

Except scowl over her shoulder.

He was indeed staring down at her ass. As if sensing her gaze on him, he glanced up and met her stare. The gleam in his smoky eyes, his small knowing smile and the lurch of his cock deep inside her made her scowl evaporate. In the distance, her follower's footsteps retraced the path. The Cigarette Man was growing increasingly alarmed. Soon, he was going to leave the path and comb the woods, looking for her.

Dylan must have thought the same thing, because he started to move. Obviously, he was in agreement with her that the only course of action was forward.

No going back now.

She winced at the friction, holding his stare, her chin on her shoulder. She couldn't look away from his rigid face. It was wrong. The man was only sixty or so feet away. He might notice some tramped-down grass and identify where she'd left the path. He could step off the trail and be upon them in a moment. It would be humiliating to be discovered.

But the moment was too volatile. What was happening between Dylan and her wasn't going to end anywhere but in explosion.

For a moment, she lost count of where the man was. Dylan wasn't thumping his pelvis against her bottom anymore. Instead, he was stopping just short of making contact, his hips moving fast, fluid, and furious. It was enough. It was more than enough. Blood was pulsing in her ears and pooling in her sex. She'd never known a man could fuck so silently, yet so forcefully. She bit her lip, stifling a moan with effort. It wasn't something she could control.

She was going to come.

Maybe Dylan sensed her agony, because suddenly he transferred one hand to her shoulder. His other hand slid over her mouth. The feeling of his glove against her lips sent her over the edge. He silenced her cry with his pressing hand. She shuddered in climax, biting down on the soft leather with her front teeth. Pleasure gushed through her, hot and forceful. He fucked her while she came, using his hold on her shoulder to power his thrusts.

She blinked open her eyes a moment later as her orgasm waned. She'd heard the snap of a twig, and then silence. Dylan thrust into her, and then went still as well. Alice held her panting breath. She tried desperately to hear past her roaring heartbeat. Slowly, and very deliberately, Dylan stepped closer, sliding his cock into her to the hilt. He pressed. Alice's eyes sprang wide at the pressure.

Her lungs burned with a need to breathe, but she was stifling her pants.

Then she heard it. The man's footsteps on the path. He was jogging in the direction of the stables. Now he was running.

A deep, ominous growl vibrated in Dylan's throat. His hand slid off her mouth. He clutched at her hip and thrust hard. She whimpered at the sensation of his cock swelling inside her. He shuddered behind her, and she knew he was coming. His warmth filled her. She tried to move, to stroke his cock a little as he climaxed, but he gave a small grunt and fixed her in place with his hands.

She clamped her eyes shut, experiencing his sweet agony along with him as he emptied himself at her farthest reaches, his big body shuddering behind her.

SOONER than either of them was ready for, he withdrew. She stung a little. He hadn't ridden her as forcefully as he had in the past, but he hadn't lied about coming deep and hard in her. The second he was gone, she felt empty.

He immediately bent and straightened her shorts and panties around her ankles. He drew them up her legs and over her hips. She straightened, helping him furtively by pulling them up. She watched him as he drew up his boxer briefs and hastily fastened his jeans. When he was nearly finished, he glanced up, his gaze moving over her face.

"I hope you thought your little game was worth getting him fired."

"You're going to fire him from Durand?" she asked, straining to mute the anger in her tone.

"No," he said, glancing into the forest. "From this assignment, though. You're coming back to the castle at night. His services aren't needed anymore."

She opened her mouth to protest his cocky assumption, but he cut her off. "Let's move before he returns. Kar Kalim is back this way," he said, referring to his horse. He gestured with his head toward the northwest. Alice nodded, too dazed following their illicit, outrageous tryst to say much of anything coherent.

She followed him, their progress slowed by brush and thick foliage. They finally reached a slight clearing. On the far side of the clearing, Alice noticed a horse path. She saw Kar Kalim tethered loosely to some low-lying bushes. He was even bigger than Quinn, the horse on which Dylan had given her first lesson last week. His coat color reminded her of Dylan's eyes—so dark brown it was nearly black and so lustrous it shone. The horse regarded them as they walked into the clearing, his gaze striking Alice as intelligent and regal.

"How did you know where I was?" Alice whispered as Dylan approached Kar Kalim and reached for the tether.

Dylan merely pointed west. Alice stepped back and saw the break in the trees. In the distance, there was a clear shot of a stretch of the beach and a pale blue Lake Michigan.

"You saw me jogging?"

Dylan nodded. "I knew Janocek would be following after a bit."

"Janocek? That's the name of the guy you've had watching me at night?"

His mouth was drawn in a tight line of dissatisfaction. "As much good as it's done me. Either I have a highly incompetent security team at Durand, or you're damn near impossible to guard," he said, his swift, annoyed glance telling her loud and clear he knew which option it was. "I saw you glance back, like you knew you were being followed. There was something on your face. Rebellion. Then you took off like a shot. I had a feeling you were about to pull something."

"I don't like being followed. I don't like being watched all night, either," Alice said thickly, finding it difficult to meet his eyes. In truth, she was a little embarrassed. Her actions suddenly struck her as juvenile.

"Then you'll just have to sleep at the castle every night, won't you."

It wasn't really a question, so Alice didn't respond. She was too embarrassed to meet his stare. Her gaze clung to his boots and hard jean-covered thighs. The truth was, she didn't want to be anywhere else at night but by his side. It was just that sometimes, she felt like if she surrendered too easily to him . . .

She'd somehow lose herself.

"I . . . I never got to tell you more about what happened that night. About what I remembered . . . about Addie," she said, her voice sounding a little congested. She'd surprised herself by bringing it up in this situation. Until that moment—until seeing him again—she hadn't realized how much she longed to share the incredible experience with someone.

Not just *someone*. Him.

She started slightly when he placed his glove-covered hand on her chin and forced her to meet his stare. She blinked when she saw the emotion that blazed on his usually impassive expression.

"I want to listen."

Her lip trembled at his stark honesty. He noticed.

"I'm not what you're making me out to be in your mind, Alice. I don't want to control you. It's a complicated situation, to put it lightly. I've told you I was in love with you. Do you believe me?"

She swallowed thickly, trapped in his stare.

"Yes," she whispered. "I think so."

"Do you need to hear it more, less . . . or not at all?"

Her heart squeezed unpleasantly in her chest at his expression of grim inevitability.

"It's not that! Of *course* I want to hear it," she grimaced. "I'm just so confused right now," she mumbled miserably, because she'd withheld the truth. Not the part about being confused. That was pretty much becoming the everyday air she breathed. No, it was that he'd told her he loved her twice now, and it was like a concise rapture on both occasions, a joy too acute for her to truly comprehend or absorb, let alone communicate.

"Do you want to be with me at night, Alice?"

"So much."

"Then *stop* fighting it," he bit out, white teeth flashing.

A small spasm of emotion shook her. She nodded. He dropped the reins and took her into his arms. His mouth captured hers. She sunk into his strength. His heat.

God, she was like a moth to a flame. Did the moths consider it worthwhile, even as they were being incinerated?

There, in that moment, under the influence of Dylan's kiss, Alice thought maybe they did.

TEN

Kuvi asked her that afternoon if she wanted to join her and some of the other counselors at the Lakeside Tavern in Morgantown that Friday night. Alice soberly explained why she couldn't. She'd agreed to meet Dylan in the woods tonight and to resume their previous routine—if being with Dylan Fall could be even remotely called *routine*.

She had all day long to anticipate seeing him, to worry about it . . .

Relish it.

Her kids were in a manically enthusiastic mood that evening because they'd come out tops in the wall climb challenge that afternoon. It seemed that Alice's initial matchup between Noble D and Judith for the zip line had been inspired.

While things might still be prickly between the pair, she noticed that the physics of attraction were definitely coming into play. D and Judith used to invariably end up on opposite sides of the common room at night, Judith regally ignoring D's curious, longing glances from afar. Now that they'd been thrown together, however, something new was happening. They were both smart, competitive kids. Scheming for success turned out to be a language they could comfortably use to communicate. The pair had masterminded the logistics of the wall climb today, coming up with a creative solution for various team members' challenges and strengths. Alice had largely remained hands-off. Relinquishing control and giving the two of them the freedom to handle the task had been a personal challenge for her—Alice. Watching them all work together so successfully had been her reward.

Something certainly *had* changed, Alice observed wryly as she entered the common room that night. D, Judith, Terrance, and Matt sat in a loose circle around a table, reliving a few exciting moments from the wall climb. Judith was silent as she listened to Terrance describe his harrowing moment on the top of the wall when he didn't know which direction he was going to crash to the earth. But as Alice approached, she noticed the girl was listening closely and enjoying herself. She was definitely allowing herself to be part of the group.

"If you stayed on top of that thing any longer, I was worried the wall would decide which direction you were going by falling over itself," D said. Terrance and Matt laughed loudly. Judith was unable to repress her amusement any longer.

"You were like a giant balanced on the head of a pin there for a few seconds," Judith snorted with laughter. They all busted up even louder. Alice slowed her pace, grinning as she observed the type of moment that comes only through achieving a goal through personal challenge and teamwork. Dylan had been right. He'd told her before that an important part of leading was delegating tasks. Alice felt the truth of that firsthand at the moment.

Judith wiped a tear from her eye. "But you pulled through, Terrance. We couldn't have done it without you."

Terrance looked pleased by the rare compliment from Judith.

"Crystal knows we're up to something, by the way. She's been watching you, me, and Justin like a hawk," Terrance said in a hushed tone to Matt after they'd all quieted. He referred to their very experienced night cabin supervisor, who had just arrived and was greeting a group of girls across the large room. "But if we're good enough to come out on top on the wall climb, there's no way we shouldn't be able to . . . you know," Terrance said shiftily to

Matt and Judith. Judith glanced up and noticed Alice slowly approaching them. She gave Terrance a repressive glance.

"Steal Bang?" Alice finished pleasantly, coming to an abrupt halt next to them.

Judith's, Terrance's, and Matt's expressions ranged from panic to convincing noncomprehension. Noble D just stared at the table uncomfortably.

"What's a bang?" Terrance asked, pointing at Alice and giving Matt an "insane-lady alert" look.

"You know," Alice said with the air of musing quietly to herself and ignoring Terrance. "It occurs to me that a team that strategized so brilliantly on the wall climb should be able to recognize that the candidate or candidates to send on a . . . oh . . . say a *secret* mission or something, isn't necessarily the obvious one or ones, because that person or persons would have the spotlight turned on them."

Terrance scowled at her cryptic statement. "You okay, Alice? Did you eat dinner? You light-headed or something?"

"I'm fine," Alice said blithely, because while Terrance and Matt were looking confused, D had slowly raised his head and Judith was regarding her through a narrowed gaze. Alice had paused behind a couch. She idly picked up a throw pillow. "And it also occurs to me that a team should consider the ultimate *goal* of any task. Is it really the *obvious* goal?" Alice wondered as if to herself, keeping her voice low so that only the four kids heard her. "Or is the real goal something symbolic? Could the goal be achieved in some alternative way without taking any unnecessary risks? Taking *anything*, really? That's what I wonder about."

"You and me both," Terrance said, rolling his eyes. Alice smiled innocently, flipping the throw pillow and catching it.

"I was just thinking about things, that's all. It's a good night for thinking . . ."

"Or going nuts," Terrance muttered under his breath.

". . . about goals, and how the most brilliant of plans often achieve more than *one* purpose," Alice continued. She abruptly tossed the pillow. Despite his hunched-over position, Noble D straightened and caught it with the reflexes of a natural athlete.

Judith blinked at the sudden move. Her stare transferred from D to Alice, her eyes widening.

Message received.

She pointed at Terrance. "We're running in the morning. Don't be late. Night, you guys," Alice said before she sauntered away.

DYLAN'S last kiss in the woods—that hot, deep, tender one—rode her consciousness as she crept out of her cabin that night at nine thirty. She'd never known it was possible to be both anxious and relieved to the point of euphoria at the idea of seeing another human being . . .

At the idea of resuming her schedule of spending the night in his bed, wrapped in his arms.

The night was still and quiet. There were a million stars in the night sky. Alice wasn't sure if it was her sharp anticipation in seeing him or if she was getting used to his silent nocturnal movement in the dark woods, but unlike most nights, when he surprised her, she turned to him just before he touched her back. Instead, his hand slid along her T-shirt and cupped her shoulder. Alice stepped toward him and went up on her tiptoes, both her hands pressed against the solid wall of his chest.

She found his mouth in the darkness unerringly. Her kiss was hungry; she held nothing back. All the feelings that she'd been stifling found an outlet in that kiss.

It only took him a split second to get over his surprise at her attack. Then his arms were closing around her, and he was joining in that wet, wild kiss.

After a delicious moment, where Alice felt her toes curling in her tennis shoes, she reluctantly came up for air.

"I'm still mad at you for keeping things from me," she breathed out against his lips.

"Exactly how am I supposed to know what to tell you and what not to tell you, when you send me so many mixed messages?"

She bit her lip, unable to answer his question as concisely as he'd asked it.

"I know I'm sending mixed messages," she conceded. "What else can I do? I'm confused."

"Understandable."

"But you shouldn't have treated Thad like that," she whispered. "You're far too protective of me, Dylan. I'm an independent person. I always have been. I don't want to live in a cage."

A breeze caught the tops of the trees that surrounded them, making them sigh softly. It suddenly struck Alice that she was having this conversation with him in the pitch black, where she couldn't see him. Maybe that made it easier, somehow. When she looked into his deep, magnetic eyes, she sometimes lost herself.

"I respect that," he whispered stiffly after a moment. "And I still don't think you should be giving anyone carte blanche with your loyalty, but I do understand that Schaefer has become your friend. For better or worse."

"And?"

"And what?"

"Why are you so protective of me? If you can't stop doing it, you at least have to tell me why. It isn't *twenty years* ago, Dylan."

"Not now," he whispered tensely. She felt his hands tighten on her shoulders and sensed he was peering into the darkness around them, searching the shadows. He really was paranoid. *Wasn't he?* "All right, we'll talk," he said finally. "But not here. Up at the house."

They were silent for the rest of the trip to the castle. Once they'd arrived at the terrace doors, he quietly told her to use her key to make sure it worked. It did. She disarmed the security system, too. When they reached the kitchen, he told her to go on upstairs and he'd bring them something to drink.

In Dylan's suite, she strategically sat on the couch in the sitting area before the fireplace. She wanted to talk to him, and didn't need the distraction of the great luxurious bed or the smoking memories of what they'd done in it on previous occasions.

Dylan entered a few minutes later. He wore a dark red plain T-shirt and jeans that emphasized his body in the exact right places. She ate up the vision of him, all big lean male, a man who was supremely confident in his physicality, who knew his power and strength, and precisely how to use it. He carried two glasses. She guessed the one with the dark brown liquid was Dr Pepper. A strange giddy feeling went through her at this evidence of mundane familiarity on his part. His favored drink was club soda with a lime twist—which he carried right now—or expensive French brandy, when he wanted alcohol. He'd never blinked once early on when she'd named her favorite unsophisticated, sugary beverage.

He set their glasses on the coffee table before the couch, reached into his back jean pocket, and plopped a box of Sweet Adelaides on the table next to her drink.

She grinned unabashedly and reached for the box. "Thanks."

Sweet Adelaides were a Durand bestseller. Along with Jingdots, they were Alice's longtime favorite sweets. Alice had recently learned that Marie, Dylan's cook, kept a huge jar filled with various Durand candies on the counter in the castle kitchen. She felt shy but happy, too at Dylan's little gift. Which was stupid, of course. She opened the box and poured a few of the caramel, peanut, and chocolate candies into her hand, giving Dylan a sideways smile.

"You really must love me if you're willing to feed my chocolate addiction."

He sat down on the cushion next to her and leaned back, draping one arm across the back of the couch. Alice paused in the process of popping the candies in her mouth, her hand stilling several inches below her chin. His T-shirt stretched over his wide muscular chest and lean torso. His strong, jean-covered spread thighs were a distraction, too, but it was what she read in his dark eyes that snagged her attention.

"I do."

She'd been attempting to be light, but suddenly everything seemed dead serious. She felt her cheeks warming.

He smiled. "I know you come by the love of chocolate honestly. It's in your genes."

A tingling sensation went through her forearms. Slowly, she opened her palm and stared at the chocolates she held there. She'd looked at similar candies hundreds of times.

She'd never *seen* them until now.

A shiver tore through her. "Oh my God," she whispered, shuddering.

"*What?*"

"Sweet Adelaides. Alan Durand named them after his daughter."

"Yes," Dylan said with the air of someone confirming she did indeed have a cobra poised at the back of her neck. "I thought you realized it the day we told you about Addie. Sidney mentioned that Alan used to tease that his daughter was usually a Sweet Adelaide but could occasionally be a Sour Citrus—" He broke off when she just stared at him blankly. He leaned toward her. "Alice?" he asked tensely.

"It's okay," she mumbled. Why hadn't she made that incredible charged connection until now? Yes, Sidney had made that statement, but it'd bounced right off her like many things had that fateful afternoon.

To a casual observer of the facts, the truth must have been obvious. But Alice was no casual witness. She was so deeply immersed in this situation, she was blinded. Defenseless. That truth now rang in her ears and pulsed in her blood. It was like two electrical circuits had abruptly joined, sizzling with power and lighting up her brain, fusing together a small part of her—Alice's—childhood to Addie Durand's.

All this, from the seemingly innocuous stimulus of a common drugstore candy.

Slowly, deliberately, she raised her hand to her mouth and placed a chocolate on her tongue. *One.* She didn't toss all of them in there at once, chew, and reach for the next handful even before she swallowed, like she usually did. She closed her mouth and eyelids, letting the sweet flavor and velvety consistency of the chocolate fill her.

Her life didn't flash before her eyes, like they said of drowning victims. That would be far too dramatic of a representation of what happened to her in that moment. But because she allowed it, because she squeezed every ounce of meaning out of that little piece of candy that she possibly could, threads from her life that she'd formally thought of as inconsequential background noise, suddenly knitted together with the Present-Day Alice.

She swallowed.

"Alice?" Dylan repeated.

She blinked, coming out of her trance. It finally hit her how anxious he looked.

"Uncle Al would bring me Sweet Adelaides and Jingdots every once in a rare while. I told you how Al was my favorite uncle," she prompted, holding Dylan's stare. He nodded. "It'd be like Christmas for me, every time he held out that plastic bag of candy. Sissy would start yowling at him, accusing him of spoiling me after I'd just mouthed off to her, or committing whatever sin I'd just committed. But Uncle Al would ignore her. And on a few occasions when she screamed too loud, he'd blaze up at her and say, 'She deserves that candy, Sis, that and a whole hell of a lot more! Are you forgetting that?'"

Alice shook her head. "I never *got* before why she'd shut up after that," she said hoarsely. The nerves in her hands and feet tingled. She blinked and started back, like she'd just taken an invisible slap.

"They *knew*," she whispered to herself. The candies she still held fell from her hand heedlessly to her knee, rolling to the carpet. Dylan reached out and grasped her upper arm. Alice appreciated his touch. It steadied her.

"Why?" she asked him. "Why did they keep me? Why did they keep it all a secret? Who knew? All of them? How much did they know?" The questions spilled out of her in a pressured rush even as more formed on her tongue. How could she not have wondered about the Reeds before? It was like a defensive dam had crashed and she was being pummeled by roaring, crashing anxiety. "*Dylan?*" she demanded desperately.

Dylan shook his head. "I'm not entirely certain which of your uncles knew or how much—obviously Al knew something, given what you just said. But Sissy knew from the beginning." She started to ask another question, but he held up his free hand. "I don't have all the answers, Alice, but I'm going to tell you everything I found out from Avery Cunningham. But take a deep breath for a moment. Slow down."

Hearing her mother's name paired with the name of one of Addie Durand's kidnappers sent another small shock through her. Her mouth snapped shut. She breathed slowly through her nose. Dylan was right. She'd felt a little dizzy there for a moment.

"Are you all right?" Dylan asked.

"Yes. Absolutely. Please go on," she said quickly, worried he'd change his mind about telling her what he knew.

He gave her that look that she now recognized as extreme caution. She'd learned that expression well over the past few days.

"I'm okay, Dylan. I want to know."

He inhaled, and she had that sense again of him forcing himself into the deep well of memories that he detested.

"I told you how Cunningham planned to throw Addie Durand's body in the creek, but as he was letting go he saw her eyes flicker open. But it was too late. She fell into the water. Realizing she was still alive, he ran down the creek bed and jumped in to save her. There had been a heavy rain that night after an extended dry spell. He said the water was moving fast and strong. According to him, he must have hit his head on something when he was struggling to get Addie from the current, because he was disoriented after he'd pulled her to shore. He claimed *that* contributed to what made him alter his plans in regard to Addie."

"You didn't believe him?" Alice asked, noticing the derisive tilt of his mouth.

Dylan shrugged. "Given Cunningham's constant cat-and-mouse games, I tried to remain doubtful about almost everything he said. Which was hard, because I craved any morsel of information he'd dangle. I don't know what actually happened that early morning twenty years ago. I never will. All I have is what he told me—and the fact that the information *did* finally lead me to Addie Durand. But Cunningham's explanation about being disoriented didn't add up, in my opinion."

"What do you mean?"

"Cunningham claimed that the reason he didn't take Addie back to Jim Stout and resume the plans for sending a ransom note to Alan Durand was that he was disoriented from a blow to the head. That, and he was somehow . . . moved by the fact that Addie was still alive."

"*Moved?*"

Dylan met her stare. "Remember how I told you a few days ago that Cunningham kept talking about Addie's eyes—the impact they had on him when he saw them open while he thought he was dumping her dead body? According to Cunningham, he was sort of—" He waved his hand impatiently. "*Converted* when that happened."

"He saw the light?" she asked, stunned.

His gaze snapped to meet hers. "Avery Cunningham was a liar, a drug addict, and a murderer. He was the lowest common denominator of society. *After* he supposedly underwent this miraculous 'conversion,' he nearly tore a man apart with his bare hands while he was high on crystal meth. Cunningham's supposed redemption didn't help his victim a bit. He was *playing* me with that story, painting a picture of himself as he lay on his death bed, trying to convince himself as much as me that he had a sliver of humanity left in him."

"What did he do with Addie after he pulled her from the creek?" Alice whispered, dread and curiosity waging battle in her brain.

"He made a phone call to an old friend."

Goose bumps rose on her arms. Something Dylan had told her last week leapt into her brain to mingle with the new information. *Cunningham was already in prison on a separate murder charge. He'd killed a man a few months before when he'd been whacked out on methamphetamines.* That, and Dylan's tight-lipped wariness at the moment told her what she dreaded.

"Cunningham knew Sissy, didn't he?" She turned to him when he didn't immediately respond. "She was his meth dealer?"

He nodded once.

Alice felt a little numb, but she wasn't surprised by the news. Not really. Men and women of the caliber of Avery Cunningham regularly pulled up into the drive of their shabby, garbage-strewn double-wide in Little Paradise. It was voices like theirs—rough, guttural, and at times, savage—that Alice regularly heard vibrating through the walls of her bedroom. That was Alice's life. She was a mouse cowering in a den of pythons, constantly trying to disguise her vulnerability, to make herself darker and tougher than she was.

"Apparently, Sissy and Cunningham went way back," Dylan said. "They met in Cook County Juvenile Detention Center back in the eighties."

Alice swallowed thickly, trying to absorb this strange reality. Jesus. Had she and Cunningham ever been in the trailer at the same time? Typical Sissy, to welcome her daughter's kidnapper and would-be murderer into their home with open arms. Cunningham had been an old crime buddy and paying customer, after all.

"According to Cunningham, Addie was pretty banged up after he fished her out of the creek," Dylan continued gruffly. "She was drifting in and out of consciousness when he put her back in the car. At some point, she must have come to, though. He said he fed her while they were on the road. I think it was at that point that Cunningham realized something miraculous had happened. Addie was amnesic not only in regard to the kidnapping and Cunningham's attempted murder, but also to her own identity. Sidney assures me that given the physical trauma she endured, in addition to all the psychological stress and fear, amnesia is a very realistic coping mechanism, especially for such a small child. Sidney thinks it also could have just been the fall that caused the amnesia, the heavy sedatives she'd been given, the trauma, or maybe it was a combination of all those things. For Cunningham, it must have been like the slate had been wiped clean of all his sins toward her. He also must have realized that in the state she was in, Addie would be less likely to betray him if they got her medical care. She couldn't even remember her own name."

"They told her that her name was Alice, and she believed it," she said dully.

"There's no reason she wouldn't," Dylan said forcefully. "She was a traumatized, injured, tiny little girl who had been ripped from her parents and almost died at the hands of a ruthless criminal."

Alice nodded, trying to disguise her unrest. "Go on."

His nostrils flared slightly as he stared at her, obviously reluctant.

"Please, Dylan."

He briefly shut his eyes and inhaled. "Cunningham put a call in to Sissy and they agreed to meet at a hotel in Michigan City, Indiana. Sissy helped him put a dark rinse on Addie's hair. Addie's hair was a remarkable color—a rose gold. They needed to hide that telltale characteristic."

Alice shook her head slowly. "For as long as I can remember, Sissy put a rinse on my hair. When I got a little older, she told me she'd been abused as a girl. She said she didn't want me to be obvious prey, there in Little Paradise. She was the one who taught me to hide myself. Darken my hair, hide my body, make myself look tougher. It was actually one of the few useful things she'd ever told me," Alice said with a rough bark of laughter. "And now, I find out she had an ulterior motive, even for that. She was trying to disguise my identity, not protect me."

"I'm sorry," Dylan said after a pause.

She pulled herself out of her thoughts and focused on him.

"Go on."

"Addie's amnesia didn't remit, and Sissy ended up taking her to a local ER. Her lack of memory made things easier. Whatever they told her—"

"Became reality," Alice filled in, anger entering her tone. "That's my first memory—or at least it *was* before coming here— waking up in the hospital," she said, staring into space as she relived that fuzzy memory, now through an unveiled mind's eye. Shivers of dread crawled beneath her skin. That feeling of belonging to strangers, to people whom she had nothing remotely in common with had started *there*, in those moments when she'd awakened in that hospital bed.

"Alice?" Dylan asked uncertainly.

She blinked. She realized she was hugging herself as if for warmth. Steeling herself, she dropped her arms.

"And Cunningham just gave Addie"—*me*, she screamed silently in her head—"to Sissy to raise after that? *Why?*"

Dylan shook his head slowly. "All I have there is speculation. I told you what Cunningham claimed. He says he regretted kidnapping and hurting that little girl . . . almost killing her. He didn't want to continue in his mission, but was too much of a coward to take her back and risk getting arrested. But I think he also needed a female accomplice, and thought of Sissy. As the only witness, I'd told the police and FBI about the two males I'd witnessed who took Addie. They wore masks and hats, but I was positive that they were both men. A woman claiming to be Addie's mother in the emergency room would have been less suspicious."

"But why then *give* Addie to Sissy to raise on a permanent basis? I know you don't know exactly why he did it, but you must suspect something," Alice implored, desperate to understand.

He was sitting forward now, his elbows resting on his spread knees. He looked down at his clasped hands.

"Alice . . . I don't think Stout and Cunningham actually masterminded the kidnapping."

"You think someone else planned it? That they were hired to do it?"

He met her stare. "Yes," he said with quiet conviction.

She chafed her hands over the roughened skin of her arms.

"I've always thought that Cunningham and Stout had been fed information about Addie's habits and activities. They chose the *ideal* circumstances to snatch her. Someone would have had to hole up in the woods for days on end in order to observe and understand the moment when Addie was most vulnerable and when their escape would be easiest."

"But that's what they did, right? Staked out the area in order to determine the prime moment?"

"That's what they would have *had* to do, but there's no evidence to show they actually *did* that. If they had, they would have left traces . . . evidence of their presence while they spied for days, maybe even weeks, in the woods and on the grounds. It had been a dry hot summer before the kidnapping. There was no rain or wind that would make evidence vanish. The FBI combed the woods and grounds on the estate following the kidnapping. They never found anything to indicate that Stout and Cunningham had been hiding out repeatedly to discover the best moment for the kidnapping, they just suspected they *must* have. Somehow. The agents did locate where they thought the escape vehicle had most likely been parked on a side road just past the bluff, but there was no indication of several trips, no multiple tire tracks. There was a single trip on the day they successfully took her. Plus, the riding lesson I planned for Addie that day wasn't our typical routine. Someone *must* have told Stout and Cunningham when and where the ideal moment presented itself."

"Who?"

He shook his head, his mouth clamped together. Alice sensed his profound frustration at his inability to answer her. "Any number of people could have informed them from the camp— employees and campers who were frequently at the stables, anyone that the Durands conversed with about Addie and her activities, like Alan's and Lynn's friends and confidants. Personally? I always had my suspicions about Kehoe, but never had anything solid to go on. I never said anything to the agents, because my suspicion seemed pretty groundless. I told Jim Sheridan about my concerns, but Jim has never really been on board with that. The problem is, I can't figure out a motive. Whoever did it not only had the means to hire Cunningham and Stout, they must have anticipated the outcome of the whole thing. As Jim has always reminded me, Kehoe couldn't benefit in any way from Addie being taken."

"So why do you suspect him?"

"I'm not sure," Dylan admitted uneasily. "It's just a feeling I have about him."

"Well, he certainly doesn't like you much." Dylan glanced over at her. "It's kind of hard not to notice. He was running the camp back then, wasn't he?"

He nodded. "I was a camper here for the first time during the second year the camp ran, and Kehoe was already the head guy. It was because of all the good work he did here that he was promoted to VP of human resources in that time period."

"What did Kehoe think of you back then?"

"What did he think of me when I was twelve, thirteen . . . fourteen years old? Very little, I'd guess. I don't remember many personal interactions with him at all. He was decent not only to me, but all the kids, as I recall it." He pressed his fingertips to his eyelids and shook his head. "Maybe it's just paranoia on my part when it comes to Kehoe, and the bad vibes I get from him are solely due to his dislike of me. Like Jim always tells me, Kehoe would have absolutely no motive for kidnapping Addie."

"Who *did* benefit monetarily from Addie being taken out of the picture? Who was the Durand's heir before Addie was born?" Alice asked.

"Lynn and Alan were both only children. Their parents were all dead. Alan's mom and dad died in a small plane crash when he was twenty-four. Lynn's mother died when she was twelve of breast cancer, and her father had a heart attack a few years before she had Addie. They had made a few personal bequeathals in their original will to friends and distant cousins, but they weren't considerable amounts, given the worth of the entire estate. Certainly not enough money that someone would take such an extreme risk of going to jail, at least in my opinion. Every one of that handful of original beneficiaries was wealthy in their own right, and couldn't have thought the bequeathals much of anything aside from a kind remembrance from Alan and Lynn. The FBI did do a cursory investigation of each beneficiary, but found nothing connecting them to the kidnapping. Before Addie was born, Alan and Lynn had planned for Durand to go public when the last of them died, and for the bulk of their personal wealth and the proceeds from the stock sale to be donated to charity."

So . . . Addie had no close living relatives. Alice squashed down with effort the feeling of loneliness that descended upon her. She forced her brain to focus.

"What about the charities Alan and Lynn favored? Isn't it possible that somebody was angling to get more money for their cause by taking Addie out of the picture?"

"The FBI considered that, too. But nothing ever panned out as a significant connection or motivation in that direction, either. Besides, although Alan's plans were for Lynn and him to give the bulk of their estate to charity, he hadn't promised the money to specific organizations at the time of Addie's kidnapping. He didn't specifically designate charitable beneficiaries until he rewrote his will after Addie's kidnapping."

"But the kidnappers planned to ransom Addie. Isn't money motive enough?"

"Maybe," he said quietly. "But personally, I think there was never any plan to actually send a ransom note. Cunningham and Stout might have *thought* that was the intention when they kidnapped Addie Durand. But at some point after the kidnapping, I believe whoever hired them told them the plan had changed. I think they—or possibly just Cunningham alone—were given orders to murder Addie . . . to make her disappear forever."

"So it really wasn't a matter of accidental death from an overdose of the sedative they gave her?"

"I don't think so. Given Stout's confession about Cunningham accidentally over-sedating Addie, and his insistence that he wasn't responsible, he might not have been involved in the murder. Then again, he might have just been pointing the finger before Cunningham fingered him."

Her entire body seemed to pulse with the beat of her heart. It was so strange, talking about these cruel facts so rationally.

"*Why?*" she asked. "What makes you think that another person was involved, and an order was given to murder her?"

He shook his head, and she once again felt his restrained frustration. "It's the only thing that makes sense to me. It's hard to explain what it was like talking to Cunningham. The guy was a sociopath. He'd mix up facts with straight-up lies, but he'd also twist the facts. I'm not even sure he was aware of doing it sometimes. He'd just automatically try to recast himself and his actions in a more positive light."

"Like the fact that he claims the reason he saved Addie from the creek and turned her over to Sissy was because he was suddenly a saved man."

"Right. Don't get me wrong. There might have been a tiny sliver of truth to that. I remember Addie's eyes. She was such a pretty little girl. She practically glowed with life. If any human being could spark a redemption, it was Addie," he said, his voice going hoarse. Alice held her breath when he paused, his focus clearly in the past. Suddenly, his gaze sharpened on her. "It wouldn't shock me to find out there was a bit of fact to Cunningham's story, enough for him to fabricate a lie around that kernel of truth, anyway. But Cunningham was a manipulator at heart, so when he pulled Addie out of that creek, he was planning for the future. That's the bottom line. He'd probably considered it before, but his scheme kicked in when he realized that Addie was miraculously alive and amnesiac to his crime. Fate nudged him in that direction. He might have gotten a sweet deal in payment from whomever hired him to kidnap and kill Addie, but how much sweeter would

it be if he threatened whomever had hired him with the knowledge
that Adelaide Durand was still alive and stashed away in a place only
Cunningham knew? What kind of blackmail money might he be
able to get, dangling the threat of an anonymous tip to the police?
With Addie alive and in his possession, there was always the chance
of a future ransom, too. Plus, although Alan hadn't yet put up a reward for useful clues that would lead to his daughter, Cunningham
must have realized Alan eventually would."

"Alan put up reward money?"

"Yeah. He offered half a million dollars to anyone who provided information that would lead to Addie's recovery. When
Addie was still missing after . . . after ten months, he raised the
award money price to one million."

She stared at him, mute with disbelief and confusion. A million
dollars of reward money, and no one stepped forward? And . . .

"Why *ten months*?" she demanded.

His gaze bounced off her.

"Dylan? What's the significance of ten months? Why did Alan
raise the reward to a million then?" she repeated, thinking he
hadn't understood her query.

"It was ten months after Addie was kidnapped that Jim Stout
was arrested and made the drunk confession he later recanted.
Before that, the FBI assumed Addie was most likely dead, given
simple crime statistics and the amount of time that had passed
without a ransom request. After Stout confessed that she was accidentally killed, they were even more certain. Despite the fact that
Stout recanted once he was sober, that incident altered the flavor
of the investigation. Almost no one held any hope after that point
that Addie was still alive."

"Oh," Alice whispered, imagining the horrible scene when the
Durands received the news that Stout had claimed Addie had been
accidentally killed.

"Alan flat-out refused to believe Stout, though. He never

stopped believing Addie could be alive, even on his death bed," Dylan said quietly. She was glad he didn't comment when she looked away and furtively wiped at a tear. For a moment, they didn't speak as Alice struggled to calm herself.

"My whole point is," Dylan continued somberly after a moment, "why *should* Avery Cunningham go along with the moneyman's plan to get rid of Addie? Between potential blackmail, ransom, and reward money, she was a precious commodity."

"But Cunningham never admitted he was hired by someone, did he?"

"No. He denied it, but in the same sly way he used to deny that he had anything to do with the kidnapping for all those years. I started to recognize when he was lying."

"If it were true that they were hired for the job, why wouldn't Cunningham just confess? He was dying and admitted to the kidnapping. What would it matter to him at that point?"

"Again, I don't know exactly. It could be any number of things. It's possible whoever hired him had some kind of hold on Cunningham or a family member. We'll never know for sure. *I* think it was some combination of the fact that Cunningham wanted to see himself as a misunderstood hero—a sort of scoundrel with a heart of gold—and that he actually *did* feel some twisted sense of liking or loyalty toward Sissy, Addie, or both. He was a convicted murderer. He was going to die in prison, and knew it. Exposing who had hired him for the kidnapping and possibly murder wouldn't get him anything substantial. Plus, if he confessed that he'd been hired by someone, it might bring into question his motives for keeping Addie alive. *Had* he kept Addie alive to blackmail whomever hired him? If people questioned his motives, then how could Cunningham continue to tell himself that he'd been a decent man, even a hero, for one brief flashing moment in his life? How could he claim any worth when he met his maker? People lie to others and the world for much less motivation," he finished grimly.

Alice leaned back on the couch. "You really *did* get to know Cunningham," she said, stunned by his concise knowledge of the psychological workings of the criminal's mind.

He grimaced. "It wasn't pleasant, listening to that asshole go on about himself. I had to make myself what he needed: an avid listener to his bravado. He was a slimy, dangerous braggart," Dylan muttered, his mouth pressed into a hard line.

"And yet you went like clockwork to visit him in prison," Alice said softly. "Thank you."

He rubbed the side of his head distractedly, brushing off her praise. "I was worried about telling you all this. I know it must come as a shock, that Cunningham knew Sissy." He exhaled heavily and leaned back next to her, their shoulders touching.

"It does and it doesn't," she said hollowly. "Does it surprise me that Sissy would associate with scum like Avery Cunningham or that she would take me in under such . . . *sleazy* circumstances? No. Not really. She collected people all the time. She liked having all those people addicted to her product, pulling up to her trailer day and night, knocking on her door. Needy people. Desperate. Sissy didn't do relationships in the classic sense of give and take, but she loved having people seek her out. Dependent on her. She was a born drug dealer. She probably thought she'd hit the jackpot taking in a child, having something so completely at her mercy. Another human being who would be"—her voice cracked, and she took a deep breath—"utterly dependent on her to survive."

Dylan winced and shut his eyes.

ELEVEN

For a moment, they sat in silence. It took Alice a moment to comprehend what she was feeling. Everything she'd said to Dylan was true, but it didn't stop the hurt that went through her: a terrible, cringing shame. *This* had been the reason she hadn't allowed herself to question how she'd ended up with Sissy. She'd been unconsciously fending off *this* pain.

If one of Sissy's whacked-out "friends" had asked her to keep a puppy as a favor, she probably would have. Sissy could be loud, outgoing, and friendly when she wanted to be and when her latest batch of meth was particularly good. She'd have fed that puppy sporadically, bragged about how much the puppy loved her, and kicked it when it got in her way. For days on end, she'd forget the puppy even existed until it suddenly showed up in front of her blurry-eyed stare.

That's what Alice had been all these years: a puppy dropped on the front door of a drug addict. At least previously, she'd lived under the misperception that she'd come from Sissy's body, that she shared some kind of primal link with her. But no. She and Sissy were strangers that fate had tossed together into a trailer for fourteen years of Alice's life. Sissy didn't belong to her any more than Alice belonged to Sissy.

It was an awful truth . . . a severing one. What Dylan had told her sickened her . . . but it had liberated her, too.

"Why didn't they turn me in for the reward money? That seems out of character for the Reed clan," Alice said darkly.

"I'm not sure. Maybe Sissy didn't have all the details as to your identity at first, but as time went on, she started to put two and two together, given the news reports and what she knew about Cunningham's character. She certainly knew what she was doing, disguising your hair color all those years. Either way, she had to realize from the beginning you belonged to someone else, and that she was keeping you illegally. Maybe Cunningham threatened to implicate her in the kidnapping and held that over her head."

"Sissy definitely wouldn't want the police nosing around our trailer."

"Even if any of your uncles were like Al, and they came to suspect the truth, they must have realized they could very easily be implicated or even blamed for the crime. From what I understand about the Reed brothers, I doubt the police would have any trouble believing they were either involved, or actually the main perpetrators."

"I can believe Sissy would do it. But *Al*. That he never told me the truth for all of those years, that he played along. That . . . sucks."

Hurts.

"I thought he cared about me, even if it *was* just a little," she finished.

"Well, he didn't sell you out for the reward money. Maybe he really did consider you family. That must mean something. People are strange. Complicated," Dylan added, reaching for her hand. He grasped it in his encompassing, warm hold and settled it on his thigh. "That's one lesson life has taught both you and me. People can be cruel, petty, self-involved, and yet they can suddenly do something that makes you see their humanity. Sometimes I think it'd be better if they didn't, because it would be easier just to straight up hate them that way."

Alice turned her head, staring into his eyes. She knew he was ambivalent about his mother, who had been a prostitute. His mom hadn't planned for or wanted Dylan, and typically treated him with disgusted anger, or merely discounted and ignored him. Dylan had been left to fend for himself in a cold mean world.

Yet Dylan had loved his mother, too, and wanted to be loved by her. It was human nature, to crave connection, nurturance and approval from a mother or father figure. Alice knew that lesson all too well.

She released her hand from his, leaned toward him and pressed her palm to his heart.

"I hate Sissy for what she's done to me," she said shakily, staring at Dylan's chest. "I don't think I'll ever forgive her. But I don't hate Uncle Al. Sissy was the worst among them. She was always the instigator. She'd whine and complain and manipulate until they finally did whatever it was she wanted, just to shut her up. As weak and ineffective as she seemed on the surface, she was the leader of them. She was the Queen of Passive-Aggressive Land. Al's and my other uncles' worst fault was weakness, but Al stood up to her the most. Almost every time he did stand up to her, he'd do it for my sake." She grimaced, lost in painful memories for a moment. "At least if Sissy were in prison, she'd be away from the drugs. She might live a few years longer away from the poison. Same for most of my uncles. But I don't want to see Al locked up," she admitted miserably. She was suddenly having trouble meeting Dylan's stare. "That makes me weak, too, doesn't it?"

"*No.* The last thing you are is weak, Alice. It's a complicated, confusing situation. I think you need time to let things settle. It's a lot to absorb."

"Do you mean that someday, I might want vengeance? I might want to see Al sent to prison?" She wasn't sure she'd *ever* want to see that day come.

"I mean that nothing is going to happen this minute. We have a reprieve, although I can't guarantee how long that reprieve will last. I wanted you to have some time, no matter how brief it is, so you can start to come to terms with things."

"That's why you didn't want Jim Sheridan to understand who I was yet," she said. She pressed tighter with her hand, feeling dense muscle and the strong steady beat of his heart resound into her flesh. A powerful longing rose up in her to be surrounded by his arms. Her throat ached. He covered her hand, and she sensed his nonverbal prompt. Uncertainly, she raised her gaze to meet his.

"If Jim finds out the truth, he'll be obligated to inform the FBI. It's their case. They'll come here to question you and me."

"And you'll have to tell them about Sissy and Al and the others," she whispered, understanding making her throat constrict more.

"Sissy and possibly some of your uncles are going to be implicated in this crime eventually. I want you to understand it's not something I can stop. Because I'm not telling the truth immediately doesn't mean I'm condoning silence forever about this. The keeping of secrets is what got us to this point. The truth *should* be told. When the time comes, I'm going to tell the FBI everything I know. Call it what you want: fate, karma, or simple justice, Sissy and some or all of your uncles knowingly harbored a kidnapped child for years and years. They lied regularly about her identity and prevented her return to her rightful parents."

"They lied about *my* identity," Alice said, staring blankly at Dylan's chest.

Shivers ran in rivulets down her body. It felt like ice water had been poured on top of her head. Dylan grasped her wrist and lifted her hand from his chest. Her gaze shot up to meet his.

"I was Addie Durand."

A muscle leapt in his taut cheek. "You *are* Addie Durand." Another shudder coursed through her. "You're Alice Reed, too," he assured roughly. "You always will be, no matter what happens."

Her eyes stung. She shut them reflexively. She wasn't so sure she wanted to be Alice Reed anymore, given what Dylan had just told her. It had always *felt* like she didn't belong as a child, the notes of her spirit clashing discordantly with her supposed kin's. Now, here was the truth. They'd never been her family. Never. It was a jarring, horrible, *incredible* truth. And yet . . .

It was starting to feel real.

She shook. His arms closed around her. He brought her against him, so that her chest pressed against his ribs and her face was buried in his chest. It felt wonderful.

This. This was the opposite of what she'd felt in Sissy Reed's trailer. This was what she'd longed for her whole life, to feel safe and prized.

She hugged him back. Hard. Thankfully, he didn't speak for several tense moments. Perhaps he realized if she was forced to respond, she'd betray her ragged emotional state . . . expose her grief.

"Alice?" he asked quietly when she'd wiped the last of her tears on his shirt and brought herself under control.

"Yeah?" she sniffed.

"You okay?"

"Yeah."

He chafed her upper arms with his hands.

"We never got to talk about what happened the night you found me under the stairs," she said.

"Are you really up to getting into that now?" he asked, and she sensed his wary watchfulness.

She nodded. She was tired, but the things Thad had said that night had been like a worm burrowing under her skin. So much had come out tonight; so much released to the surface. She couldn't bear the thought of Thad's allegations continuing to haunt her.

"Thad had said something that upset me," she began, her voice sounding congested.

"What?"

She lifted her head but kept her gaze lowered. "He said that his father had told him that the circumstances by which you became CEO of Durand were . . . suspicious."

He slid his fingers beneath her chin and lifted gently. She met his narrow-eyed stare.

"Schaefer was trying to *warn* you about me?"

"I guess so."

"Why? Does he know we're involved? Did you tell him?"

"No!"

"Then how does he know?"

"I don't know," she exclaimed, suddenly feeling like she was on the witness stand. She struggled to recall what Thad had said when she asked him how he knew she was involved with Dylan. *"Do you think a guy doesn't notice when the girl he's fallen for is completely in love with someone else?"*

She was uncomfortably aware of Dylan waiting.

"He said something about recognizing the signs because he cared about me so much . . . "

She faded off, her cheeks warming.

"Because he's in love with you himself, and bound to notice where your attentions lie?" Dylan asked incredulously. "That's bullshit, Alice. You didn't believe him, did you?"

"That he's infatuated with me?" she asked, frowning.

"No. That he knew you and I were involved because he can read the mind of the woman he loves," Dylan said sarcastically. "He's been *following* you. He knows where you go at night."

"He's not following me! That's—" She halted herself from saying *ridiculous* because she suddenly remembered those two times he'd come upon her in the woods. The Durand Estate was awfully large to just coincidentally run into her when she was alone and vulnerable.

"I refuse to believe that my two choices are either to trust in

Thad or trust in you," she said, feeling cornered. "Maybe he *has* noticed us coming up here at night, I don't know, but that doesn't mean he's got evil intentions toward me."

"So that's it?" Dylan asked, a hard gleam to his eyes. "Schaefer is trying to turn you against me because he doesn't want the competition?"

"No," she admitted reluctantly after a moment. "I think someone is telling him things, *negative* things about you."

"Who do you think it is?"

Alice swallowed thickly, Dylan's sharp question bringing the importance of her answer home to her. "He wouldn't say," she admitted. "But he said they were trustworthy. And he got at least *some* of the information from his father. I got the impression that whoever is telling him stuff about you or about you and me is friends with his father or something. Do you think it could be Kehoe?"

"It could very well be. I don't think it's much of a secret that Kehoe would like to see me taken down a peg or two. And he *is* friends with Thad's father."

Alice frowned. "So we get back to Kehoe again."

"We do," Dylan mused. "And he's on my list."

"Your list?"

Dylan nodded distractedly. "I have a list of people who were alive during the kidnapping, who had the means to hire a couple known criminals, and who had some knowledge of Addie's activities at the camp. But the essential fact remains, Kehoe would have had no motive whatsoever to become embroiled in a crime of that magnitude. So what *did* the mighty Judge Schaefer have to say about me?"

"Just that the there was more than one person who expressed their doubts about the validity of you being named CEO by Alan Durand before he died."

"Judge Schaefer implied that I coerced Alan while he was sick and fragile?"

"Something like that, yes," Alice said hesitantly.

"You don't need to look like that, Alice. Do you think that's some novel accusation? I've heard similar charges and whisperings for years now. Fortunately, Alan Durand was a very smart man. His mind remained as sharp as it ever was up until almost the very end. He'd already locked up things tight with his will and estate planning far before he weakened. The naysayers never had a chance, given Alan's foresight and brilliance. The only thing left to them was to hiss their conspiracy theories to each another."

Alice listened to this with a sense of relief. It didn't surprise her that there would be those who would dissent when the transfer of so much power went wholesale to Dylan.

"Was there something else that Schaefer said that bothered you?"

"Yes," she admitted in a small voice.

"What?" he asked, whisking his hand along her jawline and caressing the side of her neck. She shivered in pleasure when his long fingers slid beneath the hair at her nape and he rubbed the tense muscles there. Had he sensed her increased uncertainty and was trying to relax her?

"Thad probably was wrong about it," she wavered.

"Alice, just tell me."

"He said that Sidney was one of the people who questioned your suitableness as CEO."

Her heart leapt a little when his rubbing fingers never paused.

"That's true. Sidney did protest. But not for the same reason most of the dissenters did."

She met his stare, amazed by his calm proclamation.

"But why? I thought Sidney trusted you."

He shrugged. Alice slid her hands up his shirt and cupped his shoulders.

"Remember that Sidney was my psychiatrist in the years after Addie was taken. Because of that, he is of the opinion that he knows a great deal more about the inner workings of my mind than he really does."

"What does he think he knows that would bring your worthiness as CEO of Durand into doubt?"

She sensed his hesitation. His irritation.

"Dylan?" she asked when he didn't respond immediately.

"Sidney is of the opinion that I've dedicated my life to Alan Durand's legacy out of guilt."

Alice flinched slightly at the harshness of his words.

"Because of the guilt you felt when Addie Durand was taken while under your watch?" she asked slowly. He nodded once, his mouth tight. The subject clearly annoyed him. "Sidney thought you couldn't be a good leader of Durand because of this guilt?"

"No. He expressed his doubt because he was concerned about me." He must have seen her confusion. "Sidney believes I should move out of the shadow of Durand. He thinks that I've chosen to remain eclipsed by the tragedies that happened when I was a teenager. He is of the opinion that I've chosen a life of guilt and oppression instead of freedom to choose my life's path." Alice was still bewildered. "Sidney believes that I'm obsessed with the topic of Addie Durand and her kidnapping," he snapped succinctly.

Alice's mouth fell open. She suddenly felt cold. So *this* was the source of the underground current of tension she felt at times between Dylan and Sidney.

And *this* was the source of Dylan's constant worry about her well-being and safety.

As Dylan's child therapist, Sidney had been privy to the harsh effects Addie Durand's kidnapping and presumed death had on an adolescent boy's mind. It made sense.

It made *horrible* sense. What if Dylan's intense attraction toward her was related? What if his involvement with her was some kind of psychological residue of their shared trauma?

Oh God. It was too much for her to consider right now, when

the entire structure of her life—her very identity—seemed to be crumbling all around her.

"You don't believe in Sidney's theories?" she asked shakily. Hopefully.

His hands slid down to her shoulders. He squeezed the muscles gently.

"There's a thread of truth there, of course. But I also understand that I was a kid at the time. I bear no responsibility for those criminals' greed. Their brutality. I *did* feel guilty and wish I could have done more. That's not obsession. That's human nature. But I'm not *oppressed* by guilt, Alice," he said firmly, squeezing her shoulders for emphasis. "My life choices have been the result of thought and planning, not a knee-jerk reaction of guilt toward Alan or Lynn Durand. Or you."

His eyes blazed when he said the last. It was impossible not to be relieved by his steadfastness. She nodded once, and she felt some of the tension leave his muscles.

"Was that the thing that bothered you the most about what Schaefer told you? That Sidney argued against my suitableness as CEO of Durand?"

"Yes," she said honestly. "I just feel so confused about . . ."

"What?"

"Who to trust."

"I can't make you trust me, Alice," he said. "But you *should*."

"I'm trying," she whispered.

"I know," he said more gently than she deserved. She felt so frayed, so pulled in so many directions. He massaged her shoulders. She sighed in relief. The miracles his touch could inspire. "Go on. You were upset by what Schaefer had said about Sidney and me. What happened next?"

"I just wanted to get away. To escape," she blurted out, feeling a small measure of the desperation she'd experienced at that moment. "To hide. I didn't tell myself to run upstairs, I just found myself doing it. My feet were taking me to that hiding place without my brain telling them to. And as I ran down the hallway, the memory just flashed into my brain. I distinctly remembered crouching in some dark place and hearing her voice—my mother's voice—calling out to me. It was a game we played. I heard her calling out to me a few times, when I was in bed with you."

"What?" Dylan asked, his brows furrowing.

"It was just my imagination," she said quickly, recognizing how strange that must have sounded to him. "My unconscious mind spitting up some buried memory. I *saw* her that night you found me in the hall, too. She wore this delicate, filigreed gold bracelet; the same one she wore in the newspaper clipping you showed me. I saw it perfectly. I heard her calling out a name. *My* name," she whispered.

She became aware she'd gotten lost in the sad, sweet potent memory and cleared her throat. "Anyway, as I ran down the hallway away from Thad, it hit me that this memory was different. It was *connected* to all these feelings, and it felt *so* real. She and I were playing when she called out like that. I'd hide, and I'd be so excited, hearing her voice as she moved around the house looking for me. She knew where I was all along," Alice said with a small smile. "Or at least she knew I was in one of several spots. She was the one who had showed me all the good hiding places."

Dylan's hand cradled the side of her head. Alice leaned into him, instinctively craving his touch. "And it was a good memory for you, wasn't it? You said it wasn't scary like you were worried it would be."

Emotion surged in her throat. She took a moment to find her voice.

"I thought it'd feel like someone else, like a stranger was taking over my mind," she gasped. "It wasn't, though. It felt like *me*. That was *my* memory." His thumb rubbed her cheek, and she realized a tear had fallen. "Even if it's the only memory of her I ever have, it was enough. Because so many feelings came with it. She *loved* me. She cherished me. I could feel it somehow, hear it in her voice. It was the air I breathed, the security of being loved. And underneath my excitement at playing the game, I felt so safe, so trusting that the next moment was going to be nice, and the moment after that, and after that. When I was that little girl crouching under those stairs, I didn't know the *meaning* of fear or want." She shook her head in frustration.

"What, baby?" he murmured, drying more of her tears with his thumb.

"It was incredible. I'm not saying it right," she said brokenly, referring to her trouble containing the profundity of her experience in words.

"You're saying it perfectly. If it hadn't been for that memory, I don't think you would have been ready to hear about Sissy tonight."

"What?"

"You never once asked me how you ended up with the Reeds," he said, his manner a little sad. "I knew it was because you weren't ready to hear what they'd done."

"But after remembering Lynn, I was?" she whispered. It made a weird kind of sense. That brief shining memory was an unshakable bedrock to her identity, something no one could ever take from her.

He grasped her head in both his hands and leaned forward to kiss her mouth tenderly. Alice sought out his warmth and hardness, pressing closer, sliding and biting at his lips with her own. She made a dissatisfied sound when Dylan moved back slightly. She stared into his deep eyes.

"It hasn't been an easy night. Let's go to bed," he said gruffly.

"*Yes.*"

SHE cleaned up in the bathroom first and emerged wearing the fluffy bathrobe Dylan had given her. He rose from where he'd been sitting at the edge of the bed, checking his cell phone messages. Their gazes locked as he passed her on the way to the bathroom. He reached out and palmed her jaw.

"You okay?" he asked in a low rumble, leaning down and kissing her temple.

She'd be a heck of a lot better once they were in bed together. "I'm fine."

He straightened and gave her a "spare me the act" look. She winced. "I'm a little overwhelmed."

His thumb traced her cheekbone gently. "An honest admission from Alice Reed. I'm impressed. Even if you are downplaying things drastically," he murmured, his mouth curving into a small smile.

"Dylan?"

"Yeah?"

"I know you said Alan Durand never gave up that . . . I could be alive." His nostrils flared slightly at her tentative "I"; at her referral to Addie and herself as the same person. It was going to take some getting used to. "But *you* didn't, either. You kept the faith the longest of anyone. I just want to say it again—thanks."

His expression turned very sober, even grim. He just nodded once and kissed her temple again with warm, lingering lips. "Get in bed. I'll be out in a minute," he said quietly, his mouth near her ear making her shiver.

After he'd gone into the bathroom and shut the door, she walked to the bed. Her fingers hesitated at the tie of her robe. Did he want to make love? She was a little confused by his manner tonight. He was so intense. So deep. It was as if their talk had begun to expose all of his layers, the manifold meanings of what Alan, Addie, and Durand Enterprises represented to him. It took her breath away, to consider that those folds and complexities of his character had been there already when she'd walked into the dean of business's office at Arlington College and saw him sitting behind that desk.

He was a mystery to her, and yet *she* was such an integral part of his enigma. Or at least Addie was.

She thought of what he'd said regarding Sidney's concerns for him. Sidney thought Dylan should have forged his life outside the long dark shadows of the Durands' tragic past. What if Dylan *had* gone away after he'd finished college and never returned to his history at the Durand Estate? Surely Alice wouldn't be standing there right now. But *if* by some miracle the truth about Addie Durand and the lies that constructed Alice's life miraculously came to light, what would it be like if Dylan wasn't there, holding her, reassuring her . . . touching her.

The thought chilled her to the bone. She drew off her robe. Even if he didn't want to make love after their emotional talk, she wasn't wearing pajamas underneath. Since they'd started having sex, she'd never once spent the night in anything but her own skin. She tossed the robe at the foot of the bed and climbed under the soft, luxurious sheets and comforter.

"He thinks that I've chosen to remain eclipsed by the tragedies that happened when I was a teenage boy. He is of the opinion that I've chosen a life of guilt and oppression instead of freedom to choose my life's path."

She shivered with cold and snuggled deeper in the covers. What if there was more than just a hint of truth to Sidney's concerns? What did it mean to Alice?

Her anxious thoughts scattered at the sound of the bathroom door opening. She watched as he walked toward the bed, her heart sinking a little when she saw he wore a pair of thin black lounge pants that hung low on his narrow hips and left little to the imagination. He was coming to bed dressed—partially anyway. His cut, powerful torso was stunningly bare.

Their conversation tonight had been heavy and stressful. She was being shallow and needy by thinking about sex at a moment like this. It was just that . . . she *did* need him. In so many ways. Sex had always been the most natural and comfortable way to express her inexplicably strong need for him.

He walked to the opposite side of the bed. She kept herself from rolling over to face him, ashamed of her desire. Repressed air made her lungs burn. He shut out the light, and she felt the mattress give beneath his weight. He scooted toward her. A ragged sigh left her throat when she felt his arms go around her. Clamping her eyes tight, she curled into him, her back against his chest, his groin pressing to the lower curve of her ass. For several taut moments, they didn't move or speak. Alice's throat felt so tight, she wasn't sure she *could*.

"What am I going to *do*?"

She gasped, half in shock she'd said the desperate words out loud. The question had been repeating in her brain over and over, but she hadn't planned to utter it. Dylan rubbed her upper arm in a slow, soothing gesture.

"You're going to keep moving forward, one day at a time. One hour. One minute, if need be. We both are. You go for the genetic testing on Saturday. That's another step in the process. Maybe next week, if you're interested, you could start to look at Alan's will and the details of his estate, get a grip on how he planned for Addie's potential return. I could have someone from the legal department come over and guide you through the trust, if you like. It's an airtight but complex document. Alice?" he prompted when she didn't respond.

"I don't know," she said brokenly. "It feels too soon for that."

It'll always feel like it's too soon. It always feels like it's too much. *I have to move forward, despite all of that.*

"I think what I'd like to start with for now is reviewing more of Durand's annual reports and getting a firm handle on the company's history and structure," she said. "That'd feel a little less . . . personal."

"If you think it'd help." He kissed the side of her neck. She felt him inhale with his nose pressed against her skin.

"Dylan?"

He made a deep humming noise.

"I'm not sure I'm as convinced as you are that someone hired Stout and Cunningham. But given that you believe it, do you really think that whoever it was could still be around? Is that why you're so protective of me?"

"Yes. And yes," he said against her neck.

"But even if that were true, they couldn't possibly know that *I* was . . . you know. Addie."

"Listen to me," he said abruptly close to her ear. His voice was quiet, but she recognized that steely tone. "I don't have the full picture. There are parts missing. I've been over and over Alan's original will and his current will and trust document. I can't figure out a monetary motive—then or now. The truth about your identity will eventually come out when you're ready. We have to prepare for it in the next few weeks. In the meantime, I'm still trying to figure out who would have had a motive for kidnapping and killing Addie. But that doesn't mean there isn't a potential threat out there. It was only twenty years ago. *Twenty years.* If someone wanted you dead once, there's good reason to assume they'd want it again. If that person was once associated with Cunningham, there's no reason Cunningham couldn't have told him what he told me. There's no telling who Cunningham dribbled the truth out to at the end of his life. It's not like he considered me special. I merely served a purpose to inflate his ego. Talking to me was a diversion from the boredom of prison life. Who else visited him? Did he confess to another prisoner? I'm *not* just being paranoid, Alice. If you take anything away from tonight, *please* let it be that."

She turned, stunned by his intensity.

"Okay. I'm sorry. It's just . . . Alice Reed's life is a lot simpler than Addie's," she said shakily, guilt sweeping through her at the memory of how she'd constantly needled and defied him in regard to his protective measures. It was easier to do, before she'd taken her first steps on the long journey of accepting she was Addie Durand.

He exhaled and pressed his forehead against hers. "I know. I understand. Will you please promise not to try to avoid Sal and Josh while you're down at the camp?"

"Yes," she whispered.

He kissed her mouth, deep and sweet, and she felt him stir against her backside. "It's been a rough night. Go to sleep," he whispered hoarsely after a moment.

"But . . ."

"Go to sleep," he repeated. She turned her cheek into the pillow, her mind and body awhirl.

"Alice?"

"Yes?"

"I can only imagine how hard this is for you. I'm proud of you."

"Thanks."

She closed her eyes. Her world still felt off-kilter, but repeating Dylan's words again and again in her head kept her steady.

SHE awoke in a split second, the sensation of Dylan's full, flagrant erection pressing against her bare bottom yanking her quickly and completely from the realm of sleep. The room was dark. His mouth moved against her neck, hot and voracious. He bit gently on her earlobe, his front teeth scraping her sensitive skin. She shivered in pleasure. The bedside light suddenly switched on to a dim setting.

"I want to see you," he muttered roughly, pulling his arm back. He spoke near her ear, amplifying her shivers. "You're too much of a temptation. I waited for most of the night, but I have to have you before you go. I'm that selfish."

She moaned as he pressed his lips to her pulse and lowered.

"Then I'm just as selfish," she whispered. "Because I wanted this from the second you came to bed."

"I was being sensitive."

"You can be sensitive and horny at once, can't you?"

She felt his breath puff against her skin and heard his gruff bark of laughter. "We really need to communicate better."

She turned in his arms. His mouth rained kisses on her chest, making her nipples tighten. She dug her fingers into his thick hair and urged him to her breasts. He made a rough sound in his throat and rolled partially onto her, pinning her down to the mattress. He sucked a nipple into his mouth, laving it with his tongue. Her clit pinched in arousal. She tangled her fingers deeper into his hair and arched her back, offering herself to him, crying out in pleasure.

"Stop twisting around," he growled amusedly. He molded both of her breasts in his hands, applying a slight downward pressure, keeping her steady for his onslaught. He slipped her other nipple into his mouth and drew on her. His obvious rabid hunger fueled her own arousal. She abandoned herself to the need mounting inside her. It felt so hot and delicious, the wet tug on her nipple and his rubbing tongue making her clit ache. She wanted his tongue there between her thighs, slippery and firm, licking her clit until she was in a frenzy of need. Just the thought of it made her hurt. She slid a hand between her thighs, finding the cleft between her labia warm and moist. For a moment, she rubbed herself while he squeezed her breasts gently and sucked first one nipple, and then the other.

His hand gripped her forearm. He ran it down until his fingertips found her first two fingers pressing against her clit. She paused in playing with herself, thinking he'd stop her. Dylan liked to be the one to be in control of her pleasure. She loved that about him.

But instead of halting her, he lowered his hand and plunged his middle finger inside her. Alice moaned and rubbed her clit harder.

He lifted his head slightly, his lips making a sucking sound as her breast popped out of his mouth. He lashed the sensitized crest with the tip of tongue.

"Let's communicate now," he said gruffly after a moment, his lips feathering over her wet nipple. "Tell me what you want."

"Your mouth on me," she said, the truth too sharp to keep inside her for long.

"Well, I want my cock in your mouth, so we're going to have to compromise," he said, a dark thread of humor in his tone. He moved quickly, withdrawing his finger, sitting up, and spinning onto his hands and knees, his head toward the foot of the bed. Alice watched as he straddled her and positioned himself over her, his groin hovering over her face. She shifted her pillow and her head, aligning herself, and reached for him eagerly.

He didn't immediately lower between her thighs. Instead, he watched her. Feeling his gaze on her while she stared at his cock tenting the front of his pajama bottoms excited her. She started to lower his waistband.

"There's a fly. Pull it through," he instructed her gruffly.

She found the opening in the pajamas and plunged her hand in, fisting his shaft. He felt warm and hard and so good. She jacked him a few times, her fingers lingering of the bulbous, smooth head.

"God, I love your cock."

"It returns the sentiment completely." He roughly pulled her hand out of his fly.

"Hey—"

"You're not moving fast enough. I want your mouth on me. Now," he grated out. He maneuvered his naked cock through the hole and bunched the fabric around his balls. It stuck out at a right angle from his body, looking both intimidating and exciting. He cupped his erection from below. "Open your mouth."

Arousal tore through her at his harsh demand. She loved it when his control began to fray. She parted her lips, saliva gathering on her tongue. He lowered his hips, guiding his cock into her waiting mouth. His cockhead pierced her, forcing her lips to stretch. She clamped him hard. He moaned and pushed the shaft onto her tongue.

"Suck, baby. Suck that cock."

She did, for all she was worth, her mouth and lips aching at the effort. She was so hungry for him, she lifted her head.

"Put your head back on the pillow," he demanded. "I'm going to come to you. Stay still."

He pulsed his hips, pushing his cock several inches in and out of her mouth. Now that he was fixed in her, he put his hand back on the bed, steadying himself. He continued to watch her as he fucked her mouth shallowly, his tight focus driving her mad with excitement. He pulsed his hips faster, although he refrained from going deep. She sucked so hard, her cheeks hollowed out.

"Such a hot little mouth. Do you like having it fucked?" he asked, his voice thick with arousal.

She moaned her assent, her mouth too full of turgid, thrusting cock to do anything else.

"Use your hand for the bottom," he said tersely. She gripped the lower part of his shaft and pumped him in unison with his thrusting hips. "God, that's good," he groaned roughly. "Spread your thighs, Alice."

She opened her legs wider on the mattress. He used his fingers to part her labia, and then his tongue slid into the cleft. She'd anticipated the moment so acutely, but nevertheless an electrical shock of pleasure went through her at his first touch. His mouth covered her, his lips applying a firm pressure on her outer sex. He applied a slight suction, his tongue stabbing and pressing against her clit, sliding and rubbing. She screamed, his plunging cock stifling her anguished bliss.

Everything blended in her brain, the sensation of his thrusting cock, his male taste, her own exquisite pleasure. The moment enfolded her. It insulated her from the harsh realities she was learning about herself, it protected her from her grief.

She took him deeper, because his pleasure was hers, the pulse in his cock matching the hammering in her ears, his harsh groans the voice of her ecstasy. They were one in those moments, a single, throbbing nerve.

He twisted his face slightly as he applied suction, the small, taut gesture sending her over the edge. He flexed his hips back, sliding his cock out of her mouth. Climax blasted through her. The scream that had been trapped in her throat was liberated. He continued to eat her with greedy focus while she came, laving her clit hard with his stiffened tongue.

She blinked her eyes open dazedly a moment later, her shudders waning. He'd turned and was crouching over her, his head facing hers. He was naked now, the warm glow of the bedside lamp gilding his skin. His arm muscles bulged as he held himself off her. His pelvis dipped downward. She gasped as he entered her. Instinctively, she bent her knees and lifted her feet off the bed, opening her body to better fit his heavy arousal. He snarled as he slid in her to the hilt, his facial muscles tight with pleasure.

He began to move, taking her with thorough, deep strokes, their stares locked. She read something in his gleaming eyes that made her desperate. She dug her fingertips into his dense shoulder muscles, straining to keep pace with him.

"If you were feeling like you didn't belong anywhere earlier when we talked, you can stop right now," he bit out. Her face tightened with emotion. How was he always able to read her mind? She gripped him tight as he rocked her harder, their bodies crashing together now, the crescendo reaching its peak. He thrust deep, grinding his pelvis against her outer sex. She moaned shakily at the sensation of swelling inside her. "Because you belong *here*. You're mine, Alice. And I'm yours," he said, his eyes fierce.

God, she wanted to believe him.

She felt his cock lurch. As he began to climax, his eyelids clamped shut. He groaned harshly and thrust while he poured himself into her. It moved her indescribably, to witness such a strong, sure man surrender himself so completely.

TWELVE

The next day was Saturday, and her duties at Camp Durand were finished by three o'clock. Dylan was taking her to the hospital at four for the genetic testing. She knew they wouldn't get the results for over a month, but she was still more nervous about the blood draw than she was letting on. As usual, she suspected Dylan was aware of her anxiety. They planned to meet at three thirty in the woods that bordered the castle like they had the previous Saturday. Dylan had asked Sal to watch over her for the first part of the trip. Then Dylan would watch her progress through the open field.

But instead, something happened to her that had never yet occurred while she was working at Camp Durand, something that seemed to signify the fact that Addie's and Alice's worlds were indeed moving closer together.

She and Dave were gathering their equipment after archery practice. It was a few minutes before three. The kids had already gone ahead to the cabin to meet up with the weekend supervisor and head over to the beach. Alice was searching for stray arrows at the edge of the field.

"You good?" Dave called to her from a distance. He pointed to the path. "There's something I need to take care of before the kids take off."

"Yeah, go," Alice yelled. "You have most of the stuff anyway," she said, referring to the fact that he carried the bulk of the archery equipment in two nylon sacks slung over his shoulders. She waved at his departing figure and scanned the edge of the field. In the distant woods, she noticed movement. A figure emerged from the tree line.

She remained still, wariness growing in her as Sal Rigo approached. What had made her bodyguard leave the shadows and seek her out?

"What is it?" she asked when Rigo was close enough for her to see the way the sun turned his graying blond crew cut into a pale silvery gold.

"Mr. Fall has asked that I take you all the way up to the castle."

"Why?" Alice demanded. "We weren't supposed to meet for another half hour."

"He didn't say why, I'm sorry."

It must be important, for Dylan to break protocol like this.

"If you'll follow me?" Rigo asked, his manner stiff and formal. "We'll stick to the woods as much as we can."

She fell into step beside him. They entered the woods a moment later, taking a worn foot trail Alice had never noticed before. It struck her that Rigo and Peterson, her two assigned guards, must really know these woods and grounds like the back of their hands if they did surveillance in them.

"This must be weird for you," Alice said as they crossed under the canopy of the trees.

"What?" Rigo asked, turning his chin over his shoulder to see her. The path wasn't large enough for them to walk side by side.

"Hanging out with me, when you're so used to slinking around in the shadows."

He faced forward again, his stride never breaking. "I'm just doing my job, ma'am."

"Did you already know the layout of these woods? Before you came to Camp Durand to . . . you know. Follow me?"

"My job is to watch over you as best I can while the camp is under way," he corrected shortly. "And the answer is yes. A few of us who work in Durand security are trained for the estate. We provide security during a lot of company functions here. We need to know every square inch of the property."

"Do you like it?" He turned his chin over his shoulder again. "Your job. Do you like working in Durand security?"

"Yes, ma'am."

"Not very chatty, are you?" she said under her breath, jogging to keep up with his long-legged pace. He must have noticed, because he slowed.

"It's a good company. Mr. Fall is a good boss, even though he's not my direct boss."

"Kehoe is, right?"

"Mr. Hintzen is my department head. Mr. Kehoe is only my supervisor while I'm here at camp."

"When Dylan isn't overriding his orders?" Rigo gave her an impassive glance over his shoulder that seemed like an affirmation. "You don't like him, do you?"

"Who?"

"Kehoe," Alice said breathlessly as they emerged from the woods into the sunny meadow.

"It's not my place to like or dislike him."

"You don't."

She assumed she was right when he didn't argue.

She was curious about the man who had been lurking around all this time, watching her. He seemed to shy away from questions about his assigned mission, though. Undeterred, she jogged up next to him.

"What do you think of Bang?"

He looked a little startled.

"What do I think of *bang*?"

"Yeah. You know, the goat from Camp Wildwood. Do you think Kehoe will come down hard on kids if they sneak over there?"

"Why are you asking me?"

"Because you're a Camp Durand manager in addition to watching over me. You hang around Kehoe and the others all the time. You must have *some* inside scoop."

He seemed to consider this for a moment as they walked.

"No. Mr. Kehoe has a pretty tolerant attitude about it. Kids have been stealing and returning that statue for years."

"That's what I thought," Alice said as they entered the woods again. A moment later, they broke the tree line and trudged up the steep slope of the side yard of the castle.

He halted at the edge of the stone terrace and nodded toward the patio doors. "They're open. He's in the den."

"Thanks. Nice getting to know you," she added drolly, because getting to know Rigo was like familiarizing yourself with a walking rock.

"You aren't easy to guard," he stated bluntly.

"I'll try to be easier, now that we're such good friends."

"Don't be too easy. You're observant. Quick. Those aren't things you should change."

Maybe she was wrong about the rock thing, because the stone gave her a small smile before he turned away.

ALICE pulled up short ten feet away from Dylan's den when the door whipped open. Thad stalked out, looking tense and preoccupied. He halted upon seeing her, seeming as startled as she was.

"Alice."

"Thad. What are you doing here?"

She heard a solid tread on the wood floor.

"He was just leaving," Dylan said as he crossed the threshold. "I'm going to see him out. Go on in and make yourself comfortable, Alice." Before Alice could think of anything to say, she was staring at both men's retreating backs.

Dylan returned a moment later, shutting the door quietly behind him. Her heart jumped when he locked it.

Alice watched him over her shoulder as he approached and went behind his desk. He was dressed for work at the office. He wore a dark gray suit that was perfectly tailored to his tall muscular frame. His dark hair was groomed immaculately, the hairline at his nape crisply trimmed. Had he gotten his hair cut today? When he'd escorted her from the castle early this morning, his thick, lustrous hair had been mussed and wild from her delving fingers, his jaw and lip shadowed with whiskers. He'd smelled of spice and outdoor air and sex.

She was a little intimidated by the reappearance of the business mogul. Her stomach felt tight and hollow. She'd chosen to sit in one of the leather chairs in front of the massive desk. While she waited, she'd noticed his discarded glasses on the blotter along with several reports opened to various pages, as though he'd been comparing numbers. It suddenly struck as he sat why she felt anxious. The situation had reminded her of her nerve-wracking interview with him last spring.

"Why did you ask Thad to come up here? Did you threaten him again?"

"I'm more concerned about what threat he poses to us, to be honest," he replied dryly. He noticed her mutinous glance. "He's admitted to following you at times without your knowledge, Alice."

"I told you he's infatuated with me. It doesn't make him a bad guy," she said, uncomfortable with the information despite her continued defense of Thad.

"Do you ever see Schaefer talking privately or behaving suspiciously in any way with anyone on this list?"

Her pique of irritation evaporated as she leaned forward to better see the piece of paper Dylan had shoved toward her. "I don't even know who some of these people are," she said, confused. "Who's Meg Everett?"

"She was a good friend of Lynn Durand's. She still lives in Morgantown. Her husband, Rob, is a Durand exec."

"Oh, this is the *list*. The one you were telling me about last night, the list of people who could potentially have hired Cunningham and Stout, were around at the time of the kidnapping, and possibly knew our whereabouts on that day?"

He nodded. She peered again at the list.

"Why would Thad be talking to Meg Everett? Or *Sidney Gates*?" she asked incredulously, re-skimming the list. Some of the people she recognized as camp employees, but most of the names made no sense in regard to association with Thad.

"You're under the impression that Thad doesn't know Sidney personally?"

She shrugged and tossed the now memorized list back on the blotter. "I don't know." It bothered her, hearing about this secretive side of Thad. "Although he obviously knows who Sidney is, given what he told me the other night about Sidney objecting to you becoming CEO of Durand. And he seemed to recognize Sidney at the party."

He nodded, watching her from beneath his lowered brow like a hawk. "Because Sidney says he's never met Schaefer. Sidney was talking to you the other night at the Alumni Dinner. You looked upset. What did he say?"

"Is *that* why you asked me to come up here early?" she asked, bewildered.

"I'd like an answer."

She sighed. "He was saying some stuff about Alan and Lynn Durand. Just about how they had trouble getting pregnant, and how much it upset Lynn." Dylan looked especially somber. "It was fine. I wasn't upset," Alice lied. "*He* doesn't seem to think I'm so fragile that I can't hear about the Durands. In fact, he thinks I should see him on a professional basis and talk about Alan and Lynn more."

"He said that?" Dylan asked very quietly.

"Yes. Not because he thinks I'm a potential resident for the local insane asylum. Because he thinks it'd be healthy for me. Helpful. Don't you?" she asked, confused by his manner. Was he actually suspicious of *Sidney* now?

He didn't speak for several seconds, his gaze fixed on his desk.

"Yes, I suppose I do," he finally replied. He lifted one hand and gave her a beckoning gesture. "Come here."

"What?" she asked, taken off guard by his request.

"Come. Here," he repeated, quietly but succinctly.

She rose from her chair, her pulse starting to throb at her throat. Sunlight glowed through the partially closed blinds on the windows behind his desk.

She came up next to him. Holding her stare, he rolled back the large leather wingback desk chair in which he sat. She gulped at the vision of male power he made, the strength of his chest, shoulders, and thighs evident beneath his tailored suit. Her gaze lingered on his gray and white silk tie and the crisp, snowy dress shirt beneath it. She recalled how on the day of her interview, she'd had a vivid, shockingly inappropriate fantasy of unbuttoning his shirt and sliding her hand against dense, ridged muscles gloved by smooth, warm skin. Her glance lowered further still.

Had she gleaned somehow even back then, what their future held?

"What is it?" she asked uncertainly, jerking her gaze off his crotch.

"I hadn't realized until yesterday that you'd had such a clear memory of Lynn that night in the hall," he said. "Of the bracelet." He reached into his top desk drawer and withdrew a dark red velvet box. He handed it to her.

Alice opened the box, and there it was: the bracelet in waking reality.

She swallowed thickly and touched it. It was like a cuff, but it was supple and flexible. Delicate vines and leaves surrounded it, but intertwined in the webwork of finely wrought gold were interspersed . . .

"Sunflowers," she murmured. "They turn their faces to the sun. I remember . . ."

"What?" Dylan asked when she faded off.

"Someone telling me that. *Her*, I think."

She met his stare, her eyes burning. Miraculously, she'd been granted another tidbit of memory.

"There are more of her things, besides the bracelet and the pearls. They're yours anytime you want them."

"The pearls you gave me the other night? They were hers?"

He nodded once. "I wasn't sure if you were ready to know then. I am now."

She studied the bracelet intently, trying to keep him from seeing the tears that had swelled in her eyes. She cleared her throat. "I thought you gave them to me to make me look like a rich heiress or something," she mumbled.

"What?" he asked, clearly confused.

She sniffed. "It's not important. I didn't really believe that anyway," she said honestly. "Just my insecurity talking."

"Do you want me to put it on you?" he asked after a pause.

"Please." She handed him the exquisite bracelet and set the box down on the desk. She extended her arm, and he fastened the bracelet around her wrist. Alice lifted her hand and let the ambient sunlight flicker among the vines. She looked at Dylan and beamed.

"You're happy?" he asked quietly.

"Very," she said. It was impossible to stop grinning, even though her eyes still brimmed with tears.

He reached for her hand. "Come here," he said again.

She kicked off her flip-flops and straddled his legs, her bare knees pressing against the soft leather seat. She came down in his lap, facing him. He opened his hands on her ass and scooted her closer on his thighs. He enfolded her into his arms. She hugged him back tight, her chin resting on his shoulder. She felt so *full* of something: Gratitude. Wonder. Joy.

"I love you," she said in a hoarse, congested whisper.

He put his hands on her shoulders and pushed her back several inches. She resisted the urge to hide her face and damp cheeks in his neck.

"You don't have to say that because I gave you the bracelet. It wasn't even mine to give. It belonged to Lynn, so it now belongs to you."

She gave a ragged laugh and rolled her eyes. "Give me some credit. That's not why I'm saying it."

A small smile tilted his mouth. His eyes shone. Her heart seemed to squeeze in her chest. Her admission had made him happy. It had made her happy, too, despite her former anxiety about it.

"I've felt it for a while." She shrugged. "I just . . . didn't know if—"

"You could trust it?" he asked calmly, lifting his hand and cupping the side of her head.

She bit her lower lip, her gaze cast downward. "I didn't know how to say it," she admitted. "I've never said it before." He delved his fingers into her hair. Her eyelids flickered in contentment when he massaged her scalp. "Was it . . . was it hard for you?" she asked.

"To tell you I love you?"

Her heavy eyelids sprang open at the sound of his deep, rich voice uttering those words.

"Yes," she whispered.

"At first. I've told you before I've never been much of a romantic. But at some point, it starts to feel like denying the sky is blue."

She just nodded, her throat too constricted to think for a moment. "I don't know what it means, exactly."

"You don't have to sign a contract because you say you love someone, Alice."

She laughed. "I know. I mean . . . I *guess* I do, anyway. Lately, it doesn't feel like I know much of anything anymore." Her gaze ran over his face. "We have such a complicated, long history. And at the same time . . . everything feels so new," she confessed. He probably had no idea what she was talking about. Alice wasn't sure *she* did.

His thumb swept over her cheek softly.

"We'll do it just like we're going to do everything else. One day at a time."

She nodded, recognizing she was staring at him with hope in her eyes. He noticed, and his expression turned sober. He cupped the back of her head and brought her to him. His kiss started out tender, but emotion frothed in her. She kissed him back feverishly, her tongue tangling with his. She slid her hands against the solid wall of his chest, relishing his hardness and the steady beat of his heart. Beneath her, she felt him stiffen. She ground her hips down against his crotch in order to feel him better. Her fingers found the knot of his tie. She broke their kiss, gasping, and jerked, hearing the hiss of silk as she loosened it.

"There's no time. We have to leave for the hospital in a few minutes," she said against his mouth.

"Then why are you undressing me?"

She blinked in surprise when she glanced down. She'd not only loosened his tie but had the first two buttons of his shirt unfastened and was working on the third.

"Because I want to touch you," she replied honestly, wasting no time in sending her hand in the opened placket of his shirt. She caressed dense muscle and crisp hair. When she found a small, erect nipple and rubbed it, his mouth went hard. He abruptly grabbed the hand stuck in his shirt and lifted it over her head along with her other wrist. He whipped her T-shirt off over her head and arms in a second flat, tossing it on the floor. Her sports bra soon followed.

"Only a fool doesn't make time for this," he stated gruffly, caressing her appreciative nipples too briefly before he turned his focus to unfastening her shorts.

"Do you really think it's wise?" Alice asked, coming up on her knees to assist him as he jerked her shorts down over her ass.

"Who said it had anything to do with wisdom? Stand up for a second."

She scooted awkwardly back on his thighs, her breasts swaying at the movement. He growled softly and leaned forward, halting her progress by cupping her breasts in his hands, his thumbs running over her nipples.

"God, your breasts," he muttered, his mouth slanting like he'd just been stabbed by sexual hunger. Alice knew exactly what it felt like. It must have been a result of all the emotion that'd been bursting out of her, but she suddenly felt desperate. She moaned and arched her back shamelessly, willing him to touch her more. He gave her what she wanted momentarily, molding her breasts to his hands and gently pinching and rubbing her nipples until they were distended and stiff. He lifted the globes and let them fall, only to catch them again as they bounced softly. Another moan vibrated her throat. He glanced up at the sound, his eyes shiny with lust.

"Stand up and slip out of your shorts."

She stood and shoved her shorts and panties down her legs. She straightened, now naked. Dylan was in the process of hastily unfastening his belt and pants. He hooked his thumbs beneath his boxer briefs and stretched the waistband over his erection. Lifting his hips, he pushed his clothing down to his thighs, sat and reached for her in a seamless, hasty movement. Alice once again straddled him in the chair, her breathing coming in choppy bursts.

He fisted his cock, stroking it as he guided her over him.

A moment later, she stared blindly out the window clutching his shoulders as he throbbed deep inside her. He urged her with his hands. Air popped out of her lungs as she began to rise and fall over him.

"That's right," he told her, his gaze glittering as he watched her. Still setting the pace with one hand cupping her ass, he ran a palm along the curve of her hip to her waist and along the side of her body. He caressed her neck and brushed her cheek. "So beautiful. You're glowing, Alice" he muttered, seemingly transfixed.

"Dylan," she whispered, laid wide open to him. He cradled a breast and whisked his fingertips over the crest. She whimpered in pleasure, her hips moving faster.

He caught her to him, his hands at her lower back. He impaled her and kept her fixed in place. She cried out when he took a nipple into his mouth, sucking her hotly. She squirmed in his lap. His greed excited her. He was hurting her a little with his brisk suck, but pleasuring her a lot. Her nails bit into dense shoulder muscles. She pushed, desperate to feel the friction of his cock.

He grunted and lifted his mouth for a moment. He grabbed her wrists and drew them to the small of her back. Alice arched her back, bobbing her hips subtly to get friction on her clit. He firmed his grip on both of her wrists and slapped her bottom.

"Why do you always have to be so bad?" he wondered before he spread his hand on her hip and applied pressure, stifling her wriggling. He'd said "bad" but the edge of lust in his tone made it sound like he'd said "good." He sucked her other breast into his mouth, lashing the nipple with his tongue. Alice moaned uncontrollably. Her spine curved as she offered herself to him again.

His thick shaft filling her was driving her mad. It applied an indirect pressure on her clit. It was impossible not to try to shift her hips, but he held her fast. A sweat broke out on her chest and upper lip, the fever in her seeking an outlet. He continued to torture her breasts and sensitive nipples with his tongue and fingertips.

"Oh, please. Fuck me," she begged, unable to stand it any longer. She strained against his hold on her wrists, longing to grip his shoulders so she could ride his cock. He tightened his hold on her.

He lifted his head and ran the tip of his firm tongue over her distended nipple. She quaked.

"You don't want to fuck. You want to come," he said. He grasped her hip and worked his thumb between her labia. He sucked her nipple back in to his mouth while he rubbed and pressed her clit. Alice jumped in his lap. He applied a firmer pressure on her hips, fixing her in place on his lap while he played with her.

While he made her burn. Her clit began to sizzle beneath the pad of his thumb.

"Oh no. No, I want to fuck," she moaned, mindless with mounting pleasure. He continued lashing and sucking on her nipple, too focused on his task to pay her heed. "Dylan," she cried out desperately after a moment.

He lifted his head and flicked at her nipple with his tongue. Alice's feet curled in pleasure. "Come for me, and then I'll give you what you want," he assured before he ran his lips over her wet nipple slowly, as if he wanted to feel every tiny bump to the fullest. It was a sweet erotic gesture, making her clamp him tight inside her. He cursed under his breath.

"Come for me, Alice."

The hand gripping her hip pressed down and then lifted her slightly, urging her. He granted her enough movement that she could bob a mere inch up and down on his cock. When she recognized the freedom, she shifted her hips rapidly, riding him. Her tensing bottom slapped against his hard thighs, the fast, staccato rhythm betraying her desperation. His thumb moved faster on her clit, a slick, firm command.

"Oh—"

He released her wrists and pushed her roughly to him. His mouth covered hers as she began to shudder in climax. He pushed his tongue between her lips, greedily eating her cries and whimpers as pleasure shook her. She was still coming when he lifted her off him. The deprivation was cruel. She cried out at the loss.

"Hold on," he said tensely. He moved to the edge of the chair and stood, lifting her with him. When her feet touched the oriental carpet, he turned her so that she faced the desk. He pushed lightly at her shoulders, urging her. "All the way down," she heard him say. Panting erratically, she pressed her forearms, cheek, breast, and belly to the scattered Durand reports on his blotter, her bottom curving over the edge of the desk. The paper and blotter felt cool against her aroused nipples and hot cheek.

Then he was entering her. She gasped loudly at the impact.

He set a fast, forceful pace from the first. Instinctively, she reached above her head and gripped the far edge of the desk. Her lips parted and a shaky moan slipped between them. Her eyes rolled back in her head as pressure and pleasure pummeled her consciousness. Once he was ready, Dylan always ended up giving her exactly what she wanted.

He grunted roughly and grasped her ass tighter, serving her to his thrusting cock.

"Is this what you wanted, little girl?" he bit out between the lewd slaps as their bodies crashed together.

"*Yes.*"

He slipped his hand beneath her lower thigh, still thrusting his cock in and out of her. He lifted her leg, forcing her knee to bend. Alice guessed his intent and put one knee on the top of the desk, opening her body even more to him. He plunged deep, and she cried out at the fresh burst of friction and harder pressure. He fucked her faster.

"You make me crazy," he said from behind her, his tone harsh from driving lust. He grunted in pleasure, and the imagined vision of his focused, controlled savagery leapt into her mind's eye. He thrust using nearly the entire length of his cock, his strong arms propelling her, crashing her body into him in a brutally concise counter rhythm to his hips. She clamped her eyes shut, overwhelmed by sensation, emotion ready to spill out of her at any moment.

"Tell me," he demanded. "Tell me again."

"I . . . love . . . you," she gasped as he pounded into her.

His hands came down next to her elbows on the desk. He thrust at a downward angle, his strokes shorter and faster, their bodies smacking together. He shook her to her very core.

"Oh God," she moaned, gripping the desk like she thought her life depended on it.

"Alice."

He sounded as full of sensation and feeling as she was. His cock swelled in her. He plunged deep, groaning roughly. He kept his pelvis locked tight to her and circled his hips slightly, applying a jaw-popping pressure on her clit.

They remained locked like that, joined in rictus of combined, intense pleasure. Alice wished the moment could last forever. But after a dazed moment, his shudders of climax began to differentiate from hers. Slowly, the sound of their harsh breathing slowed and quieted in her ears. Alice inhaled shakily, fully catching her breath for the first time in minutes.

She felt his lips press to her spine. His cock twitched in her channel.

"Should I be sorry?" he asked against her skin.

"God, no," she whispered, confused by the question. "Why would you be sorry?"

He straightened and pulled her up off the desk, his hands on her shoulders. He wrapped her upper body in his arms. Alice closed her eyes, feeling utterly sated and content.

"Seems like it should have been a little more soulful, after what you just told me," he said, his mouth pressed against her neck. She sensed his small smile. "But you drive me crazy every damn time."

She gave a throaty laugh and clasped his forearms. "I could say the same about you. And I love it." His cock slid from her body and he turned her in his arms. He leaned down and kissed her deeply.

"Soulful and wild. Strong and commanding. Focused and

brilliant," she murmured dreamily against his lips a moment later. His taste still lingered on her tongue; her nerves still tingled with pleasure from his powerful presence in her body. "That's you, isn't it? Why would you make love any different?" She blinked her eyes open wider, bringing him into focus. "Why would I ever want anything else?" she wondered, her brow crinkling in dazed puzzlement.

His expression sobered. She recognized the hard telltale glint in his eyes. She lifted her mouth to meet his, eager to be claimed once again.

THIRTEEN

After Alice had hastily washed up, she met Dylan downstairs in the foyer.

"We should only be a few minutes late for the appointment if we hurry," she said jogging down the stairs.

He waited for her patiently, looking handsome and unruffled once again in his immaculate suit and tie. Alice took his outstretched hand when she neared him.

"What are you frowning about?" Dylan asked.

"You have a lot of nerve, looking like that when I look like *this* afterward." She referred to the fact that her cheeks were still flushed bright pink in the aftermath of amazing sex, she was panting and sweating a little from running around trying to get ready for the doctor's visit in a rush. Plus, her hair looked like a mop had been dropped on her head, it was getting so long and unruly. To make things worse, her hair color was starting to look bizarre. Parts of the dyed dark brown portion had lightened and faded in the sun, and her reddish undertones and roots were starting to shine through.

Dylan examined her calmly. "You look beautiful."

She made a disgusted sound. He smiled.

"I'm serious. Your eyes are shining and you're flushed." He lifted a hand and brushed a warm cheek. "It's my favorite way to see you."

She gave him a wry grin. "That's because you like to strut over the fact that you made me that way."

"Caught in the act, but far from guilty," he replied, dropping his hand and landing a kiss on her mouth. His smile faded as he leaned back and studied her more closely. "Can you do me a favor, though? Start wearing the makeup on your eyes again."

"What? I thought you hated it."

"I do," he murmured, his gaze still pinned on her face. "But your similarity to Lynn is starting to become more and more obvious. I don't want anyone else to notice. The least we can do is hide it a little longer."

"I . . . yeah, sure, I guess," she said dubiously, shrugging. She started toward the stairs. "Just let me run back up to the bathroom and grab some makeup. I'll put it on in the car on the way to the hospital."

"And Alice?" he called a few seconds later.

She paused mid-stride on the stairs and looked back at him. He nodded at her wrist. "The bracelet. Take it off for now. You can wear it while you're here if you like, but not outside until things are settled. Lynn always wore it. It was her trademark."

"Yeah. I know," she said, pausing a beat before she raced back up the stairs.

When she came back down, he took her hand and they headed toward the garage entrance. They both halted when there was a knock on the front door.

"What the—" Dylan headed for the door, eyebrows slanted in consternation.

A tall man in his late thirties with a thin, gaunt face stood on the top step wearing coveralls.

"I'm here from Home Guard to do the maintenance on the security system," Alice heard the man say. Dylan peered at his identification badge.

"Damn it, I forgot about this," Dylan said. "I'm on the way out. Let me get my housekeeper. Come in."

He flew up the staircase in search of Louise. His efficient, neat housekeeper returned with him a minute later.

"Were both Louise and Marie in the house while we were in the den?" Alice asked once they were on the road to the hospital a few minutes later. She'd been so *loud* while they were making love, she realized uncomfortably.

Dylan gave her a brief, amused glance, clearly guessing the origin of her concern.

"I sent Marie home early. Louise was there, but she's working on a special project for me up on the fourth floor. She was far enough out of hearing range. Even for *you*."

Alice snorted in embarrassed laughter. It was nice, to laugh a little before the stressful appointment.

"Aren't you worried about someone seeing us together at the hospital?" she asked Dylan after he'd parked the sedan and they were hastily walking to the main entrance of Morgantown Memorial.

"A little," he admitted, holding the door open for her. "But not enough not to bring you myself."

She gave him a grateful glance. He noticed, his mouth tilting into a small smile.

"Once we get to the waiting area, I'll let you check in. I'll wander around in the vicinity, but I won't be far off. That should minimize the chances of being seen."

The blood test itself was pretty anticlimactic, given the buildup of her anxieties about it. She'd assumed she'd be meeting Lynn and Alan Durand's personal physician during the blood draw, Dr. Shineburg. The doctor must know something about Alice and Addie Durand, because Dylan had asked him to confirm she was their biological child using Alice's blood sample and the Durand's remaining genetic material. Instead of a physician being there, however, she was greeted by a friendly young female phlebotomist.

She explained to Alice that Dr. Shineburg had been called for an emergency. As a result, the blood draw itself felt like more of a technical matter than the emotional one she was both anticipating and dreading.

After the procedure was complete, Alice walked down the hallway in the direction of the waiting room clutching a patient informational pamphlet from a laboratory called GenCorp in Chicago, which would perform the genetic comparison analysis and provide her with results. According to what she'd briefly read as the phlebotomist had taken blood, she'd have the results in four to six weeks, but they were going to try to put a rush on it.

Where will I be when I get the results?

The question slammed into her like a fist to the head.

"Miss? Are you all right?"

Alice blinked, rising out of a daze. She realized she was standing still next to a parked wheelchair and a middle-aged nurse was watching her with a part-curious, part-concerned expression on her face.

"I . . . yeah, I'm fine," Alice said hollowly. "I felt a little dizzy there for a second."

"Did you just give blood?" the nurse asked kindly.

"Yeah."

The nurse nodded. "Why don't you go on back to the phlebotomist station and sit down. They have juice and cookies there."

"No," Alice said, smiling stiffly. "I'm fine. Thanks."

She started down the hallway again. It hadn't been the blood draw that had made her dizzy. It was the fact that Camp Durand finished in a week's time, and she had no idea what the hell she was going to do with her life after it was over.

What if I'm not selected as a Durand manager? Should I go back to Maggie's and start looking for another job? That was the original plan. But I can't act like Addie Durand never existed, especially once I get the official testing results. What if I am selected as a manager? Wetting my feet as a Durand junior executive would be a good way to find my way in the company. In my life. But what if the position offered to me wasn't in Morgantown?

What about Dylan?

What if Dylan was wrong, and I'm not actually Alan and Lynn Durand's child?

Where the hell do I belong?

She continued her walk to the waiting room on rubbery legs, these questions and more crashing and colliding in her head, leaving her in a cloud of blank, numbing anxiety.

The waiting room was nearly empty except for an older man reading a newspaper. She glimpsed Dylan's singular form in the far hallway. He was standing next to a bulletin board and talking to someone in hushed tones. Should she just sit down, and wait for his acquaintance to leave? she wondered nervously. She and Dylan weren't supposed to making their connection public.

But then Dylan glanced around and saw her. He beckoned.

"Sidney, hello," Alice said a second later when she rounded the corner and saw whom Dylan had been talking to. She took his extended hand and Sidney leaned down to briefly kiss her cheek. "What are you doing here?"

"I had to admit a patient, unfortunately, and I was on my way out when I saw Dylan." He blinked and sobered. "Are you all right, Alice?"

"Yeah, I'm great," she said too brightly and emphatically. Hearing the psychiatrist mention having to admit one of his patients into the hospital had pricked a nerve. Not that Alice really considered herself psych ward material. Still, she was keen to prove to the two men—and herself—that she was perfectly fine. "Did Dylan mention why we were here?" she asked, quieting her voice.

"Yes," Sidney said. "Are you all set, then?"

Alice held up the pamphlet and put on her game face. "Yes. All that's left to do is wait for official results."

Sidney gave her a wry smile. "That's only step one. Working through what step one really means to you is going to be the hard part. If only it *were* as simple as giving blood and getting an answer."

"True," Alice conceded. She glanced at Dylan uncertainly. "Did . . . did you tell him about what I remembered?" she asked softly.

"I did. I hope that's all right," Dylan said.

"It's okay," Alice assured.

"It sounds as if the memory of Lynn moved you very deeply," Sidney said quietly.

Tears sprang into her eyes, surprising her. Something about Sidney's kind, compassionate gray eyes that had done it. God, she was turning into a wreck. "It was," she managed, her stiff smile quivering. "It was incredible."

"Alice—"

"I think I'll just run to the ladies' room before we go?" she said in an unnaturally high-pitched voice, looking down the hallway and interrupting Dylan.

Dylan looked like he was about to halt her.

"There's one right there," Sidney said, pointing to a door twenty feet down the hall.

"Thanks. Right back," she said with a smile that was completely at odds with her brimming eyes.

"YOU have to tell her, Dylan," Sidney said quietly when the bathroom door shut behind Alice.

Dylan frowned. "You just saw her. She's not ready for it. She likes to act like everything is fine, but she's more fragile than she wants to admit."

"I'm not so sure anymore. She's not fragile by nature. Her defenses have been compromised due to all the psychological and emotional stress. But that doesn't mean she won't be able to take it, eventually. She has to be told sometime."

"If she was ready to know, she'd ask. That's what you've been preaching all along," Dylan hissed. He glanced around warily, making sure no one was around. He and Sidney had had this conversation several times in the past few days, and it was getting more and more trying each time. "The truth about Sissy and her uncles came to her once she was ready . . . once she had that memory of Lynn to cling to. Now you expect me to taint *that* memory for her as well?"

"It's not a matter of *you* doing anything harmful to her. These are facts. It's her history. She deserves to know. Events are going to start unfolding now; things that neither you nor Alice can control. Better the truth comes from you than from a stranger."

He made a frustrated sound. Sidney was right, and yet—

"You weren't there," Dylan said edgily. "You don't know what it was like, telling her that the woman whom she considered her mother was a knowing accomplice to her kidnapping."

"No, but I can imagine how difficult it was for you," Sidney replied. "Neither of us thought any of this process was going to be easy, and yet here we are, getting through a step at a time, right along with Alice."

"What I'm experiencing is nothing compared to what it must be like for her," Dylan said grimly. His gaze sharpened on his old friend. "And since when are you such an advocate for aggressive action when it comes to this topic? Since when did you stop advising caution when it comes to exposing her past to her, or subtle nudging at worst."

"Since I met her," Sidney said without pause. "She's quite unique, and very strong in her own way. The news from the camp is that she continues to excel and demonstrate unique leadership ability. This despite what we know about all she's endured this week."

Dylan grimaced, partially mollified but not convinced. "What have you heard about Kehoe's temperature when it comes to hiring her—not that it makes an ounce of difference in the end," he added.

"She's a top runner for a position, although I get the impression Kehoe is looking for any excuse to push her down lower on the list."

Dylan shook his head. "I wish I got him. He's always performed at the highest level, for Alan and for us, but he's . . ."

"Got his own agenda. And he's not an easy man to warm up to," Sidney finished for him. "I remember Alan was ambivalent about Kehoe, but his work was always top notch. It was Lynn who admired what he'd done with the camp so much. You know the camp was always her baby. She and Kehoe collaborated on it a great deal to make it what it is today: a valuable program that demonstrates every aspect of Durand's philosophy while seamlessly benefitting children at the same time. I think if it weren't for Lynn valuing Kehoe so much, Alan might have shifted Kehoe to some foreign office years back."

"I didn't know Alan wasn't particularly fond of him," Dylan said. *Or that Lynn* was. The sound of the hand dryer going on in the bathroom down the hall distracted him. He turned toward the door.

"She's shaken some by having the testing done today, Dylan," Sidney said quietly. "It hasn't defeated her, though. I'm beginning to wonder what would. You're going to have to tell her how Lynn died eventually."

He pressed his mouth together, unwilling to promise the psychiatrist anything yet. Alice was his sole guide in this, not Sidney.

"DID you plan ahead for us to ride at Riley Stables this evening?" Alice asked him in amazement ten minutes later. They were flying down the rural route that followed the Lake Michigan shoreline, Dylan at the wheel. He'd just told her they were going to ride and then have dinner.

"I did. I have some clothes for us to change into in the trunk. You seemed a lot more comfortable on Kar Kalim yesterday morning, so I thought the time might be right for another lesson."

He referred to the fact that after she'd dodged her follower and they'd had that impulsive, scorching tryst in the woods, he'd taken her back to the stables on his horse.

"I was too busy thinking about other things to be nervous," she said wryly. "But I *was* more relaxed than I was with Quinn. Kar Kalim is an amazing horse."

"So you don't mind?"

"No," she said honestly. "It sounds nice."

In fact, it had been a unique and wonderful experience for her last Saturday, to go to the stables and their special dinner, to escape for a period of time from the shadows and mysteries of Castle Durand . . . to share stolen moments with Dylan. It'd felt as if an entire new aspect of her personality had flowered, being with him on that sunny day and romantic, star-filled night. The Durand home and grounds drew her in so many ways, but there was a darkness to it, too, an oppression that felt so hard for her to shake at times.

Presently, sunshine filled the sedan and glowed all around them like a warm embrace. Dylan looked so handsome and in control behind the wheel of the luxury sedan, his suit jacket in the backseat and his tie loosened. She felt happy. The moment of existential angst she'd experienced at the hospital had entirely faded, thank God. Dylan was right. They just needed to deal with things one moment at a time.

He glanced over at her and did a double take.

"Why are you smiling?" he asked, his mouth twitching.

"I'm just glad you planned this. That's all."

He arched his brows, staring at the road again. "Then I'm glad. I was worried about you, back there at the hospital."

"I'm fine," she assured. She was starting to feel like a tape recording, saying that over and over again.

He gave her a quick smile that went all the way to his eyes, and Alice experienced a rush of relief. He wasn't going to push her into talking about what had happened at the hospital. Not now, he wasn't.

"Do you want to try riding on your own this time?" he asked her.

"Do you think I'm ready for that?"

"With the right mount, I think you were born ready."

OF course, Dylan had already discussed with Kevin Riley, the owner of Riley Stables, what he considered to be the *right* mount for Alice. After they'd changed into riding clothes, Dylan and Kevin introduced Alice to the horse. She was a beautiful gentle mare with a glossy mahogany coat and liquid brown eyes. She was much smaller and more delicate than Quinn or Kar Kalim, which Alice appreciated. Her fear of heights and falling had not disappeared by any means, and she doubted it ever would entirely—especially now that she knew the original cause of her phobia. But the pretty mare was a lot less intimidating than either Quinn or Kar Kalim.

For Alice, it was love at first sight. Her name was Shenandoah, but Kevin called her Doah for short. Alice did, too, as she petted and murmured nonsense to the patient, appreciative mare.

"I guess you know how to pick them," Kevin told Dylan with a knowing grin before he left them to their ride.

When she first mounted alone, she had her misgivings about whether or not this was a good idea. True, Doah was a good deal closer to the ground than Quinn or Kar Kalim had been, but there was no Dylan holding her securely from behind, either.

Certainly there were no moments of Dylan providing her with mindless ecstasy to erase her anxiety, either.

He was right there, though, at first guiding Doah and Alice on the lunge line. They stayed within the confines of the large enclosure at first, Alice and Doah making circles around Dylan as he held on to the lunge and patiently instructed her on riding basics. Alice's nervousness faded by degrees, replaced at first by cautious optimism and, slowly, by the thrill of mastering a new task. Doah was extremely well trained and exquisitely sensitive to even her subtlest commands.

Finally, Dylan said he thought she was ready to take an easy ride on the path that led along the lakefront. He alighted on his chosen mount, a big chestnut stallion with fire in his eyes, and they headed at a slow pace toward the golden lake.

"Why are you so preoccupied?" Dylan asked her when they reached the portion of the path that followed the shoreline, allowing them to ride side by side.

She glanced over at him, squinting into the light of the dipping sun and the luminescent lake. "I was thinking about when you had us on the lunge there in the corral. I know it was probably my imagination, knowing what you've told me about how you trained Addie on her pony, but—"

"What?"

"It felt *familiar*. Like I'd done it before," she said, her voice just loud enough to be heard above the horses' clomping hooves. "Do you think it was a real memory?" she asked, keeping her gaze trained ahead on the path.

"Do you want it to be?"

"Yes."

"Then it was, because it definitely happened," he said. She looked over at him. Whether it was the bright, intense sunlight or her bubbling sense of happiness, she allowed herself to be on display. She was losing the ability to shield her emotions. Or maybe allowing herself to show her feelings was the real skill, after all . . . the true strength?

His expression stiffened, and suddenly he was urging his mount nearer to Alice and reaching with one hand for her reins.

"Whoa," he murmured, pulling up on them. Guessing his intent, Alice tautened the reins. The horses halted, side by side. Dylan leaned in and down several inches, his gloved hand cupping her jaw, and he was kissing her, deep and thorough.

"Do you like Doah?" he asked gruffly, nibbling at her mouth a moment later.

"You know I love her," Alice replied, her eyes closed. She felt dazed and heated by his drugging kiss and the warm sunlight.

"Good. She's yours. Happy birthday, Alice."

She blinked open her eyes. The sunlight blazed around his shoulders and head. She squinted, bringing his shadowed features into focus.

"What? My birthday isn't until August twenty-eighth."

He shook his head. Why did he look so sober?

"It's today," he said gruffly. He applied a pressure with his hand on her jaw and pressed his mouth to hers again. She kissed him back, her mind spinning. Distantly, she realized he was doing what he always did, comforting her with his touch when he revealed anything he thought she'd find anxiety provoking.

"Addie was born on July twenty-first," he said a moment later next to her lips. He leaned back slightly and studied her face. "I thought you'd want to know."

She inhaled shakily. "Of course," she said, trying to focus her attention. "Sissy would have had to make up a date, wouldn't she? Even there, at the hospital when she first saw me. Even if either Cunningham or her knew the actual date, which I doubt, they couldn't provide it to the hospital and risk the chances of authorities checking the records."

He nodded, still somber.

"Thanks for telling me," she said. He looked doubtful. "No, I mean it. It's weird to hear it, but it makes sense. Why would I share Addie's birthday? That would be odd, under the circumstances. It'll take some getting used to, but I'd rather know. I'm glad you

thought I'd be . . . you know, okay hearing it," she said, embarrassment hitting her when she recalled how weak and transparent she'd
been in front of him and Sidney earlier at the hospital.

"I know you've had to hear and absorb a lot lately. I wasn't
sure about telling you. But it didn't seem right, to let the date pass.
Not when you're back. There were a lot of birthdays that Alan
couldn't wish you happiness. Or me. It just didn't seem right, to
let another one pass," he repeated gruffly, dropping his hand and
straightening. They remained motionless on their mounts for a
stretched moment, Dylan looking out at the lake, and she at his
rugged profile.

"Do you ever think about what will happen if the test results
say I'm not their daughter?"

Would you feel the same way about me, if that were true?

His chin turned sharply. "No. Are *you* thinking about that?"

"It's always a possibility, isn't it?"

His dark eyes ran over her face.

"No," he said, finality ringing in his deep voice.

She attempted a smile. "So . . . I'm twenty-four today?" she
asked shakily.

"Yes."

She blinked, hearing the rest of what he'd said earlier as if for
the first time. "And Doah is *mine?*" she asked, disbelief and
amazement finally hitting her.

"She's yours. And *that* gift is from me."

She saw the warmth in his eyes and the emergence of that
small, deadly smile, and suddenly she was the one leaning toward
him, her fingers sinking into his hair, seeking the sweet, heady
solace of his mouth.

FOURTEEN

"Where are we having dinner?" she asked dreamily later that evening as she stared out the car window at the orange ball of the sun as it began its descent into Lake Michigan. She felt so content after their ride, like she'd not only faced a fear, but surmounted it. True, Doah had made riding seem so easy—something she'd expected Dylan made sure of when he'd generously gifted her with a mount. But it was more than facing her fear about falling, or even getting the blood test done.

She'd told Dylan she loved him today. She'd exposed her heart, and she was still living and breathing. There was no pain, only joy. The world hadn't come to an end.

"Dinner is a surprise," he said, his gaze remaining on the road. She absorbed the image of him. Again, that feeling of euphoria went through her. He was *hers* in this moment of time, and that was a wonder. He looked good enough to eat, rugged and handsome in his jeans and a fitted blue and white plaid button-down shirt that fit his lean torso and muscular chest, shoulders, and arms perfectly. It took her a moment of satisfied lusting before she recognized how intent he appeared as he drove.

"What's got you so serious? You're not still worried about telling me it's my birthday, are you?"

He blinked and glanced over at her swiftly. "No, it's not that. At least not mainly."

"What's that supposed to mean?" she asked, grinning. He noticed her smile.

"I wanted to wait until you gained your . . . equilibrium to ask, but what happened at the hospital to upset you? Did the doctor say something to you?"

"No, not at all. The doctor wasn't even there." She explained to him about Dr. Shineburg being called in for an emergency.

"I was hoping you'd get a chance to speak with him. He knew Alan and Lynn," Dylan said, his brows furrowing as he stared at the road.

"It's okay. I was just glad to get it over and done with. If I ever want to speak to him after the results are in, I will."

"Then what *did* upset you?"

"Oh, something stupid," she discounted.

He looked at her, his wry glance saying loud and clear that he wouldn't find it stupid.

"I just . . . I had this thought. *Where will I be when I get the results of the test?*"

"I don't get it," he said blankly after a pause.

"That question just brought up so much stuff. I mean, if I don't get hired by Durand, will I be at Maggie's house in my apartment when I get the call? Will I be looking for a job? If I do get the Durand job, does that mean I'll be in the process of relocating to a new office? If so, where? And what will it be like, to leave here and everything—" Her voice broke. Her seat belt tightened when he abruptly hit the brakes. "Dylan, what are you *doing*?"

He was pulling the car over to the side of the rural route. He brought it to a halt and shifted the vehicle into park. Alice blinked when he turned to her, and she saw the gleam of fire in his eyes.

"Why are you so damn stubborn about this?"

"What do you mean?" she asked, stunned.

"You are the sole heiress of Durand Enterprises. *You*. No one else—"

"Dylan, I don't want to—"

"*No*. You've refused to listen to me about this, but you can't go on blinding yourself, Alice," he grated out between clenched teeth. He leaned across the dashboard, grasping her upper arms. "I disagreed with the idea of you returning to the camp and going on as if nothing had changed, but I understood why you wanted to do it."

"I have to finish what I started! It's what I came here to do—"

"Fine," he said loudly, teeth flashing between tightly drawn lips. "But you're not going to keep persisting in this fantasy that you're going to be sent away from Durand under any circumstances."

"But—"

He shook her slightly. "You've got to stop imagining that I'm going to allow you to be sent away from *me*." She went silent, stunned by his fierce focus.

His shout echoed in her head. Her mouth dropped open in amazement.

"Now are you going to listen to this, or not?" he asked in a more restrained tone. His jaw was very tight.

She nodded. Not even she would dare to defy him at that moment.

"Good," he snapped.

He exhaled slowly, mastering himself, before he began.

"After Lynn passed away, Alan set up a trust that was to be followed to the letter while his daughter remained missing. He put sixty percent of the stock of Durand Enterprises into this trust, which included very specific philanthropic directives. He generously offered me the opportunity to purchase the remaining shares of his company—forty percent—at a discount rate. He also made me executor of Addie's trust. Sixty percent of Durand's cash, investments, dividends, and profits were annually poured back into that fund for nearly two decades. I've followed Alan's philanthropic directives to a T, but the excess has been enormous. I've managed the excess to the best of my ability, and it's done well.

Very well. Alan specified that in the event that his daughter returned, the directives for how the trust must be spent would be dissolved, and either the executor or Addie, if she was of legal age, could utilize the funds as needed. The excess fund currently yields more than six hundred million dollars a year. In total, the trust is worth billions of dollars. And it's yours, Alice . . . along with the controlling interest in Durand."

Shivers poured through her. "I can't take any of that."

"I'm not asking you to be ready now, either to assume ownership or to lead the company—"

"I'm not leading Durand Enterprises. Are you *crazy*?" she blurted, shocked to the core at the very mention. The idea of making decisions that affected tens of thousands of people horrified her. Her ignorance and lack of experience yawned in front of her like a depthless black hole, and she was teetering on the edge of it.

"I told you, I'm not expecting anything now except that you assimilate at your own pace. Take as much time as you need." He squeezed her upper arms for emphasis. "But I won't have you worrying about going back to Chicago to find a job or relocating somewhere you don't want to go. If you want to persist in this Camp Durand business, then you can be hired on as a junior executive and work in Morgantown. It's our headquarters. Why shouldn't you get your feet wet there?" he grumbled impatiently. Clearly she'd pushed him to the edge.

She swallowed thickly. "That's . . . sort of what I was thinking. Hoping for."

His gaze flickered to her face. "Then why didn't you just *say* so?"

"Because I don't know if I'm going to be asked to be a Durand manager or not!"

He rolled his eyes and let go of her. He sagged back in his seat, raking his fingers through his hair. "Jesus. Did you even hear a word of what I just said?"

"I heard you. It was sort of hard not to, you were yelling so loud!" She, too, sagged back in her seat, her arms folded across her belly. A car zoomed past, making the sedan vibrate.

"We don't even know if it's true yet," she said in a hushed tone after a tense silence.

"There is no doubt in my mind. If you aren't their daughter, why are you having all these flashbacks and memories?" he asked through a clenched jaw. "And how does it happen that Alice Reed came into being at the exact moment that Addie Durand disappeared?"

Alice closed her eyes briefly. "I'd rather see the proof, firsthand. Is that too much to ask? And in the meantime, surely it makes sense for me to continue at the camp. Don't you think it'd be more ideal if it all turns out to be true for sure, that Durand employees knew I'd been in the trenches? That I was willing to show I'm not afraid of hard work or to start out at the bottom?"

He shook his head, staring at the road ahead of them. "You don't understand. Durand is yours by birth and by law. You're not obligated to prove *anything*." She watched him grip the wheel, his knuckles going white.

"I disagree." She reached out and squeezed his forearm. He blinked and looked at her. She held his stare. "I'm not saying I'm ever going to lead Durand. But if I did, I'd want to show I'd earned the right to do it. I'd want to demonstrate to the employees I was willing to work my ass off for their company. I'd want to earn their respect." She gripped his arm. "I'd want to do it like *you* did," she whispered emphatically.

She watched as the cutting fire in his eyes banked to a warm gleam. He exhaled heavily and grabbed her extended hand. He enfolded it in both of his and rested it on his thigh. They said nothing for a moment, watching as a pickup truck barreled past them and slowly disappeared down the ribbon of highway.

"Is it really all that crazy that I want to finish Camp Durand successfully?" she asked in a hushed tone.

"I guess not," he replied. "Just stop living under the illusion that if you want to be a manager for Durand Enterprises and learn the company, that anyone has the power to stop you, including me."

"Maybe you can explain that to Kehoe," she murmured, smiling.

"Fuck Kehoe." He glanced at her, his former fire blazing high again for a brief moment. "I've heard nothing but good things about how you're managing at the camp."

She perked up a little at that. "You have?"

His brief shrug and expression seemed to say, *Of course, what else would I have heard?*

"We haven't talked about it all that much. I wasn't sure if you knew anything beyond the little bit I told you last weekend."

"I hear things. I didn't want to bring it up. I didn't want to overshadow your decisions or progress as a counselor."

She smiled. "You wanted me to sink or swim by my own merits?"

"Yes."

She gripped his hand tighter. He glanced over at her.

"That's all I want, too, Dylan," she explained feelingly, willing him to understand her point of view.

After a moment, he exhaled and shook his head.

"Is that another thing you've learned at camp? How to sway a dissenter so perfectly?" he asked, giving her a darkly amused glance and reaching to put the car back in drive. Alice laughed.

"No. I think I owe that lesson one hundred percent to you."

BY the time they returned to Morgantown, the evening had turned still, overcast, and muggy. Steel gray clouds encroached on the brilliantly lit sunset. Alice thought the dramatic, eerie backdrop of the sky especially fitting for the beautiful, silent mansion perched atop the bluff.

"Is everyone gone, do you think?" she asked Dylan when they entered the house via the garage.

"Yes. We're all alone. Louise has set the alarm," he said, pushing in the code on the keypad of the security system. He turned to her. "You go up and shower for dinner. I've got to take care of a few things, but I'll come up and get you when everything is ready."

"Why are you being so mysterious?" she asked him, grinning.

"Because it's a surprise, why else?"

Her grin widened. No matter how hard she tried to wheedle a few clues out of him as to what he planned, he was impervious. He just hustled her over to the grand staircase and urged her up the stairs.

"But . . . what am I supposed to wear?" she demanded when he'd successfully pushed her up three steps.

"The less, the better," he said. He noticed her exacerbated expression. "Anything. Don't get dressed up. It doesn't matter. No one is going to see you but me."

"Then it matters a lot."

He lunged up the first two steps, cupped her jaw, and planted a kiss on her mouth for that. That kiss didn't last long enough for Alice before he was turning her around again.

"I'll come and get you in forty-five minutes or so," he said from behind her. "No venturing out this time, armed with a golf club or not. Stay *put*."

"But—"

She tried to turn around, but he stopped her by facing her toward the staircase with his hands on her shoulders. She looked over her shoulder, and he gave her ass a playful swat.

"There are more of those where that came from. It is your birthday, remember?" he asked, that dangerous glint shining in his dark eyes. He raised his hand over her ass when she hesitated. She snorted with laughter, leaping up the stairs to avoid his swat.

After she finished taking her shower and washing her hair, she hesitated about what to wear, given the meager information Dylan had provided. She considered all the lovely things he'd given her last week. Cinching the sash tight on her fluffy robe, she wandered out of the bathroom to the closet where the items were stored. What would be appropriate for what sounded like a special dinner?

A birthday dinner. It still seemed too incredible to believe. But that wasn't the primary reason she found the day special. Today was the day she'd told him she loved him.

Several minutes later, she stood up quickly when she heard the knob turning. She'd been reading a Durand annual report that was on the coffee table. Or she'd *tried* to read it, anyway. Mostly she'd been on high alert, waiting for Dylan.

He walked toward her now, smiling when he saw her tug self-consciously at the tie on her robe.

"I thought you said I shouldn't dress up," she said, eyeing him and scowling. He looked indecently gorgeous. He'd obviously showered in another room, because there was still moisture in his thick, wavy hair. He wore a pair of black trousers and a stylish black, gray, and ivory short-sleeved polo. She caught a hint of his clean, spicy aftershave as he neared her.

"I said it didn't matter," he repeating, running the lapel of her robe through his hands. He stepped closer, his head lowering until their faces were just inches apart. She stared up at him, her mouth hanging open. It was as if it were her first time seeing him. Her body clamored with awareness. "Your robe is perfect. You might be a little warm, though. We're having dinner outside, and it's muggy out there," he said, his voice going low and gruff. His dark eyes ensnared her. She was intensely aware of his hands sliding up and down on the lapel of her robe, his knuckles brushing against the bare skin of her chest. His mouth hovered just an inch above hers.

"I'll manage," she croaked.

He smiled. "Good." Disappointment spiked through her when he stepped back and took her hand.

"Should I wear shoes?" she asked uncertainly, glancing down at her bare feet.

"You won't need them. Follow me."

She was a little surprised when, instead of leading her down the grand staircase and downstairs toward the terrace entrance, he led her in the opposite direction and down the west hallway.

"Where are we going?" she asked, even more confused when he led her up the staircase instead of down a moment later.

"You'll see."

"Oh, the back porch," she said happily a moment later when they finally arrived at the narrow set of stairs that she recognized. Dylan had taken her here last week in order to watch the sunrise. Even though the rear porch appeared to be rarely used and weatherworn, Alice had found it extremely romantic and lovely. She especially loved the huge old porch swing.

Dylan turned toward her as he reached for the door. "Close your eyes."

She followed his instructions, unable to repress her grin.

She heard the latch on the door and he tugged on her hand. She walked several feet blinded, guided only by his hand.

"Okay. Just stand there for a few seconds and keep your eyes closed. No cheating."

"Hurry up," she insisted amusedly after what felt like forever. Was that the sound of a lighter being struck? "The suspense is killing me."

"Patience," he remonstrated. She felt his hand enclose hers.

"Okay. Open them."

It took her several seconds to absorb what she was seeing. The entire veranda had been transformed into a romantic fairyland. It'd been repainted. The wood floors and beamed ceiling a soft gray that matched the limestone of the house, the railing and large porch swing were a pristine white. The wrought iron chaise lounges had been spruced up with cheery red cushions. Pots of colorful red and white flowers had been set along the railing. Interspersed between them were glowing, flickering lanterns. Several small leafy trees in large pots had been placed along the back of the veranda, and someone had intertwined strings of tiny white glowing lights on them. In the center of the porch a round cloth-covered table had been placed along with two chairs. The table was a feast for the eyes, decorated with a low crystal bowl of lush purple hydrangeas and flickering candles. Before each chair sat a silver domed dish.

A small lacy three-tiered cake and a bottle of champagne in an ice bucket had been placed on a side table. The pretty little cake was lit with candles on each layer, making it look like a glowing confectionary tower.

"Happy birthday," Dylan said, leading her toward the cake.

"It's all so beautiful," she murmured, wide-eyed, soaking in all the minute details around her with wonder. Her gaze landed on the white railing and flowerpots. He watched her reaction warmly. A heady feeling rushed through her. "You remembered what I said that day about how the railing should be white, and flowerpots should be in front of it."

"I never came up here when you were small, and I've never seen any photos," he said, his hand moving at her back. "When you said that it should be white with flowerpots, that was my only hint of what this porch looked like twenty years ago." He nodded at the cake. "Well? Make a wish."

She swallowed thickly, finding it hard to focus with so much happiness crowding her consciousness.

I wish I could live up to it all, she thought, her gaze wandering over the lovely veranda and thinking of everything it entailed. It landed on Dylan. *Please let me be what he truly wants—me—not freedom from the burden of grief and guilt he's felt all these years.*

She blew out the candles . . . all twenty-four of them.

"Do you think it was a real memory? The one about the white

railing and the pots of flowers and my love of the porch swing?"
she asked Dylan after he'd seated her at the table and sat down
across from her.

"I see no reason why not. Louise and Marie both assured me
that the color choices were ideal, one way or another." He lifted
the champagne from the ice, his brows arched in a question.

"Please," she murmured, going back to staring all around and
admiring the romantic setting. "So Louise and Marie helped you
with this?"

"Couldn't have done it without them. I had some painters come
in a few days ago. Louise did all the decorating and flowers. She's
been at it all day. Marie prepared our meal and baked your cake."
He set her champagne flute down in front of her. "The only thing
I did was follow Marie's instructions for heating the dinner. Let's
hope I didn't blow that." He whipped off the domed lid and Alice
stared down at a steaming, beautifully presented meal.

"Chicken cordon bleu, rice pilaf, and braised asparagus. They
both say happy birthday, by the way. Louise and Marie, I mean.
I gave them the day off tomorrow—I wanted the house to
ourselves—so they told me to be sure to tell you for them."

"That was nice of them. This is wonderful. Thank you."

"Like I said, I didn't do much," he assured, removing the dome
from his own plate and setting it on the serving table.

She reached across the table and caught his hand. He glanced
up in surprise.

"It's the exact opposite of nothing. You planned it all. No one
has ever given me a birthday dinner before, let alone one like *this*."

His mouth pressed into a hard line. "Never?"

"It's okay," she assured, grinning. "This makes up for it all."

"If only that were true," he said quietly.

She swallowed thickly, regretting the shadow that fell over his
features. She shouldn't have brought it up. The reminder of his
regret when it came to her—when it came to Addie—had thrown

a temporary pall upon the magical moment. She was eager to make it disappear.

"I have a little surprise, too," she said brightly, reaching for the tie on her bathrobe. She stood and went over to a chaise lounge, the fluffy robe falling past her shoulders. She laid it on the cushion and turned to face him, holding her breath. His expression went rigid as his stare lowered over her.

"You said I could wear whatever I wanted," she said tremulously, affected by the heat of his gaze. "It was one of the things in the lingerie you got for me last week," she added when he just continued to stare.

"I bought you a nightgown. You've turned it into an event."

She blushed in pleasure. What had he meant, *an event*? Whatever it was, she knew by his stare it was a compliment. "It fits really well," she agreed lamely, taking a step toward the table. It was an understatement. The dark blue and silver fitted gown might have been made for her. It dipped very low and cupped her breasts, rib cage, and waist before it flared ever so slightly, still skimming sensually against her belly and hips. An inch of elasticized black lace was the only thing that covered her nipples. The upper mounds of her breasts were fully displayed. Her cheeks warmed even further as Dylan continued to eat her up with his stare. She stepped toward the table to take her seat again, but Dylan caught her hand and pulled her toward him. His stare was fixed on her breasts.

"Turn around. Let me see you," he urged gruffly.

Arousal prickled at her clit in response to his hungry expression. She turned slowly.

"Hold still," he directed when her back was to him. She looked over her shoulder. The gown was backless. His gaze traveled downward, making her naked spine flicker in awareness. When it reached her ass, he reached and stretched the silky material over a buttock. He cupped the cheek in his palm and squeezed. Her sex tingled in excitement. Slowly, as though he was relishing the anticipation, he lifted the fabric, exposing her buttocks. He caressed the bottom curve of her ass with his fingertips. She exhaled shakily at the intimate caress combined with his intent stare.

"No panties. You really are going to turn this into an event," he said. He released the fabric. She blinked when she heard a brisk metallic sound, and then another. He'd placed the domed warmers back on their meals. His hands on her hips, he turned her and brought her closer, opening his thighs. He stopped her when she stood just inside his knees. She watched, holding her breath, as he ran his fingertips over her silk-covered belly. His expression was almost feral. A sharp thrill went through her. She didn't know why, but she loved it when he grew single-minded in his arousal. A fool might have thought he became selfish in those moments, but Alice knew the truth. His sexual hunger fed her. She loved being the object of his lust.

His hand lowered. He brushed her mound very lightly with his fingertips through the silk. Pleasure tingled through her at his touch. Her nipples tightened beneath the lace. She whimpered softly, and he looked up. The candlelight gleamed in his eyes.

"You're so lovely."

"Thank you."

"I'm going to have to have you. Your dinner will have to wait. Cake, too."

"I'm very patient," she whispered, trapped in his dark eyes.

"No, you're not. Neither am I."

Still holding her stare, he once again brushed his fingers against her mound, his fingertips finding the cleft between her labia. He rubbed gently against the silk. The subtle pressure made her tremble.

"You're like something out of a fantasy. So beautiful. So primed to my touch."

She exhaled shakily and reached for him, longing to dig her fingers in his hair. He stopped her by grabbing her wrists and placing them at her sides.

"Keep them there, or I'll tie them behind your back." His tone was mild enough, but the flash of steel in his stare told her he was serious. He cradled her hips in both his hands, then ran his palms along her waist and the sides of her body. She shivered in pleasure.

"Cold?" he murmured.

"No," she replied. The summer air was warm and a little muggy. It was his skimming hands that were making her tremble. He brushed his hands over the top of her breasts. His forefingers dipped beneath the clinging lace, pushing the fabric beneath her nipples. His low, rough growl of satisfaction caused arousal to stab at her clit.

"Look at that," he muttered, his gaze glued to her protruding nipples. "You're the feast here tonight, Alice. I'm going to savor you." His stare flickered up to her face. "And then I'm going to gorge myself on you. Are you ready for that?"

The edge to his lust intimidated her a little, but also excited her hugely.

"Without a doubt."

His mouth softened slightly at her eager reply. He lowered her gown down to her waist, baring her breasts completely.

"Good. Let's start with some appetizers and champagne." He leaned forward. With his hands at her hips, he pushed her back slightly, as though he wanted a full view of her. He grasped her wrists and raised her hands. "Touch your breasts."

Alice cupped the mounds uncertainly. His request made her a little self-conscious. Especially when he leaned back in his chair and picked up his champagne glass. He took a sip, watching her all the while like a hawk about to pounce on its prey.

"You have uncommonly beautiful breasts. Firm. Soft. Fat pink nipples that turn so hard with the slightest stimulation. Touch them now," he commanded gruffly. Alice ran her fingertips over the crests, loving the way his eyes narrowed and glittered greedily. With his elbow on the arm of the chair, he pressed his fingertips against his whiskered jaw and mouth in a manner that distracted Alice thoroughly. All the things he'd said about her breasts struck her as true for the first time. The skin felt satiny smooth beneath her hands, the mounds firm and soft. Her nipples stiffened beneath her circling fingertips and Dylan's hot, focused stare. Experiencing her power over him thrilled her. She pinched lightly at the beading crests. Recalling something he'd done in the den this afternoon that he seemed to enjoy, she lifted the mounds and released, bouncing them softly.

He groaned roughly through a snarl. "Again," he said. She gladly complied. His little game was turning her on. She bounced her breasts. He took a sip of his champagne and watched while she pinched at her nipples. His hand moved to his crotch. Alice moaned shakily, watching him while he stroked his cock through his clothing as intently as he watched her.

"I'm showing you mine. Show me yours."

A smile curved his mouth. "Would you like that?" he asked, still rubbing his hand up and down along the shaft of his cock slowly. He was killing her. She could see the outline of him clearly though his pants, his stroking fingers molding the fabric against his erection. Her mouth watered.

"Yes, please."

"How can I refuse a *polite* request from Alice Reed when the occurrence is so seldom," he said, smiling at her frown. He fleetly unbuckled his belt and unfastened his pants. He kicked off his shoes and drew off his socks before standing to remove his pants and boxer briefs completely. Alice watched in mounting excitement. He sat back down in his chair and lifted his shirt. She gasped softly at the vision of his erect cock lying against his taut belly, the candlelight casting it in a rosy gold hue.

He cupped his round, shaved testicles and slid his hand along the shaft. She shivered in excitement.

"I wouldn't have agreed to do it if I thought you'd stop," he said with a dark glance.

Alice blinked. She'd been so mesmerized by the sight of him, her hands had fallen to her sides.

"Hands back on your breasts," he instructed. "Hold them up for me. That's right," he muttered as she did what he said. He stroked his cock more firmly. "Keep holding them up and play with the nipples."

Alice did everything he asked of her, becoming increasingly aroused by her own touch . . . by the powerful vision of him stroking his cock. In one hand, he held his champagne, which he sipped occasionally as he watched her. His other hand fisted and pumped his erect cock. Alice felt very much on display, like she was putting on a show for his pleasure. Maybe it should have offended her, but it didn't. Instead, it aroused her intensely.

"Are you getting wet?" he asked her bluntly a minute later. He set down his glass of champagne and twisted in his chair, picking up the champagne bottle. He poured himself another glass and glanced at her, expecting an answer.

"Yes," she told him a little defiantly. How could she not be wet, standing there watching such a beautiful man masturbating right in front of her. His manner was that of a prince or a sheikh, a man used to having his every command followed. He wasn't playing a part, though. Dylan was a sexual dominant by nature, and undoubtedly was used to getting what he wanted in this arena. It certainly was true in Alice's case. It aroused her to do what he demanded . . . but of course, she couldn't appear to be giving in *too* easily.

"Slip out of your gown," he said, leaning back in his chair and lifting his champagne to his lips. "Prove to me you're aroused."

"*Prove* to you," she muttered under her breath a little sourly. She rolled her eyes. Nevertheless, she lowered the fabric of the gown over her belly and shimmied her hips to encourage it to fall down her thighs and legs. He grunted and began to stroke himself again at the tight shaking of her hips.

"Dip your fingers between the lips," he ordered thickly. Alice complied, a moan escaping her throat. She rubbed her clit through thick cream. "I can see how wet you are," he said, his stare glued between her thighs. She circled her fingers and whimpered. His focused attention and jacking hand were making her desperate.

Wanton.

She lifted her hand and let him see her moisture glistening on her skin. Slowly, she lifted her hand to her mouth and slid her moist fingers between her lips. His pumping hand paused mid-staff. He watched her narrowly as she sucked her juices off her first two fingers.

"Don't try to control the pace, Alice," he warned softly, his eyes glittering dangerously.

A smile tugged at her pursed lips.

"I think you need something to cool you off," he said grimly. He let go of his cock and it thumped tautly against his abdomen. "Get your fingers out of your mouth, you little witch, and come here."

She stepped between his knees, holding her breath as he cradled her hips and then whisked his hands up and down the sensitive sides of her body. He cupped her breasts and squeezed them gently.

"Just what I thought. You're very warm." Still cradling a breast with one hand, he picked up his champagne glass.

"Dylan," she whispered warningly, her eyes going wide as she watched him slowly tip the glass above the breast he held. The liquid reached the lip of the flute and dribbled onto her breast, sliding down the upper curve and dripping off the nipple. She gasped.

"Cold?" he asked, rubbing the champagne into her nipple with his fingertips.

"You know it is," she said, sounding breathless.

"Yes. I can see that it is," he said distractedly, studying the proof of her beading nipple. He tilted the glass again. Her sex tightened in anticipation as she watched the golden liquid slip over the rim and splash onto her breast. Again, he ran his fingers over the mounds and nipple, distributing the champagne.

"No, you're still flushed with heat," he said, shaking his head.

"Is that a crime?" she asked dazedly, highly distracted by watching his fingers rub her moist skin and nipple.

"No. It's just an experiment." She blinked at his seemingly innocent tone.

"An experiment in torture," she muttered, watching him pinch lightly at her nipple. Her clit gave a twinge of sympathetic arousal at the caress.

He smiled, clearly not planning on defending himself. Instead, he reached for the ice bucket and placed it on the table next to him.

"No," she whispered when he dipped his hand into the silver bucket that was beaded with moisture.

"I like my champagne very cold," he said. He held her stare and placed a small cube of ice against her nipple. Alice knew what was coming, but she couldn't prevent herself from jumping slightly. Her mouth trembled as he rubbed the hard, cold cube against her, manipulating her flesh. She shivered in a mixture of discomfort and sharp pleasure. "Look how stiff it's getting," he said, eyeing her nipple. He reached with his free hand and grabbed some more ice. Alice whimpered in anxious anticipation as he lifted both hands. He began to rub the ice on both her nipples at once.

"Stop," she whispered without any heat. Her entire body was drawn tight with tension. Her nipples ached with cold and sharp arousal. She'd never seen them so tight and erect.

"Just a moment more," Dylan replied, his thick, distracted tone telling her loud and clear how aroused he was by his task. The cubes melted beneath his rubbing fingers until they were nothing more than cool rivulets of water running down her breasts and ribs.

"Please," she whispered, even though she wasn't precisely sure for what she begged.

His gaze flickered up to her face. He lowered his moist fingers and reached for the bottle of champagne.

"You're right. I'm very thirsty."

Alice whimpered as he lifted the bottle.

"Stay still," he directed, perhaps sensing the tension coiling in her body.

She couldn't still her jump as he poured the icy liquid over both her breasts. He set aside the bottle as Alice stood there, trembling with desire, champagne dripping off her nipples and streaming down her ribs. He regarded her sheened breasts grimly, a snarl slanting his mouth. Then he was pulling her to him, his hot mouth enfolding a tight, aching nipple, his tongue laving off the moisture. Her shaky moan of disbelief and arousal twined with his rough groan of satisfaction.

He cupped her other breast, rubbing the damp nipple, while he sucked her tautly. It was unbearable. Her nipple popped free from his pursing lips, and he ran his tongue over the globes of first one breast, then the other, gathering the drops of champagne. Then he tongued her ribs and belly. Alice quaked, her thighs tightening to stifle the stabbing arousal at her sex. She moaned in rising misery. He must have heard her.

He lowered a hand between her thighs and rubbed her creamy clit firmly. Her mouth sagged open at the sharp pleasure. He returned to her breasts, sipping and licking. When he drew a tight crest into his warm mouth and sucked firmly, Alice cried out and began to come against his hand. He never paused in his actions as she shuddered in climax. The only indication that he knew she was coming was the low, rough growl that vibrated in his throat. He continued to stroke and quench his thirst on her, working every last tremor out of her.

Or so Alice had thought. Until he cradled her hips in his hands and lowered his head, sliding his tongue in the cleft of her labia. She cried out as tension leapt back into her muscles, and his firm tongue demanded another shudder of pleasure from her.

Suddenly, he was standing and pulling her tightly against him, his hands running over her hips, back, and ass, kissing her harshly with lips and tongue that tasted of champagne and her—Alice. Her body felt flushed and tingling, satiated but still ringing with desire. His strength and hardness stilled her dizziness. She craned for him, pressing her belly against his thick cock, straining against him, and squeezing the tight, hard muscles of his ass in her hands.

He tore his mouth from hers roughly a moment later, his ragged breath hitting her face. He pressed his fingertips to her upturned lips and slid them into her mouth. Alice closed around him, sucking him deeper. For several seconds, he watched with a feral focus as he finger-fucked her mouth. He slipped them from between her lips and leaned down to kiss her swollen lips.

"On your knees," he whispered against her mouth. Her heart jumped at his words and the fierce gleam in his eyes.

He grasped her hands, kicking his discarded trousers between them. He guided her down until her knees rested against the cushion of the fabric. Immediately, he cupped his heavy erection from below and guided the flushed cockhead between her lips. She looked up at him as he pulsed his hips. He grasped her head.

"That's right. Look at me while I fuck your hot little mouth," he rasped, his face tight with lust. "Do you have any idea how beautiful you look right now?"

She suspected he saw her total surrender in that moment. Alice allowed him to see it. It gave her strength, somehow, to abandon herself to his pleasure.

She raised her hand and fisted him, stroking him as she sucked him deeper. He was hard and flagrant, filling her mouth, stretching her aching lips. With one hand on his hip, she urged him to thrust faster even as she ducked her head at the same pace. He was demanding of her, but she was just as demanding of him. He held her head in place and thrust deep. She overrode her body's response to reject him, her hunger trumping instinct. His face tightened and he shuddered in pleasure.

"That's right," he grated out. "You're so sweet; you're going to let me use you for a moment, aren't you. Ah God, that's good." He thrust faster, but Alice kept pace with him, loving his low, rough grunts of pleasure. She felt his excitement mounting as if it were her own.

She felt him spasm against her tongue.

He withdrew partially as he began to climax, thrusting shallowly and ejaculating on her tongue. He groaned harshly, gripping her hair between his fingers. Her eyes sprang wide as all his coiled, incendiary power was unleashed. She struggled to keep up with him, sucking and swallowing, feeling his cock twitch and throb as he thrust, while more and more of his semen spread on her tongue.

Finally, his ejaculations waned. His still rigid, streaming cock popped out from between her pursed lips. She craved more of his taste once he was gone, pushing the tip of her tongue into his slit. She looked up at him, laving the swollen, glistening cockhead. He stared down at her, still grasping her head, his nostrils flaring slightly, his dark gypsy eyes smoldering as she lapped up every trace of him she could find.

She kissed the tip of his cock, pausing to glide her mouth against the wet skin. A grim smile pulled at his lips.

"You never give half-measure," he said, his eyelids narrowed as he studied her. "I love you for that, among other things."

"For giving good head?"

His mouth twitched. "For giving yourself so completely. Come here," he said, suddenly sounding stern. He bent to put his hands on her shoulders, urging her to stand.

"What, am I in trouble?" she joked, a little confused by his intensity.

"No. You've been very good. Exceptionally so," he said, turning to shift his covered plate and the ice bucket over to the side table. He swiftly did the same with the silver and glassware. Then he was reaching for her and lifting her onto the table.

"What are you doing?" she asked him in amazement when he pulled up his chair and sat again.

"Spread your thighs," he demanded shortly. She opened her legs and he scooted his chair between her parted knees. She yelped when he put his hands on her hips and jerked her closer, her pussy zipping to the edge of the table.

"I drank," he said, lowering his head between her thighs. He used his thumbs to spread her labia. She saw his small, grim smile. "You ate. Now it's time for my meal."

THEY finally actually *did* eat the meals Marie had prepared them. Alice remained sitting on the table in front of him, naked and flushed from multiple climaxes. She held the plate in her lap and fed him succulent bites of food from her fork, serving herself every other bite and laughing when she occasionally spilled grains of rice onto her stomach or his thighs. They talked about trivial things, and she teased him mercilessly.

"It's a lot easier than I thought it'd be," she said spontaneously a while later when they moved on to the delicious birthday cake.

"What?" Dylan asked, taking a bite from the fork she extended.

"Loving you."

He paused in chewing, his eyes flashing as he looked up at her. Still holding her stare, he took the plate from her lap and set it aside.

"I don't know how you do it."

"What?" she asked, breathless, because she recognized that gleam in his eyes. He stood and lifted her off the table.

"Be such a smart-ass one second, and so sweet the next."

She smiled. He'd told her that before.

"I don't want to be predictable."

His dark eyes glistened from amusement and candlelight. "Heaven forbid."

At his urging, they covered the cake and blew out the candles, but left everything else behind. He led her to his bedroom, where he told her to lie down on the bed. She stared up at him, enraptured, a moment later as he came over and entered her.

"Was it a happy birthday?" he asked, his muscles bulging as he held himself off her and his cock throbbed deep inside her.

"The happiest day I've ever had."

"*Alice*," he rasped.

He began to move. The truth of what she'd said filled and overwhelmed her.

It frightened her a little, too.

FIFTEEN

The next morning, Dylan awoke alone. He rose and donned some pants, concerned but not as alarmed as he'd been in the past to realize Alice was in the house alone, a potential victim to memories that didn't feel like her own.

This morning, he had a feeling he knew where he'd find her. When he reached the top steps that led to the back veranda, he heard the telltale squeak of the porch swing. Relieved, he opened the door.

She rocked on the big old swing, one bare foot on the floor propelling her, the other bent and resting on the swing. On top of her thigh rested a plate of cake. She smiled around the fork she'd just inserted into her mouth when she saw him approaching.

"I woke up thinking about this cake," she said, chewing.

He sat down next to her, his hands at the edge of the swing, and regarded her closely. Alice with the fire of defiance in her eyes was always a fierce trial on his patience and senses. But Alice's eyes sparkling with happiness as she relished a long overdue birthday cake left him lung-locked and mute for a moment.

Her brow crinkled. "Do you want some?" she asked, waving in the direction of the cake. She'd misunderstood his intent expression as he'd witnessed her glowing happiness. She started to get up, as if to get him some cake.

He caught her hand, halting her and shaking his head. Instead, he kissed her softly, the sweetness lingering on her lips more than satisfying him. After a moment, he lifted his head and leaned back in the swing, his arm around her.

"Go ahead," he instructed gruffly. "Eat your cake."

He noticed her satisfied smile as she snuggled up next to him and resumed eating. He tightened his arm around her and stared out over the railing. It would be a clear day. The sun had risen, but just recently. It cast the eastern woods in a pale gold light. Alice lingered over her last bite, carefully scraping up all the icing off the plate. He glanced at her amusedly as she sucked every last remnant off her fork.

He held out his hand with a droll expression. Laughter filled her eyes as she handed her plate to him. He returned a moment later, a hefty fresh slice of cake on it.

"It's really good," she insisted by way of explanation for her early morning hunger for birthday cake.

"The breakfast of champions."

She laughed and offered him a bite, which he took. "I hope so. The bonfire is tomorrow and they'll be announcing the team totals. I could use any edge I could get. I can't believe camp is over this Friday, and the kids leave on Saturday."

"Red Team was on top last week. I've heard it's still in the running this week."

Alice nodded, forking more cake in her mouth. "We've got a good chance, but Thad's team is always a threat, and Dave Epstein's Gold Team and Brooke Seifert's Silver have had good weeks. Everyone is really coming together and forming solid team identities."

He smiled in memory of his days as both a camper and then a counselor at Camp Durand. "You might have to do something a little out of the box to get the managers' attention. Team building is crucial, but at this point, they'll be looking for more. Some dazzle."

"Dazzle?"

He shrugged. "Salesmanship is a huge part of being a successful manager. You know that. That's how it'd be in the business world if you were competing for a contract, talking retailers into higher product numbers or negotiating for product placement, convincing a bank Durand has a high trust value for expansion loans . . . whatever. It's not enough to just show them numbers, you've got to be different from everyone else. You've got to stand out."

She looked thoughtful and grim as she took another bite of cake. "Don't worry about me. Brooke Seifert has been telling me from the start I was *different*."

"You are," he assured her, skimming his fingertips over her shoulder. She glanced at him uncertainly. "I've been telling you from the beginning, that's a *good* thing."

She ducked her head. She stuck her fork into the cake with great focus. "Thank you again for yesterday," she said quietly.

He stroked her shoulder. "It was my pleasure. It was a special day for me, too."

He saw color spread on the cheek nearest to him. She continued to study her cake like she'd discovered it held the secrets of the universe.

"You probably have had it happen a lot," she murmured.

"What?" he asked, sensing her disquietude. He continued to stroke her silky skin, silently reassuring her.

"Have women tell you they love you."

"You were the first."

Her fork plinked on the china plate. She turned fully to face him, clearly startled.

"What?"

"You were the first person to ever tell me you loved me. When you were four years old. Of course, you told Angelfire you loved her constantly, and the Raggedy Ann doll you'd fed strawberry preserves one day and had a permanent red beard and mustache as a result, and the mangy stray cat that hung around the stables . . . so I'm not sure how much your proclamation of love meant," he said, shrugging. He met her gaze, his amusement fading. "But you *were* the first."

For several seconds, she just stared at him, her dark blue eyes glistening.

"It meant something," she finally said feelingly.

He nodded. He wasn't quite sure if she'd understood how much hearing those words for the first time when he was an angry, lonely boy of fourteen years had meant to him, or if she was saying her innocent declaration of love had been more than just the passing childish sentiment of a little girl. It didn't matter.

The light shining in her eyes at that moment was all that did.

THEY spent an idyllic day together. Dylan showed her the workout facility. They did a workout together—more or less, anyway. They were in the same room, but there was no way she could have approximated his routine. The wonders of his lean, powerful body started to make perfect sense to her.

He told her to bring along a swimsuit, and they'd go for a swim after their exercise. Alice hadn't even realized there was a swimsuit among all the items he'd purchased for her. When she looked, she discovered a sophisticated low-cut black maillot that was about a thousand times sexier than Alice's practical camp swimsuit.

After their workout, he showed her to a beautiful pool that was hidden, nestled as it was among the trees and gardens at the far side of the house. There, they spent a few hours in the hot afternoon sun, sipping chilled white wine, swimming, talking, and snacking off a tray of fruit, crackers, and cheese.

At one point, Alice's eyelids started to grow heavy while she lay on a chaise lounge. They flickered open again at the pressure of Dylan's mouth brushing against hers. Her hand went to the back of his head, and their kiss deepened, turning hot, wet, and deep.

"Let's move this party to the bedroom. You're getting a

sunburn," he murmured next to her lips a moment later. His fingertips skimmed the inner swell of her breast. Despite the heat, her nipples tightened. Wearing the skimpy swimsuit, skin that was usually covered was exposed, both to the sun and Dylan's admiring stares and caressing fingertips.

"*That's* your excuse for getting me into bed?" she teased, nipping at his lower lip.

"Do I need an excuse?"

"No, but it's cocky just to assume."

He opened a big hand on her hip and ass, his fingertips sinking into a buttock. "I am cocky, though," he said, and she saw the gleam of his eyes in the shadow of his lowered brow. A thrill went through her. She loved the way he touched her: so possessive. So sure. He never held anything back. "Is this a complaint?"

"No," she whispered. "Not at the moment, it isn't. I reserve the right to change my mind though."

His small smile widened a tad.

"You go ahead. I'm going to clean this stuff up and take it in," he said, waving at the remains of their meal and wine. "Go and take a quick shower to cool off your skin. I'll meet you upstairs in a minute. Pull down the covers all the way and lay down on your back," he said, his eyelids heavy and his stare hot as he looked down at her. "I'm going to restrain you."

"Any other commands, master?"

His brows slanted. "Quite a few, in fact," he said, ignoring her sarcasm.

She laughed.

A moment later, she walked along the slate stone path alone through trees, shrubbery, and waving flowers. The workout, two glasses of wine, and the hot sun had her feeling drowsy and content. The pool area was extremely well secluded. When she reached a split on the stone path, she hesitated. They'd taken a different route from the workout facility to the pool. Knowing she'd eventually find her way back no matter what, she chose the left-hand path.

It was the wrong way. She realized that as soon as she heard the waves hitting the shore in the distance. She continued forward, knowing that when she left the trees, she could just walk through the backyard and terraced garden to the house. There was a clearing just ahead.

She emerged from the wooded area, breathing deeply of the fresh breeze. She saw the gray and white cobblestone fence at the very end of the property, and the blue, sea-like Great Lake taking up the entire horizon. A memory popped into her head of seeing Thad, Brooke, and Tory Hastings—another Durand counselor—standing at the edge of the bluff at the fence and down at the lake. She'd seen them in the distance on the evening of the counselors' welcome to Camp Durand several weeks ago. It'd been the night Dylan had found her, alone and disoriented in the castle's dining room, convinced she'd heard a gong. Later, she'd stood shoulder to shoulder with Dylan, staring down at the Camp Durand party that took place on the terrace. Thad, Brooke, and Tory had stood at this very fence.

Alice herself had never ventured to the end of the yard or the edge of the bluff. The fence was quite sturdy, though—at least four feet high and nine or ten inches thick. It was a fence made for safety, not a delicate garden ornament. Curious, she stepped forward and cautiously glanced down.

The waves collided against the shore far below her, startling her.

Of course it was all so strange, everything that had happened to her since coming to Camp Durand. But the reality of her singular circumstances seemed to crash in at that moment with as much force as the waves hitting the rocks below.

A feeling of dizziness assailed her. She'd had no idea the bluff was so high up from the shore, or that it was such a drastic drop-off from the edge. Forty or more feet below her, the waves struck an ominous-looking beach of glistening, jagged rock. No wonder she'd never wandered down here. Instinctively, she must have realized that with her fear of heights, it was a very undesirable place to be.

For a few panicked seconds, however, she couldn't move. She stood frozen, staring down as if hypnotized by the sight of the waves hitting the dramatic, stark shoreline. The sound held her in a spell, too. The rhythmic rush and slap of the waves struck her as forceful and bizarrely intense, given the sublimely beautiful summer day.

Violent.

"Alice?"

She spun around at the sound of Dylan's voice, the action unsteadying her. She faltered and reached out in a panicked fashion to catch hold of something.

"Ouch," she cried out when her hand struck a cobblestone hard, and pain shot through her. For a split second, she had the experience of falling in the direction of the shore. The wind rushed in her ears. Vertigo and blind terror struck her.

Then Dylan's arms were around her and he was pulling her away from the stone wall.

"Are you okay?" he demanded tensely.

Alice stared up at him, knocked utterly off balance. Not just physically. Mentally. Her entire being had rocked there for a moment. She stared over his shoulder, her mouth gaping open. The fence looked perfectly steady and solid. It'd just been her vertigo that made it feel as if it were giving way, and that she was falling.

"I'm fine," she mumbled. Embarrassment swept through her when she noticed his fierce, anxious expression as he looked down at her.

"What are you doing here? I thought you were going up to the house," he said sharply.

"I don't know. I lost my way." Irritation pierced her anxiety. She glared at him. "Why are you snapping at me? Do you think I'd come here and stare off the side of that bluff on purpose?"

She saw his shadowed gaze flicker from the path she'd taken to the drop off the bluff. "No, I suppose not," he said slowly after a pause. What was that she read on his rigid features? Trepidation? Caution? No . . . it wasn't that. The gate had slammed down on his expression. It was the expression he'd get occasionally when he was keeping something from her. *Wasn't* it?

Maybe it was, Alice wasn't sure. She felt confused. All she wanted at that moment was to get away from the edge of that treacherous bluff. Her fear made her irrational, in more ways than one.

"Well, I *know* not," she corrected heatedly. Her skin was prickling and she felt nauseated. "Can we please go inside?"

She broke from his arms and stalked toward the long yard that led toward the house. After she'd gone twenty feet or so, he halted her by grabbing her hand. She looked back at him.

"I know how scared you are about heights. I was shocked to see you standing there. It looked like every ounce of blood had left your head when you turned around. It just . . . alarmed me."

"Well, it alarmed me, too!"

He closed his eyes briefly. His skin had darkened this afternoon. With the sun behind him, his face looked shadowed and enigmatic to her stunned brain.

"I know," he said, opening his eyes. This time, she read the concern in his expression perfectly. "I'll ask you again, are you okay?"

She nodded, her shoulders slumping slightly.

"I think I drank too much wine," she mumbled. "I was feeling kind of dizzy and I took the wrong path and then . . ." She waved feebly in the direction of the fence and the edge of the bluff.

"And then I snapped at you," Dylan finished, his mouth slanted. "I'm sorry."

Their gazes had met and held. A silent peace was made. He stepped closer and put his arm around her shoulder.

"Come on. Let's get you inside."

THE jarring incident was soon forgotten. Alice had never been so reluctant to leave the peaceful haven of the castle and the heaven of Dylan's arms as she was that Monday morning. She'd have gladly curled up in bed with him for many days to come, basking in the newness and sensual delight of their mutually acknowledged love. It was difficult to pull herself out of her daydreams and resume her routine at camp. Although something *did* happen at breakfast that certainly sent a jolt of reality and euphoria through her.

She was standing alone at the coffee station, waiting for the pot to finish brewing and praying for an extra-strong pot. Someone spoke behind her.

"How is it that you always manage to come out on top?"

Alice spun around at the sound of the quiet, bitter voice. Brooke stood there, looking glamorous and beautiful, despite her casual camp attire. Brooke Seifert was the only person Alice knew who could do her hair and put makeup on for a hot summer day filled with rigorous activity, and still look disgustingly gorgeous and put together at the end of it all.

"I'm assuming that's a rhetorical question," Alice mumbled, staring at the coffeepot with quiet desperation. She hadn't even had caffeine yet. How was she supposed to deal with Brooke?

Despite the fact that she'd told Thad she'd try to get to know Brooke better and give her the benefit of the doubt, she hadn't really lived up to her promise. It'd just been easier to stay away from both Brooke and Thad for the past few days, although the avoidance hurt much more in Thad's case than in Brooke's.

She did a double take when Brooke shoved her cell phone in front of Alice's face. Startled, she stared at the image on the screen.

"You haven't seen it yet?" Brooke demanded quietly, obviously recognizing Alice's shock. "All the managers are crowing about it, although Kehoe doesn't seem too pleased," she added with bitter triumph. Her victory was short lived. An uncertain, sullen expression came over Brooke's face. "I suppose you put them up to it?"

Alice laughed abruptly. She grabbed Brooke's phone, peering closer at the photo. "Oh my God. That's *awesome*."

Dave came up behind them, grinning. "Is this your first time seeing it? Everyone is talking about it. They sent out texts with the photo this morning. They somehow got most of the managers' phone numbers, plus most of the counselors'. At least one kid on every team got one, too, so the photos are flying around with the speed of light. Hilarious. Nice one, Alice."

Someone called out to Dave, and he walked away.

"There's more. Next photo," Brooke said through a tight mouth.

Alice took another long look at the first before moving to the next, however. The photo was of an iron goat perched on a stone pedestal—obviously Camp Wildwood's legendary Bang. The area behind it was dark and empty. It was clearly the dead of night. Around Bang's neck was tied the Red Team's iconic flag. The goat was wearing sunglasses that Alice immediately recognized as Judith's knock-off Cartiers. Beneath it, three hands held up in the V for victory sign: one large, light brown, clearly masculine, another feminine, paler with long manicured nails, the last small and delicate. Alice suspected she knew to whom all the hands belonged.

Alice swiped her finger on the screen. Her grin widened. This was *priceless*. Now the common area around Bang was filled with people. The photo showed Noble D, Jill Sanchez, and Judith surrounded by several other teenagers and adults, most of them wearing sweatpants, shorts, T-shirts, and pajamas. They were strangers to Alice. This must be the Camp Wildwood staff and kids. D and

Judith appeared to be passing around pizza boxes, Jill handing out cans of soda. The girl's mouth was open as though she was talking, and she was grinning.

Jill? Talking to strangers with what looked like genuine enthusiasm?

The caption underneath the photo read: *How to make trouble and friends at once, Camp Durand–style.*

Alice barked with laughter, unable to stop herself despite the fact that she knew Brooke would find her pleasure annoying.

"They gave the kids at Camp Wildwood a *pizza party?*" she blurted out incredulously.

"After they snuck into camp unnoticed and took their pictures of the goat, proving they could have stolen it *if* they wanted to," Brooke said, grabbing her phone back abruptly. She looked mutinous as she met Alice's stare. "I know you must have set them up to it. It could have easily had the opposite effect, you know. All the managers could have been as pissed as Kehoe is. How did you know they wouldn't be?"

"I didn't for sure," Alice said, shrugging. "The kids wanted the adventure and the challenge, and I thought they should have it. They *are* supposed to be here to have fun, you know. I just wanted to make sure they did as respectfully and safely as possible." She nodded at the phone in Brooke's clutching hand. "They came up with all the other brilliant ideas."

"*Brilliant,*" Brooke spat. Alice's spine straightened, until she noticed that despite Brooke's bitchiness, tears pooled in her eyes and her lower lip trembled. Alice's acidic retort evaporated on her tongue.

"What's wrong?" Alice wondered, confounded by the other woman's show of vulnerability. Brooke was always in control and smug in her superior knowledge and position. Alice had been intimidated by her from the first moment she laid eyes on her. To see Brooke on the verge of tears shook her a little. "It's not a big deal, Brooke. They're just kids, having a good time."

"It *is* a big deal," Brooke corrected in a hushed, but harsh tone. "I can't win when it comes to you. I can't beat you because I can't figure out why everyone is so determined to act like you're *special* when you're really just a grubby, smart-mouthed, low-class—"

"Whoa," Alice interrupted angrily. She pointed at the other woman in a menacing gesture. "Stop right there."

Brooke inhaled shakily. A tear skipped down her cheek. "No matter what I do, I can't beat you. If I don't make it as a Durand manager, it'll all be because of you."

Alice gaped at her in disbelief. "Because of *me*. That's ridiculous. First off, there's no reason you shouldn't make the cut. Everyone knows you're a top runner. But if you *didn't* make manager, it'd be because you're more worried about yourself than you are your kids."

Brooke's expression broke. Several more tears fell down her cheek. "That's not true," she exclaimed shakily. "Do you really think that? I care about my team. A lot."

Alice stared, seeing the other woman's genuine dismay at the idea that someone thought she was selfish when it came to her team. She exhaled sharply, resisting a strong urge to roll her eyes. Suddenly feeling awkward, she turned back to pour her coffee. Jeez, she hadn't even had a single sip of coffee yet, and she had to deal with not just a regular Brooke, but an *anguished* Brooke. God help her.

"I don't really think it," Alice mumbled grudgingly, ripping the paper on a sugar packet and pouring it into her steaming coffee. "I've watched you. You're really good with them. They like you. My student team leader, Judith—you know, the one in the Bang pictures—thinks you're brilliant, the perfect example of feminine leadership. Compassionate. Strong. Put together. Always unruffled," Alice said, scowling. It was a truth she'd sworn she'd never confess to anyone, let alone to Brooke, of all people. But it was a fact. During the first week of camp, when Judith and Alice had been grinding against each other at every turn, Judith had made a few pointed remarks within Alice's hearing about Brooke's superior pedigree and education in comparison to Alice's. Now that she knew Judith better, she didn't think the girl had been doing it solely to annoy her because she knew Brooke was Alice's nemesis, either. Judith really did respect Brooke.

When Brooke didn't speak after Alice had ripped open her fourth sugar packet—she didn't even take sugar in her coffee—she glanced sideways warily. Her eyes sprang wide in alarm.

Brooke was totally unmasked. She stood there, all traces of smugness and superiority vanished, her expression open, unguarded, and undone. Her tears had smeared mascara onto her cheeks. Alice hastened to pull some napkins from the dispenser. She handed them to Brooke.

"Here," Alice said uncomfortably. "I'm sorry, I didn't mean—"

"You didn't *have* to say that about Judith," Brooke sniffed, wiping her cheeks. "Everyone at camp knows how much Judith defied you at first. It was sort of . . . well, *entertaining* to watch, to be honest," she added a little regretfully. "I thought she was going to kick your ass a few times."

"Me, too," Alice admitted.

Brooke swallowed thickly. "And you brought her around completely. She adores you now."

"Oh God, *no*," Alice insisted emphatically. "Judith worships no man or woman. She prefers to be on the adored end of things."

Brooke smiled shakily. Another tear fell down her cheek and she wiped it away quickly. "There's nothing wrong with a woman knowing what she wants."

"No. I guess there's not."

An awkward silence fell.

"Well . . ." Brooke inhaled and wiped her cheeks one final

time. Alice could almost see her willfully knitting together her fraying ends. Not for the first time, she admired Brooke. Maybe they'd never be the best of friends, but Thad had been right about one thing: Brooke had her moments.

"I'm sorry for jumping all over you like that," Brooke said briskly, tossing the napkins. She met Alice's stare levelly. "I panicked for a few minutes when I saw the photos and heard the rumor about how much the managers admired the Red Team's stunt."

"I don't think you have any reason to panic."

"I still think there's a good chance we'll beat you tonight," Brooke said, her chin tilting up.

"Maybe. I'll be fine with that, as long as my kids feel okay about themselves. It might be time for them to deal with some disappointment, anyway. They're getting a little cocky with all their wins," Alice said, suppressing a smile and not succeeding.

"Imagine that," Brooke said, her arch look reminding Alice of the Brooke of old. But then she gave Alice a small, genuine-seeming smile before she turned away.

Brooke was gone before Alice realized that neither of them had mentioned Thad. Alice was glad he hadn't come up. Maybe both of them had realized intuitively that Thad was too weighty of a topic to withstand their unexpected, delicate truce.

THAT night at the bonfire, her kids were flying high. The entire camp was buzzing with the word of Judith, Jill, and Noble D's exploit at Camp Wildwood. Terrance was telling anyone who would listen that Judith, Jill, and D were the chosen emissaries from the Red Team because they were three of the more upstanding, rule-abiding kids, and therefore under the night supervisor's radar. He assured people that the entire team was involved in the venture, though, and had agreed on the three campers to represent them.

"We all chipped in for the pizza, and it was my idea to tie the Red Team's flag around the goat's neck," Alice overheard Terrance bragging to the Gold Team's student leader as darkness fell and a couple managers started to shout for them to take their seats.

Alice started to sit down on the beach between Judith and Matt Dinorio when someone spoke from behind her.

"Alice? A word please before things officially get started."

Alice noticed Judith's concerned expression when they both turned to see Sebastian Kehoe standing behind her.

"Sure," Alice said.

Kehoe nodded in the direction of the woods. The sun had just slipped beneath the horizon, leaving the western sky a brilliant blend of magenta, orange, red, and gold, but the woods were dark. Kehoe paused just inside the shadow the tall trees cast onto the beach and faced her.

"I suppose you know what this is about?" Kehoe asked.

"Um . . ." Alice blinked. The light from the western sky gleamed red in his glasses, although his face was cast in shadow. "Bang?" she asked hesitantly.

He looked grim. "I'm *not* happy about your little spectacle. I've made it clear around camp that while Camp Wildwood forays have been condoned if not encouraged in the past, we were putting a damper on the idea this year. Now your kids have gone and made it seem even more glamorous and desirable to break the rules in subsequent years."

Alice swallowed thickly. "I didn't think there was any real danger in it, sir. My kids knew they'd have to be respectful. I wasn't encouraging theft. I made sure they understood that."

Kehoe's mouth clamped together in a tight, straight line. "I suppose you had some advice from a certain former Red Team member? Some instructions from another Durand *maverick*?"

A chill passed over the surface of her arms. He was referring to Dylan, of course. He really *did* suspect their involvement. Or possibly, he more than suspected.

But he was wrong to think Dylan had given her the idea. She raised her chin.

"No. Any ideas I did plant with the kids were mine alone, and they came up with the rest. The whole photo as a symbol of the claiming of the goat versus actually stealing it was their idea. So was the pizza party, which personally, I think was brilliant. It was a gesture of friendship, and it went a long way to mend any bad feelings that happened between Camp Durand and Wildwood last year."

Kehoe looked like he'd just eaten something bitter. "Apparently, most of the Durand managers agree with you." He hesitated. "So did the Camp Wildwood staff. Their staff supervisor contacted me this afternoon and asked all of the Durand campers and staff to come to a cookout next year at Camp Wildwood."

"That's great!"

"I didn't ask you over here to praise you," he snapped. Alice's grin vanished in a split second. He was coiled as tight as a spring. She resisted an urge to step away from him. Surely it was a trick of the fading light and shadows, but Kehoe looked a little crazed at that moment.

"You're as full of yourself as she was. As he *is*. What do you actually think is going to come of this? That you're going to ride off into the sunset with your prince?" he snarled. "It didn't happen before. It's *not* going to happen now."

She stood there, her mouth hanging open in shock, watching as Kehoe walked stiffly away from her toward the blazing bonfire.

AS she returned to the circle of the kids, she noticed Sal Rigo standing at the back of the crowd. His face looked rigid as he watched her approach. She had the distinct impression he was poised to spring into action. Alice nodded once in reassurance. For the first time, the sight of him nearby reassured instead of annoyed her. Kehoe had been beyond rude. He'd bordered on vicious. Rigo warily turned and sat with the others on the sand, keeping Alice within his sight.

The encounter had rattled her. She had no doubt the "he" that Kehoe had referred to as he dressed her down was Dylan. Had he garbled his words, by initially saying *she*? And what had he meant about *before*? Was he trying to make her believe Dylan had become involved with a new recruit before, and that Kehoe had stopped it? Because Alice had worried about that in the beginning, but in the end, she just didn't believe Dylan made a habit of this. It showed how angry Kehoe was . . . how desperate, that he'd stoop to innuendo and slander. She'd never seen Kehoe come undone. He was usually so meticulously in control.

Maybe *too* in control. Tonight, all the pressure he must exert to be so together all the time had seemed to be steaming out of the cracks in his armor.

The only thing she knew for certain was that Kehoe's feelings toward her were not the dislike and disapproval she'd suspected.

Sebastian Kehoe clearly *hated* her.

SIXTEEN

At nine thirty that night, Dylan sat in his den talking to Jim Sheridan. Since tonight was the bonfire, Alice would work late. They'd planned to meet an hour later than their usually designated time. He'd originally been glad to have a little extra time to deal with Jim's visit.

Now he was just annoyed and frustrated.

"Why did you have to push it?" he barked at Jim, his anger undisguised.

He sat at his desk, his elbow on the blotter. He pressed his fingertips against his shut eyelids. His flash of fury drained out of him almost instantly, leaving him weary in its wake. Jim had just informed him that he'd done a background check on Alice Reed. In doing so, he'd come across Sissy Reed's name, and done a subsequent check on her. Being the bullheaded, diligent cop he was, he'd eventually gone deep enough into both Sissy's and Avery Cunningham's separate criminal histories to notice that Sissy and Cunningham had both served time at Cook County Juvenile Detention at the same time.

"I'm sorry. I'm a curious son of a bitch, you know that. Always have been," Jim said apologetically. Dylan slowly opened his eyes and met the sheriff's stare. "Your reaction on the night the alarm went off set me down the path. Clearly, this wasn't some run-of-the-mill bedmate, as wound up as you were. But the more I looked at Alice . . ." He shrugged helplessly. "I'm sure you notice the resemblance between her and Lynn, too. It wasn't obvious at first, but there was something familiar that was tickling at my memory. Then it was prodding at it so bad I couldn't sleep. You're right. I couldn't let it go."

"She's not ready to face the FBI's interrogations. The press. The Durand board. The challengers to a claim that she's the long-lost Durand heiress. The result of the Reeds being implicated in the kidnapping. I was just trying to buy some time for her."

"Would anyone ever be *ready* for that?" Jim asked, compassion in his tone.

"Can you at least wait to tell the FBI until after the genetic testing is in? You could say we wanted to be sure before we contacted them."

"That would require that I lie in regard to everything you just told me about Avery Cunningham's deathbed confession, Dylan. That's a hell of a lot of withholding, for a hell of a long time, whether the genetic testing is conclusive or not. Besides, both of us know what those results are going to be."

"Just give me until the end of the week, then," he bargained without pause. "For whatever reason, the completion of Camp Durand means the world to Alice. She wants to prove that she's capable of being a Durand leader."

"If that testing proves it, she *owns* the company, doesn't she?" Jim asked, bewildered.

"Of course, but you don't know Alice," Dylan frowned. "She's very . . . stubborn at times."

"Hasn't changed that much from when she was little, then," Jim said with a small, sad smile.

"Just give me until Friday. Give *Alice* until then. That's the last official day of camp. There's a dinner and the individual awards and the Team Championship trophy are given here at the castle. You have no idea what it'd mean to Alice, to finish this before the swarm descends."

"I can't keep something this big a secret, Dylan. Not without sacrificing some pretty damn important professional ethics."

"I know you have to inform the authorities. I understand. Just give it a few days? The counselors don't know it, but the managers and Kehoe start to tabulate all their evaluations to decide which of the nine counselors are going to become Durand employees tonight, after the points are rewarded for team competition. The votes are tallied and the results are final by Wednesday. On Thursday, they start to inform each counselor who was chosen and who wasn't in private meetings. At least give me enough time so that if push comes to shove, she could see the results and know she'd been selected as a Durand manager, fair and square."

He sensed Jim's continued hesitation. Frustration rose in him.

"Sometimes, I don't think I'll ever get her to accept her legacy if she can't make the first step of successfully completing this damn camp," Dylan said, slapping his hand on the desk. Jim started at his intensity. "She's fixated on the idea. I can't sway her. But then—" He exhaled and sagged heavily back in his chair. "Sometimes, I see her point, even if I'd rather not. She's had a shitload of confusion and shock and disbelief dumped onto her. Completing the camp successfully feels like . . . some kind of tangible stepping stone for her, I guess."

"Between Addie's world and her own," Jim said.

He met Jim's stare and nodded once.

"I'll give you until Thursday evening. That's the best I can do, Dylan. I'll let on like we just had this conversation before I contact them. And I'll tell them that you were holding off in telling the truth because you wanted to see the results of the blood test first. The chances are that agents won't arrive here until the following day, if I contact them after hours. Hell, I don't even know who's going to answer the phone for the number I have," Jim said, shrugging dubiously. "For all I know, the agents who worked on the case are retired or moved on to other jobs."

"Do you think I'll be in trouble with the FBI?" Dylan asked quietly. "For withholding the truth until now?"

"I doubt it. All you did was succeed in a mission they failed at for twenty years. But there's always the chance they won't take to your keeping secrets kindly. I suggest we don't let on so blatantly that we're as convinced as we are that Addie Durand and Alice Reed are the same person. Who knows?" Jim said, shrugging. "It may turn out we're wrong."

"Not a chance," Dylan said grimly. "You won't think so, either, when I tell you about some of Alice's returning memories."

"I don't need much convincing as it is." Jim pointed toward the door. "I'm going to use the facilities first. Tell me about her memories when I come back?"

Dylan nodded. Jim didn't shut the den door when he left. As Dylan waited, he heard a distant knocking. Hammering, actually. Someone was at the front door. He quickly checked his watch. It was going on ten o'clock. Who the hell was visiting at this hour?

As he neared the foyer, he realized the knocking was persistent and loud. He swung open the heavy front door and saw Sebastian Kehoe standing on the stoop, his face fixed and pale.

"Sebastian. Is something wrong?" Dylan asked, alarmed at his unexpected appearance and tense presentation.

"She won again tonight. The team competition," Sebastian grated out without answering Dylan's question. "She tied with Thad Schaefer, but it doesn't matter. She won the team competition last week, as well. She's managed to win the favor of every manager. They'll all cast votes in favor of her."

"What's your point?" Dylan asked slowly.

"You don't even ask whom I'm talking about," Kehoe said bitterly. "You know I'm referring to her. *Alice.*"

"I figured," Dylan said with false calmness. "Alice Reed. I'm aware that she won the team competition last week."

"You're aware of a hell of a lot more than that about her."

"Careful, Sebastian," Dylan said softly. Kehoe's mouth snapped shut. Suddenly he shook his head.

"No. No, I'm not going to let it happen. I'm not going to let that know-it-all, trailer-trash upstart claim the position of Durand executive. She's completely unsuitable," Kehoe shouted.

"I suggest you calm down. As for Alice, the twelve Durand managers seem to disagree with you. And it's what the majority vote says that counts."

"It's because of your constant intrusion that we're in this situation. You brought her here. I would never have hired her as a counselor to begin with. You *contrived* to get that interview with her while we were in Chicago, didn't you? You've been manipulating me! I will *not* let this happen."

"Then you'll be out of a job, won't you?"

"I was working and excelling at this job before you knew how to drive. How dare you threaten me," Kehoe bellowed.

Dylan stepped forward, anger pouring like ice through his veins. "You really think that was a *threat*? That was reality, plain and simple. Am I making myself clear?"

Kehoe looked apoplectic. Dylan had been in more than his fair share of fistfights as a kid and young man. He had the familiar feeling of being face-to-face with a person who had reached his limit, with whom logic's hold was weakening. The word *rabid* came to mind. He tensed, fully prepared for Kehoe to physically attack him.

"What's this all about?" a mild voice asked from behind them.

Eyeing Kehoe carefully and remaining on high alert, Dylan took a step back.

"It's Sebastian Kehoe. He's expressing some concerns about some goings-on at the camp tonight."

Jim stepped into Kehoe's view. He looked pleasantly surprised to see Kehoe standing at the threshold.

"Evening, Sebastian," Jim drawled. "Nice night, isn't it? Can I help with anything?"

Kehoe flinched and twisted his mouth, like he was gargling acid. He definitely was considering spewing some nasty words. Or worse.

Instead, he did an about-face and marched down the stairs.

Dylan and Jim watched until Kehoe disappeared down the top of the road. Dylan swung the door shut with a brisk bang. Jim gave a low whistle.

"Did you hear it?" Dylan asked quietly.

"Every word."

"Good."

Dylan waved his hand and both of them headed back to his office.

After they'd spoken for several minutes about Kehoe's bizarre, insubordinate tantrum, Dylan started to calm down a little. He confessed one of his more immediate concerns about Kehoe.

"It looks as if I have to be out of town for two nights, starting tomorrow. We're opening a plant in Reno, Nevada. Originally, I was scheduled to be there for five nights. I've managed to whittle it down to two, but I'm not going to be able to get out of it. I was planning on doubling Alice's security, but after what Kehoe just pulled, I'm not comfortable going at all."

Jim frowned. "You really think he'd try to *harm* Alice?"

"You heard how crazy he sounded when he talks about her. I thought he was going to come at me out there. If you hadn't shown up, he might have. He's losing it."

"I know I've never shared your concern about Kehoe and Addie Durand, but I still feel like I'm missing something."

"Join the club," Dylan muttered under his breath.

"Do you think Kehoe *knows* Alice is Addie Durand?"

"I didn't think he did at first, but now I think he might." He filled Jim in on the details of Thad Schaefer overhearing Alice talking about having memories of Addie. "Kehoe has been suspicious of Alice since day one. He knew I considered her special. Different. I think at first, he just thought I was attracted to her, so she was an object of not only interest to him, but derision. It's no secret among the board of directors that Kehoe disapproves of me, and so I thought he was just transferring that dislike to Alice. I've heard rumors he's down on her at the camp a lot, although she's a high performer so it's hard to call her out on specifics. I don't know how long Schaefer was standing in that hallway last week, or how much he actually heard, let alone understood. I haven't been able to get him to admit that someone, quite possibly Kehoe, has asked him to spy on Alice— to influence her. I'm trying to convince Schaefer that I'm not the bad guy here, but unfortunately, he's having trouble seeing reason when it comes to Alice. He's pretty invested in seeing me as a jerk because he wants her for himself. But if Schaefer *did* hear Alice that night and if he *did* feed information to Kehoe right after the Alumni Dinner, then Kehoe might very well suspect Alice is Addie Durand."

"Kehoe is picking a strange way to garner favor with his new boss, then."

"That's my whole point. He was that pissed off tonight at the idea of Alice becoming a Durand junior executive. Can you imagine what his fury would be if he suspects or knows she's the owner of Durand Enterprises? And what if he *was* involved in the kidnapping? What then?"

Jim's eyebrows arched in understanding. Dylan had shared his feelings on that topic before, and Jim suspected there might be some truth to the idea that there was a shadowy puppet master behind the Durand kidnapping case. Kehoe was certainly a possible suspect they'd discussed over the years. Presently, Jim brought up the point where they usually ended up stuck.

"But why would Kehoe hate Addie so much? He didn't really even have any interactions with her, did he? He's been a successful Durand executive for years. Why would he risk everything by stooping to the level of child kidnapping? It's not like Alan would ever consider making *him* his heir in place of Addie."

"If I knew the answer to those questions, you would, too," Dylan said, his mouth tight with irritation at that frustrating impasse.

"It seems more likely to me that Kehoe is transferring his dislike of you to Alice, since he suspects you two are involved. He sees it as you treading on his haloed recruitment territory."

Dylan scowled. That seemed like the obvious answer, but he couldn't give his verbal agreement.

"Well, I can certainly keep a closer eye on things while you're gone, make a police presence known at the camp just to discourage anything. I'll make up an excuse about there being a theft from the lodge or something, just to explain the sheriff's department being in the area. But as far as your immediate concern about Kehoe and Reno, Nevada, I have a suggestion: Take him with you. Then you won't have to worry about Alice and him being in the same place while you're away."

"That's not a bad idea," Dylan muttered after a moment. "People are going to think it's odd, and Kehoe is going to be pissed as hell to be pulled away while his precious camp is in session, but you know what?" He leaned back in his chair, already mentally planning how he was going to orchestrate the maneuver. "I really don't give a damn what that asshole thinks."

THAT night, Dylan had expected that Alice would be flushed with excitement over her team's tied win for first place in the team competition. Instead, she seemed tense, tired, and distracted when they returned to the castle. When he suggested she take a hot bath in the Jacuzzi tub and try to unwind, she agreed immediately, making him think she realized she wasn't herself, too.

After she emerged from the bathroom a while later, hair damp and wrapped in her robe, she appeared a little more relaxed. He was reading a report, half-reclining in bed against the pillows. He set it aside as she approached and beckoned her with his hand. Wordlessly, she came down on the mattress and cuddled up to him, her head on his chest.

"That tub is amazing. My legs and arms are like cooked noodles."

"Good, you needed it."

She made a satisfied sound of agreement.

"Did something happen today that made you so tense?" he asked, sliding his hand beneath her robe and stroking the soft, dewy skin of her shoulder. He glanced down and saw her lips part, but she said nothing. Her long eyelashes flickered. He sensed her hesitation. "Alice?" he prompted.

"It was nothing," she said softly.

"If there was an 'it,' then it *had* to be something."

She placed her opened hand, palm down on his bare abdomen. His nerves flickered in awareness at her touch. She caressed him, gliding her hand toward his crotch. He placed his hand on top of hers.

"Are you trying to distract me?" he asked her.

She turned her face into his chest. "No, you're distracting me. You smell good. And you feel good," she said throatily, rubbing her lips against his skin. His skin roughened at her touch. He resisted a strong urge to push her head closer . . . encourage her. He slipped his fingers beneath her chin and applied pressure. She looked up at him reluctantly.

"What happened?" He read her anxiety like a neon sign. "Tell me," he insisted.

She shook her head impatiently. "It was Kehoe," she finally admitted.

"What about Kehoe?"

"He came down really hard on me for this thing my kids did— something that the other managers liked and he didn't."

"What did he say?"

She sighed. "I don't expect you to fight any battles for me when it comes to Kehoe," she said impatiently. "I don't expect you to do anything for me when it comes to my counselor duties, and you've said you wanted me to sink or swim on my own merits. I can handle it, Dylan."

He cupped the side of her head. "This isn't about your success or failure as a Camp Durand counselor, Alice. It's about Kehoe. And you. He came up here tonight, ranting. I've never seen him like that before."

She blinked in surprise. She planted her elbow on the mattress and propped herself up, so that she could see him better. "He came up here? What was he ranting about?"

"You. Me. He insisted that I was somehow responsible for you doing well as a counselor, implying I was coaching you. He said he was going to refuse to offer you a position as a junior executive, even if the other managers gave you the votes."

"He *did*?" she gasped. "What did you say?"

"That if he did, I'd fire him."

Her eyes widened.

"He acted like a lunatic. Jim Sheridan heard it all, and he thought the same thing. I want to know what he said to *you*. I'm not trying to fight any human resources battles for you. This is about something much more practical and important."

She sighed. "He just said stuff about how while everyone else might think I'm doing well as a counselor, he doesn't. And then he said all this weird stuff about me being dead wrong if I thought I was going to ride off into the sunset with Prince Charming." She rolled her eyes. Despite her supposed casual attitude, he sensed her anxiety though. It made him tense.

"What else, Alice?" he prodded.

"He . . . he sort of implied *this*"—she waved between them—"has happened before, and he didn't allow it *then* and he wouldn't now, either."

"What? That you and I had been involved before?"

"No." She glanced up at him warily through spiky bangs. "I

think he was implying that you'd slept with someone under his watch before . . . like a new Durand recruit or something, and that he put a halt to it." She shook her head, appearing bewildered. "Maybe I misunderstood him. I know you've said that isn't true, that you've never slept with a Durand employee before."

"You're just not sure you can believe me."

"I do believe you, Dylan. But why did he *say* that? What's he trying to accomplish?"

"Dissention. He's jealous of your success at the camp, of me, of what we have . . . everything. And he's trying to poison any happiness we might have," he said, sounding more irritated than he'd intended.

"He obviously knows about us. If he tells the other Durand managers we're involved, they'll probably withdraw their votes for me."

"He wouldn't dare," Dylan told her, his glance assuring her he was stating a fact, not an opinion. In the privacy of his mind, he was having some pretty vivid fantasies about punching away that smug, superior look on Sebastian Kehoe's face. How *dare* he try to sway Alice by implying Dylan had a history of seducing Durand employees?

Alice's anxious expression penetrated his aggressive fantasy. He cupped the side of her head and waited until her dark blue eyes met his. "You've done extremely well as a counselor. No one is going to take that away from you. I'll make sure Kehoe is solid on that point. He's taking a trip with me to Reno tomorrow. We'll be away for a couple nights, so there'll be plenty of opportunity for us to talk," he stated grimly.

Her spine straightened. "You're going away tomorrow?"

He nodded. He planted his hands at her waist and shifted her, sliding her farther up his body. When she craned her chin up and stared up at him through her spiky bangs and long lashes, their mouths were only inches apart. He maneuvered his hands between them. She lifted slightly to accommodate him, and he loosened the ties of her robe. He parted the sides of the fabric, exposing her nude body to his naked torso. He grunted in pleasure when she settled against him.

"I tried to get out of it, but I can't. I'm going to put some extra security on you at the camp while I'm gone," he said.

"Dylan, I don't want—"

"And I'd appreciate it"—he interrupted her, sliding his hands along her bare shoulders and arms, and ridding her of the robe altogether—"if you didn't lead that security on some kind of wild-goose chase. They're good people, and they're just trying to do their job, Alice."

"I know," she mumbled, looking vaguely contrite. His gaze narrowed on the vision of her teeth scraping against her lower lip. "I won't try to get away from them."

"Thank you. Now come here."

He put his hand at the back of her head, bringing the tempting distraction of her mouth within striking distance.

SHE ran through a sun-dappled hallway, laughing. The gong had just sounded, and she was so hungry. The smells of chicken and macaroni and cheese filled her nose, making her salivate. There was chocolate ice cream for dessert, too. Mommy had let Cook have the day off, and she'd made the meal herself—all of Addie's favorites. But the chocolate ice cream: That was *Daddy's* favorite, too.

"Hurry, Daddy. Dinnertime," she called over her shoulder. He was more of a feeling than a tangible man behind her. He was so big—as big as a mountain—and so strong. And he loved to laugh. There was nothing her daddy couldn't do.

"I'm right beside you, Addie. I always will be," he called.

Her scurrying footsteps halted. His voice echoed in her head. So rich and warm, love knitted into every syllable.

So real.

"Daddy?" she called out shakily, because all she saw behind her were shadows. Fear slinked into her golden world like a light-sucking serpent. A shiver tore through her. Why couldn't she see him? She peered into shifting light and darkness, taking a step toward him, hoping to see him. Craving it. Someone grasped her upper arm from behind, the hard grip making her cry out in shock. She turned and saw Mommy, but she didn't look right. Her face was pinched with fear. Her neck and ear were wet with a shiny bright red liquid, but it was the wildness in her large eyes that terrified Addie the most.

"Run, Addie. *Hide*."

ALICE awoke to the sound of her own shout. Her muscles immediately tensed and moved for fight or flight, but someone was holding her down.

"Alice. Shhh, it's okay, baby. You were having a nightmare."

The sound of Dylan's voice penetrated her thick fear. Her thrashing slowed, but she couldn't seem to stop it altogether, as though the primal necessity for flight was quieted by degrees, not entirely in a moment.

"Shhh. You're safe. Everything is fine," Dylan soothed, tightening his hold on her until her sluggish fight eased. The sounds of her ragged breathing filled her ears. "You okay?" he asked after a moment, stroking her arms, warming her pebbled flesh.

"Yeah. It was the *dinner* gong," she gasped. In her mind's eye, she reviewed the brief but vivid dream. "Mommy would ring it to let Daddy and me know it was time to eat. There was going to be macaroni and cheese and chicken . . . and . . . and chocolate ice cream."

"Your favorite meal," Dylan murmured. "And yes. You're right. That's what the gong was used for. It called you to dinner every night."

"And I heard his voice," she panted. "But I couldn't see him."

His soothing motions slowed. "Alan's?"

"Daddy's," she whispered. She flinched. "I wish I could have seen him," she cried out in frustration. Intense longing and grief flooded her. She paused to repress a powerful urge to sob. "But I heard his voice, and it was so real. And then Mommy was telling me to run and hide again, and there was blood on her ear and neck. Dylan, are you sure she wasn't there when I was taken in the woods? Are you *sure* those men didn't hurt her, too?"

She felt Dylan shift behind her. The bedside lamp clicked on. He urged her with his hands to face him. Alice scooted onto her side. She was naked. They'd made love before falling asleep, she recalled dazedly. Her skin was sheened with perspiration, but she was cold. She shivered, and Dylan pulled the sheet and comforter securely around her neck. She searched every detail of his tense, handsome face.

"It was a dream, Alice," he assured quietly.

"But his voice . . . I think it was real." She *wanted* that part to be real.

He nodded. "That might have been a real memory, or memory of emotions mixing with a dream. *Not* the part about the blood, though. You never saw Lynn like that. *Never.* She was up at the house when you were kidnapped."

"It's the first time I've ever had any memory of him. It's always been her," she mumbled, determinedly reliving that portion of her dream again. She didn't want to dwell on the expression of stark fear and panic on the woman's face.

Or the blood.

"He sounded so strong and warm. He liked to laugh, didn't he?"

"Yes. Especially with you. All of his thoughts about his business,

every worry or problem that needed to be solved: All that melted
away the minute you ran into the room. He became lighter with you
there. Happier."

"He told me he was right beside me, and that he always would
be. And . . . and he liked chocolate ice cream as much as me." This
time, she couldn't restrain her sob. She turned her face into the
pillow, embarrassed by the raggedness of her emotions. How was
it possible that so much feeling could be embedded in a brief flash
of a dream and a few words?

Dylan rubbed her back. "I know it must hurt. But isn't it better
to have the memory, as painful as it is? You're right about the ice
cream. It was Alan's favorite. You really *did* have a memory of
him. Your father adored you, Alice. I never knew a man could love
a child so much and without a shred of reservation. It was a revela-
tion to me, to see his devotion to you and Lynn."

"I'm never going to know him." She gasped and curled up her
legs. The realization had felt like a knife going through her belly.
"Those bastards took him from me. I wish I could kill them."

"I know. I know, baby."

After a moment of Dylan holding her and kissing her cheek
and the side of her head, the acuteness of her pain eased to an ache.
"I'm never going to know them," she repeated dully, as if she were
teaching herself a lesson she instinctively didn't want to learn, but
knew she must. "Never."

"You *do* know them," Dylan said, his fierceness making her
blink and rise out of her misery. "Feelings like they had for you,
and you once had for them, don't disappear, Alice. Who they were
is a part of you. It's like Alan said in your dream: He'll always be
beside you."

Another shudder of grief went through her. It was too big for
her to absorb, that dream. "I can't do this, Dylan."

"You can. Your mind knows what you can handle and what
you can't. That's the natural way of things," he soothed, stroking

her with long, reassuring caresses. "And I'm right here with you. Do you understand?"

"Yes," she sniffed. *Dylan is here.* She nodded her head against the pillow, fortified by that solid, wonderful truth.

ALICE awoke several minutes before the dawn. The dream about the dinner gong and Alan Durand still clung to her. Moving carefully so as not to rob Dylan of those precious extra moments of sleep, she eased off the bed. He was up, however, when she exited the bathroom. The bedside light was on. He stood by his dresser, wearing a pair of jeans and pulling on a dark blue T-shirt. She smiled as she walked toward him. She liked him best this way: mussed and warm from bed, his jaw shadowed with whiskers.

"What are you smiling about?" he asked, pulling the edge of his shirt down over his taut abdomen. She reached out and touched a patch of his naked skin before it disappeared.

"You. I like you in the morning, when you look like this."

He cupped her shoulder with one hand. "Then I guess that after camp is over, you'll have to get up every morning with me to ride, won't you?" he asked, a grin tilting his sexy lips. She went up on her tiptoes and kissed him.

"Is that a yes?" he asked gruffly a moment later, his hand now cupping the side of her head and their mouths brushing together.

"I'd like it to be a yes."

"Then it is," he said simply. He smiled, and she found herself smiling back, so *wanting* to be convinced by his absolute confidence.

"I'm glad you feel a little better," he said.

Alice blinked when she felt him slide something against her palm. It felt metallic and cool.

"What's this?" she asked, taking a step back and staring at what he'd placed in her hand. But Dylan didn't need to reply. It was a beautiful silver vintage lighter. On one side, the silver was smooth, on the other it was intricately chased. She ran her fingers over the tiny metallic grooves in wonder.

"It was Alan's," Dylan said. "I figured after last night . . ."

"He smoked?" Alice asked dazedly. She flipped open the cap and gasped softly. The whisking sound of the hinges sounded familiar. She repeated the action.

"No," she heard Dylan say. "I mean, he did, when he bought the lighter. He quit the day you were born. He kept the lighter out of habit . . . and because he was fond of it. He'd purchased it in Paris, when he and Lynn were on their honeymoon. He told me that once you discovered it in his pocket when you were three or so, and you became fascinated by it. So he removed the flint, so that it couldn't light. Then he felt better about giving it to you when you asked him to play with it."

"Yes," she said softly, running the lighter through her fingertips and whisking off the cap several times. It *did* feel familiar, the memory of the antique lighter a purely tactile one. The grooves in the metal felt good beneath her fingertips. No wonder she'd liked it as a child. Impulsively, she pressed it against her lips and nose and inhaled. There was no discernible odor, but she smiled anyway. She had the distinct impression she'd done that before. She looked up at Dylan.

"Is it okay? That I gave it to you now? Is it too soon?" he asked.

She shook her head adamantly. "No," she assured him, going up on tiptoe again to put her arms around his neck. "It's perfect."

When she lowered enough to see his face, she saw a shadow of tension on his face.

"What's wrong?" she whispered.

He shook his head, stroking her shoulders. "It's nothing," he grimaced and inhaled. "No, that's not true. It's something." He met her stare. "I wish this could have waited, but it can't. We need to talk about something important when I come back Thursday, okay?"

SEVENTEEN

That morning, she was extra thankful for the distraction of running with Terrance on the beach when she returned to camp. Dylan had insisted that what they needed to discuss wasn't earth-shattering, and that he was confident she could handle it. But he wouldn't say any more. About that, anyway.

He *did* tell her that he wanted her to return to the camp and hit the ball out of the park in regard to her counselor duties.

"You've been a huge success here," he'd said. "Now, just focus on going down there and sealing the deal."

His support had meant a lot to her. Enough that she was pretty successful at focusing all her attention on Terrance that morning.

Terrance was doing a lot less huffing and puffing nowadays, even though he continued to waste an awful lot of breath by talking to her nonstop.

"I still think we were robbed with that *tie* with the Orange Team," he was saying as he thundered along next to her. "We won the wall climb, Jill got top points for that painting she did, and Miguel even told her it was so good that he talked to a gallery owner he knows, and the guy said he wanted it for his gallery," Terrance said, referring to Miguel Cabrera, the camp's talented art therapist. Alice was highly gratified over the fact that Jill had finally felt secure enough to leave her safety zone in her art. The result had been three unique and moving paintings, one of which Miguel considered fine enough to sell in a top gallery in Chicago.

Jill had gone speechless again for almost a whole day when Miguel told her. This time, her muteness had come from disbelief and happiness versus residual trauma. To see Jill so silently rapturous had humbled Alice, not to mention made her almost ridiculously proud.

"We dominated with that whole Bang thing," Terrance continued. "Judith won the diving competition, and Red Team won all the football games for the week—thanks to me."

Alice feigned shock. "And they had the nerve not to give us points for modesty."

Terrance grinned slyly. "Why deny greatness?"

"Does that mean you've decided you're going to go out for football this year?" she asked casually. It was something she'd been subtly pushing for with him. Not only did she think it'd help Terrance's self-esteem enormously, she knew that the practices and a coach would continue him on a path of better health.

"Those guys are all white dicks."

"All the guys on your school's team are white?" Alice asked, surprised.

"No, I just mean they've got the littlest . . . Sorry," Terrance said quickly when he noticed her repressive scowl as he started to show a measurement with his thumb and forefinger. "I just mean they're losers."

"Do you *really* know that?"

"The size of their dicks?"

"*Terrance.*"

He laughed. "I don't know any of them personally. But those guys who do sports are all, 'Look at me, I've got a shirt with numbers on it. Look at me, I can walk in the douche parade at a pep rally.'"

Alice suppressed a grin. "So you think people who are part of an organized team with a common goal are losers?"

"Yeah," he said, as if she'd stated the obvious.

"That's what you've been part of for the past few weeks," Alice said, staring out at the glistening lake. "Seems to me, you've been pretty damn good at being a team player."

"That's different—"

"No, it's not. Do you think I was the cheerleader, student counsel type in high school?"

"No, you were definitely a loner freak," Terrance replied approvingly.

"Thanks," Alice said, rolling her eyes. "My point is, you don't have to become some kind of mindless robot to be part of a team. You can grow stronger as an individual by working with other people. Look at what you guys accomplished on the wall climb. That was all through teamwork, but it made *you* feel good. It made you smarter, too. Better."

Terrance grimaced as he stared fixedly at the beach ahead.

"Those guys on the football team aren't going to like me."

"Screw them." He glanced over at her sharply. Alice grimaced. She hadn't meant to sound so sharp or bitter. She'd automatically gone into defensive mode at just the thought of cocky teenage athletes being jerks to Terrance. Alice knew how cruel kids could be toward another kid who was different. Grasping for her elusive reasonable calm, she continued more levelly. "Even if they do act like jerks at first, they'll change their mind when they get to know you. You just have to work through that first difficult phase. It doesn't mean anything when people say cruel things except that they're immature and stupid. Let them think what they want in the beginning. Your skills will speak for themselves in the end. And if I haven't told you enough, you *have* the skills, Terrance, not just the heft. A coach will be able to polish those skills up better than I can. With some hard work, you could be amazing," she said sincerely. "Besides . . . those other guys on the team will be scared that you'll squash them like a bug if they give you a hard time."

He snorted with amusement.

"You've got to believe in yourself, Terrance."

"I know," he admitted, his grin fading. "Who else will, right?"

Alice thought of his absentee mother, of the fact that he'd essentially been his own supervisor since he first entered elementary school. She didn't reply. She didn't think she needed to. Terrance knew better than anyone that if he didn't step up to the plate and take care of himself, no one else was going to do it. He gave her a pointed sideways glance as they made a turn on the beach and headed back toward camp.

"Did you believe in yourself when you first came here, and had Brooke Seifert staring down her nose at you?"

"Well . . . I might have had a *few* dark moments when I wavered," Alice replied with grim honesty after a moment.

"Yeah," Terrance chuckled. "Okay, I'll do it."

"You'll do what?"

"Go out for football."

"Really?" Alice asked, breaking her stride to do a euphoric little sideways leap.

Terrance grinned. "Brooke is at least the equivalent of the entire defensive line of Metro Tech varsity. I figure if you can do it, I can."

Alice grinned.

"Look out," Terrance muttered under his breath after a moment. "Psychotron ahead."

"Huh?" Alice asked. She followed Terrance's stare. Just past the marina, the camp had a small fitness course on the beach. Terrance and she jogged past Sebastian Kehoe, who was doing rapid pull-ups with mechanical precision. Alice had to hand it to him. The guy was in major good shape.

She gave an obligatory wave as they passed. Kehoe never wavered an iota in his pull-ups, but his gaze was fixed on Alice, following her as she passed. The exertion he made in his show of considerable strength made his face look rigid and somehow out of alignment.

"What'd I tell you?" Terrance whispered once they were well past Kehoe. "*Psychotron*."

Alice rolled her eyes. Privately, she was thinking that once again, Terrance was demonstrating his typical brilliant powers of social observation.

WHEN she left the kids that night under Crystal's supervision, she didn't walk as briskly or purposefully as she usually did. Dylan was halfway across the nation tonight. She reached into her jeans pocket and slid her fingers across the cool metal of the lighter. She'd been doing it all day, finding the sensation reassuring. He'd given her the lighter to remind her of Alan Durand, but instead, it made her think of him. The feeling of the lighter in her pocket reassured her, but it also made her miss Dylan all that much more.

Farther ahead on the path, Alice saw Thad standing face-to-face with Brooke. In the light of the fading sun, she saw their hands clasped together loosely at their sides. Thad's head dipped and their mouths met.

So . . . they were no longer hiding their relationship. She thought of what Thad had told her, about how he and Brooke had hooked up every once in a while since they were teenagers. Would they continue to be a couple after camp was over? Something in their manner tonight, their comfort level with one another and their easy intimacy, didn't call to Alice's mind a convenient, casual sexual relationship.

Thad looked around before she had a chance to duck onto the path that led to her and Kuvi's cabin.

"Alice," Thad called. She waved a greeting and reluctantly approached the couple. "I didn't get a chance to congratulate you last night at the bonfire. Nice job," Thad said when she was a few feet away.

"Back at you," Alice said. "Hi, Brooke."

"Alice," Brooke said. Her gaze ran over her. "Are you growing your hair out?"

"Oh," Alice touched her hair self-consciously. She pushed it behind her ears. "I just haven't had a chance to get it cut here at camp."

"Only a few more days left," Thad said. He smiled, and Alice had the random thought that he seemed more like the Thad of old. A little more relaxed. She wondered if the fact that a limousine had arrived at the camp this morning and a tight-mouthed Sebastian Kehoe had gotten into it had anything to do with Thad's rediscovered easiness. Kehoe had left for Reno on the company jet today, Dylan at his side. Leave it to Dylan to alleviate his concerns about Kehoe by just picking him up and transferring him to another part of the country.

"Yeah. It's flown by," Alice said.

"How are you going to feel about relocating?" Brooke asked.

"Well, assuming I get a spot, I'll go wherever Durand wants me," Alice replied. She was a little uncomfortable talking about it. Would Thad, Brooke, Kuvi, and Dave—everyone at Camp Durand—think her disingenuous when the truth came out about Addie Durand? Would they look back on moments like this, talking to her, and consider her a lying fake?

And did Thad suspect at all, given what he'd overheard her saying in the castle hallway the night of the Alumni Dinner? If he had heard, did he understand what it meant? Was that why he felt uncomfortable? She and Thad had been largely avoiding each other ever since then. Alice felt awkward, knowing he knew about her and Dylan . . . knowing he didn't trust Dylan. Plus, Dylan had told her that Thad had admitted to following her at times. Was he still infatuated with her?

"You'll get a spot," Brooke said, her sharp, annoyed glance reminding her of the Brooke of old. She'd noticed Thad was studying Alice closely. Brooke lifted Thad's hand, which she still held.

"So will you. The other seven slots are pretty much up for grabs, though."

"That's not true," Thad said somberly, dragging his gaze off Alice. "You'll get a spot. So will Dave and Kuvi. I'm sure of it."

Alice agreed.

"Yeah, well not too long now before we know for sure, one way or another," Brooke said, shrugging. She hitched her head toward the beach, looking pointedly at Thad. Thad nodded distractedly.

"You go on ahead. I need to talk to Alice about something," he said.

Brooke's eyes widened. Alice sensed her disbelief and anger. Brooke opened her mouth, and Alice sensed whatever she said wasn't going to be pretty.

"It's not what you're thinking, Brooke," Thad said sharply, preempting her fury. He held her stare. "I'll be down to the beach to meet you in a couple minutes. This won't take long. And it's important. Trust me?"

Brooke's mouth hung open. Alice thought she saw a hint of the vulnerability in Brooke's eyes that had been there when she confronted Alice about Bang.

"Okay," Brooke agreed. She gave Alice an uncertain glance before she turned and walked away.

"That was big of her," Alice mumbled, meaning it. Brooke was definitely miles ahead of her in the trust department.

"Yeah," Thad agreed grimly. Alice couldn't think of what else to say when his gaze once again ran over her face. Alice felt like he was an artist studying her for a portrait.

"What is it, Thad?" she asked uneasily.

"I wanted you to know that I didn't understand at first. What I overheard in the hallway of the castle that night. But I do now."

His meaning penetrated. She took a step back from him. Out of the corner of her vision, she saw movement at the far left of the common area. She blinked at the vision of Sal Rigo standing on the path. It was as if he'd emerged magically from the trees somehow. He was staring at both of them, his features rigid. Thad noticed Rigo, too.

"What the fu—"

"It's okay," Alice said sharply, cutting off Thad's indignant exclamation at Rigo's blatant intrusion on a private conversation. She waved at Rigo, the gesture both an acknowledgement of his presence and an assurance that she was fine, and he needn't approach any closer. She had difficulty meeting Thad's stare.

"Dylan has asked him to watch over me," she said uncomfortably.

There was an awkward silence.

"Because you're Adelaide Durand? Because you're the Durand heiress that was kidnapped twenty years ago?"

His quietly uttered words struck her like bullets, denting her mental armor. Maybe a few penetrated. Her throat had closed. She couldn't reply. He put his hand on her upper arm.

"Alice?"

"You overheard me that night? You knew what it meant?" she asked in a quiet, choked voice. She still studied his T-shirt-covered chest, unable to look into his eyes. He was the first person outside of Dylan and Sidney who had confronted her with the truth. It felt intimidating, like her identity was too new, too fragile, and still forming to talk about it in the everyday world.

"After I overheard you and Fall talking, I just . . ." He looked uncomfortable. "I sensed how important it was, what you were saying . . . what was happening to you. But I didn't really understand it, at first. So I asked my dad about it. He didn't recall anything about the name Addie, but he did recall that the Durands had a daughter named Adelaide and that there was a tragedy that involved her. So I did some research, and I found some articles about the kidnapping. Since Fall has been so focused on you and so protective, I put two and two together. Sort of, anyway. I still don't get how Fall found you."

"It's a long story," Alice said quietly. She glanced up at him. "Please don't say anything to anyone, Thad. The truth will come out, eventually. We're having genetic testing done, but it takes time. I'm not ready for it to be known yet."

He nodded tensely. His gaze strayed over to Rigo, who still watched them with a tight focus from a distance. "I guess it's good," Thad said slowly. "That he's watching over you."

"I'm sure it's overkill. But it makes Dylan feel better."

"And it doesn't bother you? That Fall knows who you are, and started up a relationship with you?"

She stared into his green eyes, and saw only concern. A chill passed through her. "No, it's not like that, Thad. Dylan and I have a long history, together. Longer than you realize. Deeper than you realize. Don't judge him. I owe everything to him."

"You don't *owe* him anything, Alice." His mouth tightened and he shook his head, cutting her off when she opened her mouth to refute him.

"I was starting to think you were right after the Alumni Dinner, that maybe I was misjudging Fall. He can seem decent enough at times. But over the weekend I found out . . . *everything*. I figured out why he's so focused on you." He glanced aside, making sure Rigo remained in the distance before he continued in a more hushed tone. "Don't you remember, what I told you the first week of camp? About how the majority of Durand shares are tied up in a trust, and how Fall is hamstrung in his control of the company without being able to touch that wealth?"

"Yes, I remember," Alice said, anger making it easier to meet his stare. "Dylan explained it all to me. He's not making a secret of it. Why would he?"

"Because he got you into bed within months of finding out you weren't only worth billions of dollars, but were the key to controlling Durand Enterprises. Isn't it obvious how much he'll benefit by having you in his right pocket? No one more so than Fall."

"Be quiet," she spat in a hushed tone. She glanced over at Rigo. He looked ready to walk over to them, so she held up her hand again to reassure him. A cool calm had come over her, hearing Thad spout something so vindictive against Dylan. "I'm hardly in his right pocket. That's insulting. And you don't know Dylan like I do. His motivations are far from selfish in this."

Thad gave an incredulous bark of laughter. "Right. He gets to sleep with a gorgeous woman who also just *happens* to be the heiress of the company he leads, but can never completely control. Does Fall strike you as the type of guy who wouldn't want total and complete control of his domain? He's drawing you closer into his circle of influence. By the time the news breaks about who you are," Thad hissed, "he'll already be in the most prime position of power when it comes to you. God, Alice, can't you see what he's—"

"Stop it!"

This time, she didn't care when Rigo lurched toward them. She spun and started toward her cabin.

"Alice—"

She ignored Thad. "It's okay, Sal," she said quietly to Rigo when he approached her. "I'm going to my cabin now. Good night."

She was done listening to Thad Schaefer.

Or she *wished* she were, anyway.

His accusations kept repeating in her head over and over. She didn't believe a word of his allegations.

So why was it she cringed each time she recalled them as she tried desperately to sleep that night?

MAYBE it was her sense of growing unrest that made her do it, or maybe it was a weak sentimentality that she didn't know she

possessed until that summer. Probably, it was just the fact that her
unsettling conversation with Thad had told her one thing loud and
clear: The storm was on the horizon. It was coming, whether she
was ready for it or not.

Whatever the cause, the next day during the lunch break, she
returned to her cabin and grabbed her cell phone. She headed
toward the back terrace.

"Uncle Al?" she asked quietly a moment later, staring out
blindly at the sunlit beach. There was a long pause on the other end.

"Alice? Is that you?"

"Yeah. It is. How are you doing?"

"Good. All right, anyway. Can't get rid of this cough," he said,
clearing his eternally congested throat and coughing a few times
as if to prove his point. She didn't like the sound of his lungs.

"You smoke too much," Alice said out of pure habit. Sadness
swept through her. She always said it.

Al never listened.

"Gotta have some vices," he croaked.

"Yeah, because you're such an angel otherwise," Alice laughed.
He joined her, his familiar rough bark of amusement making the
ache in her chest swell.

"Your mom and I thought you'd fallen off the face of the earth.
We haven't heard from you since last Christmas."

"I know. I've been really busy with finishing up my program
and trying to find a job."

"You got yourself that fancy degree. I hope you ain't going to
find out it was all for nothing."

"No," she said quietly. "Uncle Al, it wasn't for nothing. I *did*
get a job. With Durand Enterprises."

This time, the silence stretched even longer. She could almost
hear his mind going into overdrive.

"Uncle Al?" she asked, damning the tremor in her voice. She
scrunched her eyelids closed when they started to burn. "I think

maybe you better go away for a while. Leave the trailer. Maybe take that trip you always wanted to take to see Arizona and New Mexico. You . . . you don't have to tell anyone else. Just *go*."

"Are you saying what I think you're saying, Alice?"

"I am. I . . . I won't be able to control what happens in the near future, Al. Please. Just leave there."

"Do you want to talk to your mom?"

"No," she cried out sharply. The thought of hearing Sissy's voice panicked her. "Please don't tell her I spoke to you. Don't let on what we talked about. I don't want to talk to her. I don't think I ever want to talk to her again."

She heard Al's heavy, wheezy exhale. "I suppose you want an explanation," he said after a moment. "I'm not sure I can give it. I more suspected all these years than knew anything concrete."

Alice couldn't respond. Her throat had tightened uncomfortably.

"If it helps any to know it, I'm glad you found out. You should have the life that was taken from you. You deserve it. You never did belong here. I think you knew that better than anyone. That didn't stop me from wishing sometimes that you did belong with us." His voice broke slightly at the last, increasing Alice's misery. She'd never heard Al show any emotion aside from anger or gruff fondness.

"Will you *please* go, Uncle Al?"

"It's going to be all right. You listen to me about that."

"Okay," she whispered. "Take care of yourself."

"You do the same. Don't you let anyone else do it, either. That's one thing the Reeds taught you. Don't trust anyone else to your happiness. It'll only lead to misery."

Alice shut her eyes and felt a tear skitter down her cheek.

God, Al was right. They'd taught her that lesson so well, she wondered if she'd *ever* be able to unlearn it.

EIGHTEEN

Upon his and Kehoe's return to Michigan Thursday afternoon, Dylan immediately went to his office at Durand headquarters. The trip and the new plant had generated a mountain load of work for him. It was after five by the time he entered his office. His administrative assistant, Mrs. Davenport, was waiting for him. Mrs. Davenport was a very efficient, spry woman in her mid-sixties. She'd been Alan's secretary for ten years before he'd passed. She had a sharp eye and an even sharper tongue, the latter of which she used on Dylan on a daily basis without an ounce of fear or compunction.

He absolutely couldn't function without her.

She sprung up from her desk the second before he crossed the threshold, her notebook in hand, and started ticking off tasks for him.

"Marcus Jordan needs you to call him right away about the latest numbers from Indonesia. Jason Stalwalter has called three times in the past two hours in regard to a new junior exec recruit from the camp," Dylan's rapid pace toward his office flagged, "Janice Ahehorn from the new plant is having some major staffing issues—"

"Hello to you, too, Mrs. Davenport."

"We've spoken several times already today. Do you really require the niceties?"

"I certainly don't *expect* them," Dylan replied dryly. "Have

Kehoe handle Janice. He's been doing it well enough for the past two days." At Dylan's command he had been, anyway, and completely unwillingly. Kehoe had been a surly and unpleasant companion in Reno and on board the company jet. Dylan had ignored his hostility and loaded him up with work. "I just walked with him to his office, so you should be able to find him for Janice. What's this about Stalwalter? Have the managers at the camp made their selections for new hires?"

"I think so, considering Stalwalter already wants one of them."

"Fine," Dylan said, opening his office door.

"Should I get Stalwalter on the phone first, then?" Mrs. Davenport called after him.

"No," Dylan said, tossing his suitcase on a nearby couch before he rounded his desk. "I have another call I need to make first." He ignored Mrs. Davenport's sniff. "And close the door!" he yelled as she started to walk away.

She did so with a muted bang.

Dylan checked his watch. It was five forty-five. He *might* be able to catch Alice as she finished her dinner. They'd agreed a while back not to communicate by cell phone, but he had her number, and made sure she had his. Counselors were discouraged from using their cell phones or texting except for emergencies while they were on duty, but Dylan thought this rated an exception. Yes, he'd be seeing her in person later tonight, but he knew how important this was to her.

The phone rang once, twice, then three times. She might not be carrying her phone. He let it ring a few more times. Disappointed, he started to hang up.

"Hello," he heard her distant, hushed voice.

He jerked the phone back to his ear. "Alice? It's me."

"I know," she said, and despite her exasperated tone, he sensed the smile in her voice. The excitement.

"They offered you a position, didn't they?"

"Yes."

He grinned full out. It was impossible not to be affected by the barely restrained happiness in her voice. "I'm in the kitchen pantry. Red Team had dinner duty tonight. I ducked in here when I felt my phone ringing. I can't talk long. It just happened . . . they made me the offer right before dinner. They called us in one by one. It was nerve-wracking. I feel really bad for the people who didn't get a spot, but the managers told them that everyone had done an outstanding job, and that they'd be giving them excellent recommendations. They also invited them to apply at Durand through regular channels in the future, if they were still interested. Kuvi got a spot! So did Thad and Dave and Lacey Sherwood . . ." She paused, as if something had occurred to her. "Did you already know? Before you called?"

"Not firsthand. We just arrived back in Morgantown, and Kehoe and I haven't been too chatty, even though I'm sure he's had the final list since last night. I didn't want to ask. Him or anyone. I didn't really need to. I was confident we'd want you," he said. He didn't elaborate. He thought Alice understood he wanted her to win this challenge completely on her own merits.

"I'm so glad Kehoe wasn't here when the managers told us." Even her whisper brimmed with happiness. "The managers were so *nice* when they reviewed my performance and offered me the position. They said I approached things in a fresh, innovative way and that I wasn't afraid to take chances. Course they were wrong about that. I was scared shitless most of the time. They also said they were impressed by the connections I'd made with my kids in such a short period of time."

"They weren't being *nice*, baby. They were being smart. We want you for purely selfish purposes."

There was a pause.

"Alice? Everything okay?"

"I should probably go," she whispered. "Someone is going to hear me."

"Okay. I'll see you in a few hours, then?"

"Yes." She didn't hang up. "Dylan?"

"Yeah."

"Thanks," she said in a muffled voice.

"I had *nothing* to do with them hiring you, Alice. That was all you. Surely you believe me when I say that. If anything, given Kehoe, I might have been an anchor around your neck."

"I know," she said, and her voice broke slightly. "But no matter what the circumstances, I'm standing here at Camp Durand because of you. And it's . . . just . . ." She cleared her throat. "Really been an incredible day."

Something inside him gave a little. She really had the power to stir him, and yet she seemed so unaware of her ability.

"I'm glad. Because you deserve it. And so many more special days besides."

"Thanks," she muttered, suddenly sounding embarrassed. Self-conscious. She'd never stop fascinating him.

"I'll see you soon," she whispered.

"Not soon enough."

He hung up, still smiling. He quickly checked his messages and noticed that Jim Sheridan had called sometime between when he'd arrived and hung up with Alice. His grin vanished. All the warmth he'd been experiencing talking to Alice evaporated, to be replaced by a grim sense of dread. He quickly redialed Jim's number. He'd been waiting for the call.

A few minutes later, Dylan hung up his phone and sat heavily in his chair. The truth was indeed out, although not entirely. Jim had just informed him that he'd called his contact at the FBI and left a message, but hadn't yet spoken to anyone in person. Jim had given them a few extra hours by calling the FBI in the evening.

He was definitely going to have to tell Alice tonight. The Durand kidnapping case was about to officially be reopened.

Elbow on the desk, he rested his forehead in his hand, rubbing his closed eyes with the ridge of his palm. Without his bidding, the image of how she'd looked several nights ago when she'd awakened from her nightmare flew into his mind's eye. He'd never seen her so vulnerable . . . so afraid . . . so aware of her loss, and therefore never more grief stricken.

"He told me he was right beside me, and that he always would be. And he liked chocolate ice cream as much as me . . . And then Mommy was telling me to run and hide again, and there was blood on her ear and neck."

The last part echoed, it's effect like an igniting spark on his brain.

Slowly, he lowered his hand and opened his eyes. A tingling sensation scurried down his back and arms.

Why would a doting mother encourage her four-year-old daughter to hide in a dark, scary hole beneath the stairs? Or in any of the other castle hidey-holes, for that matter?

Why hadn't he thought of that before? True, Dylan had always been closer to Alan than Lynn. He'd never known Lynn as an adult, only as a teenager. Still . . . the hide-and-seek scenario Alice had described seemed completely out of character from what he knew of Lynn Durand. Addie had been the prized princess of the household, adored and loved and protected. Lynn hardly ever let her out of her sight. That was one of the reasons Dylan had felt so guilty about the kidnapping for years; because the Durands trusted less than a handful of people with their daughter, but they'd given it to Dylan.

Why the hell was Lynn sending Addie off to cower in dark, hidden places, spots where most small children would be terrified to be alone? It clearly hadn't scared Alice, though. She'd found the game fun. It'd been that memory that had first returned, hearing Lynn playing that game with her.

What if it had only been a game for Addie, though? What if it had been a dead-serious exercise for Lynn?

What if Lynn had been preparing her daughter, *training* her for potential danger?

"Dylan, are you sure *she wasn't there when I was taken in the woods?"*

Lynn Durand had *definitely* not been in the woods on the day Dylan was stabbed and Addie was kidnapped. But had he been wrong in telling Alice she'd *never* seen Lynn that way? What if Alice really *was* remembering something traumatic that had happened, something that had occurred on another day . . . not the day of her kidnapping? What if someone had hurt Lynn and threatened to harm Addie? And being fearful of it, Lynn had trained Addie to run and hide in one of the *good* spots?

Again, Alice's voice came to him: *"They were her hiding places, too."*

A moment later, he flung open his office door.

"Janice Ahehorn called again, and I can't find—"

"Not *now*, Mrs. Davenport," he growled, charging toward the door. He got a glimpse of his secretary's openmouthed shock at his harsh interruption. For once, she gave no snippy reply.

THEY had a mandatory camp-wide meeting on the marina beach following dinner, after which there would be a big inter-team beach party. Their evening meal had been especially light because Mira, the camp cook, would be providing food and drink for the festivities later tonight. The kids bubbled with anticipation and good spirits. A DJ had been hired to play music later, and there would be a bonfire. A lifeguard was present and the beam lights would be turned on in case any kids wanted to swim.

Like the kids, Alice was wired tonight, still ebullient from her hiring meeting and the prospect of meeting Dylan in a few hours.

She'd missed him so much, despite the uncertainties she'd been having thanks to Thad's accusations. From experience, however, she knew that as soon as she saw Dylan, as soon as he touched her, that all her doubts would be forgotten.

Because of her keyed-up state, she was standing a few feet back from her seated group of kids, too excited to sit still.

After the meeting, the managers all undertook the task of handing out a photo booklet to each camper and counselor. It was like a camp yearbook, filled with photos and commemorations of memorable events, both serious and amusing ones. There were blank pages where the kids could have staff and friends sign. Other managers were walking among the kids, carrying boxes with Camp Durand keepsake pens. A few other managers were passing out T-shirts and hats.

A party atmosphere prevailed. She watched as Sal Rigo passed out the booklets to her kids, feeling happy but a little melancholy, too, at the idea of saying good-bye. She'd grown so fond of them. Their faces all looked alight with the setting sun and excitement, but Alice thought she recognized something else. They looked . . . *proud*.

She thought back to her interview with Dylan. Finally, she understood what he'd meant. Camp Durand really wasn't about strutting corporate philanthropy, publicity, prime photo ops, or even hiring the best and brightest managers. It was about the kids. Communities and people-building didn't have to be kept in a separate realm from corporate success and growth. In many ways, this camp was like the lifeblood of the whole organization, the origins of its driving principles, the source of its yearly renewal. Alan and Lynn Durand had recognized that. They'd nurtured that ideal, and so had Dylan.

Standing there on that beach as the kids' excited chatter and shrieks grew to a dull roar, she suspected that maybe . . . just maybe, she could *really* belong at Durand Enterprises. This was Alan and Lynn's legacy. It was Dylan's.

A newly born sense of pride swelled large inside her.

She beamed at Sal as he walked toward her.

"I see they've got you doing some honest work tonight," Alice told Rigo with a grin as she accepted her booklet.

"We're a little short-staffed," Rigo said, keeping his voice low.

"Yeah, I noticed that. Jessica Moder still isn't feeling well? Someone told me she was sick after I was called in for my meeting with the managers," Alice explained when she saw the question in Rigo's eyes.

He nodded. "Yeah. Flu bug or something. Elle Perez just went back to her cabin with it, as well. And Kehoe is still gone. Congratulations on your hire, by the way."

"You didn't think I had it in me, did you?" she joked, leafing through her book.

"No. I knew you had it in you." She glanced up, surprised by sincerity of his tone. His eyebrows went up. "If we could ever catch you, that is."

Alice laughed. She saw Sal's tiny, fleeting smile before he turned away to pass out the books to the Orange Team.

NINETEEN

Moving with a rapid sense of purpose, Dylan strode down the castle's downstairs hallway. Marie, his cook, must have heard him coming because she was staring at the entryway, holding a covered plate in her hand, when he entered the kitchen.

"I thought you said you wouldn't be home until around eight," she said. "I was just about to put your dinner in the fridge and take off."

"I changed my plans. And that's fine, you're free to go. Lock up on the way out, will you?" He glanced distractedly around the large kitchen. "Where do we keep the flashlights down here?"

"In the pantry, right side, top drawer," Marie said, giving him a curious glance as he hastened to the pantry.

"Night, Marie," he called before he headed for the back stairs and charged up them two at a time.

A moment later, he once again peered into the compartment beneath the stairs, the location where he'd found Alice hiding last week. Disappointment went through him as he swept the flashlight beam all around the dark three-by-five-foot space. It was mundanely empty, save some cobwebs in the corners. If Lynn Durand *had* ever used the castle's secret places to hide anything besides her daughter, it wasn't in this spot.

Several years ago during a visit, Deanna Shrevecraft had shown him not one, but five secret hidey-holes in Castle Durand. Deanna owned a bed-and-breakfast called the Twelve Oaks Inn down the coastline. The Twelve Oaks had been built by the same architect as the castle, but on a smaller scale. When Deanna had visited Castle Durand once, she'd demonstrated to Dylan how alike the two houses were, right down to several secret rooms and compartments.

The door to Addie's old room opened with a loud squeak. He immediately walked toward the large wall unit he'd had built during redecoration. It covered one entire wall. The new unit was constructed from glowing cherrywood, and included an entertainment console, deep cupboards, and bookshelves. Most people wouldn't realize the unit had been designed around a smaller original built-in bookcase. Dylan had asked the carpenters to apply new exterior woodwork that matched the rest of the unit, leaving the interior intact.

He opened the second drawer, stuck his hand into the back of the cabinet, and found the latch. There was a muffled click.

The entire nine-by-four-foot section of the shelf swung forward several inches. He pried open the heavy door.

He exposed a much larger hidey-hole than the one beneath the stairs. Dylan had never discovered if the architect of Castle Durand and Deanna's bed-and-breakfast mansion was just secretive by nature, or if he'd designed the hidden spaces by request.

He stepped over the threshold, an odor of dust and stale air entering his nose. He'd only been in here twice, once when Deanna had cheerfully revealed the secret to him, and once just before the carpenters came to build the new shelving unit. There hadn't seemed to be much of interest inside the little room; the hidden quality being its only real curiosity. Deanna had been of the opinion that bootleg liquor might have been stashed in here during Prohibition, but Dylan doubted it. A much more likely candidate for that use would be the secret little room at the back of the kitchen pantry.

Nothing much had changed, Dylan acknowledged as he pointed the flashlight into every corner, revealing dusty wooden floorboards and chipped plaster walls.

This had been a dead end, too, he realized grimly, starting to back out of the dark space. His flash of insight hadn't been so inspired after all. There were three other secret places—that he knew about—in the old house, although he was losing the steam of enthusiasm and curiosity by the second.

His flashlight skimmed across the floor as he turned to leave. He did a double take. Walking to the far right corner of the little room, he ran his light over a board that was slightly raised above the ones next to it.

He knelt and pried his fingers beneath the floorboard. It gave, and he lifted. He was expecting resistance, but someone had loosened the nails that had originally secured the board in place. The entire three-foot-long board rose as though it had a hinge on one end. He shone the flashlight into the opening beneath the board.

There, nestled between the joists, were four cloth-covered books. His flashlight revealed nothing else of interest, so he gathered up the volumes and replaced the board.

It was probably nothing—some long-forgotten diaries of a lovesick teenager or the hidden financial accounts of a crooked accountant. This was a very old house, after all, with a very long history.

He replaced the façade door and walked under the full light of the glowing chandelier. Immediately, he noticed that while the volumes were old, they weren't ancient. He opened the first page of the top one.

No. It *was* something after all.

He stared down at the front page of the top book. There, in a sloping hand were written the words *Lynn Charlotte Durand, July 1990.*

He turned the page and began to read. Lynn's journal writing was evocative. It called up an image of her clearly in his mind: her kindness, her elegance . . . her sadness.

Yes. As a boy of thirteen or fourteen he hadn't understood that sad, poignant quality of a grown woman's character. But his memories, the part of her soul that was instilled forever in her written words, and the present-day understanding of an adult man all combined, allowing him to see Lynn Durand clearly for the first time.

It wasn't until the fourth entry that the bombshell struck.

Of course I've been a fool and unworthy of an excellent man's unwavering, passionate love. To say this is stating the weary obvious. They say that people sacrifice everything for the sake of romantic love, but I sacrificed everything in the name of one selfish, heartless goal: to call myself a mother. To give Alan a child. God answered my prayers and gave me a beautiful baby. But he's making me pay for my sacrifice—he's making me pay for my cruelty and unfaithfulness to Alan—by putting the two things I hold dearest in harm's way: my marriage and Addie.

I put myself in league with the devil. Isn't that what the devil is famous for? He knows your secret desire, and he does whatever he can to give it to you. At a price. He played the part so well. I thought he shared my dreams, and that's powerful stuff to a woman who imagines herself doomed to a barren life.

Sometimes I'm afraid Alan knows about my infidelity. Worse, sometimes I'm afraid he knows, and not only understands, but accepts because of his medical issues and our trouble conceiving. He knows better than anyone how I've suffered. That he would forgive me in this is the sharpest and deepest of my pains.

But Alan doesn't really know, thank God. That's just my guilt surfacing and haunting me.

As it should.

Dylan felt sick, like he'd just taken a punch to the chest that reverberated through his heart, gut, and brain.

He'd insisted Alice go for the genetic testing. He'd never even thought to consider what would happen if he'd dangled this story in front of her about whom Addie Durand was—about who *Alice* was—and it all turned out to be wrong. If it all turned out to be a lie.

He walked out of the room feeling dazed. In his bedroom suite, he found a pair of glasses. He turned on the lamp in the sitting area and sat down on the couch. He put on his glasses and turned his full attention back to the journals.

He made sure he arranged them in the proper chronological order. The journals ranged from the year before Addie was born to three years after the fact. These were the entries that Lynn had chosen, the ones she'd felt compelled to leave behind in one of the secret places she'd shared with her daughter.

These were the shameful confessions of a heartbroken woman. Like everyone else, Dylan had believed that Addie's kidnapping and suspected death were what had driven Lynn to end her own life. Dylan was just beginning to realize that the secrets he held in his hands right now had been an even more precise, cruel prod to her suicide.

He still had several hours before he was due down at the camp to meet Alice. With a grim sense of purpose, he began to read, doing his best to ignore the dread that weighed on him, heavier and heavier by the minute.

"WHAT?" Alice asked, grinning widely when Dave Epstein approached her, carrying two cases of soda. The DJ had started and a raucous rap boomed, making conversation nearly impossible. Kids were dancing on the sand, swimming, exchanging camp books, and posing for pictures. Almost everyone who wasn't in a swimsuit wore his or her new Camp Durand T-shirt, including Alice.

"Mira took a call for you up at the kitchen. She knew I was headed this way, so she gave me the message."

"*What?*" she repeated when Dave handed her a folded piece of paper. She'd understood Dave's shout this time, but was still bewildered by the actual message. Mira was the camp cook. Why was she taking messages for Alice?

"Hold on," Dave said, rolling his eyes. He went and deposited the two cases of soda on a serving table in front of Kuvi. Kuvi was bopping around to the music, but gave Dave an appreciative wave before she started to load the sodas into a huge tin receptacle filled with ice. While he was gone, Alice read the message in the light of the brilliant sunset.

To Alice Reed,

Mr. Fall phoned the kitchen. Apparently, he knew you'd be on the beach and hard to contact, so he called here. He's received some news, and wants you to come up to the castle immediately. He said not to worry, it's not an emergency, but it is important. He suggested you take the main road, and come now, while it's still light. He also said to make sure Sal Rigo accompanied you, and that he'd be waiting for you in his den.

Mira

Alice blinked in amazement. This was strange. She saw Dave reapproaching. Kuvi had handed him a Camp Durand T-shirt. He'd pulled off his old one and was shrugging on the new one as he approached her. The T-shirts were black with a neon green design and print. Alice suspected the shirts would glow in the dark.

"*Mira* gave this to you?" she yelled when Dave got close enough.

"Yeah. No way anyone could hear a phone out here. Did I hear Mira right? Was it Dylan Fall calling?" Alice could tell that by his incredulous expression that Kuvi hadn't betrayed her secret to Dave, even though she suspected Kuvi and Dave were growing closer and closer. "Was Fall contacting you about some kind of emergency? I thought I heard Mira say he needed to see you. Is everything okay?" he asked, nodding at the note she clutched.

"It's about something from home," she lied, thinking intently.

"Nothing serious, is it?" Dave bellowed.

"I'm sure it isn't," Alice replied, smiling gamely for reassurance. She glanced around the beach, looking for Sal Rigo.

KUVI hauled Thad onto the beach to dance. The sun was starting to dip below the shimmering blue lake by the time the song ended. Another loud dance number immediately started again.

"Wait. What about me?" someone called good-naturedly from behind him as he and Kuvi walked through a swarm of kids and staff. *"Thad?"*

Thad was aware that it was Brooke trying to get his attention, but something had caught his eye. He saw Alice at the edge of the crowd. She was on her tiptoes, shouting something into Sal Rigo's ear. Rigo's brows furrowed and he nodded. Alice ducked behind a grove of saplings planted just past the sand. He saw her long bare legs moving rapidly in the direction of the cabins, and then she disappeared. Lots of counselors were making runs back and forth from the beach to the dining hall to keep the food table stocked, so that wasn't what set off Thad's mental alarm. It was more Alice's furtive manner that had caught his attention.

No sooner had he thought that her actions were suspicious, Sal Rigo also slipped behind the grove of trees.

"Thad!" He turned and saw Brooke standing on the beach, smiling. She looked radiant tonight. She beckoned to him. "Celebration dance with me?"

He read her lips and manner instead of actually hearing her. The noise level at the beach party was out of control. "Sure," he said distractedly. She was referring to the fact that they'd both been offered positions as Durand managers, he knew. But instead of going to join Brooke, he turned back to scan the shore. An uneasy feeling had come over him.

"Thad?"

"I'm sorry, can I take a rain check?" he asked, pointing significantly toward the kitchen and making a face. He was pretty sure that Brooke didn't understand him, but since he was purposefully being evasive, he didn't really expect her to. He plunged into the crowd of shouting, celebrating kids in the opposite direction from Brooke.

ALICE trudged up the last part of the road, watching as the castle floated fully into her vision. There was enough light left in the sky for her to see the grand, elegant home. She knew it was her imagination, the remnants of a child's fanciful mind when it came to the house, but it often struck her as sentient: always ageless and waiting, sometimes mysterious in the sense of a wondrous fairyland, occasionally secretive, threatening, and dark.

Maybe it was the boisterous sounds and music of the distant beach party reaching all the way up the bluff, but tonight, she got no ominous vibes from the castle. Of course it was hard to be anxious with a man of Sal Rigo's heft at your side.

"When I'm with Dylan, I usually enter at the back," she called to Rigo when he headed toward the front door.

Rigo nodded and fell into step behind her as they walked toward the side of the house. Earlier at the party, she'd thought he seemed a little more approachable, wearing his Camp Durand T-shirt, talking with the kids as he passed out the photo journals, and helping out the counselors and employees setting up food and beverages. Presently, he'd switched back to his somber professional persona. She noticed him studying the side view of the castle through a narrowed gaze.

Was he worried about Dylan's note? Alice was, a little, although probably not in the way Rigo was. She was definitely mystified. Dylan had already indicated that he needed to speak to her about something important tonight. What had happened that had made him want to speak with her earlier? Or was the note about something different altogether?

Rigo paused at the perimeter of the stone terrace.

"I'll watch and make sure that you get in all right. Then I'll take the woods back to the party."

Alice smiled and nodded in the direction of the distant music. "They'll need you down there. If anyone asks where I've gone—"

"I'll just tell them the truth. That Mr. Fall received some emergency information for you and wanted to give it to you in person. I doubt you'll be missed, though, in that swarm. Besides, the night supervisors took over responsibility for the kids a half hour ago."

"Thanks for walking me up, Sal. Night."

"Night. And congratulations again about today."

"Thanks."

She used her key. She glanced over her shoulder as she entered, giving Rigo a wave. As she closed and locked the French door, she saw him fade back into the gloom. The sun had dipped completely into the lake, and dusk was descending fast.

She quickly keyed in the memorized code into the security alarm. Silence clung thickly around her as she made her way through the dim media room. The music and sounds from the party didn't penetrate the thick walls of the castle. She flew up the three stairs that led to the kitchen level and headed toward the hallway.

She had no prescience of threat or fear. When the moment came, she was thinking of how much she was looking forward to seeing Dylan, despite whatever emergency had occurred. They'd face whatever it was together.

Addie's past crashed into Alice's present in a single jolting second via a disabling blow to the left side of her head.

TWENTY

Dylan left the house at around nine twenty that night to meet Alice. His head was ablaze with what he'd just read in Lynn's journals. How was he going to tell Alice? It was bad enough he had to tell her that it was a matter of hours or days before the FBI appeared to question them. Now, Dylan had even more damning information to give the investigators. He'd have to contact Jim Sheridan as soon as Alice was up at the castle with him. Lynn's journals would definitely rattle some old bones in the Addie Durand kidnapping case . . . and Dylan finally grasped that elusive motive.

But Lynn's journals' effect on Alice was what worried him most.

By nine thirty-three, he was starting to get concerned when Alice didn't show up at their assigned spot in the woods. She was usually very prompt. He'd heard the music emanating from the marina beach as soon as he walked out of the house, of course. It was the traditional beach party they held on the next to the last night of camp. It was usually a pretty crazy affair, so at first, he figured that was why Alice was late. More than likely, she was celebrating the victory of her Durand job offer with the others and had lost track of time.

By nine thirty-five, he wasn't so convinced, however. He was worked up by the contents of Lynn's journals and more than a little anxious. For only the second time since Alice had arrived at the camp, he stalked up to her cabin front door, heedless of the glowing lights in the empty common area that could easily reveal his identity to any onlooker. He knocked, the first time sedately.

The second and third times, not so politely. He was about to run down to the marina when someone spoke from behind him.

"Mr. Fall?"

He spun around at the male voice. He saw a tall dark-haired man that he'd seen hanging around Alice at castle events alongside Kuvi. They stood a few feet from the cabin stoop, the male's arm looped around Kuvi's waist. They both looked a little taken aback at seeing him there.

"Kuvi," he said, glad to see someone close to Alice. "Where's Alice? Is she still at the party?"

"I think so. I haven't seen her for a bit, though. Have you, Dave?"

The tall man shook his head. "No, she's not at the party. She's up at the castle."

"*What?*" Dylan asked, descending the three steps.

"Yeah, she got a note with a message," Dave said, eyeing him uneasily. "From *you*, right? I overheard Mira on the phone taking part of the message while I was getting supplies in the kitchen earlier."

"Tell me everything. What did the note say? *Quickly*," Dylan emphasized when Dave just looked perplexed by his request.

"I didn't read the note myself, but I gave it to Alice maybe twenty minutes ago, just before sunset. I heard enough of Mira's phone conversation to know it was from you, and that Alice was supposed to go to the castle because there was a family emergency or something like that."

"Is Sal Rigo still at the party?" Dylan asked, barely restraining his feet from taking off down the path.

Kuvi and Dave exchanged a dubious glance. "I don't know, to be honest. It's kind of a madhouse down there."

"Go back to the beach and look for him." Kuvi nodded. "If you find him, tell him I never called Mira and that the note was a trick. Tell him to get up to the castle. I'll call Jim Sheridan on the way up."

"But—"

"Just do it," Dylan interrupted Dave.

"Mr. Fall? Is Alice all right?" Kuvi asked, her eyes wide with alarm as he moved past the couple.

"She'd better be. Just do what I asked, Kuvi. *Now*," he insisted before he took off down the path to the castle.

SOMEONE was dragging her, his hands beneath her armpits hurting her. No, it wasn't dragging. Her feet were moving—weren't they? Her legs felt loose and heavy as rocks at once, as if they were attached to her body inexpertly and malfunctioning at their task. Just as she thought it, they failed. She felt herself drop several inches.

"Stand *up*, you stupid bitch."

"Leave me . . . alone," she mumbled between gritted teeth. The sharp tugging on her arms and a knifing pain in her head *had* to stop. It was unbearable. Opening her eyelids took a monumental effort. Darkness and dizziness assailed her.

She retched.

"Don't you dare throw up on me," someone snarled in disgust.

She was shoved. Instinctively, she put out her hands to break a fall, but she was too late to do much good. Her palms collided against hard stone, and almost immediately her jaw and then her cheekbone struck the unforgiving surface. She fell to the ground on her knees, whimpering as white-hot pain raged and ruled over her entire body and brain. For a moment, she couldn't tell up from down or left from right. She couldn't draw breath.

Then someone was grasping her shoulders and lifting her once

more, and her lungs unfroze. She inhaled raggedly. The new, fresh
wave of pain had sliced through her vertigo some. As it remitted,
she found the wherewithal to think.

This isn't a nightmare. The pain is way *too real. I'm being*
attacked.

It was the first clear thought she'd had since being struck earlier. It came back to her in a split second, walking through the
hallway of the castle, looking forward to seeing Dylan . . . a flash
of pain and then nothingness.

Adrenaline shot through her at the incomplete memory, making her veins seem to burn. She elbowed her attacker in the belly
as hard as she could.

He grunted and shoved her again. This time, she caught herself
better, but the skin on her hands had been torn on her previous
fall. She cried out at the impact of striking the stone with open
flesh.

"Go on, hold yourself up if you want to. You always did imagine yourself strong and *feisty*. It certainly didn't help matters, the
way Lynn treated you. By the time you were three, you expected
all of us to fall on our knees in worship in front of you. But you
weren't *strong*. You were just a spoiled little brat."

Alice gasped. Only star shine provided any light, and it'd been
too dark to see her attacker clearly. Her dizziness wasn't helping
matters. He was just a swooshing tall shadow to the right of her.
Sometimes there were two of him. But she'd recognized the thick
disdain in his tone just now. Tonight, it had grown exponentially
from what she was used to at the camp.

"Kehoe," she muttered.

"That's right. Let's make everything crystal clear tonight, of
all nights. And you're Addie Durand. Forgive me if I don't drop to
my knee in worship tonight, Addie."

She closed her eyes, panting, trying desperately to still her vertigo and gather her wits. Kehoe had disabled her pretty badly. She

just needed to steady herself sufficiently to fight. Run, if need be. Rigo had told her she was fast, hadn't he?

She just needed to buy time to still her dizziness and for the pain to fade some.

Run, Addie. Hide.

"How did you know I was Addie?" she asked between ragged pants. Where was she? Was that the shimmer of water in the distance? Her fingers clutched at the surface where they still pressed. *It's the stonewall.* Kehoe had dragged her down to the bluff. That rushing sound wasn't just her blood pounding in her ears, but also the waves rushing the beach and crashing against the rocks.

"I didn't, at first. Then I started to get the picture, as unlikely as it all seemed. Fall was too focused on you. Of course he'd want to make sure he got his hooks in you, just like he got them into Alan Durand. At first, I couldn't believe it. But you look like her, without all the ugly makeup. Lynn, I mean. I noticed when it washed away after you swam. You're taller and rougher than her. Did you honestly think you could compare to her by wearing that fancy dress and her pearls. *Her* pearls. You couldn't hold a candle to Lynn Durand; you're nowhere near as elegant. Every bit as full of yourself as her, though. There's *something* of her in you, all right. I should know. I knew her better than anyone alive. Your mother and I were very close. As close as a man and woman could be."

That sliced through her shock and disorientation more than anything.

"What?"

"Don't sound so incredulous," he hissed. "We were two of a kind, Lynn and I. We had the same philanthropic dreams, the same generous bent. We created Camp Durand together. We carved out the ideals that later became the driving principles of this whole damn company, even though Alan Durand took all the credit for what we'd done. *I* gave Lynn what she needed, more so than that defective husband of hers. She was lonely, you know. So beautiful. So sad."

"Prime pickings for a predator like you?" Alice couldn't stop herself from saying. "Ow. No, *stop*."

He'd grabbed the hair at the back of her head and snapped back her neck. It hurt so much.

"You're not the prized little princess anymore, do you *hear* me?" he spat near her ear. Spittle struck her skin. Despite her pain and discomfort, the sound of his voice sent pure fear through her. He was a crazy man, shouting in her ear, a man so enraged, he no longer held any fear for the consequences of his actions. "Did your lover, the great Dylan Fall, tell you how your mother died, Alice?"

His snide, taunting tone—or perhaps the question itself—sent fury and panic through her. He'd stepped closer to grab her hair. She elbowed him again, but this time she didn't hit him as squarely as before. He cursed and tightened his fingers in her hair, stretching her neck and forcing her back into an arch. His forearm pressed to her throat. She gagged at the pressure. She started clawing at his arm to free her airway, but he wouldn't budge.

"She went right off this bluff, Addie. They found her body on the rocks below, bloody and broken."

"Did . . . you. . ." She gurgled when he pressed the bone of his forearm tighter against her trachea.

"No. I didn't throw her off, if that's what you're wondering. I'll tell you a little secret though, Addie," he whispered in her ear, causing her shivers of fear and disgust to amplify. "I was right here when she did it. You might say I had a front-row seat. And I didn't stop her. It was her guilt that killed her, not me. She wanted a baby so bad, she *chose* to be unfaithful to her husband. She chose me. I hated seeing her suffer when we stood here together at this bluff, so I thought it would be cruel to stop her once she'd made up her mind. What else would she do, once I told her that all the rumors were true? Her precious little Addie was *definitely* dead. Or she was *supposed* to be, anyway. That's what I paid those worthless idiots, Cunningham and Stout, good money for. But at the time, when I stood here with Lynn on this bluff, I thought they'd done their job. I felt bad, telling Lynn that Addie was dead. But your mother had it coming. She'd left *me* bleeding and broken years before by abandoning me. And then later, by telling me what she did about you. She actually believed she could go back to Alan, and the three of you were going to live out her little dream, the rich king, and the beautiful queen and the darling little princess, all of you so happy," he mocked. "Well I couldn't let that happen, Addie. Not after Lynn had led me down the path she did. I *didn't* let it happen."

Rage at what he was saying had made Alice's mind go blank. All she wanted to do was hurt Sebastian Kehoe in that moment, and she didn't care how she accomplished it. She pulled with all her might on her head and sunk her teeth into his forearm. Kehoe shouted in pain and surprise.

She clamped her jaw, her teeth cutting into flesh. The taste of his blood spread on her tongue.

He howled in agony, but she held as fast as a furious dog with its prey in its jaws. He clumsily struck her temple with his free fist. Sensing the break of his hold, Alice loosened her jaw and dropped to the earth. She rolled on the ground away from him.

"I'm going to kill you for that, you worthless, snot-nosed little bitch," Kehoe seethed. "This time, I'm not going to be a spectator, either. I'll send you over the bluff myself. Maybe I'll follow you, and we can be broken and bleeding together. Would you like the company, Addie? I wouldn't mind. I'll die with the satisfaction of knowing that Dylan Fall will find you, and be as wrecked for the rest of his miserable life as Alan Durand was when he found Lynn."

Alice scurried farther away on the lawn, wild to put distance between herself and the sound of his ranting voice. Horror filled every cell of her being. He was completely mad.

Her fall to the ground and rolling away amplified her disorientation. A distant, blaring alarm began to pulse in her ears. She
sat in the grass, the darkness her only cloak, trying her mightiest
to steady herself so that she could stand. It was only a matter of
seconds, however, before Kehoe's shadow lurched above her. Panicked, she scuttled several yards on her hands and feet. She gave a
wild, frustrated cry when he followed her with ease.

"I see you, Addie," he laughed.

Shit. He could see her glow-in-the-dark Camp Durand T-shirt.
She cried out in anguish when his hands clamped on her shoulders
and squeezed. God, she was really going to die.

"Get up, Addie. You lived twenty years longer than I planned.
What have you got to complain about?"

"No!" Alice resisted, one fist punching at his neck and head as
he leaned down over her, the other hand reaching for the ground,
digging into the grass in desperation, seeking a firm hold that
wasn't there. She would lose. He was strong, and he'd weakened
her so badly. "Dylan. *Dylan!*" she screamed.

He slapped her face. Hard. She gasped in shock.

"Your suck-up knight in shining armor isn't going to save you
this time. In fact"—she whimpered in shock when he hauled her
roughly to her feet—"you have him to blame for all your misery,
Addie. If Fall would have left well enough alone, you'd be safe and
sound right now, wouldn't you? You would have never returned
to Morgantown. You have him to thank for tonight, even. I knew
he was getting suspicious of me, forcing me to go on that damn
trip to Reno, laughing at me under his breath the whole time
because he thought I was helpless. Well guess what? I don't give a
damn about whether or not the mighty Dylan Fall wants to *fire*
me. Fuck him and his *job.* The job was never as important as Lynn.
She was what counted." He shoved her in the direction of the
beach, and she cried out. "Don't be a coward, Addie. Your mother
wasn't, in the end. She was beautiful and brave when she went over

that bluff. I should have followed her then. I should have ended it with her, not with *you*. I would have, but I kept on living for her. I wanted to make sure her dreams came to life. Everything I've done since she died, I've done for her."

He pushed her and she staggered in the direction of the sound of the crashing water. Terror seized her chest, gripping so hard that Alice thought she'd die of a heart attack in that very moment instead of falling to her death.

Falling . . . falling.

"No," she grated out, gripping both her hands tightly in front of her, preparing to throw her balled hands and all her weight against him in one last desperate attempt at survival. The thudding sound of a fist striking flesh entered her ears, followed by a grunt of pain. Kehoe's hold on her loosened. What was happening? She'd been preparing to lash out at him, but her hands hadn't moved, had they?

Another thud of bone against flesh and Kehoe's grasp broke completely.

"Run, Alice. Get out of here."

"Thad?" she gasped, amazed. She squinted, making out the shadow of another figure. There was another thud, and Thad's shadow staggered back. Kehoe had retaliated for Thad's surprise attack. Alice hesitated. If Kehoe had wanted to throw Alice over the bluff, he probably wouldn't hesitate to do the same to Thad for interfering.

"You dumb-ass, Schaefer," Kehoe said, his tone thick with exhausted disdain. Alice thought she saw Kehoe's hand push back roughly on Thad's shoulder. Thad's shadow stumbled. Kehoe's daily workouts must really work. But it was more than that. His strength was that of a madness long held in check, and suddenly liberated. "No wonder you're father thinks you're such an idiot. God, is it impossible to hire anybody decent these days?" Kehoe wondered disgustedly.

She heard another thud and a grunt of pain.

"Thad?"

There was another surprised grunt, and this time, Alice thought it was Kehoe. Thad had got in a good one.

"*Go*, Alice," Thad seethed.

This time, Alice didn't hesitate.

She whipped the telltale shirt over her head and tossed it aside. Wearing only a black exercise bra now, she lurched in the direction of the castle. Her feet held her, but barely. She kept veering unintentionally to the left. Kehoe's blow to her head had done something to her brain's steering mechanism. The vertigo wouldn't go away. She crashed into some shrubbery and went to her knees.

Somehow, she managed to get herself upright again. There was a horrible, pulsing wail in her head. Her trip through the backyard was the blurry, claustrophobic, fear-soaked stuff of nightmares.

Her feet hitting the stone terrace was a major triumph. It only struck her as she staggered toward the back doors of the castle that the wailing claxon wasn't in her head. The castle alarms were blaring. They seemed to pulse in rhythm with the pain in her head and jaw. When she finally reached the French doors, she realized one of them was hanging open.

God, she was so confused. And she was so nauseated. She was never going to feel right again.

Where was *Dylan*? She needed him so much . . .

Kehoe could be right behind her.

Run, Addie. Hide.

The thought galvanized her. She entered the castle like a drunkard, staggering and bumping into furniture. One thought consumed her: Find the closest secret place and hide. Her feet took her to the kitchen. She reached for the pantry door. Without turning on the light, she shut the door behind her. In the closed room, the security alarm was muted a bit. It mingled with the sound of her harsh breathing.

"I can do it in the dark. Do you want me to show you how?"

Mommy could do everything. But *she* could do it, too. The dark wasn't scary. The dark could hide you. Her hands outstretched, she found the back wall of the pantry. Her fingers traced the edge of a shelf and sought.

No, you were littler then. Lower down.

Again, she couldn't find it. Was that a banging sound in the distance? Someone was coming. Panic rose in her. *Lower still.*

Using the shelves to support her wavering body, she bent and finally found the lever. She pulled. There was a click, and the back wall of the pantry loosened. Alice pushed, and the shelved wall swung inward. She hastened into the revealed space and pushed the wall back into place.

Her entire body began to shake. Or maybe it'd been shaking all along, and she hadn't stood still long enough to feel it. Her rubbery legs gave way and she sunk onto the floor.

"There. You did it. You're safe now, Addie."

That was her imagined mother's voice, talking to her. Alice wanted to believe her, but she wasn't entirely convinced. Her body was finished running, however. She could go no further. She scooted a few inches, finding the corner of the hidey-hole. Her head fell back against the wall. She finally succumbed to the heavy, thick haze of unconsciousness.

THANKS to the loud beach party, Dylan didn't hear the castle's alarm blaring in the distance until he reached the horse path. He'd been running already, but he picked up his pace even more when he heard the alarm.

Something's definitely wrong.

He'd already contacted Jim and told him to meet him at the castle, but hopefully the knowledge that the house had been breached would rush him all the more.

When he reached the terrace doors, he realized one was hanging open. A quick check informed him that the pane near the lock had been broken. Someone had busted the pane.

"Alice?" he bellowed as he entered, the screeching alarm obliterating his voice.

You've lost her. Again.

He willfully quashed down the unhelpful, panicked voice of doom. He sprinted through the media room toward the hallway.

ALICE'S eyelids fluttered open. The pain in her head had diminished to a throbbing ache, but her face, jaw, and hands burned like acid had been poured on the skin. Is that what had brought her to alertness? Where was she? In the distance, she heard the pulsing alarm.

Memory came sluggishly.

Kehoe.

He'd tried to kill her. All those horrible things he'd said about Lynn. What if the things he said were *true*? Did that mean that Kehoe could be her . . .

No. Don't think about that right now.

Thad had been there. He'd saved her, and she'd dragged herself to the hidey-hole in the pantry of the kitchen. The childhood memory of it must have been triggered by the trauma and her fear.

In a pause of the throb of the alarm, she heard a thump outside in the pantry. The outer light switched on. Icy tendrils slithered beneath her skin. She stared in frozen horror at the slit of white light shining beneath the fake wall at the back of the pantry. Did the wall vibrate, or was that Alice's entire world shaking?

The fingers of ice reached all the way to her heart and clutched as she watched the wall slowly swing inward. Light flooded the secret space. Someone stepped into the opening.

Kehoe stared down at her, looking like a horror with blood

streaming from his temple and his right eye swelling. His preppy glasses—the very symbol of Kehoe's fastidious personality—were now bent askew on his face. There was a smear of blood on one of the lenses. Alice couldn't breathe.

A disgusted frown tilted Kehoe's lips.

"Did you really think I wouldn't find you? You're bleeding like a stuck pig. Your tracks led me straight to you. I knew you were much stupider than Lynn, but I have to say, I'm disappointed, Addie."

She hated her weakness; despised it. But she was paralyzed as he stepped into the little space, breaching her zone of safety. That was when she noticed what he held—a heavy meat tenderizer. He must have picked it up in the kitchen from the jar of utensils on the counter. The vision of it galvanized her. She braced herself on her hands and kicked at his legs as he stepped closer to her.

He kicked her back in her solar plexus, his manner almost casual. Alice made an *oof* sound. Her lungs locked. Pain splintered her hazy consciousness yet again.

"Don't you just want to get this over with? I know I do," Kehoe said with a weary grimness that terrified her almost as much as the weapon. He raised the arm that held the meat pounder. Everything seemed to go into slow motion.

She watched, as if in a dream, as Dylan slid sideways into the cramped space. Her heart lurched. For a split second, their gazes met. She only had a flashing image of him. He wore a suit with no jacket, his tie was loosened, and his thick hair was mussed, his bangs falling onto his forehead. His narrowed gaze was trained on Kehoe. He looked furious and glacial, focused and dangerous.

Kehoe's eyes sprang wide when the meat pounder suddenly altered directions. Dylan shoved Kehoe's arm back at the same time that he hooked his thumb and fingers beneath Kehoe's chin. Gripping his throat, he pushed Kehoe's head and wrist at once, banging Kehoe against the wall with a force that rattled the surface behind

Alice's back. The meat tenderizer fell from Kehoe's grip, clattering to the unfinished concrete floor. Before Kehoe could recover, Dylan lifted Kehoe's head and smashed it again into the wall.

It was a brutal blow. There was a crunching sound. Alice suspected the back of Kehoe's head had splintered the plaster. That . . . or Kehoe's skull itself had cracked. Air popped out of Kehoe's lungs.

Dylan pulled Kehoe's head forward and whacked it against the wall yet again. Kehoe's body went slack. He sagged down the wall several inches, but Dylan still had his neck and jaw in a squeezing grip. Dylan pulled his head forward yet again.

"*Enough*, Dylan," a man shouted breathlessly. "You're going to kill him!"

It was like she was watching the scene through a ten-foot tank filled with water. Everything was hazy and muffled. She saw a man peer around the opened back wall of the pantry. He wore a uniform. It was Jim Sheridan. He was too big to squeeze into the already overfilled space.

"*Dylan*," Sheridan barked.

Dylan stilled.

Slowly, Dylan turned and met Alice's gaze. In that quick second, she knew that killing Kehoe was precisely what he'd planned to do before Jim found them. She didn't flinch from his savagery, but she was struggling to keep her eyelids from drooping and losing consciousness again. Dylan's grip on Kehoe's throat loosened. Kehoe's body slid and crumpled to the floor.

Alice stared fixedly at Dylan's face as he drew closer to her. He crouched over her and gently touched the skin at the side of her ribs. She recalled hazily that she'd flung off her T-shirt because it had betrayed her in the darkness.

All the focused savagery that had frozen Dylan's handsome face before melted away, only to be replaced by a poignant, helpless pain. That mysterious, inexplicable bond they'd shared even as children pulled tight. He was feeling her pain in that moment, and she hated it.

"It's going to be okay, baby," he murmured, his hand moving and his gaze flickering over her anxiously, searching for wounds.

"My deputy has called an ambulance. Don't move her, Dylan," Jim Sheridan said, but Alice's stare didn't budge off Dylan's face. She didn't want to stop looking at him.

"It's okay. I'm fine. But *Thad*," she whispered hoarsely. Dylan's expression stiffened.

"What *about* Thad?"

"He fought with Kehoe down by the bluff. Maybe he's still down there . . . hurt," she managed to get out. The effort of speaking exhausted her. A tear leaked down her cheek. God, what if it was worse. What if Kehoe had killed Thad? She shouldn't have left him. He'd saved her, and she'd abandoned him.

"Shhh, baby, it's going to be okay," she heard Dylan say, but his voice was very muffled. He said something to Jim in a clipped tone, and Jim replied, but she could no longer decode their words.

She went into the darkness without a struggle. It was an escape, she knew, an avoidance of all the ugliness. But this time, she didn't fear succumbing.

Dylan was there, and it was safe.

TWENTY-ONE

The first thing Alice saw when she awoke in the hospital was Dylan. He was staring directly at her, as if he'd known she was rising into consciousness . . . as if he'd been waiting for the event. Her whole body ached with a dull throb, but it hardly mattered. All of her focus was on him. For a moment, neither of them spoke as they looked at one another. For Alice, it was like she was drinking him in. She vaguely recalled, like she might a hazy dream, that he had been wearing the exact white shirt, dress pants, and tie last night . . .

. . . in the pantry.

She winced when the graphic, terrifying memory rushed her consciousness. Desperately, she tried to focus on the moment. On Dylan.

There were smears of blood on the front of his shirt. The bright crimson seemed to blaze against the snowy white background. She realized the stains must have come from her. She couldn't recall the ambulance or getting to the hospital, but at some point, he'd leaned over her and gotten some of her blood on him.

He stood slowly, his dark eyes gleaming as he looked down at her. She lifted her hand to touch him and realized it was bandaged and she had a tube inserted into her arm. She frowned. He caught her forearm and gently placed her hand back on the bed. He kept his hand there. The warm pressure of his touch comforted her.

"You're going to be fine." He sounded distant. Muffled. She

shifted her head. He must have read the question in her eyes. "They have an IV in to keep you hydrated, since you were unconscious for quite a while and couldn't take in any liquids. Your head took it the worst. You've got plenty of scrapes and bruises, but nothing that time won't heal just fine. Their biggest concern is the head injury."

"You're . . ." She swallowed. Her throat was very dry. Dylan noticed her difficulty and reached for a pitcher on her side table. He poured her some water. He raised her head off the pillows and held up the cup to her lips. Alice swallowed, the cool liquid feeling like nirvana to her parched throat.

"You're okay?" she finished asking a moment later when he'd laid her back on the pillows and set aside the cup.

He gave her a small smile. Her heart gave a little spasm at the sight. She'd missed him. She hadn't seen him since he'd left town on Tuesday, but it was more than that. It was as if that ordeal on the bluff and in the pantry had taken up a year of time in her brain.

Last night had aged her.

"I'm completely fine," he said, placing his hand on her forearm again. "A good deal better now that you've woken up," he added.

"Thank you for coming," she whispered feelingly.

His hand curled around her forearm, and then he immediately loosened it, as if he thought he'd break her. She could tell by his expression he'd understood she was thanking him for saving her life, not for coming to the hospital room.

"I'm just sorry I wasn't there sooner."

She glanced around the room, taking in her surroundings. "Do you remember everything that happened, Alice?" he asked cautiously. "The doctor is worried there might be some memory loss."

She nodded. "I think I remember everything. I still don't really understand it all, though."

"We've been trying to figure out the chain of events. I know from Dave Epstein that Kehoe had sent that message to you through the kitchens, saying it was from me." He grimaced, as if a pain had gone through him. "Alice, I think I was *there* in the house, when he first attacked you. Upstairs. I left for our meeting, but that must have been in some quiet interim before Kehoe took you to the bluff and Schaefer set off the alarm."

"When he first hit me, I blacked out. I'm not sure for how long," she admitted. "When I came to, he was dragging me through the yard, and it was dark. If he heard you coming, he might have waited in the house until you left."

She regretted saying it when she saw the angry tilt of his mouth. The vision of him disabling Kehoe so utterly flew into her mind's eye. A shadow crossed his bold features, and she wondered if he'd just recalled the same thing.

"Kehoe?" she rasped.

"He'll live," he replied, his expression conveying he wasn't exactly pleased about that news. "He's in stable condition."

"Is he . . . is Kehoe here? In this hospital?" she wondered uneasily.

"No. The ambulance took him over to County General. That's where the county jail inmates get medical care. They're more used to police guards than Morgantown Memorial."

She exhaled shakily, relieved at the idea that Kehoe wasn't in the same facility as her. Dylan's mouth went grim, and she realized he'd read her anxiety and subsequent relief at realizing Kehoe was at another hospital and under guard.

"He's a horrible, sick man," she muttered.

"He's never going to bother you again, Alice. Never."

She had so many questions to ask him, but exhaustion weighed on her. How had Kehoe gotten past the security and into the house? Was he talking to the police? Was he admitting his guilt? Was anyone else hurt?"

"Is Thad okay?" she managed weakly.

"Thad is banged up a bit, but he's going to be fine. They'll be discharging him this afternoon." He held up his hand when she opened her mouth to ask another question. "I know you have questions, baby. So do I. But now's not the time. I need to go and tell the nurse that you woke up. The doctor wanted to be called when you did so she could do an examination. I promised I would call the second you opened your eyes. So for now, know that you're safe and will recover soon enough. Okay?"

She nodded, but grew uneasy when he started to walk away.

"I'll be *right* back," he growled softly before he leaned over the railing and brushed his mouth against her lips. Alice closed her eyes, savoring the contact of his skin against hers. Then he was gone.

She tried her mightiest to stay awake, but she would have sworn her eyelids weighed thirty pounds each.

SHE didn't succeed in holding up the eye weights. She awakened at around noon, ravenous. Dylan stayed with her while she ate a meal of chicken noodle soup and a grilled cheese sandwich. She was so starved, that sandwich was the best thing she'd ever eaten in her whole life. She was glad to see some of the stark worry leave Dylan's face as he watched her demolish her simple meal. Afterward, a Dr. Sheldrake examined her and declared that she showed no overt signs of neurological damage. She explained that more testing was required, however, and she'd ordered an MRI for later that afternoon.

"When will I be finished? I have somewhere I need to be tonight," she told the doctor as she completed her examination. The doctor's brow furrowed and she glanced at Dylan.

"I'm afraid you won't be going anywhere tonight, Alice. You'll be with us at least until Monday morning, maybe longer, depending on your test results. You took quite a blow to the head. We want to make sure there's no serious damage to your brain."

Alice looked over at Dylan, panic sweeping through her. "But my kids! It's the last night of camp. They're giving out the team trophy tonight. If I don't see them tonight, they'll be gone . . ." She faded off because her voice had grown shaky at the mere idea.

"I'm sorry, baby, but you heard the doctor."

"But—"

"There's no but about it," Dylan said more firmly this time, but there was compassion in his dark eyes. The doctor murmured some platitudes and medical facts about brain injuries, which Alice ignored, and left the room.

She sagged back on her pillows, desolate. She couldn't believe it. After all she'd experienced at that camp—all the effort, anxiety, risk, and triumph—and she was going to miss the most important day. The Red Team had such a good chance at winning the Team Championship trophy, and she had so many things she wanted to tell her kids before they left. She might never see them again. She wanted to cry. God, she despised Sebastian Kehoe for a lot of reasons, but this particular robbery from her life had to be right up there at the top of the list.

"Can my kids maybe come see me before they go home tomorrow?" she asked Dylan, her voice cracking.

He looked a little slain. "I don't think you realize what you've been through."

"I have a concussion and some cuts and bruises! You said so yourself."

He inhaled and closed his eyes. Suddenly he stood and walked away.

"Dylan?"

"I'll be right back."

He returned a minute later, carrying a hand mirror. He looked very solemn as he handed it to her. Alice grasped the handle dubiously with a bandaged hand. She held it up to reflect her face.

Her lungs froze. She stared in disbelief for several seconds before she handed the mirror back to Dylan wordlessly. He set it down on the bedside table. Tears swelled in her eyes in the silence that followed.

"The police want to speak with you, and so does the FBI," Dylan said quietly. "Dr. Sheldrake wouldn't let them in to talk to you until after she'd completed her examination and gave the okay. I seriously doubt that she's going to allow a bunch of teenagers in here. The only reason *I'm* allowed in is because . . . well, I wouldn't take no for an answer, number one. I'm guessing Durand's donation for the new children's wing here at the hospital probably helped my cause some," he added dryly under his breath. "But the real reason I think Sheldrake made an exception in my case is that you kept saying my name over and over when they brought you in. I was the only thing that quieted you, so I guess she saw my worth. But she's not going to okay a roomful of kids."

Alice didn't argue. Her mind had changed in an instant when she looked in the mirror. The last thing she wanted was for them to see her like this. Her face was a bruised, bloody mess after slamming into that stonewall. She looked like a bandaged ghoul.

"Are you sure none of the damage is permanent?" she asked shakily, ashamed of her vanity at a moment like this.

"*Yes,*" Dylan assured, touching her shoulder. "Don't worry about that. It'll take a while for the abrasions to heal and the bruises to fade, but it's surface damage. No bones were broken, thank God. They don't think there'll be any serious scarring." He stroked her. His warmth made one of the tears spill out of her eye. "I'm sorry for breaking it to you like that, but I thought you should understand."

She nodded. It was very hard to contain her disappointment. "What are my kids being told about why I won't be there for the trophy presentation?" she asked.

"I've briefed the Durand manager of human resources—Guy Morales, he's just under Kehoe and will be taking over his duties for now—to hold a meeting with the managers, key camp employees, and the other counselors about the basic details of what happened up at the castle last night. Guy is going to determine which of the managers is most familiar to your kids, and have that person break the news to them. The media was informed that an arrest was made last night, and that there were two assaults and a break-in at the castle, but no names or specifics have been released yet. This should be the first your kids hear of it, and then a more generalized announcement will be made to the whole camp. Whoever tells your kids the news will assure them that you're going to be fine."

Alice sniffed. Dylan handed her a tissue wordlessly.

"Jessica Moder knows them best, but I don't know if she'll be up for it. She came down with the flu on Thursday night," Alice said. "I'd rather Dave Epstein and Kuvi told them. And . . . and please have them make sure they keep an eye on Jill Sanchez. She'll probably be more unsettled than any of the others. Can you put in a special request to have them ask Judith Arnold, the team leader, to especially look out for her? Although she probably will anyway."

"I'll tell all that to Guy. Alice, do you think you can talk to the police about what happened now?"

"You said the FBI, too. Earlier."

He nodded. "That's what I planned on telling you after we met last night. It seems Jim Sheridan did some digging on his own, and made the connection between Sissy and Avery Cunningham, which confirmed what he already suspected about you being Addie Durand. When he confronted me, I told him everything I knew. He contacted the FBI with the information last evening. Two agents arrived in Morgantown to interview us this morning, only to find that you were here at the hospital, and their dead case file had come back to life in the biggest way possible." He grimaced. "They've already interviewed Thad and me. They're very eager to speak with you."

"I don't want to talk to them."

"I'm sorry, Alice. I really am. But I can't put them off—"

"No . . . I just mean I don't want to talk to them until I talk to you," she said hastily. "About the things Kehoe said last night, when he attacked me." The memory suddenly fresh in her brain, she winced and gagged.

"Alice?" Dylan said, standing and leaning over her. "Are you going to be sick?"

She shook her head, bringing her instinctive reaction under control as best she could. "I think . . . I think Kehoe might be my biological father," she said quickly, before the nausea rose in her throat again.

"No," Dylan said with abrupt harshness.

Misery overwhelmed her. She'd known Dylan would never want to believe that she wasn't Alan Durand's daughter, but she hadn't thought he'd deny it so stringently. She *had* to tell him before she told the police and FBI, or worse yet, Kehoe confessed it and Dylan discovered the truth in some roundabout fashion. It'd been toward *Alan* that Dylan had felt so much loyalty. It'd been Alan's grief at the loss of Addie for which Dylan had felt a lifelong guilt and experienced a personal mandate to set things right.

It was agony for her to tell him that all of his guilt and his mission to see her returned to her rightful place as Alan Durand's daughter had been for nothing.

"You don't understand," she whispered shakily. "Kehoe said that he and Lynn Durand had had an affair. She wanted a baby so bad that she betrayed Alan because he couldn't get her pregnant."

"I know," Dylan said calmly. "I know all about it."

"What?" Alice asked, sure she'd heard him incorrectly.

"I found some of Lynn's journals last evening. I started to wonder why Lynn would tell a three- or four-year-old child to hide alone in dark, scary places. It seemed completely out of character from what I knew about her. She doted on you, and rarely let you out of her sight. Then I remembered you saying that the hiding places were hers, too, and I don't know . . . something clicked for me. I went back to the castle and inspected a couple of the secret compartments in the castle. In your old bedroom, I found four of Lynn's journals in a secret room Deanna Shrevecraft had shown me once. I think Lynn placed them there on purpose because of their contents, to be found some day."

"What did they say?" Alice asked, amazed.

"Special Agent Clayton and Agent Rogers have them right now. They're holding them as evidence, but I think they'll let you look at them whenever you're ready. But I read them all, and know this right off the bat," he said pointedly. "You are *not* the daughter of Sebastian Kehoe. Lynn broke things off with him months before she learned she was pregnant with you. In her journals, she mentioned that the time of her affair with Kehoe was close enough to her pregnancy to make her worry at first."

"So, he still *might* be my father?"

Dylan shook his head resolutely. "No, the timing was off once she understood how early in the pregnancy she was. Unfortunately, the timing *was* close enough to make Kehoe question it. But she had more evidence he wasn't the father. Despite her insistence to Kehoe that he wasn't the father, Kehoe persisted in believing he *was* for years after she stopped seeing him. Lynn had told him during their affair that Alan had some medical issues, and the chance of their conceiving a child was so negligible as to be an impossibility. Maybe it all related to the fact that Alan later was diagnosed with testicular cancer." He shook his head. "I don't know. I *do* know that Alan and Lynn always referred to you as a miracle. I sensed the amount of emotion behind it when they said it. If all this is true, then for *them*, it was true in the literal, not the figurative sense. Especially for Lynn, who would have given up all hope of having a baby after she'd broken things off with Kehoe and resolved never to be unfaithful to Alan again. But since Kehoe was armed with the knowledge of Alan's supposed inability to have a child, he wouldn't let go of the idea that he was the father.

"He harassed Lynn about it for years. He was obsessed with her, and wrecked by her breakup with him. Unfortunately for Lynn, Morgantown isn't a huge city, and the Durand executive enclave is even smaller. She was thrown together with Kehoe on several occasions at business dinners and functions. The more she avoided him, the more Kehoe's obsession with her grew. Lynn was terrified that he'd expose the truth of their affair to Alan. I think she lived in daily, maybe hourly fear, but did everything in her power to hide that fact from Alan and you."

"Is that why she taught me to hide? From him?" Alice asked, shivers snaking under her skin. It was incredible to believe, but twenty-some years after the fact, that was precisely what had happened. Alice had been attacked by Kehoe, and hidden in one of the spots Lynn had taught her. It probably would have worked, too, if she hadn't been so disoriented that she didn't realize she was leaving bloody tracks that led Kehoe straight to her.

Dylan nodded. "Lynn grew terrified of Kehoe. The real proof that you weren't Kehoe's child was that given your blood type, Kehoe couldn't have been your father. Several months before your fourth birthday, she finally showed Kehoe your medical records and some articles on ruling out paternity through blood type. She'd called Kehoe up to the castle for a private meeting while Alan was out of town on business. Kehoe became enraged when she presented him with the facts. There was no way he could continue to hold on to the delusion that he was the father of the love of his life's child . . . or that she'd ever come back to him."

"He hit her, didn't he?" Alice asked numbly.

"Yes. Apparently, he clubbed her on the side of her head." Instinctively, Alice touched the left side of her head. That's where Kehoe had first struck her to disable her. It was the blow the doctor was most concerned about. To think that Lynn—her mother—had endured a similar injury from the same man was another sad but firm bond between them. Dylan noticed her gesture and his expression went hard.

"Go on, please," Alice insisted.

He inhaled. "You were with a babysitter, but you heard Lynn cry out when she was struck. You ran into the den. She was bleeding from her ear, and—"

"She was terrified to have me in the same room with him, and she told me to run and hide," Alice finished.

"It was another true memory. Maybe the earliest one you've had," Dylan said quietly. "I was wrong to tell you that it never happened."

"Why didn't she speak up?" Alice blurted out suddenly. "Why didn't Lynn tell the police when I was kidnapped that Kehoe might be responsible? He *was*, by the way," she added quickly. "Kehoe admitted to it out there by the bluff, that he hired Cunningham and Stout."

Dylan froze. "He did?"

"Oh, he did all right. But why didn't Lynn say anything after the kidnapping? Was she afraid of Alan finding out about her affair with Kehoe?"

"No. I don't think anything would have stopped Lynn from exposing her infidelity if she thought it'd help in bringing you home to her."

"*Why*, then? Why didn't she say anything about Kehoe?" she asked, frustrated and angry with a woman of whom she only possessed the smallest glimpses, and yet with whom she shared the most elemental of bonds.

Dylan cupped her shoulder, grounding her swell of helpless fury. "He'd hit her in a fit of rage when she presented him with proof that you weren't his child. Maybe he'd hit her before, and she was ashamed of it. I don't know. She never specifically said that in her journals. I got the impression from her writing that their original relationship was sexually intense at its best, volatile at its worst. They argued a lot; Kehoe wanted her to leave Alan, and Lynn refused.

"But the main reason I think she didn't say anything is that she didn't believe Kehoe could be capable of kidnapping a child. Like it or not, she believed herself in love with him for a brief time in her life. She didn't believe he'd make *you* the target of his fury at being rejected by her. She might have worried he'd hurt *her* if pushed, and that you might be harmed if you were in the vicinity. The two of you were together almost all the time. But I don't think she ever believed he'd plan and plot *exclusively* against you, let alone try to kidnap and murder you. Her journals indicate that she never knew a side to his character that was *that* dark."

Because Lynn had been unable to see it, Alice had been forced to. It was an uncharitable thought to have about a woman who had suffered so much . . . about a woman who was her biological mother. Alice knew this. She scrunched her eyelids tight. The action pulled on her facial abrasions. She immediately opened her burning eyes.

"Lynn knew the truth about him," she said. "At the end, she did. Kehoe told me by the bluff that he couldn't let it happen. He couldn't watch while the rich king and the beautiful queen and the little princess lived out their idyllic dream in the castle. He actually *said* something like that," she said in a hoarse voice, disgusted at the memory. She dabbed carefully at the corner of her eyes.

"He probably hated you enough for what you symbolized after he realized you weren't his," Dylan said after a pause, caressing her shoulder. "But beyond that, he knew that by depriving Alan and Lynn of you, he guaranteed their misery."

She inhaled and shuddered, holding the tissue to the corner of her eye to stanch the flow of tears. They made her cuts burn.

"Why didn't you tell me she jumped off the bluff?"

"I'm sorry," he said gruffly. "You never asked how she died. I was trying to follow Sidney's advice and tell you things only when you seemed ready. I suspected you must know, deep down, that she'd died tragically, given the circumstances. I thought you'd even caught hints of it from that damn ghost story the kids tell. But even though I thought you might suspect, you never asked." She looked up at him. He looked as miserable as she felt.

"He was there with her. Kehoe. When she fell."

"*What?* Did he—"

"No, he didn't push her. Or at least that's what he said. But he *did* kill her."

"What do you mean?"

Her lip curled at the memory. Things were starting to fall into place in her head. "What a fucking bastard," she whispered. "He knew that rumors were flying around that I was probably dead at that point. You told me after Jim Stout confessed, that the police and FBI were convinced I was dead. That's when he confronted Lynn out by the bluff, when she was so full of dread and grief, vulnerable because of what the FBI suspected."

"She sunk into a severe depression after you were taken. She believed she was being punished for her infidelity. It was in her journals."

"That's when Kehoe told her everything, when she was at her weakest," Alice said. She shut her burning eyelids. She wanted to weep full-out, but her body wasn't providing her with enough energy to grieve so forcefully. "He told her that he knew for a fact that Addie was dead," she paused, suppressing a sob, "because he'd been the one to hire and give the order to the kidnappers. And then he didn't stop Lynn from going over the bluff once she'd heard that news.

"He *was* going to throw *me* over that bluff last night. He said he'd join me, and we'd be broken and bloody together. It was like it was happening all over again for him, what happened with Lynn. He said he wished he'd committed suicide with her, so that they could have been together. That's how warped and twisted he was. He kept acting like he hated her more than anything, and in the next second, he talked about her like she was perfection itself. He planned to commit suicide after he killed me, I think. He knew you were suspicious of him, and that he might be under fire if the kidnapping investigation started full force again because I'd come back. He already was jealous and hateful of you because of your relationship with Alan," she said, looking at Dylan.

"He *despised* the idea of you and me being together happily, controlling Durand Enterprises, especially after all he'd been through to cancel Lynn and Alan's happiness. That's why he told me the other night at the bonfire that he wasn't going to let it happen *again*. He wouldn't watch me ride off with you into the sunset." She gave a bitter laugh and it mixed with a restrained sob. "Instead, he wanted to see me end up in the same place as Lynn, and you in the same place as Alan. He said something about dying satisfied of your misery when you saw me on those rocks. The fact that he was considering committing suicide last night must mean he'd given up on disguising his hatred and obsession . . . his sickness anymore."

"Jesus." Alice glanced up. Dylan's rigid features broke briefly. He pressed his lips to her temple. She sensed his fierce misery. She reached with her bandaged hand and touched his shoulder, absorbing the shudder of emotion that went through his powerful body.

"Do you want me to talk to the FBI and police now?" she asked him weakly after a moment.

He straightened and shook his head.

"No?" she asked.

"Rest now," he said, his gaze running over her face. She hated to think of what he saw when he looked at her. "You can barely keep your eyes open. I'll fill them in on what you told me, so the officers and agents aren't complete blank slates when they interview you. It should make it a little easier for you. If you feel up to it after you rest and your testing later, you can talk to them then."

Alice nodded. He was averting his gaze from her, which bothered her deeply. She opened her mouth to question his preoccupation, but he halted her with a soft, firm kiss on her lips. Her heart
sunk a little when he turned and left the room.

Deep down, was he worried that she wasn't really Alan
Durand's daughter? Vague former worries returned to haunt her,
now clarified and flashing like neon signs in her brain. Dylan
wanted to believe she wasn't Kehoe's child, perhaps as much as
Alice wished it. The idea of being that monster's progeny turned
her insides to ice. But because it made Dylan and her uncomfortable, they couldn't just assume that it wasn't still a possibility. Even
if she wasn't Kehoe's child, wasn't it possible Lynn had slept with
someone else? Wouldn't that be a more likely scenario, than that
Addie Durand was a miracle baby?

What would happen if the results of the genetic testing came
back, and she learned she wasn't Alan's daughter? She'd be so
disappointed, after hearing Alan's voice in that dream, after feeling so much emotion associated with him. *Daddy.*

But Dylan would probably be devastated, too.

He'd been focused to the point of obsession for most of his life
with the idea of finding her. Now that he knew the truth, would
it change the way he felt about her?

ALICE gave her statement to the police and FBI that night after
her early supper. When the agents first entered her room, carrying
cases of what looked like electronic equipment, Dylan came with
them.

"What's all that stuff?" Alice asked uneasily after she'd been
introduced to Special Agent Clayton and Agent Rogers. The older
agent, Clayton, gave Dylan a pointed glance. Dylan stepped closer
to her bed, and Alice had the uncomfortable feeling the agents had
asked him to break some news to her.

"What is it?" she whispered, studying his lips closely for their hushed exchange.

"Alice, the agents need to photograph you."

Alice blanched. "I look like hell," she whispered. The last thing she wanted was to have strangers take her picture.

He grimaced. "Your injuries are evidence. If Kehoe pleads not guilty to your attack—"

"He's going to plead not guilty?" she asked in a high-pitched voice.

"We don't know yet. He's still in the hospital, and he's been out of it a lot. When he is awake, he's not saying much. The point is, if this *does* go to trial," Dylan continued quietly. "Your condition is important evidence. Even if it doesn't go to trial, it's valuable information for Kehoe's sentencing. I'm sorry, honey. I can't see any way around it."

"No, it's okay," she said after a pause. "If all these bruises and bandages make it more likely for Kehoe to get the most severe sentence possible, then it'll be worth it."

"I was hoping you'd see it that way." Alice glanced up at him when he didn't move away. "There's something else. They want to videotape the interview."

Alice's mouth fell open. She wanted to do whatever she should to nail Kehoe for what he'd done to her . . . for what he'd done to Lynn and Alan. But she'd never felt more vulnerable.

Dylan's mouth curled into a small snarl when he saw her reaction. "I'll tell them if they want to tape the interview, they'll have to do it another time."

"No, it's okay," Alice said softly.

"Are you sure?" he asked quietly. "Because I can't stay in here with you during it. I guess they don't want to take the chance of me influencing your story."

Alice strained to hide her disappointment at that.

"Of course. I'll be fine," she assured. She saw his hesitation.

"Besides, you need to go home and shower and get some rest anyway," she told him. Her gaze lowered significantly. "My blood isn't the ideal accessory on you, you know." He hadn't left the hospital, even when she was being tested, so he still wore the bloodstained shirt.

"An accessory I'll gladly never wear again." Alice strained to hear his quieted voice. He straightened, glancing at the agents darkly. "She tires very easily," he told Clayton. "Don't push her."

Clayton nodded. "Just tell us if you grow tired, Alice, and we can finish up in the morning."

Dylan seemed partially mollified. He surprised her a little by turning back and kissing her mouth, ignoring the agents. Her heart jumped at the sensation of his warm, firm lips against her own. She joined his slow, delicious rhythm, kissing him back for a fleeting moment.

"Are you sure you're okay to do this now?" he asked, his mouth brushing against hers.

She nodded. "I want to get it over with."

"I'll be back later tonight, then," he assured her gruffly.

"Don't you think you should get some rest at the castle and come back tomorrow?" she whispered.

"I'll be back later tonight," he repeated.

A feeling of uncertainty went through her. She'd read his lips to understand him. Was he talking *that* quietly? He straightened, giving the agents what Alice could only call a warning glance, and left the room.

Alice wasn't sure what to make of that kiss in front of the agents. Were they now declaring their relationship to the world? She suspected maybe he was telling her not to be self-conscious about revealing their involvement. There hadn't been much opportunity for them to discuss her statement to the agents. That kiss heartened her more than anything had since awakening and seeing him sitting next to her bed. It seemed to say, *Just tell the truth. The time for secrets is done, and you have nothing to be ashamed of.*

* * *

SHE was pretty tired by the time the agents packed up their equipment and left. It'd been difficult talking about Sissy and the Reeds, knowing that the agents were viewing them strictly in terms of potential collaborators to Addie's kidnapping. While to Alice, they had been much more. They were a family she was horribly ashamed of, and despised at times . . . but they were family, nevertheless. Or at least she'd thought they'd been. She sent up a silent prayer that Uncle Al had left the trailer, like she'd asked him to. As for the others, it felt grimly inevitable and completely out of her control to do anything to stop the hand of fate or justice. It all seemed so much bigger than her.

It was even harder, at first, to talk about every detail of her encounter with Kehoe, but it got easier once she got a momentum going. When she got to the part about Kehoe planning to throw her over the bluff, the agent paused her. He asked her to recall exactly what Kehoe had said, as best as she could, toward the end. Wincing, Alice repeated what he'd said about Lynn, her suicide, and his threats against her—Alice.

Special Agent Clayton nodded when she'd finished. "That matches up well with what Schaefer overheard as he neared the bluff. Did you realize that Schaefer had been following you regularly, under Kehoe's orders?"

"No. I mean, I knew Thad was following me sometimes, but I didn't know it was under Kehoe's directions. Are you saying that Thad followed me up to the castle last night because Kehoe told him to?" she asked, confused.

"No. Last night, he claims he did it because he was concerned about you. It seems he was no longer entirely convinced that Kehoe had good intentions toward you."

"He uh . . . said he had a thing for me," she admitted uncomfortably. "That's why I thought he was following me, at first."

"Did you ever reciprocate the interest?" Clayton asked.

"No. I made it clear from the beginning I just wanted to be friends."

"It seems Kehoe had given Schaefer orders to keep an eye on you as much as possible, get close to you, report back to him about anything noteworthy. According to Schaefer, his father and Kehoe are old friends, so he had an implicit trust in him from the first. Plus, Kehoe was his top boss there at camp . . . the man he needed to impress to get hired as a Durand manager. He felt obligated when Kehoe asked him to get close to you, although he didn't start to put together until more recently why Kehoe was so focused on you."

"Do you think Thad just acted like he liked me so that he could follow me easier . . . give Kehoe more information about me?"

"Schaefer flatly denies that, but I wouldn't be surprised."

"But he saved me," Alice said, frowning. "He fought Kehoe, and made it possible for me to escape out there by the bluff."

"He was starting to not trust Kehoe. He started to feel pressured by him to do things he didn't want to do, and thought that Kehoe seemed like he was losing control. Recently, he realized that his motives were not at all honorable when it came to you. Of course," Clayton said wryly, "Schaefer was pretty dishonorable himself. On Kehoe's orders, he intentionally set off Dylan Fall's home alarm one night a week or so ago."

"*Thad* did that?"

"Schaefer himself admitted to it," Rogers replied.

"But *why*?"

"That was all Kehoe's planning. Apparently, Kehoe was familiar with Fall's security system. He's been up to the castle a lot for business and social functions over the years, enough to notice details about the security system. The security company is called Home Guard, and the headquarters are right here in Morgantown. Kehoe managed to either ingratiate himself with an employee there, pay him off, or blackmail him; we're still looking into that. The employee hasn't been so forthcoming on that angle, so I'm guessing blackmail. At any rate, Kehoe somehow got this guy to do some of his dirty work." Agent Rogers paused and checked his notebook. "A man by the name of Chester Greeson. The plan was for Schaefer to rattle doors and windows to set off the alarm. Kehoe would have him do it as many times as it took until Fall asked for the alarm to be serviced and checked by Home Guard for a glitch. It seems Fall was vigilant enough to call after the first occurrence. Greeson showed up to do the service check, and programmed an additional disabling code into the system."

"Which he then passed on to Kehoe, giving him access," Alice said.

"That's right," Clayton replied. "After Schaefer told us what he knew, we paid a visit to Greeson early this morning."

"Will he admit what he did and point the finger at Kehoe?"

"He already has. That's how we have the information," Clayton said.

Alice was relieved by his air of confidence. "So Kehoe had already disabled the alarm when I showed up there because of that fake note?"

"He was inside, waiting for you to arrive. We're not sure if he knew Fall was upstairs or not. He might have just waited until the cook left and disabled the alarm, then entered. At some point, he put in a call to the camp, though, claiming to be Fall."

Alice winced, picturing it. "Kehoe got lucky. Dylan had told me there was something important he wanted to discuss with me when he returned from Reno. When I saw the note, I thought it related to that. It was stupid of me to trust it, but Dylan's earlier mention of something important in combination with the fact that in the note he seemed concerned about my walk up to the castle, telling me to take the safer route and have Rigo escort me . . . well, it sounded like something Dylan would say.

"What will happen to Thad?" she asked Clayton after a pause. She was pissed at Thad for colluding with Kehoe, but thankful he'd saved her. She didn't trust Thad as much as she had at the beginning of their friendship, but it sickened her to think of him working for Kehoe. . . even if he had eventually seen through Kehoe's sane act.

"The local sheriff has arrested Schaefer for trespassing after he admitted to setting off the alarm. Sheridan could have come up with a more severe charge, given all that Schaefer confessed. But Schaefer did cooperate fully, and he seems to have come to the realization that Kehoe wasn't the respectable, high-powered executive his father would have him believe he was. Plus, when he first arrived and heard you screaming down by the bluff, he purposefully broke into the castle. His intent was to set off the alarm—"

"So the police would come," Alice finished. "Then he confronted Kehoe, giving me time to get away."

Clayton nodded. "Schaefer claimed he would have been there sooner. But you and Rigo took the road up to the house. He had to give both you and Rigo some distance, or risk being caught. The road up to the castle is a long, clear view. If you or Rigo turned, you would have seen him on it, so he had to stay back and wait until both of you were all the way to the top of the bluff. His account of what happened is probably our best account of how long it was between when Kehoe first knocked you unconscious and when he dragged you out to the drop-off. It sounds as if Schaefer almost didn't make it in time to stop Kehoe."

She thought of all the times Dylan had warned her about Thad. She shut her eyelids, suddenly feeling very tired.

THE agents left at about seven that night. Maybe it was her pain medication, but she found herself in the strangest state of mind. She wasn't quite sure if she was half-asleep or awake, but her ruminations had a nightmarish quality. For half an hour, she just lay there, thinking . . . reworking the tapestry of her life.

The thread she worried and picked over the most was Dylan.

Was he feeling regretful that there was a chance she wasn't Alan Durand's biological daughter? And if that were true—if she in fact wasn't Alan's daughter, only Lynn's—how did that affect the trust document and Dylan's powers as CEO of Durand? It wasn't that she thought he was only interested in her potential power or money. It wasn't that at all. She loved Dylan. So much. It was just that Lynn's journals and Kehoe's confessions would drastically alter how he'd considered his life . . . his preoccupation with finding *her*. He must be struggling with some major re-envisioning of his past as well.

What if he was re-envisioning his relationship with her?

She felt cut wide open, vulnerable to anxiety and doubt. She thought repeatedly about Sidney Gate's worries about Dylan's pre-occupation with finding Addie Durand, and how he'd sacrificed his own dreams to lessen the burden of his guilt.

When she heard a light knock at her door, her heart leapt with anxious anticipation.

"Come in," she called, assuming Dylan had returned. She was eager to see him, despite her dark turn of mind. Or perhaps because of it. Dylan's presence always had a way of scattering her doubts.

"*Thad,*" she said when he walked into the room. "I thought—"

"That I was arrested by Jim Sheridan? I was. But it wasn't a serious charge. I'm out on bail."

She stared at him, and he stared back. He had a black eye, a bandage on his left temple and a cut, swollen lip.

"Kehoe knocked me out down by the bluff in order to chase you," he said, touching the bandage briefly.

It'd taken him a second or two to gather himself before he spoke. Alice knew he'd been put off by her appearance.

"That son of a bitch packs a wicked right hook," Thad continued uneasily.

"Not news to me, unfortunately." she murmured wryly. "You look horrible, but at least you look better than me."

He shook his head, clearly speechless over her light handling of the situation of her condition.

"This is the part where you're supposed to say, 'You don't look that bad, Alice.' Don't worry. Dylan gave me a mirror. I know I look like something out of *The Walking Dead*."

Thad's eyes shone with emotion. Alice felt a little regretful at her flippancy.

"Fall told me that the doctor thinks you'll be fine. I just hadn't expected," Thad gestured helplessly at her face. "I'm so sorry, Alice."

"For thinking Kehoe was so ace?" she wondered sarcastically.

"For everything. To think, he did *this* to you. To think . . . this is what he intended all along."

"I don't know if it was *all along*. When he first contracted your services," she said with a frown, "he didn't realize I had any connection to Addie Durand. He was just curious and suspicious because of Dylan's interest in me. Once he did figure it out, he wanted to do worse than this," she said, pointing at her face.

Thad sunk into the chair by her bed as if his legs had just given out on him. "I'm the one who ultimately confirmed it for him."

"Confirmed what?"

"That you were Addie Durand," Thad said. His stark regret was obvious. "*That's* what Sheridan should have arrested me for. I mentioned it to Kehoe before I understood fully what it meant: what I overheard you saying in the hallway the night of the Alumni Dinner about Addie Durand," he said, his manner that of a penitent man making a painful confession.

"For what it's worth, Kehoe already suspected I was Addie by that time, anyway. Why else would he plan to get into the castle?

When you told him what you heard at the Alumni Dinner, it was probably just a confirmation, and maybe not even the first one for him. Kehoe understood quite a few more things than you did when he started pushing you around his chess board."

"As his pawn." Alice didn't disagree. "He understood how much I'd want to please my dad. So much so that I blindly helped a mad man almost kill the woman I—"

Alice realized she'd flinched, and that's why he'd abruptly halted. For several seconds, they just stared at each other.

"I know that given everything, you must think I was lying about how I felt about you. But I *wasn't*, Alice," he said gruffly.

Alice nodded. She didn't want to dissect it all with him. It wasn't worth it, and it'd be too painful. She was never going to start a relationship with Thad. The grim, set expression that came over his face seemed to say he had accepted that reality, too.

"You set off the alarm so that the police would come to the castle that night," she said quietly. "You fought Kehoe. I might be hurt that you colluded at all with that asshole, but at least you redeemed yourself. You were my friend, in the end."

"I don't deserve your forgiveness. Kehoe was right to call me a dumb-ass," he said in a muffled voice.

"Fuck Kehoe. He's a lunatic."

"Sounds like good advice," Thad said, attempting a small smile.

"I do forgive you, but I *am* still mad at you," Alice clarified with a dark look. "I can't *believe* you were willing to get involved in something so insane, all for the sake of getting the job your daddy wanted you to have."

He flinched at her scorn. "Yeah. Well . . . I deserve that. And more."

Her eyebrows arched when she saw his uncertainty as he stared at her.

"Come on, Thad. Do I look like a woman who feels up to kicking your ass?" she asked with disgusted amusement.

"I wouldn't put anything past you."

She laughed softly and his smile widened. Something occurred to her. She sat up slightly in bed. "Hey, how come you're not at the castle? For the Team Championship trophy presentation?"

He shook his head, looking sober again. "I'm not going to be a Durand manager. I'm not a counselor anymore, either."

"*What?* Did Dylan—"

"No, no one fired me. Although after the mistakes I've made in judgment for the past few weeks, I wouldn't have been shocked if Fall did kick my ass all the way back to Greenwich. I quit. Just before I came back here to see you, in fact."

"Why?" she asked, stunned.

He shook his head, clearly embarrassed. Worse than embarrassed. *Ashamed.* Despite her irritation at him, her heart went out to him.

"If anything could teach me the stupidity of blindly following my dad's ideas about what's best for me in life, it's this. I couldn't trust my own instincts before all this happened. I had to be told by authority figures what the right thing to do was." He shrugged. "Look where that got me."

"So . . . does that mean you're going to listen to your own judgment now?" she asked hopefully. "And become a teacher?"

"It means I'm going to look in to finding out what I'd need to do to make that happen."

"No, Thad. Just *make* it happen. You. No one else."

He nodded once, and Alice had the distinct impression he was going to follow through.

"You always did have what it took to be a good executive," he said after a pause. "A phenomenal leader. You're so strong," he said, his voice breaking at the last.

"You can be strong too, Thad. You were brilliant with the kids. Everyone says so. You just doubted yourself. But in the end, you saved my life. You and Dylan did."

She saw his throat convulse as he swallowed, and knew he was choking back emotion.

"What are you going to do about Brooke?" she asked quietly after he'd brought himself under control. "Is there any kind of future with her?"

"Maybe. She sort of shocked me by not putting down the idea of becoming a teacher when I talked about it with her the other night."

"That's good. Both that she was receptive and that you were comfortable enough to tell her."

"Yeah. And I was thinking . . ."

"What?"

He grimaced. "Up there on the bluff, that was the first time I really ever fought for something," he said starkly. "Everything's always just been given to me."

"Including Brooke, right?" Alice asked wryly.

"Yeah, to be honest."

"That doesn't mean she's not worth trying for . . . fighting for. Brooke's all right," Alice conceded. "It's not every day a guy meets someone as pretty and smart as her, that's for sure. And she's crazy about you."

Thad nodded. "You're right. Actually, she's incredible. Maybe it's time I saw her as more than a convenience."

"If you're really trying to be a bigger person, that's exactly what you should do."

He nodded and met her stare uneasily. "There's something else I need to apologize for," he said. "I've watched Fall quite a bit, here at the hospital. He's crazy about you. I . . . uh . . . I might have been unwilling to see much good in him before because he had what I wanted. But from what I've seen, the first thing he thinks of in every situation is your safety and comfort. Your happiness."

Alice's smile trembled. "Addie Durand's happiness, or mine?"

Thad blinked. "They're one and the same, aren't they?"

Alice didn't reply. Her throat had gone tight, because she didn't know how to answer that question.

"Is there going to be some kind of press conference or something?" Thad asked.

"About Kehoe's arrest?"

"No . . . his name broke on the news just this evening. I heard about it on the radio on the way over here. I meant is there going to be a big announcement about Addie Durand's return . . . what it means to Durand Enterprises?"

"Oh. I don't know," Alice replied blankly, disconcerted by the question. Was that what she really wanted? To stand in front of the world and flashing cameras, and be introduced as the lost heiress Adelaide Durand?

She couldn't imagine having the strength to do it. Not until she at least had the genetic test results in hand . . .

And possibly, not even then.

TWENTY-TWO

She awoke to the sensation of someone nuzzling her ear.

"Wake up, beautiful."

Recognizing Dylan's muffled, gruff voice, she opened her eyes, smiling tiredly. She was never more confused about their relationship and what it meant than she was at that moment. But that fact didn't stop her heart from jumping at the sound of his voice, or dampen her craving to see his bold, handsome face in the slightest. He remained leaning over her when she opened her eyes, his face just inches from hers. Her gaze ran over him warmly. He'd showered and changed, and he looked amazing to her tired eyes. He wore a blue button-down and a gray sport coat. She inhaled his familiar, spicy scent and made a satisfied purr in her throat.

"I tried to stay up for you," she whispered.

"I'm sorry. I got caught up with something at the castle. Now the nurse is threatening me to keep this short. I wouldn't have wakened you, but I thought you'd think this was worth it."

"What?"

He straightened. She realized his hand had been behind his back. He moved it to the front, showing her what he'd been hiding. She stared at the Team Championship trophy.

The Red Team flag had been tied beneath the clasping hands.

"The team that wins usually can't keep their hands off the trophy on the last night of camp; it's a major coup, you know. They only get the one night to crow over it," Dylan said, smiling.

"Your team immediately asked Guy Morales if the trophy could be sent over to the hospital. Over to you."

Emotion hit her like a tidal wave. She choked. Tears shot from her eyes. Dylan looked alarmed, but she couldn't seem to stop it. The storm of emotion had slammed into her unexpectedly.

"Shhh," Dylan soothed a moment later. She realized he'd set aside the trophy and lowered her bed railing. He sat on the bed and his arms came around her. She pressed her right temple against his chest. She shuddered with feeling. Happiness. Anxiety. Hope. Anguish. Bewilderment. Desire. Loss. Grief. Triumph. Fear. All of it mixed together, everything she'd been experiencing since she'd first set foot on the Durand Estate weeks ago.

"They shouldn't have done that. It was theirs. *They* won it."

"They wanted you to have it. It was their way of saying they were thinking about you. And to thank you," Dylan said, stroking her back.

"I can't do this," she muttered miserably against his chest. Why had the demonstration of caring and support from her kids sent her over the edge, and not Kehoe's homicidal actions? Dylan would think she was crazy. Maybe she *was*. "I'm not who you think I am, Dylan. I'm not who *anybody* thinks I am."

She felt him gently press his lips to the top of her head. His hand ran up and down her spine, as if he ironed out her emotional upheaval. "Who I think you are is Alice. And Alice has been through more than most people could imagine in the last few weeks, let alone bear."

"I'm *not* bearing," she gasped between shudders. "I feel like everything is crashing down on my life. It's such a fucking mess."

"All the crashing is done, baby. All the catastrophe is over. Now comes the hard part."

"What?" she muttered, her attention caught.

"Now you have to clear aside the rubble and decide what you want your life to look like."

Minutes passed. Slowly, the onslaught of emotion subsided. She was left exhausted in its wake, her body aching with a dull throb. Dylan continued to hold her. She clung to him. They didn't talk. Nevertheless, it was his voice she kept hearing in her head.

What *did* she want her life to look like?

THE next morning, the agents returned with some follow-up questions, most of them in regard to the Reeds. Alice became highly uncomfortable when they asked her for details on the physical layout of the trailer where she'd grown up and whether or not she knew of any weapons on the property. They were asking her for specifics because they were planning on sending agents there to arrest the Reeds. Dylan was in her room when the agents arrived, and they didn't ask him to leave. When he saw Alice's hesitation over answering the questions, he stepped in.

"I know it's hard, Alice. But the details you give them will help insure that no one gets hurt."

Alice nodded. He was right. She answered all the agents' questions to the best of her ability.

LATER that morning, she went for more tests. Just as she was finishing her lunch, Dylan popped his head in the room.

"Hi," he said.

She laughed. She recognized his look. He had some kind of surprise in store for her. "Hi. What are you so smug about?"

"You have a visitor," he said. He moved aside to make room for someone to enter the room. Alice thought maybe it was Kuvi or Dave, even though she knew the kids' buses didn't leave until after lunch today. But instead of Kuvi or Dave, Maggie Lopez entered the room.

"*Maggie*," Alice cried, overwhelmed at seeing the familiar face of her mentor and friend. Maggie had been her graduate school advisor. She'd been so proud of Alice for getting hired as a Camp Durand counselor. Alice rented the apartment above Maggie's garage, and they'd become close.

"Dylan called me last night," Maggie said, coming over to the bed. She reached to hug her, but paused, looking worried about Alice's injuries.

"It's okay," Alice assured, extending her arms. Thankfully, they'd removed her IV that morning. "I'm *so* glad to see you."

Maggie hugged her delicately, laughing. She planted a warm kiss on her right temple to make up for her weak embrace. Her heart went out to Maggie when she straightened and studied Alice's face. She wasn't able to entirely disguise her concern and anxiety.

"I look a lot worse off than I actually am," Alice assured. "Right, Dylan?"

Dylan still stood in the doorway, watching them. "The doctor says all indications are good. She's not going to have any lasting damage. She'll heal, in time." Alice held his stare for a moment, gratitude in her eyes that he'd called Maggie. How had he known that she was precisely the person Alice needed at that moment.

Why do you have to be so perfect? Not perfect in some objective way. Perfect for me.

Dylan nodded once, as though he'd understood her thanks, even if he probably hadn't decoded her longing for him. Her confusion. He pointed down the hallway. "I'm going to make a few calls, give you two some time to catch up."

Maggie turned and gave Alice her familiar game face. Her gaze flickered to the trophy on the bedside table. She grinned.

"Dylan told me all about your big win," she said, picking up the trophy and looking at it proudly.

"Since when are you two on a first-name basis?" Alice asked, amused.

"Since he called me last night and told me everything," Maggie said, giving her a sharp glance. She set down the trophy. "Or almost everything. Surely a story of this magnitude can't be told in a forty-five-minute conversation. I kept thinking I'd heard it all, and then Dylan would spring some new shocker on me."

"You're telling me," Alice said, rolling her eyes.

"So . . . *Adelaide Durand?*"

Alice shrugged and nodded in agreement at Maggie's incredulity.

Maggie cast a glance over her shoulder toward the doorway. "And *Dylan Fall?*" she added, eyes wide.

"I know. That's the part no one else can believe either, including me."

Maggie gave a bark of laughter and squeezed her forearm. "That part is actually starting to make more and more sense. I saw the way you two were looking at each other just now." She pulled the chair behind her closer. "Now, I can only stay a few nights because of Doby."

Alice smiled, all too familiar with Maggie's rambunctious Irish setter.

"How *is* Doby?"

"Healthy. Which means he's bound to eat my Aunt Janine into poverty if I don't get back to Chicago by Monday. So . . . talk to me, Alice."

AN hour and a half later, Dylan looked up from making a call and saw Maggie enter the waiting room. He hit the disconnect button, halting his call in progress, when he noticed the dazed expression on Maggie's face.

"Is everything okay?" Dylan asked her when she plopped down in a seat a few feet away from him.

"Yeah. It's just a lot to take in. I'm glad you told me about how beat up she was before I saw her." She met Dylan's gaze squarely.

"This son of a bitch who did that to her, are they going to nail him good?"

"I just got off the phone with one of the agents a few minutes ago. The FBI is building evidence against Kehoe even as we speak. The U.S. Attorney's office is confident they're going to have a solid case against him if Kehoe dares to plead not guilty."

"*Good,*" Maggie snarled.

He sagged down in the chair next to her. He'd already decided he approved of Maggie Lopez, but seeing the evidence of her tight-lipped, steaming fury, he liked her all the better. But Maggie's hurt and anger also lit a match to his guilt and helplessness. He kept reliving the seconds when he'd rushed through the house that night in order to meet up with Alice at the usual designated spot. She and Kehoe had probably just been feet away from him: Alice unconscious, Kehoe silent and watching. If only he'd known and intervened then, he might have saved her that horror down by the bluff . . .

. . . and in the pantry.

He winced.

"No offense, but you look like crap. When was the last time you slept?" Maggie asked him.

He opened his eyelids. "Lots of fronts to fight on, lots of fires to put out," he muttered. Maggie's gaze on him was kind, but shrewd.

"That's odd, because Alice said you've hardly left her side."

Dylan grunted noncommittally.

"You know . . . I have a cousin who lives in the Logan Square neighborhood in Chicago. He's a cop—a big strong guy like you," Maggie began in a conversational tone. "Four years ago, he was put on the night shift, and so he and his wife had to do some major resetting of their lives. They'd only been married two months at the time. One night while he was working, two assholes broke into their townhouse with the intent of burglary. Tony—that's my cousin—had taught his wife, Sheila, how to use a gun. So Sheila confronts one of the men with the weapon, but she doesn't realize the other jerk is behind her. He disables her. Long story short, these two end up pistol-whipping her within an inch of her life. It was brutal what they did, and what's worse, they seemed to enjoy it."

"Did they catch them?" Dylan asked.

"It took two and half years, but yeah . . . they did. My point is, Tony was in a living hell. He was the strong, powerful guy—a cop, no less—but he couldn't predict that situation, he couldn't protect his wife. Why? Because a sane, normal person can't predict what a criminal or crazy person is going to do. Tony had to go to work, just like most people. He couldn't sit around, staring at his wife every second of their life. Shit happens, Dylan, crap that's not in your control. You just have to deal with the consequences the best you can."

Dylan sagged another inch in the chair. "I knew there was a moral to this story."

Maggie gave a bark of dry laughter. "You're not all powerful. No one likes facing that fact." Dylan peered at her sideways without moving his head. She arched her brows. "Besides, you were lucky compared to Tony. You saved Alice from the bad guys. Both on Thursday night . . . and eventually, from what they'd done to her twenty years ago."

"Unlike your cousin, I've suspected *this* bad guy for a long time, but couldn't prove any wrongdoing on his part. Sebastian Kehoe is considered a successful, law-abiding man."

Maggie sighed, crossed her arms over her belly, and slouched in her chair next to him. "Yeah, well what were you going to do without any solid proof? Go vigilante? That's not going to help Alice any, either, to have you in thrown in prison."

Dylan thought about his brief, blinding bout of vigilante justice in that pantry. Alice had witnessed his savagery. She'd seen a part of himself he kept hidden. He'd nearly murdered Kehoe right in front of her.

For the thousandth time in the past few days, he cringed inwardly at the thought.

ALICE slept solidly and deeply that night. When she awoke the next morning, Dylan was sitting next to her bed in a chair, long legs crossed. He wore jeans, a button-down steel blue shirt, and his glasses, and was reading the *Wall Street Journal*. She didn't say anything, and just submitted to the luxury of watching him for a moment.

He was in the process of refolding his paper when he noticed that her eyes were open.

"Morning," he said, flipping his folded paper onto the bedside table.

"Hi," she murmured. She stretched experimentally. Her body was stiff and it hurt, but there was noticeable improvement compared to yesterday.

"How's the pain today?" Dylan asked.

"Better. Not so sore. I slept like a rock," she said, yawning.

"Having Kuvi and Dave here yesterday afternoon wore you out," Dylan said, standing.

"Telling Kuvi and Dave about the drama of Alice Reed's life was what wore me out." She vividly recalled the expression of blank incredulity on their faces when Alice finally got around to explaining that Dylan had found her because he believed she was Adelaide Durand.

"It was too much, to have to explain it all, first to Maggie, and then to Kuvi and Dave," he said, dark brows pinched in a severe expression. "I want you to take it easy today."

Her gaze ran over him warmly. "Stop lecturing me. It's turning me on."

He shook his head. But she'd made him smile, and inexplicably, the vision made her throat tighten with feeling.

She needed him so much. It embarrassed her, this rampant *want* he inspired, but she couldn't stop it. She held out her arms. He gave a small smile and sat on the edge of her bed, his arms going around her gently. She couldn't wait for the day when he didn't have to hug her like she was made of fine china. A feeling of nostalgia—or was it loss—rose in her. Would things ever be the same, after that horrible night? She pressed her nose against his sternum and inhaled him.

"I wish I could clean up in your huge, gorgeous shower and use some of your soap. You always smell so good. And I'm so disgusting after only a bed bath and then being hosed off in that gross bathroom down the hall. I felt like a horse, except Doah probably has better facilities than that," she muttered, frowning. Thinking about Doah had sent another spike of emotion through her.

He kissed the top of her head. "You still smell like Alice."

"If my normal smell is sweat and antiseptic and hospital stench." She buried her nose further into his chest. "I love you."

His low chuckle made her want to cry. She really needed to get ahold of herself. Her emotions had been alarmingly fragile lately.

"Do you love me, or my clean shirt and steam-showered body?"

"It's *all* good, trust me," she muttered thickly.

"Excuse me," a woman said.

Alice withdrew her nose from Dylan's chest reluctantly. She saw a nurse's aide standing a few feet inside her room, a wheelchair in front of her.

"I'm here to take you for your hearing test," the aide said, smiling.

"Okay," Alice groaned, starting to extricate herself from Dylan. She'd never wanted to leave a place as much as she did this hospital, and at the same time . . .

. . . she dreaded leaving there. She dreaded the decisions she needed to make.

"Why is she going for a hearing test?" Dylan asked the aide, standing.

"I'm not really sure," the aide said. "Doctor's orders."

"Did the doctor say something to you?" Dylan asked Alice, his brow furrowed. The nurse wheeled the chair closer to her bed and helped Alice into it. It gave her a few blessed seconds of avoiding Dylan's eyes.

"Alice?"

"It's no biggie. The doctor thinks I have some hearing loss in my left ear."

"What?" Dylan asked. She hated that look in his eyes. "What made the doctor think that?"

She sighed. "It's not a major deal."

"What made her think it?" Dylan demanded. "Was it something on the brain scans?"

"No."

"Then why the hell—"

"She thought it because I *told* her," Alice said, feeling cornered.

She watched his expression go blank.

"It's not too bad, Dylan. There's just a muffled quality on that side. My other ear is fine. And it might remit over time," she reasoned.

Dylan nodded. Alice knew what he was thinking. It was yet another thing he'd feel guilty for. She struggled for something to say. The aide started to wheel her out of the room without waiting for Alice's okay. Her inability to even *move* of her own volition only amplified her sense of helplessness.

"Stop," Dylan barked from behind her.

The aide abruptly halted. Dylan stalked around her chair, giving the aide a pointed glare. He looked down at Alice.

"I love you," he said gruffly. He leaned down and kissed her mouth.

"I love you, too," she whispered.

*   *   *

AFTER her testing, both Maggie and Dylan were waiting for her in her room. She ate her lunch in their company, and then was drifting off to sleep to the sound of their muffled, murmured conversation, when the doctor came to talk about the hearing exam.

Alice had mild to moderate hearing loss in her left ear. She wasn't shocked. That's pretty much exactly how she would have described it. Dylan asked the doctor several questions. Dr. Sheldrake explained that they'd need to do more diagnostic testing on the ear on an outpatient basis to know whether or not the damage was permanent. She'd be referring Alice to a specialist.

"Now for the good news. The rest of your tests came back clear, so we'll be discharging you tomorrow. You're going home," Dr. Sheldrake said with a smile.

"Hallelujah," Dylan muttered.

"Amen," Maggie seconded.

Alice could only manage a shaky smile. She didn't know where "home" was.

TWENTY-THREE

That afternoon when she woke up from her nap, Dylan wasn't in the room. A nurse poked her head in the door and said that the doctor wanted her to do a supervised walk. She'd been up from bed to use the bathroom, but this would be a much longer walk, back and forth down the hospital corridor.

"Got to get you back in shape for your marching orders tomorrow," the nurse joked.

Alice was mortified by how stiff, weak, and painful her muscles were. She felt like every inch of her body had been beaten. Fortunately, her joints started to loosen with the movement.

When she reached the waiting room, Alice immediately noticed Dylan. He sat next to Sidney Gates. She paused. She nearly called out to them. Something stilled her tongue. Dylan sat with his back to her, his head lowered, his broad shoulders stiff. For some reason, his pose called to mind solitude, despite the fact that Sidney was right there. Sidney's face was turned partially in profile. He was talking quickly and soberly. Alice thought he was trying to convince Dylan of something. Whether it was her damn hearing loss, or there was just too much bustle around the nurses' station, Alice couldn't quite make out what Sidney was saying so emphatically. She suspected one thing, though.

Dylan wasn't buying it.

Suddenly, she made out one of Sidney's words: *Guilt.*

A sharp pain went through her that had nothing to do with the physical.

"Are you all right?" the nurse asked.

Alice nodded. "I'm just a little tired," she said, turning to head back to her room.

"I'VE contacted Durand's VP of legal, Charlie Towsen," Dylan told Alice later that evening after she'd finished her dinner. "He's going to be calling up at the castle tomorrow to schedule a meeting with you in regard to the trust. I want you to have someone in your corner who can work with you and answer all your questions. Charlie knows that document backward and forward."

"I thought we weren't going to be worrying about that until I got the genetic testing results," Alice said uneasily.

"That was before all of this stuff happened with Kehoe. Kehoe was a member of our board. His arrest and some of the circumstances behind it have gone public. Even though we've managed to keep *your* name out of the papers so far, it's just a matter of time before that breaks, as well. I've had to communicate some of the basic details of what's happened to the other members of the board. I'm not the only one who has been bothered by reporters. We had to make a unified front. There's no saying what Kehoe is going to reveal or claim when he's charged. Kehoe runs a large international department at Durand. We needed to inform some of the people directly under him of some basic facts as well, so they aren't totally unprepared when this story explodes."

"So . . . this man, Charlie Towsen, and several other people at Durand Enterprises . . . you told them you think I'm Addie Durand?" she asked with shaky incredulity.

"*You* think you're Addie Durand. It's not a horrible truth. It's an amazing one. Don't let what Kehoe's done take that away from you."

"I don't know if I'm Alan Durand's daughter, and it was his company, not Lynn's," she said sharply. The news that other people knew something she'd been hiding for weeks left her feeling vulnerable. She was irritated at Dylan for initiating her exposure without her permission. Panicked.

I'm not ready.

"What was Alan's was Lynn's, Alice. But that's not the crucial point. You *are* Alan's daughter," Dylan said.

"You don't know that I'm Alan's daughter, no matter how much you want to believe that I am."

"What's that supposed to mean?" Dylan asked slowly, and she saw anger flicker in his lustrous eyes.

"It means that I know you want it, I know it would justify all you've done in finding me. But that doesn't make it *true*, Dylan."

"The trust is left to Adelaide Durand. *You're* Adelaide Durand," he bit out. "The document doesn't say anything about requiring genetic testing. That's just something I thought we should do for your peace of mind."

"You told me that Durand executives would demand it when the time came!" *Oh God, that time is* now. Why hadn't she realized Kehoe's actions would pop the lid off everything so quickly?

"That was before I read Lynn's journals. I didn't think it could be a potential sticking point then. But if I tell them that you're Addie Durand, then they'll just have to damn well take my word for it. *I'm* the executor of your trust, not them."

Alice stared at him, jarred by his outburst. "Is it *that* important to you? That I'm her? Is that why you're willing to shove the fact that I'm supposedly Alan Durand's daughter down the board's throat? Do you want me to be his heiress *that* much?"

He looked bewildered. Then his anger returned, redoubled. "Are you implying I just want you for the purpose of claiming the trust? Do you think I've done all this because I was motivated by *money*?"

"*No*. I don't think that for a second. But I think you might have done all this because you were motivated by honor," she said, her voice a choked shout. "And duty. And *guilt*. And so to admit that I might not be Alan Durand's real daughter is hard, because then you have to wonder why the hell you did it all."

He turned his head, hitched his chin, and shut his eyelids briefly.

"It was bad enough having to hear this shit from Sidney all these years. Now I've got to hear it from you?"

"Well maybe Sidney and I are seeing something you're not," she cried. "I know he was here in the hospital today, talking to you about your guilt."

"What?" He turned and looked at her, clearly caught off guard. "Sidney wasn't talking to me about my old guilt—the regret I felt as a kid in regard to the kidnapping. He was talking to me about dealing with my guilt for letting Kehoe hurt you."

"You weren't responsible for that! You can't control everything, Dylan."

"I realize that," he replied angrily. "But it's also completely natural that I'd regret it. Even Sidney thinks so. Do you have any idea how helpless I felt, seeing you slumped in that pantry, covered in blood?"

"I'm tired of being the thing you have to feel guilty about all the time! It's like Sidney has always told you, guilt isn't a healthy emotion to base your life on. It's certainly not the key emotion to build a *relationship* on," she exclaimed heatedly.

His eyes narrowed. She gasped back a rush of emotion. She immediately wanted to take it back, and at the same time, experienced relief at finally voicing her worry.

"Is *that* what you think?" he asked after a billowing silence. "Sidney doesn't understand the way I feel about you. I don't really expect him to. I thought *you* did though. Maybe I was wrong about that." He stood.

Alice wanted to scream so bad that he *wasn't* wrong. But she was so *scared* Sidney was right. Doubt assailed her, choking off her voice. Maggie came up to the door just as Dylan stalked out. She crossed the threshold, her eyes wide.

"I heard shouting," Maggie said in a muted tone.

"Sometimes I wish I'd never heard the name Adelaide Durand," Alice blurted out hoarsely. "No, I wish *Dylan* never had."

Her face crumpled.

"Oh no," Maggie said, rushing to her side.

THE next morning, Dylan arrived at the hospital by eight. He'd calmed down a lot since last night.

Yeah, Alice's doubt had hurt. He wished he were so confident about caring for another human being the way he cared about her that it hadn't hurt as much as it had. But he also understood Alice was scared. Why wouldn't she be? Her entire world had been shaken by learning she was born another person, she'd been forced to provide the FBI with details so they could more easily arrest the people she'd thought were her family, and she'd been brutally attacked and almost killed by a crazy man. All of that had happened within the last three weeks of her life.

Add to that, she'd told Dylan she wasn't sure she trusted him, only to tell him she loved him the following week. He knew enough about Alice to realize that alone would have rattled her world, forget about all the other crap.

He'd known going into this whole thing that it would take a lot of patience and fortitude. Alice hadn't realized that since Kehoe had gone over the edge, a lot of Dylan's power to protect her privacy and anonymity had vanished. He'd taken her by surprise with that fact. Maybe he'd disappointed her. He'd try to make her understand today, without losing his temper this time.

He saw Maggie at the vending machines on his way to Alice's room. He paused when she looked up and caught his eye.

"Any word when her discharge will go through?" he asked Maggie.

She walked toward him, a cup of coffee in her hand.

"They're just finishing up the paperwork."

Dylan frowned. Why was Maggie having trouble meeting his eyes?

"So she's up?" he asked, referring to Alice.

Maggie nodded. "She's waiting for you in her room."

A foreboding went through him.

"What's going on?" he asked slowly.

Maggie shook her head. For the first time, she met his gaze squarely. "She's just really confused. It's a lot for her to take in. It'd be a lot for *anybody* to—"

"Maggie?" he interrupted.

"Just go talk to her."

Alice was sitting on the edge of her made bed. Kuvi had brought her some clothing and her computer from their cabin, plus Dylan had brought her some things from the castle. She wore a pair of jeans, running shoes, and a short-sleeved fitted T-shirt—none of the items ones he'd provided for her. Her hair was clean, and brushed back behind her ears. Her face looked tense and wan beneath the discoloration of bruises and healing cuts.

In her lap, she held what looked like a folded piece of lumpy paper with staples around the edges.

"What's going on?" he asked, taking several steps toward her. He saw the misery in her dark blue eyes when she looked at him. *Shit.*

"I'm going back with Maggie," she said hoarsely.

"No."

She winced. "I can't keep doing this, Dylan. Camp is over. The kids are gone."

"I know you came here for the camp. But are you really going to sit there and tell me after all this, that it's the only reason you'd stay?"

"No," she said in a choked voice. He felt like a bully, seeing the silent entreaty for understanding in her shiny eyes.

"I need time to heal and to think about everything and what it means to me." He opened his mouth. "I need time," she repeated, sounding desperate.

"Away from me," he clarified harshly. "Do you think I don't know you, Alice? You're a loner. You dive for cover when you're feeling vulnerable. It's as natural an instinct to you as breathing."

"I can't just change who I am in a few weeks."

"I realize that. But I also know that once you've found cover, you're going to want to stay there. You're not going to be able to hide this time, though. This is too big for you to blend into the background. It's already begun to change you. You can't go back to your old world and fit yourself into it again."

"I have to!" she said, standing. She swayed slightly, and he reached to steady her, his hand cupping her shoulder. Misery and helplessness went through him when he saw her pain.

"You're not running away from Addie Durand's world. You're running away from me. I know I've disappointed you—"

"You have *never* disappointed me," she exclaimed, shuddering. "I love you. You're perfect."

"But you're still going to run," he realized with a sickening sense of finality.

She sniffed and brought her trembling under control. "You can contact me on my cell phone if there's an emergency. But I called that man—Charlie Towsen, the chief legal guy for Durand—this morning. You can correspond with me about anything you think is crucial in regard to Addie through him—"

He shut his eyes. Jesus. She was back to saying Addie's name like she was another person.

"—and I've promised Towsen when I find out the results of the genetic testing . . ."

"*Don't* do this, Alice. Do you really think I give a damn whose *daughter* you are?"

"Do I think it'd make a difference to you whether I was Alan Durand's or Sebastian Kehoe's daughter?" she flared. "Yeah, I do, given what I know about your past. You were like Alan Durand's adopted son. You would have done anything to prove yourself to him."

"You're wrong. You're mixing everything up in your head."

"I don't want to fight with you," she insisted shakily. She paused, trying to gather herself. He sensed her slipping away, and he'd never felt so defenseless. "Being with you was like being in a dream . . . the *best* dream in the world," she gasped. Looking undone, she thrust the piece of paper she was clutching against his abdomen. He grasped it without thinking. She started to walk past him.

"*Alice.*"

She paused a foot away from the door, her head lowered. She didn't turn around.

"Do you think you're the only one that this is hard for? I'm no more of an expert at trust, or relationships, or the long haul than you are. But I've figured out one thing. What's between us is real. You feel it. I know you do. You and Sidney can call it some kind of residue from our past, or guilt, or fucking insanity if you want to, but it's not going to change what's there. I loved Addie Durand because she was the first person in the world who loved me without question or thought. *That's* what came to *her* as natural as breathing. But I *fell* in love with you, even though you fought me and questioned and distrusted every step of the way, because I loved your strength and your independence, and yeah . . . even your goddamn prickliness. The bond between us isn't going to break," he assured her grimly. "No matter how much craziness we might have to deal with from Durand Enterprises or the press or Sebastian Kehoe's sentencing or trial. It's sure as *hell* not going to break if you walk away right now."

She stood there, her shoulders slumped and her head lowered. After a moment, she straightened her spine, lifted her head, and walked out of the room. He wasn't surprised she did it, necessarily. He knew her well.

That didn't stop it from hurting like fire.

He just stood there, feeling hollowed out in matter of minutes. Eventually, he noticed that he held something.

He separated the paper from two staples and tilted the makeshift envelope. Alan Durand's silver chased lighter landed in his hand. He carefully opened the piece of paper. She'd only written two sentences.

It's from both of us, Alan and me. You will always be my knight in shining armor.

TWENTY-FOUR

THREE WEEKS LATER

Doby frisked around her legs as she tried to help Maggie carry in the groceries.

"Cut it out, Doby," Maggie scolded as she heaved multiple bags on the kitchen counter. "You're going to put the girl back in the hospital, tripping her up that way. Silly dog, come here."

Alice laughed as Maggie's beckoning cleared the path for her. "I'm not that fragile anymore. Thank God. How did the test go?" she asked, referring to an exam Maggie gave her grad school class in statistics. Alice had helped her make up the test.

"I haven't even looked at them yet. I'll get to them tonight," Maggie said, putting away a gallon of milk.

"I'll grade them for you," Alice said, lifting some bananas out of a bag. "My bruises are almost faded, so I'd be happy to teach a few classes for you early next week, too, if you like. Earn my keep."

She looked around when the refrigerator door closed with a loud thump. Maggie regarded her solemnly. "What's wrong?" Alice asked uneasily. "I was your grad assistant, I used to teach a couple of your classes every semester. Do you think I'd be out of practice?"

"Of course not. But I already have a grad assistant. You aren't a grad student anymore. You graduated with top honors and you've been offered a position at Durand Enterprises by that Stalwalter guy. If you don't want to work for him, I'm sure there are plenty of other companies that would give you a spot. And of course, according to some reliable accounts, you *own* Durand Enterprises," she added drolly. "You've sort of moved past grading papers and doing my least favorite lectures, Alice."

"But this is just a temporary thing. I wanted to help out while I was here with you, that's all," Alice said, frowning.

Maggie sighed and stepped toward her. "And I appreciate it. But you're here as a friend. You don't have to *work* for me. You needed time and space to heal and figure things out."

"So you've decided my time is up, huh?" Alice asked with a dry laugh. "Are you kicking me out?" she asked, smiling despite her uneasiness at the turn of the conversation.

"No. I'm just . . ." Maggie shrugged and made a helpless sound. "Prodding you a little?"

Alice exhaled and leaned against the kitchen counter, her arms crossed beneath her breasts.

"I saw an article in the *Tribune* this morning about the Durand Enterprises press conference next Friday. I assume you know about it?" Maggie said.

Alice nodded mutely. She'd suspected Maggie would see the article.

"And you weren't going to tell me about it?"

"I . . . I didn't know how to," Alice said, frustrated because she felt guilty for not being forthcoming with Maggie. She felt like she had this huge, enormous thing inside her, and she wanted to get it out. Problem was, she didn't know how to expel it properly. She was like an overdue mother desperate for relief, bursting and helpless in the face of nature.

"*Wait.* Are you saying what I think you're saying? Did you get the test results?" Maggie asked tensely.

"I got them," Alice said, studying the tile floor. She'd gotten the call from the genetics lab two days ago.

"And?"

She met Maggie's gaze hesitantly.

"As it turns out . . . I'm a miracle after all."

Just saying it caused shivers to rush down her arms. Her awed reaction hadn't lessened any since she'd first given the news to both Special Agent Clayton and Charlie Towsen.

"You're Alan and Lynn Durand's biological daughter."

"It would seem so," she said, shrugging disbelievingly.

"*Wow.* Does Dylan know?" Maggie asked cautiously after a pause.

Alice swallowed. "I would think he does."

"But you don't know for sure?"

"I told Charlie Towsen the news and e-mailed a copy of the lab report. Dylan is Charlie's boss. I'm sure Towsen told him." She inhaled and straightened, starting to unload groceries again because she knew what Maggie was going to say next and she needed a distraction.

"Dylan hasn't called?" Maggie asked, sounding a little confused.

"No," she replied briskly, putting a loaf of bread in the bin and slamming the door down too hard. "But I asked him only to call me in case of an emergency."

Besides which, he's probably so furious at me that he's avoiding contact at all costs.

"He doesn't consider the fact that you're definitely Alan and Lynn's child major enough news? Or Kehoe pleading guilty not only to the kidnapping, but to giving the order to have you murdered twenty years ago, or attempting to kill you recently? That doesn't qualify as serious enough information for him to call?"

"You know that Clayton told me all about that before the story broke on the news," Alice said, moving mechanically and averting her gaze from Maggie's. Both Clayton and Towsen had actually been great about keeping in contact and filling her in on all the minutia of unfolding events.

She'd been disbelieving and relieved to the point of physical weakness when she'd learned that Kehoe wasn't going to drag this tragedy out further into a trial. It still seemed impossible to believe, that the trauma he'd caused Alan, Lynn, and Alice herself, was finally going to come to an end. The news had especially been welcome because several days after she'd arrived at Maggie's, Agent Clayton told her that Sissy and two of her uncles—Tim and Christopher—were in FBI custody. She was going to have to testify at Sissy's trial, a fact that never ceased to get Alice's heart beating into anxious overtime.

She had no news of Al or her other uncles, but Alice knew there were warrants out for their arrests. There was a good possibility that insufficient evidence would allow them to go free but the future was highly uncertain when it came to the Reeds. She'd cried herself silently to sleep for two nights in a row after finding out about their arrests, unsettled enough by the news. But more than that, she'd been grieving the loss of the only person who might understand her ambivalence and misery when it came to the idea of the Reeds going to prison because of her: Dylan.

As for Kehoe, Alice understood from Special Agent Clayton that he was a broken man. After he'd recovered enough to be interrogated by the FBI, the first thing—and for a while, the *only* thing—he confessed to was betraying Lynn Durand years ago. Strangely enough, he confessed to killing her as well, although it came out later in interrogation that what he'd told investigators is what he'd told Alice. He'd goaded Lynn into suicide with the news that Addie was definitely dead.

Apparently, Kehoe was capable of guilt, and it had caught up to him in the end. Alice had to agree with Kehoe's confession: He might as well have thrown Lynn over that bluff, by taunting her until she jumped. She had also received the news from Clayton that Kehoe had been put on suicide watch after he'd attempted to hang himself in his cell. Alice wasn't necessarily surprised, given the things he'd said to her that night.

Kehoe had been obsessed with Lynn, consumed by the idea of making her as miserable as he was without her in his life. When he'd been caught, his remorse, grief, and guilt crashed into him. All he seemed to be able to do was confess his sins toward Lynn Durand over and over. It'd taken the agents time and patience to eventually get him emotionally steady enough to admit to his crimes against Addie.

Against Alice.

Maybe it was possible for a man like Kehoe to repent. Kehoe certainly seemed consumed by guilt. Alice didn't pretend to know the answers. She was only thankful that *something* had urged Sebastian Kehoe to confess and end this nightmare after nearly twenty-five years.

"And yes, I'm *positive* Dylan knows about the genetic testing results," Alice told Maggie presently, pulling herself out of her thoughts.

"How come?"

"Because I know Dylan," she said, thumping a bag of potatoes on the counter. "And because that press conference next week in Morgantown was organized by him after I gave Charlie Towsen the results. Everything is coming to a head now that Kehoe has made his plea, and his sentencing is scheduled."

"You'll be going to that, right?" Maggie asked softly.

Alice nodded. She was expected to testify about Kehoe's attack; she would have to face him in a courtroom. Her input would help the judge make his decision on Kehoe's punishment. Not just the technical details, either. The judge would want to know what the kidnapping and attack had meant to her emotionally, the impact of Kehoe's crime on her entire life . . . what Sebastian Kehoe had taken from her . . .

. . . What he had cost her.

When this had all been explained to her, Alice took on the task of tallying that price somberly.

It did something to a person, being asked to put an actual weight on one man's actions. What would her life be like if Sebastian Kehoe hadn't plotted against her and the Durands in cold blood twenty years ago?

While soul-searching those answers in solitude, Alice had realized there were losses and costs she'd never suspected. It'd hurt realizing that, but it'd cleansed her somehow, too. It'd started her true healing and built the beginnings of a solid bridge between the child she'd been and the woman she was now . . . between Addie and Alice.

"Dylan will be testifying, too. And Thad. It's happening the Monday after the press conference," she told Maggie.

"And Dylan planned this press conference?"

"Yeah. Towsen told me all about it. The FBI will be making a brief statement, the U.S. Attorney's office will take questions about Kehoe and sentencing, Dylan will speak, as well, on behalf of Durand . . ." She tipped a pound of sugar onto a cabinet shelf. "And I will."

"You're actually going?" Maggie asked in a hushed tone.

Alice placed both her hands on the edge of the counter, her back still to Maggie.

"I don't really see that I have much of a choice anymore," she said. "See . . . despite the fact that you and Dylan both think I'm just burying my head in the sand lately—"

"I didn't mean that," Maggie said earnestly. "I don't think Dylan thinks that either, to be honest."

"I *have* been thinking a lot about what I'm going to do with my life," Alice continued shakily.

"What did you decide? Are you going to accept that job offer from Jason Stalwalter in New York? He sure seems eager at the idea of having you."

Alice gave a bark of laughter. "A memo has gone out to the top executives at Durand about Adelaide Durand's return. I'm sure Stalwalter would be very eager to have Alan Durand's daughter working in his group."

"It would give him the opportunity to cozy up to the owner of the company," Maggie added dryly. "But in all fairness, Stalwalter didn't know any of that when he offered you the job, did he? He was just impressed by some work you did for Dylan . . . by you in general. And he can't be *too* much of an ass kisser. He's persisted in offering you a position, even though I'll bet Dylan is royally pissed at him for trying to lure you away to New York."

"Yeah. I was just kidding. Stalwalter seems decent."

"So . . . you are going to go with Stalwalter, then?"

"No," Alice said softly. She opened her mouth, closed it, and then opened it again. "When I go to Morgantown for the press conference . . . I'm going for good. I'm going to ask to be assigned as a junior executive in the marketing division at Durand's head-quarters. If not there, I'll go anywhere they can use me. I want to discover as much about the company as I can. Alan poured his sweat and tears into that company. By learning it . . . I'll learn *him*."

She turned around at the loud sound of a single clap. Maggie's two hands were still pressed together. She pressed them against her chest and beamed at Alice. It was like she'd been waiting for Alice to say those exact words every minute for the past three weeks.

"I think Morgantown is my home," Alice admitted tremu-lously. "Not because of Durand Enterprises, or because of Alan and Lynn. Because Dylan is there."

Compassion filled Maggie's face. She stepped forward and gave Alice a big hug. Alice squeezed her back, hard.

"Of course, Dylan probably doesn't want anything to do with me," she mumbled against Maggie's shoulder. "He probably thinks I'm a big fat coward. I hope I can make him understand—" She broke off when her voice caught. Maggie patted her briskly on her shoulder blade. She leaned back. Alice recognized her game face.

"I had to tell you once, before you went into a meeting with Dylan Fall, that you needed to stiffen up the spine and just do what's necessary. I'll tell you that again," she said with mock severity, referring to that fateful interview Alice'd had with Dylan months ago. They shared a smile. That interview felt like a lifetime ago to her. It seemed like she'd been turned inside out since that time, like she was the same person, but forever different, too. "Like I told you before, you've got to trust in yourself," Maggie continued. "But you're a world luckier than you were last spring, Alice. Because now, you've got Dylan to trust, too."

"I was lying to myself, so I was lying to him, too. What kind of a person am I, that I would choose to believe in doubt and guilt and fear, and not this amazing thing between us? I told him I didn't trust him," Alice admitted, that simple, harsh truth piercing her yet again.

"Ah, honey," Maggie said, touching her cheek. "That's because you didn't know what trust was."

ALICE arrived at Camp Durand before sunrise that Friday. The sound of the rental car wheels crackling against the gravel filled her ears. A sense of poignant nostalgia went through her as she peered through the window. The camp was lit precisely like it had been when camp was in progress, so she could make out familiar landmarks. Everything seemed so quiet and empty though, so in opposition to the bustle and laughter and the sense of purpose she'd felt while she was there.

She parked and alighted from the car, the cool, fresh predawn air bracing her. She could have parked at the castle, but she wanted to walk through the grounds. This was her opportunity to finally say good-bye to one of the best experiences of her life. She hoped camp had changed all of the kids who'd attended in a positive way, even if it was just a little. In her case, she felt like the weeks spent on that shore, and the weeks in Dylan's arms, had changed her forever.

She walked through the desolate camp, past the main lodge, and past her and Kuvi's cabin. She knew from texts and e-mail correspondence that Kuvi had accepted a position at Durand's London offices, while Dave Epstein had taken a position in New York. They had grown so close, they were going to attempt a long-distance relationship and see how it worked out. Alice was glad her two friends were finding happiness with each other.

She paused by the Red Team's cabin. The fact that she'd never been able to say good-bye to her kids still pained her hugely. Had they begun school yet? Terrance would be trying out for football, and Judith triumphantly starting her senior year. She almost went up to the door and tried to get in. Perhaps the custodian had accidentally left it unlocked?

But no . . . that was part of her past now. And the present was calling her in the direction of the woods.

Hopefully, her future was, as well. As she followed the path to the stables, however, Alice was having some major doubts and misgiving about that.

The stable door was unlocked, which meant that Dylan was there already. Before her anxious anticipation had the chance to mount even higher, she immediately caught sight of him. She'd interrupted him as he lifted Kar Kalim's heavy saddle. He looked around, saw her, and immediately dropped the saddle back onto its stand.

For several lung-burning seconds, they just stared at one another.

He wore jeans, riding gloves, boots, and a rust-colored T-shirt. His biceps still bulged with tension beneath the short sleeves, even though he'd released the heavy saddle. He'd grown a goatee since she'd last seen him, and his hair was a little longer. The dark facial hair was neatly trimmed and highlighted his hard, sensual mouth. His dark eyes were as compelling as she remembered. More so. Those lustrous gypsy eyes slowly moved over her now, making her intensely aware of every square inch of her body.

"What are you doing here, Alice?"

She wilted a little at his brusque tone. He *was* still mad at her. She wasn't expecting anything different, really, but the evidence of his anger dented her waning courage.

"I came for the press conference, and . . ." She swallowed thickly. Her uncertainty swelled now that she stood here face-to-face with him. The bond she always felt with him remained, that electrical physical and sensual awareness of him. But his expression was so cold and forbidding. The combination of connection and distance pained her.

"And?" he asked, letting go of the saddle and unsnapping a glove. Her confidence faltered even more in the face of his cool reception. He glanced up after he'd pulled off both gloves and shoved them in his back pocket. His dark eyebrows quirked up in a gesture that seemed to say, *Well?*

"I walked through the camp. It seemed so empty," she said with a fake smile, waving at the camp.

"So you came to see the camp?"

"I came to see you," she blurted out. "I . . . I wanted to talk to you."

"About what?"

"Dylan, why are you making this so hard?" she asked, her frustration and anxiety getting the best of her.

"Because I don't know what you're here to say," he replied succinctly. Their stares held, and this time, she felt the edge of his emotional state. He wasn't as cold to her arrival as he'd first seemed. She hesitated, overwhelmed by longing for him and her sense of frustration at expressing herself. She wasn't *good* at this. His nostrils flared slightly as he watched her struggle.

"I can't do everything, Alice," he said roughly, his mouth hard. "Some steps, you've got to make on your own."

She stood there, awash in helplessness, as he lifted the saddle with one sure movement, turned, and walked away.

HE'D arrived at the stables a little early that morning. It was going to be a long day. His nerves were frayed, for more reasons than one. The press conference was scheduled for eleven a.m. in the ballroom of a large local resort hotel. The Durand public relations department and his admin, Mrs. Davenport, had things running smoothly.

On his end, the waters were pretty choppy, though. It seemed that every Durand department head and manager, both national and international, wanted to talk to him, making for some hectic days and nights of late. There was an unsettled feeling in the large company, and people wanted reassurance. He'd told Mrs. Davenport when they made the press conference public, and rumors started to leak, that he would handle all the calls personally. If he could assuage any anxieties by talking to people one on one, he would.

Today would be the most hectic day of all. Charlie Towsen had diligently been keeping him apprised of his interactions with Alice, so he knew she'd agreed to the press conference. The fact that he'd see her later at the press conference had him pretty edgy. Not knowing what she was thinking about their meeting—what she was thinking about *anything*—was driving him crazy.

A vigorous ride on Kar Kalim would clear his head.

Maybe.

There wasn't a chance in hell.

He reached for the saddle. He heard the stable door open and glanced around in surprise. It was only five thirty in the morning.

She stood just inside the closed door. A mild shock seemed to pass through him and he let go of the saddle without intending to. They just stared at each other, the moment stretching tight.

She'd mostly healed, he realized numbly, his eyes eating up the vision of her. There was still a little fading discoloration from bruising on her right cheek. It only seemed to make her lovelier, somehow emphasizing her finely made, delicate bone structure and the smooth radiance of her skin. She looked the same, but *different* as well, to his stunned gaze. Her hair had been cut and styled, the color returned to what he'd guess was her natural one—a shining auburn with gold highlights. She'd had it cut in a short, asymmetrical style that highlighted her elegant neck, large eyes, and beautiful face, to say nothing of her nonconformist spirit. The haircut was surprisingly crisp, chic, and professional-looking. It made her look more sophisticated he realized. He was glad to see her newfound maturity, but also saddened a little. He knew what had aged her. She'd changed while away from him, and that in itself was sad.

He thought maybe he'd aged right along with her on that night in July. And in the days since then, he'd sometimes felt ancient.

Using all his will, he resisted the urge to go to her. No matter what he was feeling, he didn't know what she was experiencing. Watching her walk away had cut him to the bone. He couldn't watch her do it again with his defenses lowered.

"What are you doing here, Alice?"

"I came for the press conference, and . . ." She swallowed thickly. He'd thought it so many times before; that she was like a wild creature. But this morning was different. Always before, he'd wondered if Alice would show her feral nature by baring her teeth.

Today, there was more of a doe-like, skittish quality to her wildness. His heart went out to her. She was vulnerable.

But so was he.

"And?" he asked briskly. Needing something to distract him, he started to take off his gloves. *Why didn't she speak?* He looked at her with edgy expectancy.

"I walked through the camp. It seemed so empty," she said with a shaky smile, waving at the door.

"So you came to see the camp?" he asked bluntly. He felt like a man poised in front of a firing squad with someone who was hesitant about giving the order to fire.

"I came to see you. I . . . I wanted to talk to you."

"About what?"

"Dylan, why are you making this so hard?"

"Because I don't know what you're here to say," he bit out in frustration.

Their stares held. He perfectly sensed her desperation and vulnerability. She wasn't any better at this than he was. No, she was worse at it, the truth be told. He *knew* that about her. The desire to go to her nearly overwhelmed him. But these were steps Alice needed to make on her own, whether they were ones toward him . . . or in the opposite direction.

"I can't do everything, Alice," he said, his voice vibrating with emotion. "Some steps, you've got to make on your own."

Steeped in frustration, he hefted Kar Kalim's saddle and started back toward the stalls.

"Dylan. No . . . wait. Damn it, will you *listen* to me?"

It was the reemergence of Alice's characteristic acerbic tone that made him turn to face her, more than anything. He tossed Kar Kalim's saddle to the floor in irritation.

"What? What do you want to say, Alice? Spit it *out*, for Christ's sake."

She'd hurried after him when he walked away. Five feet was all that separated them now. She made a huffing sound at his challenge, her eyes wide in outrage at his harshness. She opened her mouth, as if to give him some smart-ass retort. He resisted a strong urge to close the distance between them and thrust his tongue between her lips, shut her up in the best way possible . . .

Maybe she caught a sense of how violently chaotic his emotions were at the moment, because her mouth snapped shut.

"I told you that I needed some space. Some time," she began.

He merely nodded once, waiting, his lungs burning, his muscles clenched tight in order to still his urge to move.

She shut her eyes briefly, as if summoning strength, before she continued.

"I thought a lot about things while I was at Maggie's. With Kehoe's sentencing coming up, I thought about what my life would have been like if he'd never entered the picture," she said hoarsely. "I thought a lot about what he'd cost me: a father and a mother, a loving home, a normal, secure, blessed existence."

"You're right. He took all that from you," Dylan agreed.

He saw her elegant throat contract as she swallowed. She stepped closer. His heartbeat started to pound in his ears.

"He took more than that. He took you," she said shakily, even though her gaze was steady and fierce. "For twenty years of my life, he took you. I don't want to let him take anymore, Dylan."

For a moment, everything narrowed down to her large, entreating eyes, her beautiful, soft mouth, and the roar of his heart in his ears. *She isn't going to run again.*

"I don't want that, either," he admitted, steeling himself. "But it's not Kehoe's choice anymore. It's yours."

"I know that. Now. That's why I'm here. I'm sorry I left. I was just so confused. And I'm sorry that I said I didn't trust you. I'm sorry I didn't trust in us. I shouldn't let people like Sissy or Kehoe rule me, to believe that everything is potentially bad or ugly. Or wrong." She met his stare, clearly undone by the strength of her emotions. "Because you're beautiful to me, and it *was* wrong. It was *so* wrong of me to turn away from something so right because I was afraid—"

"Alice," he interrupted, wincing. *Screw* caution. He started to breech the distance between them.

"No, no let me finish," she said, sounding almost panicked. She impatiently wiped a single tear from her cheek. It was as if now that the dam had broken on her hesitancy, she was determined to get everything out in a rush. She swallowed thickly and met his stare.

"Remember how I told you that after I had that dream about Alan and me, and how I was running to dinner and he was right behind me? Such a common, mundane memory, and yet when he spoke to me, there was so much love." Another tear spilled down her cheek. "Or when I had that memory of playing hide-and-seek with Lynn, there was *no* fear. Nearly every second of my life must have been filled with happiness and trust and love.

"And then when I was here with you, I would think: How am I supposed to ever come to terms with the idea that I once was Addie Durand? I'm so different from her. *I* don't trust. *I* don't hope beyond the ordinary," she said shakily, touching her breast. "And *everything* about you, everything about us, was so extraordinary."

"Baby," he muttered gruffly. Her struggle had become unbearable to witness.

"No, it's okay," she assured, her face turning luminous. Tears brimmed in her eyes now. "Because that's when I realized."

"What?"

"That every night I spent with you, every hour, every minute . . . Addie must have been with me. Because the truth is, I've *never* been so trusting. I've never felt so loved, than when I was with you. And you realized that all along, didn't you? See . . ." She took a step toward him, her expression eager, like she was wild to make him understand. He felt like his heart was breaking a little, seeing her in that moment, bearing witness to her strength and her courage. "With Lynn and with Alan—with my mother and father—I only had those tiny glimpses of what it was like. But with you, I feel it all the time. Addie could trust, so *I* can. Do you see? Despite *every-thing.* Despite Kehoe, and Cunningham and Stout, despite being ripped away from my family and all of this—" She gestured around the stables. "Despite all the years with Sissy, it's *not* too late," she said, reaching out and placing her hand on his chest.

He winced in pleasure at her simple touch. "If you don't think it is, I mean," she added after a moment, studying his face anxiously. "I'm sorry that I hurt you by leaving. I wish I could make you understand, Dylan."

He reached and grabbed her hand. He pressed his mouth to the back of it. "I understand better than you think," he said. "I knew you trusted, and I knew at the same time you doubted that trust."

"I don't doubt anymore," she whispered, stepping closer. "*That's* why I came."

He touched her cheek, amazed all over again at how soft she was. How precious. For all those years, he'd sought her, and yet he'd really had no idea just how precious she was. He cradled her jaw.

"The ability to trust is granted only to those who are well loved," he said gruffly. "That's why I always said you should trust me. Because I don't think anyone could be loved as much as I love you."

He swooped down to capture his name on her tongue. Her taste and texture flooded him. So sweet. So familiar.

Ever new.

Without thinking, reacting purely on instinct, he lifted her in his arms and headed toward the closed office door.

SHE'D started to get used to it before being with Dylan; so many layered, complex, and yet inexplicable feelings mingled with single-minded sexual need. Now as she experienced it again in that moment in the stables, Alice was able to put a name to what had happened to her . . . what still *was*. It was love and a deep, enduring connection, a bond that was too mysterious to dissect.

Her hands outlined his hard chest and shoulders with lust. With reverence. He tasted so good. She pressed closer to him, so hungry to fill her senses with him. Had she been out of her mind to deprive herself of this? She moved her hips in a tight circle, feeling his arousal mount. He groaned, rough and deep, his arms tightening around her.

He lifted her against him and they began to move. A thrill went through her. She'd always loved his strength and his dominance during lovemaking. Even their first time, here in these stables, he'd positioned and taken her with a single-minded focus that had left her stunned and intensely aroused.

Addicted.

Once they'd entered the office, Dylan tore his mouth from hers in order to slam the door and flip the lock. He turned back to her, his heavy-lidded gaze lowering over her flushed face in a way that made her crane up to taste him again. He placed his hand on her shoulder.

"Maybe we should go up to the house and do this right," he said, even if the way he was staring at her mouth with a slight snarl on his lips was making it clear it was a halfhearted offer.

She shook her head. "You *always* do me right. I don't need candles and violins right now. I just need you," she said, tearing at the first buttons of his shirt. She unfastened them to just above his bellybutton, shoved open the plackets and pressed her face against his skin, inhaling him. Tasting him. She ran the edge of her teeth along his side and felt his skin roughen with the tip of her tongue.

"You're always such a greedy little thing," he growled. She heard the edge in his tone, the evidence of the savage in him that she loved. To show him how accurate he was, she bit at a dense, succulent pectoral muscle and slicked her tongue over a small dark brown nipple, making it stiffen. He groaned and sunk his fingers in her hair. His skin roughened beneath her lips and seeking fingers. Applying a slight pressure on her head, he moved her over his chest and ribs, down onto his ridged abdomen. She lost herself in the glory of him, kissing and licking and using her teeth until she'd hear that growl in his throat, the one that both told her how much he liked her caresses, and was a thrilling warning, too.

Their desire pulsated around them, encapsulating them in their own small world. She was unoffended and eager when he urged her lower, her fingers sinking beneath the waistband of his jeans. He steadied her as she sunk to her knees before him. Then she was jerking at his button fly, her excitement mounting at the sensation of his cock pressing against the denim. Unable to wait, she pressed her hand along the length of it. She moaned, made feverish at the feeling. She sunk her head and clamped the column of it between her upper and lower teeth and twisted her head slightly. He groaned and pressed her head to him tighter. His jeans protected him from the rough edge of her teeth. She stimulated him like that for a moment. He seemed to appreciate the sharp pressure, groaning roughly in pleasure. But like her, he was impatient. He lifted her head and hauled down his jeans and underwear.

Her mouth parted as she watched him fist his erection from below and stroke his rigid length. He looked so beautiful. She made a choked, desperate sound in her throat as his scent pervaded her nose. She craned for him.

"I know, baby," he rasped, tightening his fingers in her hair into a gentle hold. "I missed you, too." He stepped forward slightly. Sensing what he wanted, she kept her mouth parted while he pressed the smooth, warm tip of his cock around the circle of her lips. Then he caressed her cheek with it. She looked up at him as he stroked her, helpless in her desire. His nostrils flared slightly as he looked down at her.

"You're so beautiful," he said.

"So are you," she whispered, turning her chin and licking the succulent head of his cock. She waggled her tongue. He let his hand drop. His firm, heavy erection bobbed in the air under the influence of her tongue. She looked up and met his stare while she played with him, licking just the head and making his cock twitch.

He made a rough sound in his throat, palmed his cock and her jaw at once.

"Always pushing it, aren't you?" he asked thickly. He pushed his cock between her lips, stretching them to make way for his girth. Their gazes held as he slid onto her tongue and slowly filled her mouth. Made bold by the depth and expression of her feelings, she ducked her head forward and took him deep, recovering from the daring stroke as she sucked and pulled her mouth back on his length.

"Jesus," he groaned when she did it again. "Alice—"

She was a woman on fire, her lust fueled by love. All she wanted to do was show him. Nothing could stop her, especially when she heard his incredulous groans and growls of approval. Sure, she'd made a breakthrough just now by talking honestly about her emotions, but Alice was most at home in the physical realm. This is how she expressed herself with him naturally. It always had been, and would be.

She sunk him deep again, squeezing the base of his cock with her fisted hand, then pulled back, sucking hard on the shaft of his cock. God, he drove her crazy. She popped him out of her mouth, batting gently at his jutting erection with her hand, and then sucked him back into her mouth with greedy abandon.

"You little—"

Suddenly his cock was gone and he was hauling her up, his

hands below her bent elbows. His face looked flushed and hard as he pushed her toward the desk. Poor Gordon Schneider. They were about to desecrate the stable manager's desk for a second time. Dylan jerked her sweater down over her arms, and then her cotton shirt was blinding her as he whipped it off over her head.

"Get your pants off," he ordered tersely, pulling off his riding boots with haste.

"That's what I always loved about you," she said, kicking off her flats. "Once you get in the zone, nothing stops Dylan Fall."

After a record-breaking strip on both their parts, Dylan pulled her to him. His arms enclosed her. She had a flashing vision of his rigid features descending and then he was kissing the living daylights out of her, his hands moving over her naked body, rediscovering her, taking her breath away. Once Dylan got going, he hit her like a tidal wave every time.

He palmed her buttocks and squeezed them for a moment before he lifted, and plopped her on the edge of the desk.

"It's been too long, baby," he said, and she wasn't sure if he was apologizing for his forceful desperation or just stating the obvious. They were both bursting with need. He stepped between her open thighs and bent her knees toward her shoulders. Grunting once in acute dissatisfaction, he scooted her closer toward the edge of the desk.

"Brace yourself," he instructed. Glancing down and gauging the angle of things, Alice put her hands behind her on the blotter and tilted her upper body back. She also shifted her pelvis up, tilting her pussy into a slightly upward angle. "That's right," he growled, his expression almost angry as he stared between her thighs. He guided his cock to her entrance and thrust. He groaned in mixed agony and pleasure when he sunk into her partially and halted. Alice thrust her hips upward, so desperate for him. It'd been more than a month now since she'd been with him. Her mind was more ready for him than her body was. She whimpered in frustration.

"Shhh," he soothed, nipping at her mouth, plucking at her lips hungrily. He always melted her with his forceful, greedy, coaxing kisses. She grew so focused on reciprocating that her body relaxed around him as he sawed his hips. He clasped her rib cage in his big hands as he worked his cock into her with gentle but firm deliberation. He cupped a breast and ran his thumb and forefinger over the nipple, caressing her beading flesh. She moaned, feeling her body heat around him. "That's right," he said next to her open lips. "Let me in, beautiful girl."

He flexed his hips. A rough groan tore from his throat. She cried out when he drove all the way into her, two halves of a whole sliding home. She saw his eyes roll back in his head.

"*Way* too damn long," he grated out through a clenched jaw.

"I agree," she whispered, because the sensation of him filling her and throbbing so deep was stealing her voice.

He looked up and met her stare.

"Never again," he stated simply.

"Never again," she promised.

He reached around her, his hands at the small of her back and his strong arms squeezing her knees until they touched her shoulders. Her legs were spread and immobilized between their straining bodies. Alice bit her lip at the intensity of the pressure of his piercing cock. He'd put her in a very vulnerable position. She was at his mercy.

She had been on other occasions before, too. But now, she knew she trusted him, and she was so much stronger because of it. She looked into his deep, lustrous eyes as he began to move, and knew there was no going back.

ALICE had had only a shadowy idea of what would be involved in the press conference. It turned out that it was probably a good thing that she hadn't understood the implications of what was what about to occur, or she would never have agreed to attend it.

After Dylan's and her emotional and passionate reunion in the stables, they'd returned to the castle and continued their celebration in a more leisurely fashion in bed. Alice couldn't think of anyone or anything but Dylan. Discovering her ability to love and trust left her liberated. Reborn. Dylan seemed equally as awed, and she was reminded again that despite his superior confidence and faith in their relationship, he, too, had once been a loner. He had once been that wary, angry boy who had let down his guard for an innocent girl of four.

In those moments, she never understood more clearly how doubt and uncertainty could have caused her to lose him.

She'd never risk that happening again.

Lying there in bed together entwined, touching and talking and making love, Alice felt like she'd been given the gift once again of innocence, to look at him and wonder, to admire him, to love him without the burden of anxiety.

She wasn't even concerned when it came time for them to rise and get ready for the press conference, still encapsulated as she was in the bubble of their intimacy. She decided to wear a dress that Dylan had bought for her, a cobalt blue wrap dress that was professional-looking but still complimented her figure and eyes. When she saw Dylan choose a dark blue suit, she walked into his enormous walk-in closet and chose a cobalt blue tie. She draped it around his neck, grinning.

"So we look like we go together."

He quirked his dark eyebrows and slid the tie beneath his collar. "We more than just *look* like it."

His reply made her giddy. She grinned wider and started to turn away to put on her shoes. He caught her hand. She turned around, her eyebrows arching when she realized how sober he looked.

"You don't fully grasp it yet, Alice, but your life is about to change forever," he said quietly. Her smile faded at his intensity. "You're about to be acknowledged as Alan Durand's sole heir. You're a very wealthy woman. People are going to question our involvement. They're going to insinuate and assume a lot of things about us."

"I don't care about that—"

He held up a hand. "Let me finish."

Alice nodded.

"I want a future with you," he stated simply.

"I want one with you, too."

"Because of that basic truth, I will never, upon any occasion, ask you for or share a penny of the money or estate your parents left you. Never. That's not a shifting promise, Alice. Starting tomorrow, I'm going to step down as the executor of your trust. You can take it over yourself, or hire a legal and financial representative or a team to handle it. If you want advice on who to hire, I'll give it, or I'll point you in the direction of someone else who can advise you on some different candidates. The point is, you are the sole beneficiary. It's your choice to make."

Alice flushed in discomfort. "Do we really have to talk about this now?"

He squeezed her hand. "*Yes*. Don't let the topic of money make you wary. You, of all people, are going to have to learn to talk bluntly about it. It's not crucial to our relationship, but it *is* important in a general sense to your life. Very. I want you to know right up front that, thanks to Alan and the success of Durand, I'm not doing too badly myself."

She exhaled in exasperation. She knew a thing or two about Dylan's financial standing, thanks to the research study she'd done. "You're worth hundreds of millions of dollars. I realize you're hardly pauper material, Dylan. Do you think I care?"

"I'm proud of what I've been able to accomplish at Durand. But if some day, you decide you want to take the helm—"

"Oh God," she groaned. "Dylan, that's such a ludicrous possibility at this point."

"At this point, it may feel like it," he said quietly. He reached up and touched her cheek. She moved her chin, assured by his touch, and looked up at him in quiet desperation. "I assure you, with your talents, it won't always seem so bizarre. I just want you to know, I'll be okay no matter what. I could have a whole new future somewhere else."

"I don't want you *somewhere else*," she said emphatically, alarmed at the mere thought.

He smiled that smile that always made something pull tight inside her, the one that made her feel so cherished. "When it comes to you and me, I'll *always* be here. A job is something different. You know that."

She nodded, a measure of relief seeping through her. "I can't do this without you, Dylan. Don't leave me just when I'm taking my first steps."

"I'm *not* going to leave you," he assured, his eyes flashing. "I just don't want you to ever have to think twice again, like you did with Thad Schaefer, when he started in with his insinuations about me."

"I didn't ever believe you only wanted Alan's money," she denied hotly.

He quirked one brow. "You thought about it, even if not for long, and even if you did discount it in the end."

"I never—" She cut off her defense, frowning as she considered how miserable she'd been the night Thad alleged Dylan had ulterior motives when it came to her. Maybe Dylan was right. The insinuations had created a splinter, one that could have easily grown into a giant wedge, if she'd ever let it.

"You see what I mean?" he asked, reading her expression. "Money can easily get between people and split them apart. It happens before they even realize it is. I won't let that happen to us, no matter how unusual our situation is." He leaned forward and kissed her brow. "That's why I'm telling you right now." His dark eyes gleamed with determination. "It will never, ever happen, that I will take anything from your estate; so you never, ever have to think twice about it. Alan left you a legacy—"

"One that you've more than tripled with your brilliant investments," she inserted.

"—and I'm too proud of what I've accomplished on my own to start living off heiresses at this point in my life."

"Dylan," she remonstrated, scowling severely.

He laughed and stroked her cheek. "Do we agree on it?"

"Yes," she grumbled. She found the conversation highly unsettling.

"Good, because now that we have that out of the way, I have something to say about us."

"What?"

"I want you to live here with me."

Her eyes went wide. In typical Dylan-like fashion, he'd stated his case with blunt succinctness. No beating around the bush with him. She reached for his other hand and stepped into him.

"Are you sure? You don't think people will talk? If I take a junior executive position at Durand and move in with the CEO?"

"Oh, they'll talk, all right," he assured bluntly. "That's a guarantee. Rumors are going to be off the charts, so if that's going to bother you, then we'll have to come up with another arrangement. I think we both have to be prepared for some major gossip and backlash when it comes to us. We can't let it pull us apart."

"That would never keep me from something that's so important to me," she insisted fiercely.

He touched her cheek again. "This is your home. It has been from the beginning."

She squeezed his hand. "You're right," she said feelingly.

He looked mildly surprised at her easy acquiescence, and then very pleased.

"But not because it was Alan and Lynn's house," she added

softly. She went up on her toes and brushed her mouth against his. "Because you're here."

THE first flickering of panic occurred as they drove to the press conference, and Alice noticed news vans parked on either side of the road a good half a mile from the hotel entrance. She heard a muted, familiar noise and peered upward through the windshield to see one hovering helicopter, then another.

"What's going on?" she asked.

Dylan gave her a quick, flickering glance, and suddenly he was putting on the brakes and sliding the sedan behind a white van. He put the car in park and turned toward her.

"The story itself actually broke this morning. The Durand public relations staff drafted a statement and sent it out to the major press outlets. It'll have circulated by now. The statement basically said that Alan Durand's kidnapped daughter is alive and has returned, and that the details relate to the recent attack of a woman named Alice Reed by Durand Vice President Sebastian Kehoe."

"Oh," she said numbly. "I thought *that* was what was going to be released at the press conference."

"More details will be addressed there, but the staff thought it would be helpful in distributing the story if the media was informed of at least the basic facts before it began." Alice nodded, the muted *rat-a-tat-tat* noise of the helicopters making it difficult for her to focus. "The press has been given strict guidelines that they can't bombard you with questions," he said firmly. "You can make a general statement, if you like, but you don't have to. Then someone from Durand media relations will call on three or four reporters to ask you questions. Answer as briefly or as fully as you want. If you don't know the answer, just say so. There's no crime in that. This is all brand new to you, and if the press doesn't get that, screw them. Sound okay?" he asked, cupping her shoulder.

"I just didn't expect there to be so *many*," she said, staring out the window as a news crew bustled past them on the side of the road.

Dylan grimaced. "Yeah, well . . . as much as I hate to admit it, it's a sexy story. Young, beautiful heiress returned to her legacy after being kidnapped as a child of four."

"*They* don't know who I am. And how is any of this *sexy*?" Alice asked, frowning in disbelief out the window.

"I know. Being kidnapped, told you were another person for twenty years and attacked isn't sexy, but for the media, this is a gold mine. I'm sorry, honey, I didn't write the rules," he added when she rolled her eyes. He quirked a brow and stared out the window as a woman and a man holding a camera passed. "Look at it from their perspective. For one thing, you're one of the wealthiest women in the world and they're about to get an eyeful of you. They might not know what you look like yet, but once they do." He gave her a droll glance. "Welcome to the circus."

"I'm reconsidering accepting the invitation."

His fingers inched to the back of her neck. He stroked her nape softly. Despite her rush of anxiety, her nerves tingled in awareness.

"Do you want me to take you back to the castle?"

"What?" she asked, eyes going wide. She hadn't expected him to say that.

He shrugged. "It's fine with me if you don't want to do this. It's not going to change the basic facts."

She stared at him for a moment, seriously considering taking the out he'd generously given her. After a moment, she slumped back in her seat.

"No. I might as well get this over with," she said resignedly. "I'm Alan and Lynn's daughter. This is all part of their world, and

I guess I have to get used to dealing with it. Besides, I'd just be postponing the inevitable." She looked over at him. "Thanks for saying you'd take me back, though."

He smiled and reached into his pocket. He reached for her hand, and she felt the cool metal against her skin. A moment later, she held up her wrist to examine Lynn's bracelet sparkling in the sunlight. The vision heartened her. It would be the first time she'd wear it in public. There were some advantages to not keeping her identity secret anymore. She gave him a grateful glance.

"For courage," Dylan said, putting the car into drive.

SHE could hear the manic-like chatter emanating through the door even before Rick Preston from Durand's public relations department opened it for Alice, Dylan, a Special Agent Lee, Guy Morales, and Darla Sparrow, the region's U.S. attorney. Alice felt a little numb as they walked toward the head table. The ballroom had gone hushed at their entrance, the exception being the repeated clicks of hundreds of cameras. Dylan pulled her chair out for her, then sat directly next to her. As he seated her, his fingertips skimmed against her back. His touch helped to clear the hazy, surreal feeling that pervaded her as she looked out at the crowd of people.

Rick Preston made a brief statement, and then introduced Dylan.

Listening to Dylan speak, Alice was slowly able to filter out a good portion of her surroundings and anxiety. With a strange sense of nostalgia, she recalled how last year, she'd spent so much time researching Durand Enterprises and its CEO for her graduate research project with Maggie. She'd become a little obsessed with Dylan Fall, even then, looking at photographs of him, watching news footage of him speaking. She was reminded acutely of how commanding a speaker he was, how confident and firm, brilliant and sharp without ever seeming cocky or domineering. Kehoe's crowd—if, indeed, Kehoe had ever really *had* any following at Durand—could rumor-monger, insinuate, and scoff all they wanted. Alan Durand had known *exactly* what he was doing in designating Dylan as his company's leader.

Dylan spoke in his straightforward, succinct yet eloquent manner, never hesitating as he related more personal details than he ever had before in public—to Alice's knowledge—about his relationship with Alan, Lynn, and Addie Durand and about his presence at Addie's kidnapping. He didn't elaborate on his lifetime pursuit to find that little girl, saying he would leave those details up to the U.S. attorney. Alice found his sidestepping of the issue remarkably modest of him, since he was the sole reason she sat there at that moment. But that, too, was typical of Dylan.

He went on to make a statement in regard to how Alan Durand had provided for his daughter, should she ever return. He threw firm support behind Alan Durand's heir, and provided believable reassurances for Durand Enterprises continued growth, global leadership, and fiscal success.

The energy level in the room had mounted noticeably as Dylan spoke. By the time Dylan said he'd take a few questions, almost every camera was turned on Alice. She wished she could disappear. The hazy sense of unreality she'd been experiencing only amplified.

"You mentioned that the majority of shares are held in a trust that was to be returned to Adelaide Durand if ever she should return," one male reporter began. "What does that mean for the management of Durand and the many charitable projects it supports?"

"I can respond in regard to the management of Durand, because the trust and Durand Enterprises' functioning assets are two separate entities. As for what will happen with the trust, that's not up to me. It's up to Alice—Addie. She can decide today, or she can take her time. She can alter her plans at any future date. It's entirely up to her. Whatever she decides," Dylan paused and glanced over at Alice briefly. Alice's racing heart gave a little leap. "The public should know that Durand Enterprises will continue to function and flourish as it has in the past decade. The trust was earmarked by Alan Durand for his daughter, and whether or not employees and the public realize it, daily operations at Durand have been carried out since his death with that legacy kept intact. Absolutely no impoverishment or strain will be incurred on the company itself."

A roar had started up in her ears. She understood that everything Dylan was saying was true, but there was a difference between logical understanding and emotional *getting* that she was the sole mistress to a vast fortune.

Just give it time. And Dylan assured her he wasn't going to abandon her.

Dylan waved aside further questions. "I realize that I'm not the one you really want to hear about," he said into the microphone with a small, dry smile. "So I'm going to turn things over to Guy Morales, who is our acting vice president of human resources. He's going to tell you a little more about Alice Reed." Alice shifted uncomfortably in her chair as the cameras started to click rapidly again. What did Guy Morales have to say about her? She'd only been briefly introduced to him by Dylan. She glanced at Dylan with a question in her eyes when he came and sat down next to her.

"I'm honored to be able to stand here before you all today and relate a truly amazing story about a young woman who, despite a relative lack of available resources and funds, managed to graduate with her business degree with honors from the University of Illinois, Chicago and her master of business administration, summa cum laude, from Arlington College. From an early age, she demonstrated remarkable skill in mathematics, winning a coveted scholarship to the University of Illinois. During her academic career, Ms. Reed contributed to one of the most talked-about research studies ever conducted about the correlation between corporate philanthropy and profit. Unbeknownst to her," Morales paused for effect and gave Alice a brief smile, "she was vindicating the principles long held by Durand Enterprises . . . and by her parents, Alan and Lynn Durand."

The cameras began popping like mad again. Alice felt a little queasy as Guy went on to describe her time at Camp Durand and how the managers had chosen her team—without knowing her identity as the Durand heir—as the championship team. She saw Dylan glance cautiously at her sideways, and wondered if he realized how uncomfortable she was, having her praises sung this way in front of a roomful of cameras and strangers.

As Guy continued, describing how Alice had been hired—again, without the managers' knowledge of her true identity—as a Durand junior executive, Alice's attention was drawn to the back of the room and a flicker of movement. She recognized a face that towered above the crowd. She sat up straighter, disbelieving. A shiver tore through her.

Dylan leaned over and whispered directly in her ear. "I knew how terrible you felt, missing their final night. Judith and Noble D volunteered to drive a carful each of them down," Dylan whispered near her ear. "It looks like the majority of them made it."

"I don't believe it," she whispered.

She noticed Noble D next, whose head was nearly as tall as Terrance's. Terrance waved at her cheekily. Another hand flew up and pressed Terrance's hand to his side. A smile flickered across Alice's mouth when she saw that it was Judith who contained Terrance. A grinning Noble D stood behind Judith, his hands on her shoulders. Between Terrance and D, she spotted Angela Knox and over to the side, Justin Arun. An eager face peered up over the crowd. It was Jill Sanchez, who appeared to have sprouted several inches even since Alice had last seen her. Matt Dinorio suddenly jumped up over the heads of the audience, hand in the air. Judith hissed something at him, bringing him to order, too. Alice repressed an urge to laugh.

Seeing their faces made the entire experience shift for her. She listened to the end of Guy Morales's introduction with a dawning sense of wonder. The new human resources VP was *right*. This was an *incredible* story. A couple that loved one another and who were seemingly blessed with everything, longed for a child more than anything else. After strife and struggling, they were given that child, only to have her ripped away from them by a man's single-minded greed and jealousy. Because a lonely, scarred boy's life had been touched indelibly by a man's kindness and a child's innocent love, he'd never given up on finding that girl.

A young woman, ignorant of her roots and the love she'd once breathed like the air surrounding her, had followed the tendencies and talents inherent to her blood, studying business and mathematics, even undertaking a research project that would have swelled her parents with pride, had they ever known of it. The young woman had come to a place where she could make a difference, and had touched the lives of unique children, and been touched by them, in turn, just like Dylan Fall had been altered forever by Alan Durand.

She looked over at Dylan as Guy Morales came to the conclusion of his introduction. Tears burned in her eyes, but her smile reflected genuine happiness.

And the woman and the man met, and everything came full circle . . .

Dylan stood to pull back her chair when Guy Morales introduced her. He grabbed her hand briefly as she rose, squeezing it for reassurance. This time, when Terrance put both hands up and waved and Matt jumped up, Alice grinned and gave them a wave back.

*   *   *

SHE approached the podium. The sound of her clearing her throat in the microphone sounded abnormally loud in the absolute silence that followed. She gripped the podium to steady herself.

"First off, let me just say that while you all may have a lot of questions, the chances are I can't answer them. Most of you probably wonder if you should refer to me as Alice Reed or Addie Durand. The fact of the matter is, I don't have an answer to even *that* question at the moment. A name . . . one of the most basic things a person knows about themselves, and yet I'd have to claim temporary ignorance. That's how new, incredible, and earthshaking this all is to me.

"I'd like to personally thank Dylan Fall, and the Durand board, for being so supportive and patient in guiding me through what's ended up being a really confusing time. I'll let Special Agent Lee and Ms. Sparrow answer any questions associated with the kidnapping or the FBI's investigation. But I just wanted to make one thing very clear. I'm here today because of one man. If it weren't for Dylan Fall never giving up on finding Addie Durand, I would have died believing I'd been born Alice Reed. Thank you for not giving up on me, no matter how tiny the odds of Adelaide Durand ever being found," she said thickly, looking at Dylan. She paused, emotion tightening her throat. She took strength from Dylan's steady, lambent stare. Cameras snapped like crazy in the tense silence.

"Because of the involvement of Durand Enterprises and the trust and the money, I know there's going to be a tendency for this story to become about all that," she continued shakily. "But for me, this is an extremely personal story, and it's got nothing to do with money." Her gaze ran over the teenagers standing at the back of the room. Judith appeared both anxious and rapt, watching her. "For me, the past several weeks have been about making connections with some incredible people, about learning to trust . . . about finding the faith to hope . . ."

Awkwardness suddenly crowded her conscious at the realization of how emotional and raw she sounded. It wasn't really like her, to be so transparent in a public venue like that. Rick Preston caught her eye and she nodded once.

"A few questions," Preston said. The room exploded with shouts, scuffling chairs, and waving hands. Preston pointed and called a name.

"Danny Zarnoff, the *Detroit News*," an older, heavyset man called out. "Given the fact that you're the owner of Durand Enterprises, how likely is it that you'll be happy working as a junior executive in marketing?"

Alice blinked at the brash question.

"Very likely," she replied. She glanced at Rick Preston expectantly. Danny Zarnoff looked nonplussed by her simple answer and started to call out a follow-up, but he was eclipsed by the cacophony of shouting reporters. Alice glanced aside nervously. Dylan arched his eyebrows slightly. Even though his face was otherwise impassive, she would have guessed he was amused.

Preston called out a name and one woman was left standing.

"Katie Jordan, *Crain's Chicago Business*. You're now the largest shareholder of Durand Enterprises, and it sounds as if you've got a brain for business and a knack for leadership. Any plans to take Dylan Fall's place as CEO of the company one day?"

Alice braced herself.

"Dylan Fall has made Durand Enterprises the most profitable and fastest-growing company in our industry. As a shareholder, I wouldn't want to do anything to hinder the growth or value of this company. Alan Durand was smart enough to see his potential, and since then, Dylan has proven himself as worthy of that trust again and again. I told you all that I wouldn't be able to answer a lot of your questions, but I *can* tell you this for certain: Dylan Fall will continue as the CEO of Durand Enterprises for as long as he wants the job."

By the time she finished with two other questions and sat down, Alice's legs were rubbery from adrenaline running weak in her blood.

Dylan's full attention appeared to be on Special Agent Lee making the FBI's statement. Beneath the cover of the white cloth that covered the table, however, his hand closed on Alice's knee. He gave her a squeeze. As always happened at Dylan's touch, Alice's tottering world slowly steadied once again.

A party-like atmosphere prevailed in the anteroom of the ballroom after the press conference came to an end. Not all of the Red Team had been able to come, but the ones who had were escorted back. A few of them looked a little tongue-tied at first by the news of Alice's discovered identity and past. As soon as Alice hugged them each warmly, however, the hesitant ones quickly slid back into their former camp comfort levels. Dylan had surprised her—yet again—by having someone bring the Team Championship trophy. Alice and her kids finally got their opportunity to pass it among themselves, admire it, and share stories about what had led to their victory.

After they'd reminisced and caught up for a while, Judith covertly asked Alice if she could talk to her alone for a moment. Alice agreed and they went over to an empty corner.

"You did a good job up there," Judith told her. "It must have been hard."

"Yeah. I always was telling you guys that public speaking isn't my forte," Alice agreed dryly.

Judith shifted on her feet, clearly hesitant.

"Is everything okay, Judith?" Alice asked.

"It's just . . . I know what it's like. To go from one world to another," Judith finally said reluctantly. She noticed Alice's confusion. "My mom, grandma, and I lived on Wyoming Street in Detroit while my mom finished her college degree and first started out at the bank. When she got promoted to a management position, we moved to Sterling Heights. It was like moving to another planet. Maybe my leap wasn't as huge as yours, but still—I at least have a *hint* of what you're going through."

"How long did it take you to adjust?" Alice wondered.

Judith shrugged and crossed her arms beneath her breasts. For a few seconds, Alice thought she was going to go aloof on her again.

"I never really did," Judith blurted out suddenly. She gave Alice a sheepish glance. "Not until recently, anyway, and I've still got a long way to go. Look, I know I was a bitch when I first got to camp. I'm sorry I gave you such a hard time."

"Apology accepted. I probably could have been a little more patient with you."

Judith rolled her eyes. "If you were too patient, I would have walked all over you. You know that."

Alice grinned in agreement.

"I wasn't sure where I belonged. My mom wanted me to cut off all my ties with my friends in the old neighborhood and start out fresh in Sterling Heights. It was like she wanted to wash off the taint of Wyoming Street and never think about it again. Part of me agreed with her. I wanted to blend, just like her."

"And the other part?" Alice asked softly.

"Felt like a hypocrite," Judith said, her mouth twisting in anger.

"That's understandable. I know I felt that way when I first went to college. I didn't tell anyone where I'd grown up. It was one of my deepest shames."

"Yeah. But even though I felt that way, I sort of wanted to get back at my mom for turning my whole life upside-down, too. I was always doing things to piss her off."

"Like applying for Camp Durand?" Alice asked. She'd long wondered why Judith had insisted upon defying her mother and attending a camp that was largely populated by impoverished kids, especially since Judith had acted so superior and above everyone once she got there.

Judith's chin went up in a familiar gesture of defiance. When Alice didn't say anything else and just waited, the girl's rebellion seemed to drain out of her. For a few seconds, she looked exactly like what she was: an intelligent, pretty, very vulnerable teenage girl.

"How pitiful am I?" Judith wondered gruffly under her breath.

"It's not pitiful at all," Alice said. "I think it makes sense. There's nothing to be ashamed of. Know what else I think?" Judith glanced up at her uncertainly. "I think maybe you thought getting back at your mom was the only reason you applied to Camp Durand, but I think there could have been another reason. I think you felt alienated and missed your old neighborhood, and your friends, and your roots, and part of you just wanted to connect again. And you *did*, Judith. In the most amazing way. Personally, I think you'll be able to do it anywhere from now on. Wyoming Street. Sterling Heights . . . wherever you want to make a difference, you will."

"So will you."

Alice shrugged and grinned. "As far as Durand goes, they're sort of forced to put up with me, at this point."

Judith gave a bark of laughter. "Well, it's like you were always proving to me. Sometimes the best leader isn't the obvious one."

She gave Alice a brief, but fierce—and unforgettable—hug before she walked away.

HER kids, Dylan, and a few members of the Durand staff weren't the only ones to show up at the little impromptu party. She was happy to see Sidney Gates and Jim Sheridan when they arrived. As she was talking to Jim, Terrance, and Judith about the now famous Bang pizza party, Dylan stepped up to her while escorting an older but fit-looking blond woman.

"I wanted to introduce you to someone who's been dying to meet you," Dylan said. "Alice Reed, meet Virginia Davenport. She's my right hand, and never fails to remind me of it. She was Alan's administrative assistant for years, too."

"It's so nice to meet you," Alice said sincerely, putting out her hand. Instead of shaking it, however, the woman grasped it warmly in both of her hands.

"Call me Mrs. Davenport. It may seem more formal, but it's not. It's what Dylan and Alan both called me. I'm surprised Dylan even knows my first name." Alice grinned at Dylan's forbearing expression. She noticed Mrs. Davenport searching her face and realized her blue eyes were shiny with tears.

"Is everything all right?" Alice asked quietly, concerned, especially because Mrs. Davenport seemed like such a formidable character, certainly not someone prone to public displays of emotion.

Mrs. Davenport nodded briskly. "It's just that you remind me of him."

"Of Alan?" Alice asked, touched. "Thanks. Most people seem to think I look like Lynn."

Mrs. Davenport sniffed and started searching for something in her handbag. "You do. It's not your looks that remind me of Alan," she admitted thickly, pulling out a plastic bag of Kleenex.

"What, then?" Dylan asked, clearly curious.

"It's your manner," Mrs. Davenport said before she blew her nose. "Alan had the kindness of a saint and was a real gentleman, but he could be sharp as a knife to someone who was rude. That Danny Zarnoff from the Detroit News? He always did get Alan's goat. Alan would have *loved* to see the way you put Zarnoff in his place out there."

EPILOGUE

SIX WEEKS LATER

No, no! My treat," Alice cried out excitedly when Dylan reached for the bill. "You're always buying. My turn, now that I've started getting paychecks."

The waiter looked at Dylan. Dylan nodded once, although he appeared a little exacerbated.

They were having lunch at a sleek new Chinese restaurant called the Great Wall. They made a point of having lunch together during their workday whenever they could. It was gratifying, to no longer have to hide their relationship. They didn't flaunt it, by any means, but the days of sneaking around were officially over for Dylan and her.

With great excitement, she withdrew the credit card from her wallet. She held it up next to her cheek and struck a pose.

"My first credit card ever," she said.

Dylan reached across the table and grabbed the card. He looked exceptionally handsome today, wearing the new bronze and black tie she'd bought him yesterday—also with her new card. She thought the colors made his eyes look especially lustrous and mesmerizing. He peered at the credit card, a grin softening his firm mouth. He handed it back to her.

"You got it with the new name," he said as she tucked the card into the folder and held it up for the waiter.

"I did. What do you think?"

"You know I like it very much." He reached across the table and she put her hand in his. "Are you sure you don't want an expense account from the trust? It could be arranged in a matter of hours. I'm sure Dick has told you," he said, referring to the new executor of her trust, a financial guru by the name of Dick Everhill. She and Dick, with Dylan's helpful input from years of experience, had decided for the time being to not make any changes to the trust. Alan had supplied such worthy directives, and Dylan had done a brilliant job managing it. Alice couldn't think of anything better for it than to keep it just as it was.

"He did tell me. But don't ruin my fun. I'm happy being a working girl and earning a paycheck."

"Heaven forbid I suggest anything that defeats your happiness. But I don't want you going overboard, buying things for me," he told her sternly, briefly touching his new tie.

"I like buying little bobbles for you," she joked. She sighed when his dark look didn't remit. "You spoil me constantly, Dylan. There's no reason I shouldn't be able to return the favor, in my little way."

He stroked her thumb and palm, looking thoughtful. Prickles of pleasure danced across her nerves at his simple caress. She reached and ran her finger over his knuckles, admiring his masculine hand. When she encircled his forefinger and squeezed, he blinked and met her stare.

"You'll definitely be home early tonight?" he asked, his deep, quiet voice and the heat in his eyes telling her loud and clear that he shared her amplified sensual awareness of him. Since they'd begun living together, Alice had reaped the benefits of not only fewer restrictions on how much time they could spend together, but Dylan's considerable imagination and energy when it came to lovemaking. She was a very lucky woman.

"If I get through the analyses on the Sweet Adelaide campaign . . . and Gabriel says I can," she added with a wry smile, referring to her boss in the marketing division. Alice liked her new job a lot. She was learning so much, sometimes it felt like her head was going to explode at the end of the day. It was a lot to take in, learning the ropes at a demanding new job while also trying to assimilate all that it meant to be Adelaide Durand. She was slowly, but steadily, going through all of Alan's and Lynn's remaining personal effects on the weekends, a process that could be intense and wonderful, yet emotional and exhausting, as well. She also was absorbing as many of Durand Enterprises' financial reports and historical information as she possibly could.

Fortunately, Sidney Gates had referred her to a counselor in Morgantown. It'd helped Alice, to have somewhere to go every week where she could just spill everything to an objective listener. Slowly, she was starting to rework all the confusion and discrepancy of her dual existence into a single new identity that increasingly made sense to her.

That she was growing to love.

Dylan's gaze narrowed. "You'd think the fact that the product Gabriel is having you work on was named for *you* by the founder of the company would have some weight on the whole matter."

"Well it doesn't," she said crisply, squeezing his finger again and running her fist up and down it suggestively. She smiled when his eyes flashed. "And that's the way I want it, remember?"

"You won't let me forget."

"What are you thinking about?" she murmured after a moment, recognizing his preoccupation.

"Your name," he said bluntly. "Now that you've legally changed it, I don't suppose you'd ever consider changing it again?"

Her heart gave a little leap.

"Absolutely not," Alice replied. "I mean . . . I had to live without it for twenty years of my life. I'll never surrender it willingly again."

He nodded, keeping his face impassive. Still, she sensed her answer had subdued him. She laughed softly and stroked the back of his hand.

"I may, however, consider hyphenating . . . if the right offer came along."

Frustratingly, he didn't say anything else. *"Dylan."*

"What?"

"Are you asking me if I'll marry you?" she blurted out irrepressibly.

"I was testing the waters," he said, arching his dark brows and giving her that smoky, knowing look that always reminded her of a pirate.

"But—"

"Don't push it, little girl," he murmured, his mouth tilting in amusement.

She shook her head in mock disgust. She knew him so well by now. He'd ask her to marry him all right, in his own special manner. Dylan never did anything halfway when it came to her. He was forever surprising her, whether it be with a gift presented at just the right moment or by thoughtfully including one of her friends, like Maggie, for a dinner.

He had become a lot less strained in his worry over her in the past weeks, but she had a feeling he'd always be cautious when it came to looking out for her. It was their history that had made him that way, and she understood. It was the same reason he never seemed to cease celebrating her presence, as well. She could hardly complain about his solemn, poignant gratitude about her very existence, even if it did surprise her anew every hour of every day.

Alice tore her gaze off him when the waiter returned. She took the folder, now finding it impossible to hide an ebullient grin. She was having more and more trouble disguising her joy behind a mask of tough indifference these days.

Could my life be any more amazing? Could I be any luckier?

"About those waters . . . " she murmured in an offhand

manner, pretending to be preoccupied about adding a tip to the bill. "Just my opinion, but I'd say they're pretty damn inviting."

She looked up at his warm, gruff chuckle. She saw it there in that moment, in Dylan's gleaming eyes: a whole future of wild heat and sweet, quiet moments of sharing. Their unusually strong bond was only going to grow unbreakable. Alice still doubted, at times. She still silently second-guessed herself, and she sometimes wondered if her sarcastic tongue and ever-ready cynicism could ever be fully vanquished. But one thing had forever changed. She now knew that her doubt and mistrust could potentially be the slayer of her bond with Dylan, if she let it be. And there was no way in hell she was ever going to let that enemy win on that particular battlefield.

Her parents had gotten it right. Her life really had been miraculous, in the end. Alice trusted, and she loved with all her heart. For her, there was no greater miracle than that.

She squeezed Dylan's hand. Turning to the bill, she signed her new name with a proud flourish.

Alice Durand

ABOUT THE AUTHOR

Beth Kery lives in Chicago where she juggles the demands of her career, her love of the city and the arts, and a busy family life. Her writing today reflects her passion for all of the above. She is the *New York Times* and *USA Today* bestselling author of *Because You Are Mine*. Find out more about Beth and her books at BethKery.com or Facebook.com/Beth.Kery.